Origins

The Snook Saga   *Book One*

MOLLY BLAESER

Origins

The Snook Saga: Book One

e-book ISBN-13: 979-8-9930812-0-5

Paperback ISBN-13: 979-8-9930812-1-2

Hardback ISBN 13: 979-8-9930812-2-9

Cover design by: Ben Mirabelli

Edited by: Lynn Picknett

Layout by: Jason Roach

Printed in the United States of America

Dedication

Dedicated to preteen Molly, who once read
'Eragon' and said, "I can do that."

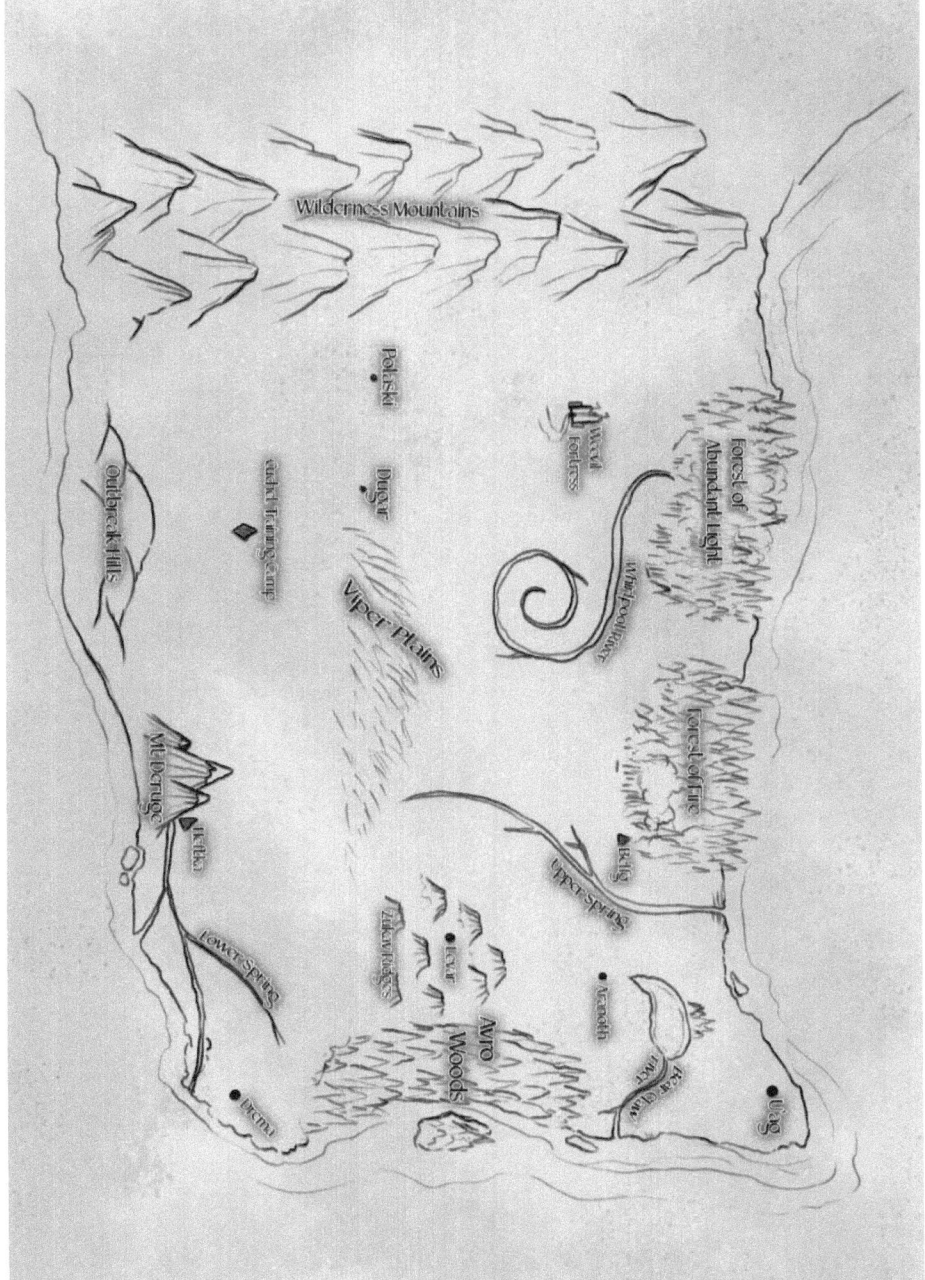

To Begin

Snook lay in his master's yard, chained to a post by a tree. As if dusted with flakes of gold, his fawn-colored coat shone in the warm light of both suns, with his smooth and short hairs keeping him from overheating – yet Snook felt a chilling fear gripping his heart.

For several days, he watched the harbor, waiting for his master's boat, while his cropped ears had listened in hopes of catching his young master's voice. But there had been no sign. People passed him as they went about their day-to-day duties, but no one approached, unless they were children, who brought him snacks when their parents weren't looking. No one wondered about his owners – fishermen often took days, sometimes weeks, to fish. And a friend of his master's kept his bowls full, so Snook was never without food or water.

He tugged at the dreadful chains, as he'd done every day, tired of waiting, wanting to wander the town with his young master. All day he tugged, his giant muscular body straining, to no avail.

With a sigh, Snook put his dark muzzle between his paws, eyes on the distant harbor. Once he fell asleep, his dreams consisted of his young master returning, laughing and arms wide.

1

"Shu surg tuk!" echoed across the Viper Plains. In response came the dry crackling of lightning.

Vic raised his eyes, in both surprise and recognition. At the age of seventeen, he had lived long enough to know what had just happened: someone nearby but out of sight had shouted a cuchel dahla, or magic spell. Most likely, Vic told himself, it was a student from the Cuchel Training Camp. The pupils there often traveled northward to the Viper Plains so as to practice their lessons – away from civilization and free to test their magic skills.

One day, Vic hoped to train in that very camp, as it was once where all young men were expected to learn cuchels and dahlas, magic and spells. Of course, these days, the sons of rich men were the ones who could afford to attend, in more ways than one. As in Vic's case, poorer families needed their sons at home.

He smiled at the possibility of learning cuchels one day – of one day mastering the ancient art of magic – if only he could convince the world he deserved that chance. *Many, if not most, will say that it's an impossible idea…yet I can't wait to prove them wrong,* he thought. But then he sighed, remembering now was still the present moment. And in that present moment, Vic had archery to practice.

He nocked an arrow, raised the bow. Inspired, an idea struck his mind: *I've learned the words to some basic cuchels from hearing them practiced out here. It might not be allowed, but…could I perhaps use one with my arrow – and make it work?*

Possibility filled him, energized him. Without a second thought, he shouted the words: "Beu shu!" In a blink, the arrow glowed with a faint red light.

It worked! Vic thought with a laugh.

Taking aim, he shot his arrow, straight at one of the wooden targets lined up in the field. The governor's guards used these to practice during their off time, and Vic had, with discretion, memorized their schedules so that he could use the targets when no one was around. Like clockwork, they were deserted today.

He held his breath, hoping not to jinx his almost perfect shot – and when the arrowhead collided with the wood, the target exploded. Pieces of wood flew through the air, flung everywhere.

Vic ducked.

Maybe, just maybe, that wasn't the best idea.

After stowing the remaining pieces of the target behind a grassy knoll, he picked up his bag of game from his hunting earlier then headed toward the town of Dugar. There he lived with his cousin Zurze, the village carpenter. As he trudged toward home, both suns began their descent, their fiery globes ducking toward opposite rims of Lilligrav. By the time Vic caught sight of the wall protecting Dugar from intruders, dusk hung around the land.

Vic quickened his pace at the sight of the gate. He had to get inside soon – strange things haunted Lilligrav at night, and he wished not to be a part of them. Stories from his childhood, of the Dark One's dæmon creatures, came to mind, but he swallowed them back, the taste bitter on his tongue.

A voice pierced the twilight mist, breaking up Vic's thoughts. "Who goes there?" A dark form hunched over the top of the gate wall, with squinty eyes peering into the incoming darkness.

"Ruthgar, it's me: Vic Hemonia."

The guard raised a lantern. "Ah, there you are, Vic. Your cousin was looking for you when he returned earlier today. Drisco was on duty then and told him you left in the morning headed for the Plains. Your bow was on your back then – as it is now."

"Aye, Ruthgar."

"Yet you return with a small catch," and Ruthgar laughed. Vic bit his tongue, not daring to explain his practicing, or else the governor's guards would be suspicious of him in the morning.

"I've still a lot to learn."

"Aye, and one such thing would be to return to Dugar before nightfall. You know well as I that strange things happen on the Plains at night, Vic Hemonia."

Vic said nothing.

"And tonight gives me a strange chill in my bones, boy. You had best come inside the gate." Hooking his axe on a link of chain, he pulled down. The chain struggled downward, opening the gate at a slow pace.

Vic ducked inside as soon as the gate had opened wide enough, forcing the lingering childhood stories farther into the back of his mind.

"Aye, Vic!" came Ruthgar's shout again, as the gate creaked shut – faster this time – while the chain shot back upwards. "Seems to me you spend more time out on the Plains then learning your cousin's craft."

Vic fingered his bow, glancing up to see Ruthgar peeking over the other side of the gate at him. "I have no interest in carpentry, Ruthgar."

"And why's that, lad?" The guard's tone held a hint of judgement.

With a shrug, Vic replied, "Some of us, like me, would rather play with the magic of our world."

Ruthgar laughed a harsh sound, reminding Vic of the whiskey-heavy laughs in the village tavern. "But lad, you would have to enter the Training Camp – and not only are you not of age, but your pocket isn't laden with gold! No, Vic, marry a nice girl and settle down." He pointed his axe toward the village huts. "Go home and ease Zurze's worry. May your supper still be warm!"

Vic dropped his gaze and headed to the hut he shared with his cousin. *No one understands that I would much rather dedicate my life to magic than settle for the life of a peasant,* he mumbled to himself.

The town of Dugar sat nestled in twilight. Smoke curled like grey scarves from chimneys made of stone, which only the rich could afford. The rest of the village burned wood inside firepits in the ground with smoke creeping out of holes in the roofs. Some lanterns in windows were lit; other homes had no lights at all. Vic assumed most of these were farmers, who went early to bed and rose with the suns.

Once Vic passed the village's central hub, he soon came upon the hut belonging to him and Zurze. Pushing open the front door, he stepped inside, avoiding the jumble of logs stacked by the entrance, then hung up his bow and quiver in the side room.

From the back room, he heard Zurze's pounding hammer.

Zurze looked up as Vic entered the back room – Zurze's workplace – and a worried crease formed in his brow. "Vic, I told you not to be outside the gates at night. The guards said you'd gone hunting, but I hoped you'd have enough sense to return before dusk." Zurze laid down his hammer and stepped toward his cousin, hand outstretched. "Are you all right?"

"You need to worry less, cousin. I'm fine. Nothing ever happens."

"But something could. The Dark One—"

"I know, I know—the Dark One prowls about at night." Vic sighed, shaking his head. "I wish you wouldn't treat me like a child. Don't you trust me?"

Zurze paused, one hand on Vic's shoulder, then sighed. "You're right. But I swore to my cousin, your father, that I'd take care of you. We're the only family left, Vic."

With a crooked grin, Vic replied, "No matter what, Zurze, I'll stick with you – family has to stay together."

"And I will stick with you," and Zurze swallowed, with a brisk nod of his head. He turned back to his carpentry but gestured toward Vic behind him. "Now, come, what did you hunt today?"

Vic leaned against the doorway, lifting his bag of game. "Grouse. I caught two just south of Frinh Woods."

"That makes two successful cousins, then," Zurze joked with a teasing wink. "I brought back fresh mahogany – once smooth, it will create the most beautiful woodwork!"

Vic laughed. "Your travels went well?"

"Aye." Zurze picked up a cloth, wiping his hands clean of dirt and splinters. "Save one for tomorrow – you can start plucking it after dinner."

"And the other?"

"You promised Gale something for his inn, no?"

"I did." Vic flicked a thumb toward his quiver. "I do need some new arrows, if the grouse feathers will work." He glanced around Zurze's workroom. "Any spare pieces of wood?" *Though he always volunteers to fletch them himself,* Vic knew. *I think he doesn't like me using his tools!*

"Somewhere." Zurze shrugged. "I promise you'll have arrows for your hunt tomorrow. Come, let's eat," and Zurze led his cousin back into the main room, where a clay pot hung over the open fire. As the pot's contents bubbled, Vic cleared the simple table while Zurze finished preparing their food.

The savory smell of cooked vegetables filled the air, and Vic looked up. "Stew again?" In response, Vic's stomach growled, and Zurze laughed. "I suppose stew is better than nothing," Vic said, embarrassed, "even if I've eaten most of the week while you've traveled."

Bringing two bowls filled with steaming broth, Zurze chuckled. "Well, I've lived off bread for most of my travels, meaning both of us will appreciate roasted grouse tomorrow."

Vic chuckled and tried to sit down – but his chair cracked beneath him, splitting right through the center of the wood. Vic yelped in pain when the cracked wood ripped his pants and poked his skin.

Zurze laughed harder than before. "I'll make you a new chair. Do you want grouse feathers on that, too?"

"No need," Vic said with a lopsided grin, rubbing his bottom. "I've used that chair since I was ten years. I do need another one."

"Unless you prefer sitting on the floor!"

Vic laughed. Getting up, he changed his pants in the side room before rejoining Zurze at the table. Zurze had replaced the broken chair with a stool from his workroom.

When both cousins had had their fill, Zurze leaned back in his chair and lit his pipe. "Vic, I overheard some unfortunate gossip while in Polaski."

Vic pushed aside his empty bowl. "Oh?"

"The news along the coast is that the Blood Bearer dwarfs are back."

"But from where? They disappeared off the coast after their banishment years ago."

Zurze shook his head, puffing some smoke. "The dwarfs are a mysterious race, Vic. They are like the rocks of the earth – hard to move and tough to chip away at." Zurze paused, stroking his beard. "I met with Kristoff, the Storyteller of Armoth. He told me that fishermen haven't been returning from trips to the far waters. It can't be coincidental."

"What about our ntéhs? Can't they protect our people?"

"They will protect us – as much as they can. But even our ntéhs, as heroic as they may be, are limited in their abilities. Remember, Vic: they are only human." Zurze paused. "And don't forget the Dark One. You know as well as I do that he seeks out and kills our ntéhs."

Upset, Vic pounded his fist against the table. "We need the Training Camp to step up and banish these dwarfs – before they kill more innocent people!"

His cousin sighed. "If only. You know as well as I that the Training Camp doesn't want to help."

"There are some like me who want to!" Vic took a deep breath. "Zurze—I—there are days when…"

"I know, Vic. I know. But we must abide by the laws set by the Six… Especially their taxes. If it weren't for their taxes, our lives wouldn't be so limited." Zurze sighed and took a long drag of his pipe. "Someday, someone will rise up and change our world, Vic. We must believe in those words, for the spirits told us so."

Glancing at his cousin, Vic took a breath. "I have to tell you something, Zurze. I didn't just go hunting today."

Straightening, Zurze eyed him. "Go on."

"I memorized the guards' archery training. And today, when no one was there, I went to practice. No one saw me!" Vic protested, noting Zurze's intake of breath. "I made sure of it. But I overheard a cuchel practice, and I just had to try one myself, Zurze. Please understand—"

Vic stopped in surprise when his cousin leaned forward, lowered his pipe, and looked at him with a strange glimmer in his eye.

"What happened, Vic?"

Catching himself, Vic continued, "I lit the arrow with the energy shock cuchel, and it destroyed the target. I hid the evidence – no one will ever suspect it was me – but, Zurze: it worked!"

His cousin smiled. "I have a gift from your father to you."

"From my father? You always said he disliked me."

"He made foolish decisions, but he was still a good man." Zurze stood and went to the handmade bookcase resting against the far wall. To Vic's surprise, Zurze picked up an ornate tome that he recognized. All his life, Vic had been scolded for touching it, told time and time again how priceless of a family heirloom it was.

And yet all his life, he had longed to open it. *Is he…giving it to me?* Vic wondered with a flicker of hope.

Returning to the table, Zurze laid the book in front of Vic. "This belonged to your great-great-grandfather. When your father left, it became your inheritance."

A million questions exploded inside Vic's mind, but only one actually formed: "What is it, Zurze?"

"It's about cuchels, Vic." Zurze leaned closer. "And even more important: elves."

Vic stared at the cover, incredulous. *The most elusive and mysterious beings!*

"I—Your father wanted you to have it when you were older. Today, you've shown me you're ready."

Holding his breath, Vic brushed his hands along the jewels set into the leather cover. "Thank you," he somehow managed to say.

Zurze clasped Vic's shoulder. "Remember this, Vic: books are for everyone, but to be safe, you should still read this one with discretion. Most people would expect a young man to learn about magic through the Training Camp but—"

"I'm not of age," Vic interjected. *Not yet. Soon – but even then, we couldn't afford it.* He swallowed. "Would the Six punish me if anyone were to find out?"

His cousin exhaled. "I'm not sure, Vic. Next time I'm in Armoth, I'll ask Kristofer how he and the other Storytellers learned magic. After all, they study countless books, so perhaps they learned in a similar way." All of a sudden, he looked up, out of the hole in the roof. "Vic! Both suns have set! Come, or we'll be late for the Storyteller's fire." Standing, he moved to the front door, grabbed his wool jacket off a hook, and went out into the street.

Torn, Vic glanced from the door to the book before him and back again. *I mustn't take it with me. But I'm dying to read it!* Reluctant, he tucked the book under the animal furs that made up his bed. Then, stringing his bow across his back along with his quiver, Vic grabbed the bag of grouse and went out to join Zurze.

His cousin stood in the cold outside, his breath forming clouds of white in the brisk air. Upon seeing Vic, he moved forward, headed for the center of the village, and Vic fell into pace beside him. "You know, Vic," Zurze said as they trudged along, "some people want to rid us of our oldest traditions – such as the Storytellers at the fire."

Rubbing his hands together for warmth, Vic shook his head. "That's absurd! Our oldest traditions are what formed Lilligrav. We'd be throwing away our history if we let them go!"

Zurze looked up toward the slice of moon in the grey sky. "I agree."

Vic paused for a moment. "Is that why you made me attend every Storyteller's fire as a youngster, even when you could not – because I had to know our history?"

"Aye." Zurze wrapped his arms around himself as the biting chill nipped at them. "You had to know our past. People – they will try and distort it. It's what your father would have wanted: for you to know the truth of our history."

Knowing not to touch the subject of his father, Vic ignored the feeling in his gut. "Thank you."

Zurze laughed. "For what?"

"For making me go."

Zurze gave his cousin a pat on the back – or rather, tried to, as it was covered by his quiver and bow. "We're safe inside the village walls, Vic," Zurze said, nodding toward the bow and quiver. "Those aren't necessary."

"With all the stories of the Dark One, I find it best to keep my bow with me at all times."

Before Zurze could answer, the village's central hub came into view, and the two cousins were lost in a sea of villagers. Ahead, Vic could see the giant fire, atop a mountain of logs, flaring in the very center of town. Behind the flames towered a wide and tall platform – the place of the Storyteller.

Sitting cross-legged, three children tossed smooth rocks into a ring of white chalk. Vic could smell their stench of manure and dirt, identifying them as shepherds' sons. A scruffy mutt lay at their feet, growling at anyone who stepped too close. With a smile, Vic remembered enjoying the same game with his village friends.

Vic glanced around, searching for Zurze, whom he'd lost in the shuffle.

"Hello, Vic."

Surprised, he looked to his left. A pretty young woman with her blonde hair brushed back stood beside him, smiling.

"Hello, Tasha."

"I haven't seen you in a while," she said, with a smile.

Vic shrugged, went back to searching for Zurze. "That's funny," he replied, not paying attention to her, "I never miss the Storyteller's fire."

"Oh." From the corner of his eye, Vic noticed Tasha stepping closer. "Maybe I didn't recognize you – you've really…changed into a man."

He chuckled. "Archery will do that to you."

"Remember when we were younger? You said you were going to join the Camp."

Vic caught sight of Zurze toward the front of the fire and turned to tell Tasha goodbye – but paused at the sight of her standing so close to him. She was smiling, twirling some strands of hair with her right hand. Ruthgar's words pounded in the back of his mind: "Marry a nice girl, Vic, and settle down." But then Vic's own thoughts followed: *I don't want to settle down just yet. Tasha would never understand that. No girl would.* "I still am," Vic answered.

Tilting her head, she giggled. "You can't afford it, Vic. You're just a carpenter."

Vic bristled and turned away. "Even the son of a carpenter deserves a chance to prove himself. Now if you'll excuse me, Tasha, my cousin is calling me."

He heard her say, "Vic, wait—" But then he was gone.

Zurze looked up, startled, as Vic came to a halt beside him. "When I lost you in the crowd, I figured you would be with your friends, Vic."

"They had different ideas. Have you seen the governor?" Vic asked, placing his bag of grouse at his feet.

Zurze shook his head. "Why in Lilligrav would he come, Vic?"

At that moment, the crowd fell into a hushed silence as two soldiers marched up the platform. Taking their positions on each corner, they faced the crowd, faces expressionless. The air hung with anticipation and then the Storyteller appeared, walking to his position at the front of the platform. He wore a navy robe decorated with dazzling crystals that caught the light of the fire. The crystals were set in the fabric in the positions of the stars; Vic could make out certain constellations – there, the Giant Bear; over there, the Unicorn. Being one of the oldest men of the village, the Storyteller's smile was almost hidden by a smoky-grey moustache that matched the beard trailing down his chin.

Raising his hands over the fire, the Storyteller shouted, "Ralas!" The fire crackled as it gushed upwards, raging above them, before shrinking back down. The Storyteller bowed, robe rustling, to appreciative shouts and applause. Closing his eyes, he clasped his hands and hid them in his sleeves. He seemed as if he'd stopped breathing. But in a flash, his eyes were open, and the story began:

"You stand on Lilligrav, sacred island created by the spirits. For unknown reasons, they began to form our world. They twisted rivers out of water droplets. The clouds they formed out of fluff. The mountains they pulled from the ground. The seeds they scattered and shaped into plants. Both suns they blasted into the sky. The moon they hung from the stars.

"And then came the dragons. By great magic, they awoke from the rock and burst into the sky – the great sky dragons. Wandering through lush forests – the slender land dragons. Dusted with snow, the furred dragons. They soared with the wind, flying on the breath of the spirits themselves." As if on cue, the fire sent out snapping fireworks which exploded into fiery dragons. Vic grinned as a child in front of him reached out in wonder, two spark-dragons dancing around his head.

"His immersive storytelling magic never ceases to amaze me," Vic whispered.

"Hush," Zurze scolded.

"The dragons ruled the sky," the Storyteller continued. "The elves ruled the land. They were the second race to appear, having been created from pure light. And because magic courses through elf blood, the spirits entrusted their own language – cuchels – to the elves. So, they brought words into our world, names such as the Avro Woods that we still use today.

"Then a new race emerged: the dwarfs, each clan named for the color of their beards. Back to the rock they went, mining the mountains for precious gems." The fire wisped into the face of a grunting redbeard dwarf before vanishing in a puff of smoke.

"Time passed. Animals came into being." As the Storyteller named each creature, their fiery forms bounded around the fire before being whisked away by smoke. "Deer, flocking the forest. Antelope, bounding across the Plains. Wild goats, leaping across the mountains. Birds of the air, soaring with dragons. Ducks, gliding across the lakes. Wolves, stalking the forests. Wild dogs, prowling the Plains. Lions, padding along Mount Deruge. Our world was brimming with life."

The Storyteller paused, looking over the crowd. A young boy appeared out of nowhere, pushing through the crowd, carrying a goat horn dripping with water. Vic could almost taste the beads of water on his lips. Once at the platform, the boy reached up, and the Storyteller took the horn, refreshing his voice.

"Now was the time. Man. The spirits drawn to water created man with water in their blood: Refeonamas, our ancestors. The spirits drawn to earth created man with earth in their blood: Zukavnamas, our cousins. The two lived together on Eosld, far out to sea.

"But, in time, our ancestors began to separate, obsessed with differentiating themselves. Eosld became too small of an island. Seeking a new home, our cousins landed on Lilligrav first. The elves welcomed them as Allies and entrusted them with sacred tasks. Hence their homes: Heftka and Belfg, nestled among the woods of the north and the mountain's shadow to the south.

"From an unknown origin emerged the weevils, bald and blue-skinned. In their beginning, they roamed as nomads before building their terrifying fortress – forbidden and as dark as night. Within they hide until their bloodthirsty terror drives them out." The smoke spat out weevil warlords that charged at startled villagers before being swallowed up by the night air. Around him, Vic could hear the whimpers of children, who feared the terrible stories of death at the hands of weevils.

The Storyteller's voice deepened with pride: "Now came our ancestors: the Refeonamas. Upon finally realizing the Zukavnamas had vanished from Eosld, our ancestors followed. The elves accepted them; our cousins grew wary."

All of a sudden, a piercing shriek erupted from the fire, startling Vic. In the flames appeared a rearing stallion. His body was black smoke, fire wisps forming his mane, eyes burning with flame. On his back sat a hazy man, waving a grey smoke sword above his head. Again, the stallion screamed.

"Our cousins' fears came true. Greedy and cruel like before, man plundered for riches and power once again, now on Lilligrav soil instead of Eosld. After tiring of war amongst themselves, they turned on the dragons. Thus, began the two-hundred-year Dragon Wars. Blood nourished the soil. Elfin Dragon Masters tried to bring peace, but man and dragon continued to kill, stealing gold from each other.

"Desperate, the elves made a compromise. They ended the Dragon Wars with the promise of men becoming Dragon Masters. Man regretted his choices, and the dragons cooled their tempers. Peace returned. A thousand years passed, then a new chaos began."

The Storyteller paused, opened his eyes, and snapped his fingers. The fire wavered before bowing before him, sending out waves of sparks. The throng of people held their breath.

"Instead of dragons, our ancestors had a new enemy in mind: the elves. Man wanted the elfin horses, the elfin riches, the elfin kingdom. So, the elves vanished. To this day, their location is unknown. But after the Mad King's spiral, our ancestors recognized how vital the elves are to Lilligrav. So, for centuries, our greatest ntéhs have vowed to seek them out. Ntéhs such as…"

There was a hush as a hooded figure stepped up beside the Storyteller. Lowering his hood, the intruder let the fire light up his face – to the cheers of the villagers.

Like those around him, Vic recognized the stranger from his portrait posted at the village's central hub, alongside proclamations and other news.

"Zurze! It's Manno!"

Vic's cousin blinked. "I can't believe it. An actual ntéh, here, in our village."

Beaming, Vic took in the travel-dusty face of Manno, who nodded at the crowd, his solemn expression unreadable. From a distance, Vic couldn't make out the miniscule details, but he knew one thing: *Someday, I will be as renowned as Manno across Lilligrav. Manno doesn't settle down!*

The Storyteller raised his arms, hushing the cheering crowd. "Manno is just one of the many ntéhs our people have seen. The others have been lost to the Dark One who haunts our Plains."

Once more came the whimpers of children – along with the hushed tones of the adults' concern and fear. Everyone knew the stories, passed down from childhood to childhood, of ntéhs slain by the Dark One. But even simple peasants had lost friends and family to the Dark One and his dæmon creatures.

Manno raised his hands, drawing the crowd's attention. "Hear my promise to you: I've come to seek out the Dark One and destroy him. If I can kill a mountain bear with my own two hands, then I'm confident I can rid Lilligrav of this curse!" The crowd cheered again, but Manno silenced them with a wave of his hand. He raised his hood and stepped back into the darkness at the rear of the platform.

The Storyteller cleared his throat. "When Manno defeats the Dark One, then he shall seek out the elves and make peace with them. The dwarfs, also vanished, shall return, and the dragons will once again rule the sky. For the spirits have foretold that a ntéh will bring back peace to the land and reunite the races.

"Until then," and the Storyteller's voice lowered, but still audible, "Dugar, like each and every village, is under the care and protection of our individual governor, one of Six Tines. Together, the Six are all descended from those who overthrew the Mad King. One's opinion of them differs from their neighbor's."

Mumbles, muffled and subdued, droned like a crowd of bees around the fire. Vic glanced through the corner of his eyes as his ears burned with the sound, his own mind disgusted with thoughts of their present rulers. Beside him, he felt Zurze shift – knowing his cousin felt the same disgust.

Vic realized the two guards had moved closer sometime during the storytelling, their spear tips in dangerous proximity to the Storyteller's face. He felt anger burning inside him: *The governor sent them. He knows the seeds of rebellion have been sown: that we look to our ntéhs now.*

"But I shall say," came the Storyteller's chilling voice. "Our great Lilligrav is headed for ruin. For until a ntéh defeats him, the Dark One is the curse that haunts the Viper Plains. He ensures we are a world torn apart by differences. We're like a tapestry, torn and frayed by war and greed. Until then, we spend our time listening to the stories of old, told by the village Storytellers, recited and memorized from books of old – stories of life as it used to be."

His story complete, the Storyteller clasped his hands together and shuffled away, the guards following close behind. The crowd watched him fade into the darkness, the stars of his robe becoming ever distant, before moving home.

Zurze turned to Vic. "If Manno is here in our village, that means he'll be staying—"

Beaming, Vic picked up his bag of grouse. "Don't wait up for me: I have an errand to attend to with the innkeeper."

His cousin winked in encouragement, turning towards their hut, and Vic moved past the platform toward the village inn, which doubled as the village tavern.

Inside, the place was bustling with activity. Two women served the men, all of whom had clearly had more than one beer. Some of the men were guards still in uniform, enjoying drinks off duty. At the counter stood a man with a scar across his cheek: Gale, the proprietor.

Vic plopped his bag atop the counter. "How much for one grouse?

A cock, at that."

Gale ran his thumb along his chin, just brushing his scar. "Seven copper coins."

"Deal." Pushing the bag across the counter and accepting the coins, Vic leaned forward. "And Manno?"

"Sitting in the corner there," and Gale jabbed a thumb over his shoulder in the hooded figure's direction. "Plenty of beer and a steak sandwich – ntéhs be the hungry type."

Vic thanked him and, with discretion, took a seat at a table behind some guards at the center of the room. They were young – new recruits, Vic figured – and still wearing their uniforms bearing the governor's crest. He dropped his gaze while eavesdropping on the nearby conversation but kept Manno in his peripheral.

"It's ridiculous," one young guard was saying. His blond hair was unkempt, after removing the helmet that now sat on the table beside his beer mug. Vic recognized him as the son of the village bookkeeper. "Captain Navarre demands so much. If I must practice whipping again, my arm will fall off. Fifty strokes a day hurts!" He rubbed his arm, as if to prove his point.

To Vic's delight, Manno turned around from his seat in the far corner. "Your pathetic whining has gone far enough!" the bear killer shouted.

The young guards gulped, and the bookkeeper's son blushed. Vic realized they had been aware of the ntéh's presence but had hoped their tones were low enough not to be heard. *They're embarrassed, as they should be,* he told himself.

Manno pushed aside his plate and stood, gripped his beer mug with one strong hand. "You're being pushed to become men and you complain about it. When I was part of the guard, it was considered an honor to have been chosen. Nowadays you lot are so ungrateful, it's astonishing!"

The young guards didn't answer.

"If the young men of the villages don't want to become men, then where will the ntéhs come from? Do you think I sprouted from the earth, like the Wound of Tears?" He grabbed at the leather cord around his neck, from which were strung bear claws – from the mountain bear he'd wrestled to death and still stained with his own blood. "Do you think I just cut these from a bear's paw, or do you think I earned them with a fight?!" He finished his beer with a swig, banged the mug back on the table.

Vic held his breath.

"Being a man – being a *ntéh* – means risking your life to prove yourself." Manno went to draw his sword. "When I faced that mountain bear—"

An older guard stood up. "A mountain bear may be frightening, Manno – but nothing compares to the terror of the Dark One."

Manno's hand froze atop the sheath of his sword. Across his face swept different emotions: first surprise, then comprehension, then outrage. The great bear killer lifted his hood and stormed outside, slamming the door behind him. Vic didn't pause: he was out the door behind Manno within seconds. As he stepped back outside into the moonlight, he glimpsed Manno heading across the square.

Ducking into an alley, Vic considered his options: *He's much too angry to approach directly. Perhaps I can follow him and wait till his temper cools? But where is he going – and at such a late hour of the night?*

His heart leapt to his throat at the piercing neigh of a stallion. Vic peeked around the corner to see Manno trotting away, astride a chestnut steed. *Outside Dugar so late at night?! Has he gone to hunt down the Dark One already?* Sticking to the alleyways, Vic followed until the gate was in sight. He peeked around a barrel to find Manno in a heated discussion with the guard – at this hour, Ruthgar's replacement.

"Sir, you can't go out there!" the guard protested. "The Dark One—"

"Open the gate, or I shall wake up the governor himself!" Manno shouted back.

Vic's jaw dropped as the guard relented and tugged the chain to open the gate. Manno burst through, despite the guard's continued protests. Taking advantage of the distraction, Vic ducked through and hid in the shadows to avoid catching the guard's eye. Ahead, he could see Manno slowing down the stallion, and he kept to the various rocks bursting through the long grass, following the hoofprints and trampled weeds.

The Viper Plains was quiet in an eerie way, with only the whisper of a breeze rustling through. The moon had disappeared from view some time ago, and without the moonlight, darkness overpowered the distant village lights. All the creatures of the Plains were asleep, except for a few bats whisking through the night sky. But most strange of all was the mist that rose from the ground – a mist that made one shudder.

Then Manno came into view. The killer of bears had dismounted, his horse grazing a few steps away. Vic ducked behind a rock and peered over the edge. "I'm ready for you, Dark One! Those boys may not be men yet, but I can promise you that I am!" Manno's words were loud and drunken, and Vic could feel his heartbeat racing in his ears.

Only the wind trickling through the long grass answered Manno, who picked up a pebble and flung it as far into the mist as he could.

Is he mad? What could have possessed him to drunkenly confront the Dark One?

Manno laughed – a rough, coarse sound. He kicked at the ground and turned back to his steed.

But in that moment, Vic felt a chill go down his spine. Glancing to his right, back toward Dugar, he froze.

Coming toward them, silent and slow, was a hooded figure, blending into the darkness and seeming to float on the mist. All of a sudden, the moon reappeared from behind the night clouds, casting the figure into shadow.

About to mount, Manno paused, his hand flying to the hilt of his sword. Perhaps he'd felt a chill too, at the startling return of the moonlight. Within a moment, he caught sight of the intruder and backed away. "Who goes there?" he called out. But the hooded figure continued approaching in silence, and Manno drew his sword. "Know, stranger, that you face Manno, hero of men, slayer of bears and beasts, and I shall not be frightened like a child!"

The breeze picked up, sending another chill down Vic's spine.

"Manno!" came the icy voice from within the cloak. It was a voice that could freeze both suns. "You're just in time."

With a great cry, Manno rushed at the figure and thrust his blade with a mighty swing.

Yet with a single gesture, the figure knocked Manno's sword from his hand – without even touching him.

Manno stepped back, now weapon-less. "Magic." Manno let out a sharp breath. "Who are you?"

The hooded figure stopped moving, hovering over the grass "Who I am is for only myself to know, nąma."

Vic shuddered as Manno vomited blood all over his tunic. "Dark One, if you must kill me" – and Manno vomited again – "then do it now."

The Dark One smiled, his perfect white teeth slashing the moonlight. "I already have."

For Vic, time seemed to stop as the Dark One raised his arm, pointing one finger at Manno. Words Vic did not understand – magic words – came out of the Dark One's mouth, just as easily as his breath. At the same time, Manno began shaking in a violent manner, choking on his own blood. Vic saw green sparks dancing across Manno's chest, by his heart. Then, a black void appeared – right where his heart would be.

Eyes widening, Vic caught his breath. *He's killing him!*

All of a sudden, Manno's eyes glazed over, and he stopped shaking. For a moment, he stayed motionless where he kneeled. But then, he fell backwards, twitching all over the ground.

Vic's grip tightened on the rock he hid behind.

The black void spread across Manno's body, consuming him. And as he watched the gruesome sight before him, the Dark One chuckled. "A befitting death for a namatéh – your inner darkness consuming your soul.

Wouldn't you agree, Manno-nama?"

But there was no reply. The black void had swallowed up the man, leaving behind only his bear claw necklace.

"No!" Vic moaned, choking on his words, collapsing against the boulder.

The Dark One floated over to stop and pick up the necklace. As he straightened, he snapped his head left, such a quick movement that it caught Vic off guard. His heart stopped as he felt the Dark One's red eyes glare right at him. Ducking behind the rock, Vic whispered a prayer to the spirits above that the Dark One hadn't actually seen him. *Please, spirits!*

In the fog around him, Vic saw a wolf's head appear. A wolf with red eyes and razor-sharp teeth dripping with blood. Snarling, it stepped out of the mist, and Vic held his breath, certain now was the end. But with a single bound, the wolf leapt to the top of the boulder, threw back its ebony head, and howled at the moon.

Vic squeezed his eyes shut.

When he opened them, the Dark One was gone, and the wolf's pawprints led some distance away before vanishing altogether. Manno's horse left no hoofprints – but a pile of bones instead.

Vic ran.

He only stopped when he reached the gate to pound on it, over and over, until the guard heard. Once he had opened the gate enough, however, Vic broke into a run again.

"Hey, wait!" called the guard, but Vic was running too fast to hear him.

Vic ran until he reached his hut. Ducking inside, he caught his breath at the table, leaning over it and panting for air.

His cousin Zurze lay snoring in the side room. Vic sighed, hung up his bow and quiver, and took a seat at his own bundle of furs – when he felt something obtrusive underneath him. It was the tome Zurze had given him much earlier. Vic let out a shaky breath as he touched the book's cover. *If it's true the elves are hidden away somewhere, then surely, they must be more powerful than the things I've seen tonight. And if Zurze is right, then this book knows where they are,* Vic reassured himself.

His hands shaking, Vic flipped the book open to the first page, and his eyes landed on the opening text: *The world has its secrets.*

With a thud, he closed the book, tucked it away, and lay awake – too frightened to close his eyes and relive the scenes on the Plains in his dreams. *After tonight, one thing's for certain: Zurze won't ever have to worry about me being outside the gate at dark,* Vic thought.

Rock Womb

The creature breathed in his first taste of air and opened his eyes. As his vision adjusted to the darkness, he discovered that he stood atop a pile of rocks, a makeshift altar built like a womb. Underneath the rocks burned a fire, but he felt no pain.

All of a sudden, a shout from below caught its attention. Looking down, the creature took in the forms of others. They were staring up at him, and the creature bristled, unsure if they posed a threat.

"Ako's sacrifice worked: Afis has awakened!" croaked another voice – but now, the sound came from right behind him.

Startled, the creature shifted to find a long-legged man watching him. There was an unsettling grin on the stranger's face, a crazy spark in his eyes. And, despite having no memory before waking up, Afis felt a strong sense within him that, already, he did not like this man.

"I made you," the man said, but Afis blinked back. So, the man repeated: "I created you, Afis. I am your master."

I have no master, Afis thought – a declaration that shocked him, for he'd never spoken before. It seemed his instincts had somehow taken on words of their own.

Stepping forward so that their shoulders were level, the stranger grabbed Afis' arm and raised it. Afis noticed his arm was glowing red, albeit faintly. Glancing down, he realized that so was his entire body, every inch of his skin.

To the others below, the man called out, "Blood Bearers: the spirits gave us precisely what we desired! Without the moon above, Afis glows the color of human fear, a beacon to terrify all of Lilligrav!" He grabbed Afis' chin with force and pulled down, revealing fangs among his teeth. "The mouth of a predator, for ripping apart human flesh – and we will ensure Afis feasts well on our enemies!" Stepping away, his eyes glinting in the fire, the man appraised Afis and grinned. "I give you: Afis the Bloodthirsty One!"

Below them, the others cheered and chanted their battle cry, raising swords and clubs into the air. One smeared blood all over his face and tunic, screaming war phrases.

But Afis looked beyond them, for his sharp vision had noticed another group. At the back of the throng, shorter men – each no more than four feet tall – stood in silence, flint-like eyes gazing up at the new life form, brooding as they sharpened daggers.

A nearby croak caught Afis by surprise. "Get some sleep," the stranger told him. "Tomorrow, your training begins."

Overwhelmed, all Afis could think was: *What am I?*

The morning after Manno's death, Vic waited until Zurze entered his workroom before taking his bowl of porridge into the side room. Taking a seat among his jumble of furs, he set down his breakfast and pulled out the book.

Brushing two fingers across, Vic admired the several exquisite jewels encrusted into the cover. At the center was a large oval gem, colored a ruddy brown with fine swirls of a darker shade. Below that were six more, all different colors: black, red, blue, green, yellow, and one consisting of a rainbow of hues.

At each corner, there was fine etching in the thick leather. Vic couldn't make out whatever they said or represented. At the top were several etchings shaped like vines, surrounding odd shapes.

Elfin letters! Vic exclaimed.

His heartbeat quickened.

Zurze was right: if there's elfin on the cover, then this book must discuss the elves! he told himself.

With a shaking hand, Vic flipped the book open to the first page — wherein he read, in shimmering calligraphy:

The world has its secrets. Several of these shall never be found out, for they belong to the knowledge of the spirit world. But with the spirits' help, their humble servant shall uncover the ancient history of magic and its use for living beings. There is history in the magic, and for Lilligrav, her splendor lies in the magic. Thus, with magic, it shall begin.

Above the human words lay elfin lettering, and Vic realized it had been translated into both languages. Turning to the next page, he yawned from lack of sleep and shoveled porridge into his mouth.

The mind is a large power in itself. All living beings have the power to control their own thoughts.

Control our thoughts? Vic repeated to himself.

All living beings have a spiritual part of the brain: the mind. The mind is a fingerprint of the spirits themselves: a grand gift so that beings are granted a taste of the spirits' infinite power. With the mind comes the focus point for magic. Magic comes from spirits, but the mind is where it is focused. Thoughts make the magic happen.

In every living being is its mental core. All sources of information can be found in the mind. Names, place of birth, memories, images, fears. Pictures are the easiest mental way of communication, as images take less strength to send than, perhaps, a thought of body. In animals, the thoughts are few and weak. But in higher beings, the thoughts become stronger and accessible.

Because the mind is such a wellspring of information, one must take careful precautions to avoid valuable insight to be "stolen" by other Magic Masters. With the mind, higher beings can block thoughts, share them, and use them. The mind opens a web of communication.

All higher beings can touch each other's minds to communicate, but this connection is always brief. The cuchel to use depends on the wielder's desires. For the most basic mental communication, the words are: gérté'pe stref qe yoi chinel'pe stref. *Translation: "my mind communicates to your mind." With these simple words, the speaker will be able to project a few words mentally to the chosen being.*

However, furthermore, higher beings may communicate on a more intimate level in mental communication. With a special spell, two beings may become "mental friends" with continuous connection. The cuchel may seem random, but the spirits see beyond what mere mortals can comprehend.

Fate chooses the two to bond. And Fate is never wrong.

The words for this cuchel are simple: stref mä jerda.

His heart beating faster, Vic's thoughts flashed, seeing the possibilities of having another living being to communicate with on the most intimate level. The idea intrigued him, tantalized him. He spoke to himself: *Imagine the possibilities! But my one concern: for as it says here, the other is chosen at random, by the spirits themselves. What if I end up with someone incredibly...boring? And yet, the possibility could be in my favor – and what an experience!* And just like on the field, without a second thought, Vic said the words, before he could change his mind.

Nothing happened.

But then, in a blink, Vic felt his mind on fire, pulled in all directions, before throbbing with what seemed like another heartbeat, second to his own. A dizzying feeling filled his head, and he fell backwards, the furs tumbling around him. As if he were without arms and legs, he lay there, his mental core bursting out of his skull, pounding at the back of his head.

He'd never been so aware of his own mental core inside him.

A tremor shook his body, and then he fell unconscious.

Afis hadn't slept. His newborn mind, juxtaposed with his advanced instincts, had kept him up until dawn: *How do I know words? How is it that, upon seeing his face, I already disliked my—my "master."* He rolled his eyes. *I have no master. Who is my creator?*

"Ah, you're awake," came a familiar voice, and he bristled at the sound. As if he'd heard Afis' thoughts, the long-legged stranger was approaching him.

Irritated, Afis grumbled incoherently.

"Speak, Afis," the man croaked. "You know you can. Ako's sacrifice ensured your instincts would be more advanced than a newborn's, to save us time."

So, Afis uttered his first words: "Who are you?"

The man laughed. "I am your master. Master Rudolf. The Blood Bearers are my men. And you," he added, the unsettling smile returning, "are my creation."

"How—how did you create me?"

"Dark magic, a blood pact, and Ako's sacrifice – all of it pleased the spirits enough to grant you to us." He gestured to the altar Afis sat on. "This is where you were conceived last night, but we have long awaited your arrival."

Eyes narrowing, Afis squinted at Rudolf. "Why? For what reason did you create me?"

Rudolf frowned. "Years ago, the Six Tines came together to banish us. We made camp here but knew we'd return someday. We swore it. And then Ako foresaw you at the forefront, the key to our narrative. For years, we let the blackbeard dwarfs serve as our image – humans fear what they do not understand – but now *you* will become synonymous with the Blood Bearers." He rubbed his hands together. "Everyone in Lilligrav will grow to fear Afis the Bloodthirsty One, and we will have our revenge."

One last question, Afis thought. "You keep mentioning Ako, but I don't know that name." *...and yet, maybe I do?*

When he heard the name, Rudolf's eyes glinted with the same crazy spark. "Our visionary, who sacrificed his life so that yours would begin. You mustn't disappoint his legacy." He gestured to the camp below. "Come: we have much to prepare you for."

Following him down the pile of rocks, Afis mulled over Rudolf's answers. The name Ako meant nothing to him, yet deep within his mind, Afis felt as if he knew the dead man's intentions. As if Ako were planting seeds inside him. *But why? And how?*

There was the soft touch of someone's palm on his cheek, and then Vic heard his name being called. Like drifting out of a dream, he listened to the distant voice, wondering to whom it belonged.

And then it dawned on him: *Zurze!*

Awaking with a start, he jolted upwards then groaned when his head throbbed. Wincing, he grasped his head, his vision gradually coming into focus. *How long was I unconscious?* he wondered.

Vic found himself looking at Zurze's concerned face. His cousin was squatted next to him, beside the tumble of furs that made up Vic's bed. "Vic, can you hear me now?"

"Aye," Vic groaned, wishing his head would quit pounding.

"Are you hurt?"

Vic shook his head. "What happened?"

Zurze's gaze hardened. "I was hoping you'd tell me. I heard your porridge bowl clatter and rushed in to find it broken in pieces on the floor."

I haven't been unconscious for long then. Vic glanced to his right and indeed, there lay his porridge bowl in broken pieces of clay. *I must have dropped it – and yet I don't remember much at all,* he thought, followed by immediate mental pain: *Ow! My head still hurts from that cuchel!*

"Perhaps lying back down will jog your memory – I'd guess you sat up too fast." Zurze reached for him, but Vic pushed him away.

"No, I'm fine." He found himself unable to return Zurze's severe and steady gaze.

"Vic?"

His mind scrambling for a story, Vic took a deep breath. "On the spirits above, Zurze, I—I don't recall. It must be lack of sleep – I was tossing all of last night." He looked straight at him. "Strange dreams that kept me awake – and your snoring didn't help!"

His cousin didn't crack a grin as Vic had hoped. Instead, Zurze continued staring at him, a grim frown turning down the corners of his mouth. *He thinks I'm lying. Surely, he won't turn and see—*As if he'd read Vic's thoughts, Zurze's gaze dropped to the book at Vic's feet.

The pages fluttered as a breeze floated through the room, and Vic let out a breath. *He won't be able to tell which cuchel I chose – if that thought has even crossed his mind.*

Zurze paused, watching the pages flip back and forth, before looking back at him.

"I'm fine, Zurze," Vic insisted, staring long and hard at his cousin, never flinching from meeting his eye.

"Cure yourself, then, Vic. It's clear you don't want me to, and I have to get back to work." With a grunt, Zurze got to his feet and marched out.

As soon as he heard Zurze's hammer, Vic reached for the book and flipped back to the page he'd been reading. Nowhere did it explain the curious reaction he'd had to the spell. With a deep sigh of frustration, he closed the book, lay back, and shut his eyes, concentrating. *Let's see if it worked,* he said, somewhat nervous, as he tapped into his mind, a place he'd never really been before. He breathed a sigh of relief when there was no physical reaction this time.

Connected to the core of his mind, he found, was a glowing white string, thin and weak. Hesitant but also curious, he touched it, and in response, felt a burning sensation – but at the heart of the sensation: a connection. Not quite sure what to do, Vic projected, threw, a word forward:

Hello?

The string strengthened, thickened, morphed into a strongly-glowing white tube.

And there was an answer.

Hello?

Magic

Vic basked in the feeling his mental companion's response gave him – a feeling he couldn't quite describe. *I—I suppose I should explain my sudden presence. But first, who—*Vic paused. *Who are you?*

The answer was instantaneous: *I am Snook, son of Kell, a mighty warrior, and Lady-borne.*

Are you nama? Elva?

The answer wasn't as sudden – but shocking: *I am dog.*

Outside his mental being, Vic gasped, opened his eyes. The connection weakened, as he stepped away from his mind. *A dog? My mental friend is a…dog?!*

Snook had been half-asleep, gazing out at the harbor in boredom, when he'd felt an annoying buzzing at the back of his skull. Stronger and stronger it became until he felt his head was full of angry bees. Then came an urgent and persistent tugging – pulling at him from behind with an invisible string – before a word of greeting echoed into his mind.

Startled, he'd perked up, looking all around and sniffing, before realizing the speaker was telepathic.

Now his strange mind reader seemed shocked to discover just who Snook was – while Snook was shocked to discover his mind had…this possibility. He'd always felt different than other dogs, as they seemed to think from pure instinct alone, while he'd always been able to ponder things, debate things – but only with himself. Of course, no one had ever heard or listened – humans couldn't hear, and dogs didn't…well, talk. Yet now he was having a conversation – a mental conversation, at that – with someone else.

Yes, I am a dog. I don't understand how this all came about, but you must be human, yes? Only humans can do magic, to my comprehension. I would try, if I knew the words.

His telepathic companion was silent, but Snook somehow still felt his presence. Moments later, there came a reply, and Snook felt himself tingle all over, as if someone had touched a hot iron – the ones he'd seen humans press to horses – to him. It was warm in a good way, but Snook had to lie down from the overwhelming sensation.

I am Vic. And yes, I am nama—I mean—human.

Why – or perhaps rather, how – have you spoken to me in my mind?

It was a cuchel I recited, Vic explained. *You are my mental friend now – we can contact each other through our mental beings, through our thoughts. But how—how I am able to contact you is beyond my understanding. Only creatures of magic are known to…speak. But you're just a dog!*

Snook barked. *And you're a human. And since you're the sole human thus far to understand me: I need your help, Vic.*

All of a sudden, Snook's mind was filled with an image: of a man pounding a hammer onto a plank of wood before looking up with a kind smile. *What was that? Is that you?* he asked.

I—I don't know. I wanted to send you the feeling of—of me being able to help you. The one person I trust to help me is my cousin, and before I could understand what was happening, I was projecting my image of him. But I will help you, Snook.

My master and young master have not returned. I cannot escape confinement without help.

Why haven't they returned?

They went to sea and have not come back, but it has been many, many days! I am unable to tell those who come to feed me that I have lost hope in their return. Humans cannot understand my persistent barking.

Why can't you escape on your own?

Snook whined. *I am chained.*

Why are you chained?

Because the humans…do not trust me, Snook admitted.

…why? Vic eventually asked.

I am not like other dogs. I am not interested in them, and they avoid me. So, the humans, they think I am some sort of…curse, and therefore, I am chained when my masters are gone. I cannot explain why I am different to the humans – until today, I did not know how to speak!

Why didn't your masters take you out to sea with them?

Snook was starting to worry Vic wouldn't come, for all the questions he kept asking. *I cannot explain it, but I am afraid of the sea. My master would have discarded me, for I am no fishing dog like my mother, but my young master has always wanted me.*

Where do you live?

Drema, near the sea, Snook replied.

Well, that is across the Viper Plains.

Somehow, Snook could sense, almost hear, the hesitation in Vic's voice. It was as if his emotions had become visual pictures, and Snook could grasp the hesitation from what Vic had sent. For the moment, he didn't understand how it worked. Perhaps he would later.

Where are you? I cannot understand the maps my master shows my young master.

I live in Dugar with my cousin. That's quite far, Snook – you know that, right?

Snook ignored the question. *You can do it. I can sense these things. I suppose you could call it my sixth sense.*

There was a long pause, but Snook could still feel Vic's touch on the strange string connecting them. And then the string rippled with Vic's response: *I will come.*

A few days later, Afis found himself being swept off his rocky island home. That fateful morning, he stood talking with one of Rudolf's closest friends and, Afis guessed, advisors. He was picking up on the human interactions quickly – *perhaps a side effect of my given intent in life?* he pondered.

Brandi whittled a slender twig between his yellow teeth. "Yessir, Afis, the plan is to leave Glasiea for Lilligrav tonight." He spat onto the broken ground. Afis snarled as some of Brandi's spit sprayed his arm. Brandi looked up at him, grounding on the stick, and regarded Afis. Only Brandi and Rudolf seemed not to fear Afis' bestial tempers.

"So, why are we leaving? This island is fine."

"That's because it's all you've ever known!" Brandi said with a chortle.

Afis growled.

"You'll see that Lilligrav is far better than this rotten island, and that's because of one thing: gold, Afis! Gold!" Brandi's eyes flashed. "Plenty of it, too. Rudolf hasn't told me which city he desires to plunder, but any good coastal town will do. Besides," he added, stroking his knotted beard and raising an eyebrow at Afis appraisingly, "we might as well test your strength."

Afis sighed, reflecting on the multiple training sessions the Blood Bearers made him go through. How to sneak up on enemies and then tear them apart. How to scream terror into the hearts of men. At first, Afis had enjoyed it – but it was all he'd ever known. And then, as the hours blended into days, he grew tired of the repetition.

There must be more to my life than training, he grumbled.

"Where do we plan on going? That large landmass to the west so far off?"

Brandi shrugged. "Lilligrav isn't so far off, Afis. Besides, traveling on ship, you'll be thankful for wherever we land. I can bet you on that."

Afis scoffed. "How do you know what I enjoy and despise?"

Brandi's lips curled up into a sly smile. "Every new trainee struggles with finding their sea legs. As for the former: I've watched your training. You enjoy killing and destroying. You'll find that plundering will give you such an energy beyond what you know — an energy you can't get enough of."

In his mind, Afis could picture himself at the front of the Blood Bearers, roaring fear into the hearts of those they attacked. He could taste the thrill, breathed in the excitement.

And yet, somehow Afis felt Brandi was wrong: *If the training no longer pleases me, how will leading the Blood Bearers please me? What if there's more than being feared?* "I'm going to find Rudolf."

Brandi shrugged, his fingers sliding along the stick. "And you're going to want to board the ship and get comfortable as soon as you can. Best get going."

Afis moved off. The Blood Bearers' base was a pure mess of people, animals, and things to load onto the vessel — completely hectic. Pens stood erected all around him, and a few animals filled their small spaces. Bleating miniature goats — bred by dwarfs — stood grouped in one pen. Afis counted five of them, and his stomach growled. The Blood Bearers didn't feed him enough.

Another pen held a pair of war dogs. Afis recalled Rudolf informing him that these two canines — among the many others bred by the Blood Bearers — were trained to rip apart human survivors and scare off intruders. However, Afis was here — Rudolf firmly believed, and the rest of the Blood Bearers hoped — to replace their growing pack of dogs.

The dogs whimpered and retreated to the far corner of the pen, their tails tucked at the very unrecognizable scent Afis gave off. The hair prickling on the back of his neck, Afis leaned down and growled at them, showing off his sharp teeth. He was getting comfortable with the idea of everyone fearing him. Everyone except —

A blackbeard dwarf, his stained dagger held between his teeth, crossed Afis' path. Afis turned to glare down at the dwarf, and a snarl caught on his lips. But the dwarf glared back, granite-like eyes sparking.

If the blackbeard dwarfs don't fear me, am I as terrifying as Rudolf boasts? Should I doubt my own destiny?

Afis let the dwarf continue leading a miniature goat up the plank onto the ship before following. After forcing a young boy to tell him where Rudolf was, he entered the captain's cabin.

Rudolf lolled in a chair inside. Two other men were standing over a table, poking daggers into a map, speaking in angry tones and gesturing toward Rudolf. The leader looked up as Afis entered and cleared his throat. The two men sheathed their stilettos and pushed past Afis out the door, which he shut behind them.

"Welcome, Afis."

He resisted the urge to cringe at the sound of Rudolf's voice. It was so unnerving, like pebbles scraping each other. Other times, Rudolf seemed to croak like a frog – and a very bad-sounding frog at that. "Rudolf."

The man stood, his long legs knocking over the chair in the process. He brushed the map off the table and replaced it with another one which had been leaning, rolled up, against the wall. "Come, Afis."

He stifled a growl. *I'm not one of his war dogs.*

Approaching the table, Afis peered down at the map. It was painted on thick parchment, the edges tattered. Crinkles covered the drawings, no matter how much Rudolf tried to smooth them. The details were extraordinary – even the seas had the terrifying faces of monsters. Compared to the simple maps Afis had seen in the possession of other Blood Bearers, this map was beautiful. *Either it was quite expensive or – more likely – Rudolf stole it.*

"It's time you learned geography." Rudolf pointed his dagger toward the map, hovering over the boundaries and pen lines.

Afis leaned over the parchment, studied it closer. "Start here." It was the farthest point north on the map.

"The town of U'ag. Quite the splendid town, I've heard, but we never could breach it. The snow there is fierce – men have died from the cold when we've tried to ransack it. We've never even found it among all the snow." Rudolf's eyes glittered. "Think of all the gold they must hide."

Afis shrugged and pointed to another dot. "Here?"

Rudolf almost crowed. "That is Levar, the richest city on the entire island. I'd love to get my hands on the governor's gold – he must be bloody rich! But the city is like a fortress, with merchants who protect their money with blood and hounds. It takes a huge inside job."

Afis blinked. "What geography am I learning, anyway?"

"Lilligrav. The main island. You've only known this rock pile Glasiea for your few short days of life, but there's more out there, Afis. Lilligrav is the largest island. The other landmasses are the Lone Isles, including Glasiea, and the hidden Isle of the Dragons. That last one's legend though."

Afis nodded, his mind still buzzing with newborn thoughts.

"Now," Rudolf continued, absorbed in his presentation, "the reason Levar is so rich is because of this town: Polaski. Oh, what a find! Polaski is the mining village of Lilligrav. Though this town, Dugar," and he slammed his finger atop yet another dot, just east of Polaski, "claims to do a bit of mining as well. However, back to the point: Polaski mines the gems and gold that hide in the Wilderness Mountains here." And he brushed his hand along a cluster of wavy lines along the far coast.

"What about here? Right beside…" Afis leaned closer, trying to read the scraggly writing that spread across the map. "Beside Mount Deruge?"

Rudolf nodded slowly, as if turning something over in his mind. "The native village of Heftka. Don't ask me what the difference is between us humans and those savages. Other than skin color, I have no idea. Only those who study history know – and I never liked history! Those blasted savages sure do think of themselves all high and mighty like, as if they are the very elves themselves!"

Elves? Afis repeated to himself.

"Now, Afis, as I was just discussing with some of the fellow…Blood Bearers, I think attacking a coastal town is our best bet. What do you have to say about that?"

Afis coughed. "Do you always destroy the village?"

Rudolf raised his head and looked him over. But his stare made Afis uncomfortable: *As if he's never quite looked at me before. Does he realize my internal conflict?*

Never breaking his stare, Rudolf responded, "Unfortunately, the people of Lilligrav are stubbornly resilient. Even if we burn…say, Drema to the ground, they always rebuild."

"So why attack at all?"

Rudolf's eyes narrowed. "To remind the Six that we were never extinguished. The blackbeard dwarfs' recent attacks have set the scene for our return, and you will mark our comeback." Rudolf smiled. "You'll be all we need to make the people fear us. Stories of dark creatures like you spread like wildfire."

"How?"

"We have connections – scouts, you could say – planted all over. They are loyal to the Blood Bearers and will help spread the story of Afis the Bloodthirsty One. Once you help us plunder Drema, the villagers will talk – and our scouts will help fan the flame. Think of the weevils, the Dark One."

"Weevils? Dark One?"

"Children's stories, to keep them inside during the night."

Afis blinked. His head was spinning: *A whole new world out there – and perhaps more to the life Rudolf and the Blood Bearers envision for me. Perhaps…perhaps there is more to being Afis than killing and plundering.*

Rudolf cut through his thoughts. "I'll summon you when I have planned the invasion. You shall be given your assignment then."

But Afis wasn't listening. He was staring at the map, a newfound curiosity blooming inside him.

Vic scooped up his quiver – filled with new arrows carved by Zurze – and grabbed his bow. Zurze appeared out of his workroom, wiping sweat from his brow, and stopped in surprise at the sight of him. "Cousin, you're up early." Zurze laid down his hammer and grabbed an apple. "Still not sleeping well?"

With a shrug, Vic turned to the front door. "I wanted to get an early start on the hunt today. There's a doe that has been dodging me for a fortnight, but today I'm going to snare her."

Zurze smiled in encouragement. "Bring back more birds and roots for tonight's stew, and I can make you more arrows. You're hunting faster than I can whittle."

Vic laughed and put a hand on the door. But then he paused, looked over his shoulder. "Zurze?"

His cousin looked up from picking up his hammer. "Yes, Vic?"

"What do you—what does it take to be a ntéh, in your mind?"

Zurze bit into the apple, chewing slowly. "I'm no expert, but…well…" He paused, swallowed. "Well, take Manno, for example. He killed a mountain bear with his own two hands. He had to trust in himself, Vic. If he hadn't been as strong as he knew himself to be, that bear would have eaten him instead. But he risked his life to do something brave." Zurze tossed his apple to Vic, who caught it and grinned. "At least, that's what my simple mind can fathom." He picked up his hammer, paused, and looked back at him. "Just out of curiosity, why do you ask?"

But Vic was gone, the door closing shut behind him.

Outside, both suns shone brightly, waking the late risers from their beds. A trio of shepherds led their flock out of an overnight pen; two herding dogs darted among the sheep, playing chase with each other. Vic could hear the men inside the tavern, while across the street rang out the sound of the blacksmith's hammer against iron.

A muscular stallion snorted from the public stables. He stood tethered outside while a tall groom brushed his coat. Another stable boy led out a mare and brought her over to the town fountain. The stallion trumpeted, tugging at the rope. A lone dark figure leaned against a pillar supporting the stables, watching the groom handle the feisty stallion. Vic figured he was the horse's owner, and from the man's dirt-dusted clothes, he again guessed the stranger was a traveler. The man's skin was bronze-colored, and both suns shone on his silver-blond hair.

Beside the village fountain sat a group of boys. Most were younger than Vic, but one was his age. All of them sat slicing apart a watermelon, laughing at the juice dribbling down each other's faces. "Vic! Come join us!" one of them called out. He looked over. The one his age pierced the watermelon with his dagger, pulled out a chunk, and held out the stiletto toward him.

"Where did you get it, Robin?" Vic asked while Robin, the leader of the boys, sucked droplets of juice off his fingers. Vic and Robin had once been playmates – ever since Vic could remember – but Robin now preferred his gang over him. The younger boys accepted Vic as an honorary leader – for, like Robin, he could outrun and outhunt any of them.

"Tasha and her father are selling fruit outside of town." Robin winked in a knowing way at the younger boys, who chuckled. "Let's just say, she can't resist this rogue's charm. When her father wasn't looking, I managed to convince her to slip me some fruit."

"Aye," another boy cut in, "she may be the prettiest girl of the village, but she's not smarter than an ass!"

Vic shook his head. "How proud of yourselves you must be," he remarked with disdain.

Robin swallowed a piece of watermelon. "What are you saying, Vic? That we shouldn't be proud of a free bounty?"

"That you shouldn't be proud of playing a girl that way."

"What do you know about girls?" Robin snorted. "I saw the way you walked out on Tasha at the bonfire."

Annoyed, Vic gripped his bow tighter. "I know not to treat them like idiots."

The boys quieted. "It was all just in fun, Vic," Robin put in.

Best not to waste food, however, Vic decided and moved closer. "I'll take a piece."

Robin handed over an entire watermelon. "Take it, Vic. We've had our share. Come on, boys!" They jumped off the fountain wall, heading in the direction of the tavern, and Vic knew they intended to flirt with the

"Five bronze coins and a strip of meat will do." women who worked there. Any other day, Vic would have joined them, to listen to the men's talk. But today, he had other things to prepare for.

Vic continued through the village, carrying the watermelon with one arm and his bow in the other. All of a sudden, the mixed-blood traveler stood in his way. "You, lad."

"Yes, sir?"

"How much do you want for that?" said the traveler, nodding toward the watermelon.

Vic glanced down at it. "Well, to tell you the truth, sir, I was going to trade it to the butcher for some meat."

The man laughed – a rich, hearty sound. "Why, I'll give you both gold and meat for it."

"It's just a watermelon."

The stranger stroked his stallion's nose. "I and my steed need provisions for our travels ahead of us. Watermelon is one of our favorites. How much?"

"You're too humble, lad." The stranger dug into his tunic, pulling out a money pouch, and dropped the stallion's rope. "Steady, Filo." The stallion snorted but stood still, eyes still locked on the delicate golden mare.

Vic raised his brow. *A well-trained horse,* he observed.

Clutching the money pouch in one hand, the man opened his stallion's saddlebags and pulled out a long strip of jerky. At the smell of the smoked meat, Vic's mouth watered. The traveler laid the strip on his arm, took the watermelon, and stuffed the fruit into another saddlebag. After handing the jerky to Vic, he dug into the pouch and produced five bronze coins and a shiny silver one. "Keep the extra."

Vic stared at the silver in astonishment. "Won't you need it?"

The man laughed again. "Not as much as you, lad. Besides," he added, mounting, "I can tell you'll be doing a bit of traveling yourself."

How—how did he— "You can?"

"Aye. Good luck, son." With a snort, the stallion trotted toward the gate, and the man waved farewell to Vic.

Well, that was a sign direct from the spirits, Vic figured, grinning.

The Healer

Snook, are you there?

Still half-asleep, Snook twitched his nose at the sound of the voice before realizing the soft touch at the back of his mind was Vic contacting him. Reluctant, he opened an eye and took in his surroundings. With both suns inching closer and closer to their midday meeting point, the distant harbor was busy with fishermen hauling in their fresh catches. His stomach growled, and he glanced at the empty food dish, licked clean from a generous stranger's dumping of leftover porridge last night. *What is it?* he asked.

I've decided to leave tonight. I'm coming, Snook.

Snook barked, wagging his tail in a frenzy. *Thank you, thank you, thank you, Vic!*

Hours later, Vic returned to the village fountain. He cupped water in both hands, splashed his face, and gulped the rest down. A tremble shook his knees: he'd just come back from running. While he and Snook had discussed the plan, Vic knew he was right to prepare for a trek across the Viper Plains. He'd been going on runs every day he went hunting. In Vic's reasoning, this was not just to keep in shape for a long journey but also to outrun bandits he might encounter on the way. *Though I'm sure there aren't many,* he assumed, *if the rest of Lilligrav is anything like Dugar. And if they think I'm an outcast, then they should leave me alone.*

Yet, Vic hoped for a little challenge. After all, that's what Manno had said: "To be a man – to be a ntéh – means risking your life for something." *Isn't this how I become a man: risking my life to save a dog on the other side of Lilligrav?* And thus, he'd agreed to trek across the Viper Plains and save his new mental companion. He wasn't quite sure how it would happen, but the thought of undergoing the journey energized him.

Again, he splashed water on his skin, feeling the refreshing liquid mingle with his sweat. Picking up his small bag of rabbit, he moved in the direction of his hut. Halfway there, he heard a shout: "Make way! Mad pig! Mad pig!"

Vic turned his head in surprise. Sure enough, villagers flung themselves to either their left or right, heeding the cry. Then, out of nowhere it seemed, a boar came rushing through. Its fur was thick with flies, and its tusks came to deadly points. Screams filled the air as villagers hurried to get out of its way. An angry boar was not a creature to be messed with.

The boar snorted as it came to a halt right in front of the fountain. Vic grimaced: *Don't you dare go into the water, you filthy pig!* Wild boars were considered unclean and unfit to eat, as well as their female mates. Even their domesticated relatives had to go through intensive cleansing cuchels before being declared suitable for supper. As if heeding Vic's thoughts, the boar trotted around the fountain.

A man hiding in an alley shot a rock at the boar, which hit it right in the side, knocking it over. The boar squealed but still stumbled to his feet.

Following the man's example, other villagers began tossing pebbles off the street at the boar. As more and more stones beat at its hide, the creature's eyes filled with fury. With an angry squeal, the beast shook its tusks, scraping the ground with a hoof.

You idiots! An angry boar is more dangerous than a confused one! Vic thought, recalling the one time he'd encountered one while hunting. The creature had been spooked by Vic running after his target and charged him. He had climbed a tree to avoid being trampled and torn apart by its tusks. It had taken the boar hours to give up, and by that time, Vic's chosen prey was long gone.

In the present moment, the boar rushed at those throwing stones before wheeling around at the last minute. And then he turned to Vic's direction – the one person without a stone. With a ferocious squeal, the beast lowered its snout and charged at Vic.

He dropped his bag of rabbit and nocked an arrow. The boar continued charging.

Steadying his bow, Vic released. The arrow made its mark: hitting the animal right between the eyes. With an angry snort, the creature stumbled and fell onto its side.

But it wasn't dead – yet. Villagers huddled in the shadows and in the alleys, more stones at the ready.

With caution, Vic approached the boar, kneeled, and reached for his arrow between its eyes. They were lit with furious hatred at the sight of him, but the animal did not rise. Letting out a breath, Vic grasped his arrow and pulled. The boar squealed in anger and pain. Blood spilled onto the cobblestones below, and the villagers inched forward. Vic plunged the same arrow into the pig's shoulder, and it went taut and froze. Cheers erupted around him. Getting to his feet, Vic found himself patted on the back by the many who'd seen his victory. From the corner of his eyes, he saw Robin and his gang. Robin stared hard at Vic, who swallowed, self-conscious all of a sudden.

"Vic," came a voice, and he turned to find Kerimo, the tanner. "Sell me the boar, and I can skin it after cleansing spells."

"Five silver coins."

Kerimo grinned. "A big price for a big kill." And within moments, the tanner thrust the coins into Vic's hands. "Oi, tie up the boar's legs and drag him to my shop, boys!"

Vic ducked away, his heart pounding. As his hut came into view, he paused outside the front door to catch his breath. *I'm ready, Snook.*

"Land ahoy!"

Grunting, Afis trudged to the deck. Almost a week had passed on the Blood Bearers' ship, and he'd regretted every minute of it. At first, Afis had been curious about the ocean, but that feeling hadn't even lasted a day. Instead, he was annoyed by the constant tossing of the sailing craft. *Brandi was right,* he begrudgingly admitted.

But now, at long last, land – Lilligrav – had been sighted.

Afis steadied himself against the railing along the steps to the deck. The ship rocked, and as he wobbled, a few curses came out of his mouth.

"Afis, come here!" shouted a voice, and he turned to the sound. Rudolf was motioning him over.

Walking over, Afis bumped into a Blood Bearer. With a growl, the man pushed past and ran off, having clearly not recognized Afis. Then Afis bumped into another Blood Bearer – this time, a bad-tempered dwarf. Turning his head, Afis realized the Blood Bearers were gathering at the edge of the ship. *Is it really that exciting?* he wondered.

Rudolf smiled down at Afis. "We've decided to attack Drema, Afis. As you can see, land is still far off. We'll stay a good distance away and then surprise attack at night, when the harbor will be less guarded, the guards more drunk. When we do attack, you'll lead the charge and kill the survivors. With you at our side, the Blood Bearers will strike fear into the very heart of Lilligrav – one city at a time!"

Absentmindedly, but for Rudolf's behalf, Afis nodded. As before, his mind buzzed with orders and questions: *Perhaps I was created to kill – but as that far-off landmass proves, there may be more to my life than what Rudolf desires. How will*

I know unless I explore it myself – make my own decisions? I've been tossing around the idea every moment on this godforsaken ship, and tonight is my one chance.

Rubbing his palms together, Rudolf turned away and began yelling out orders. Afis took his chance. With the Blood Bearers still gathered at the edge of the ship, he backed away. *It's now or never,* he decided.

Snook gazed out at the harbor, feeling one sun's final rays tickle his back, while the other sunk below the distant waves. The rising moon gave him a new sense of hope – for tonight's moon meant Vic was on his way. *Then I'll be free!*

He'd given up on his young master's return, and it had lost him a night of sleep, with all the sorrow he'd felt upon the realization. His sixth sense told him that the boy and his father weren't returning, though he didn't know why. Humans told him nothing.

But strangest of all: ever since he and Vic had become bonded, it seemed he was forgetting his young master more and more. *As if Vic is more than just another human to me.*

A young girl walked by. Snook wagged his tail at the sight of her – she always brought him a snack and would talk to him, telling him about her day. She'd said he was a great listener. "Hello, Snook," she said. "It's me, Ettalia. Remember me?" Out plopped his panting tongue, and she giggled. "You always do. Here – I brought you something."

She stuck out her hand, and Snook prodded it with his wiggling nose. *Fresh bacon!* Though the pieces were small, Snook savored them as if he wouldn't eat again for a while – which was probably true. *At least, until Vic comes!*

Ettalia giggled again and scratched Snook between the ears, glancing over her shoulder. He knew why: she'd once told him that her mother would spank her if she caught the young girl outside alone. To comfort her, he licked her cheek. She tasted sticky, and there was a bit of strawberry jam stuck to the corner of her mouth.

"Want some water?" she asked.

He whined, tail wagging.

"I'll bring some later – I have to go back now, and Momma will notice if I slip out again. But I promise. I'll bring some soon." With a kiss to his muzzle, she got up and went home.

Snook watched her leave before dropping his head down between his paws. She was the only one who took time to talk to him; others who took pity on him merely fed him and patted him once before leaving. He liked her, and now she was gone.

Without intending to, he let out a slow whine from deep in his throat. Stretching lazily, he plopped onto his side and dozed off.

Vic stretched out underneath his fur blankets, his legs ready for the long night ahead of him. Propping himself on his elbows, he watched Zurze finish carving Vic's new chair before also coming to bed.

"Goodnight, Vic."

His hands behind his head, Vic stared at the simple ceiling of their hut, realizing tonight might be the last time he'd have a shelter above his head – at least, until he crossed the Viper Plains. His eyes darted across the blankness above, the planks of wood serving as the ceiling, before noises caused him to look back at Zurze, who was shifting, restless, under the furs.

"Unable to sleep?"

With a dark chuckle, Zurze flipped onto his side, facing Vic, who caught his stern look.

"Yes, Zurze?"

His cousin sighed – a sharp outtake of breath that sliced through the air. "I just—blast it all."

"Zurze?"

"Vic, have you met a girl?"

"No." He chuckled, recalling his encounter with Tasha, unsure if Zurze had witnessed that exchange or not. "I'll wait a few more years before *that*."

His cousin pounded his fist into a fur, and Vic recognized his frustration. With a groan, Zurze shut his eyes and pinched the bridge of his nose between two fingers. "You've just been…so—so…distant."

"Zurze: I'm still just me."

His cousin shrugged, lying on his back and staring at the ceiling. "I just—just could swear that…" With a final sigh, he rolled onto his other side, back to Vic, and forced the furs up to his chin. "Forget it. Goodnight."

Vic waited until Zurze began to snore, lost in dreams. Then he retrieved his cousin's pack for traveling. *I promise I'm just borrowing it, Zurze.* From under his furs, he pulled out his book and the jerky from the stranger. He stuffed both inside then turned to his cousin.

He sighed, torn.

Goodbye, Zurze. At the head of Zurze's pallet he laid a small figurine: a slender leaping deer. When Vic was a few years old, his father had carved it – then disappeared in the night. So, now, his cousin would know what it meant: *I'm going to catch that deer, Zurze. Just like my father.*

Ducking into the main room, Vic grabbed his wool jacket off a peg on the wall and donned it over his outer tunic. He flung his quiver over his shoulder, seized his bow, and with one last look, went out the front door.

He raced for the outskirts of town, hoping to make it unseen to the gate. Not wanting to run into Ruthgar again, who would send him back home, Vic headed for the east gate, where the night guard often slept soundly on the job.

A chained herding dog twitched its ears, raised its head. As Vic passed, the beast jumped to its feet, growling, fur standing on end. In reply to the dog's ferocious barking, a goat bleated not far off. But no one emerged from the owner's house, and Vic ducked away.

Once at the tall wooden gate, he took a deep breath and murmured,

"Beu shu." Shining a brilliant ruby, the gates flung open, pieces of wood flying off.

There was a snort above, but no movement. *Thank the spirits the guard's a heavy sleeper.*

The red light illuminated everything around it, shining brilliantly into Vic's eyes and spreading his shadow far behind him. As the light dimmed from the spell, there were muffled shouts as villagers in nearby huts awoke. Footsteps filled the air.

Without hesitation, Vic ran through the open gate and looked back only once with Zurze on his mind, hoping his cousin would fare well without him.

At that moment, a loud shout boomed throughout Dugar, followed by a flare of light. Vic stumbled. Hunched over on his knees, he steadied his breathing, his own heartbeat echoing in his ears. *Torches – a search party! But I've got to keep moving –* as the nightmarish memory filled his mind, the Dark One's voice chilling his veins.

He got to his feet and swayed. *My head...*

Cradling his head, Vic ran as footsteps rang out behind him. Deep voices thundered: "The gate! We'll catch the thief!"

Vic cursed as the tome pounded against his back with each step. Looking around in desperation, he searched for a place to hide. *I'm not a thief, but that won't stop them from bringing me back!* he reminded himself. With a grunt, he thrust himself to the side and rolled behind a clump of spiny plants. On one knee, he strung his bow and waited.

The footsteps passed, as did the torches and voices.

Vic moved to his feet before slamming back into the ground. Navarre, captain of the governor's guards, loped past atop a stallion. Cracking a whip over his head, he shouted, "The boy is mine!"

Vic shuddered. *That boy is me.*

As the hoofbeats pounded away, he inched to his feet, hunched over, and slunk off into the shadows.

There was a rustle in the grass behind him. Vic halted, tense. *The Dark One? Help me, spirits!* he prayed before a human form leaped from the darkness onto a slab of rock ahead. Thinking quickly, Vic seized a stick and said in a hushed tone: "Ralas." The stick ignited, illuminating the stranger's face – and the dagger he clutched in one hand.

"Vic?"

He released his breath. "Robin?"

"What are you doing here? Does Zurze know?" His eyes trailed Vic's figure, resting on the faint outline of his pack. "You're traveling?"

Vic lowered the makeshift torch. "Robin, please understand. I have to go."

"I think I should tell Zurze," Robin said.

"No! I don't want him to worry." Vic sighed. "I'll be home before the Storyteller's next fire. To Drema and back, I swear."

"Drema!" Robin exclaimed. Then he grabbed the fiery stick and pushed Vic to the ground.

The horseback captain came trotting past, his whip dragging on the ground. "You, there!" he called to Robin, who held his torch high. Vic lay behind a cluster of rocks, watching with wary eyes.

"Aye, captain!"

Navarre cursed as he halted his horse, staring down at Robin. "What are you doing out on the Plains, boy? The Dark One could come at any moment."

Vic shut his eyes, forcing the memory of Manno to the farthest part of his mind.

Robin puffed out his chest. "I was with the search party, sir. I broke off to follow a shadow, which turned out to be a stray goat."

Rubbing his chin, the captain considered. "I see. Did you see who left Dugar?"

"I did, sir. I saw the boy running to the gate. The blacksmith's apprentice. He'd been stealing and tried to run!"

51

Navarre swore and snapped his whip. "I knew it!"

He knew what? Vic asked, recalling the blacksmith's apprentice: a nephew sent from Polaski to learn his uncle's trade.

"I'll be on my way then. You, too, boy – who knows what nights the Dark One chooses to roam the Viper Plains. The search party has already returned to the village." And Navarre galloped away.

Robin kicked at loose stones as Vic approached him. "The blacksmith's apprentice?" Vic asked.

"Yes and no," Robin said with a shrug. "I've seen him steal before, but I haven't found his hideout. Perhaps now Captain Navarre will." He frowned. "But Vic. Are you mad? Drema is across the Plains, by the sea! That's more than a week, *if* you stick to the roads."

Vic didn't respond.

"And then the trip back – if the Dark One doesn't kill you first!" Robin gripped his dagger tighter. "He may even be out there now."

Vic forced himself not to think about it. "I'm going, Robin."

Robin shook his head. "I've never understood you, Vic. The boys—" He sighed. "Zurze deserves to know, Vic."

"I left him something," Vic replied, "which he'll see when he wakes. But to quell your uneasiness, will you give him a message?"

Robin nodded.

"Tell him—tell him: I'm risking my life. He'll understand."

Robin shook his head. "I'll never understand you, Vic. But I'll tell him."

"Thank you."

"Run, Vic. The Dark One roams at night, but once you get past Antelope Rock, you'll be safe."

Vic disappeared into the shadows.

It was pitch-black when Snook awoke, all of a sudden. *What—what woke me?*

He yawned, tongue lolling out of his mouth, before realizing – his sixth sense, again – that something was wrong.

When a scream filled the night air, startling him into attention.

Four more screams echoed, and Snook tensed as he sensed the coming of mortal danger, his sixth sense ringing deep within him. The danger crept into his nose, sending him into a mad fit of whining, driving him to his feet, pacing back and forth. Danger had the strange sense of death and—

Fire! Snook realized, catching sight of the harbor. It was ablaze: ships burned, men running about with torches, and then the screams filled the air as huts everywhere caught the flame.

Vic entered his mind: *Snook, what's wrong? I felt your*— But then Vic's voice was gone as everything began happening all too quickly, like the blur of chaotic flames.

Behind him, Snook heard rustling, and a straw hut burst into flame. He spun around, the chain links clinking. The angry red flames crept toward him, and a quick glance at his bowl confirmed that Ettalia still hadn't brought him water.

Facing the harbor again, Snook began barking over and over – and his great voice echoed across the village but was lost to the screams. Snook felt something hot tickling the back of his legs, and he leaped forward, the chain choking him, but he had to get away from the flames.

The string between them went taut then seemed to break; Vic's voice disappeared.

Straining against the chain, Snook grew dizzy, his eyes stung.

Around him, people ran about, screaming, some with burning body parts. He caught sight of a dark-haired man – one of his master's acquaintances – who shouted, "Bring your buckets!" Then he pushed through the smoke and flames toward the harbor, to appear again with a bucket of seawater, which he sloshed toward buildings. Other men joined him as women escaped town with the children.

Snook's fur stood on end when he caught sight of someone with a torch, ducking behind huts and setting them aflame. Snarling at the culprit, Snook tugged harder at his chains, wanting to tear the destroyer from limb to limb. *How dare he! He's lucky I have these chains.*

But then more voices rang out – strange voices Snook did not recognize, voices that caused him to snarl. Voices that shouted out orders and attacked. More villagers screamed. The water dousing stopped. The dark-haired man thundered: "The Blood Bearer dwarfs! Run!"

Despite the distance between him and the action, Snook could sense it all: people cornered, people screaming, people dying – and the killers behind it all.

Snook began to howl. But there was no one left to come to his aid.

Again, he strained against the dreaded chain. Smoke crept into his nose, blocked his sight of the harbor, and fire crackled in his ears. He could feel it in dangerous proximity to him, like a ring of flame that inched closer and closer. Shouts rang out, shouts of war, and Snook whined. Bracing himself, he opened wide his mouth and barked – a thundering bark that seemed to almost shake the ground.

Out of the smoke came a figure now. Snook barked again – like thunder. As the smoke cleared, his vision adjusted, and he began to recognize the figure: *Ettalia.* "Come, Snook," she said, coughing and voice cracking. "I have to get you out of here. Drink—" But she fell at his feet, dead.

Snook whimpered, his one true friend gone. Bending down, he nudged her, licking her face – her cheeks were still sticky with jam. Somehow, he could taste the smoke within her that her body was too weak to fight.

And then, the darkness overcame his mind, and he collapsed.

Rising to the surface of the sea, Afis gasped for air.

After his encounter with Rudolf, he'd snuck into the supply room to fill an empty barrel with necessities for himself. Then he'd gone back up to the deck, doing whatever Brandi had ordered him to do – trying his best to look ferocious and prepared for the attack. But just as the chaos had begun, as the Blood Bearers jumped from the ship to the waves below – Afis had instead snuck below deck and grabbed his barrel. Then he'd thrown it overboard, jumped in after it, and saluted his masters – just because he'd felt like it.

Now, he bobbed above the surface, shivering in the cold water. He shook his head, scattering droplets of water from his tangle of hair. He strapped the barrel to his back and swam north.

As waves met sandy beach, he'd thrown himself on the shore, taking in mouthfuls of air. The Blood Bearers had never taught him to swim – for all he'd known he would have sunk like a rock – but he'd made it and it'd taken more breath than he'd anticipated.

He raised his head to take in the sight ahead of him. *Trees.* Something that his island home had lacked. Rudolf's map had shown trees to the north of Drema, and the silver lettering had read…something, but Afis couldn't recall.

Chest heaving, Afis stood on aching legs and glanced around. A way off, two trees bent in the wind atop a dune, guarding a small dirt path.

Breathing in more air, he straightened his spine and headed for it. Once he climbed the dune, Afis turned to survey the battle scene. Below, far to his left, was Drema: a pitiful sight. The huts bowed to a roaring fire, and doomed bodies scattered the ruined streets. He bit his lip at the sight of a small body, fingers wrapped around a metal collar and chain.

And they wanted me to be part of that. He waited to feel something, some sort of regret for missing the attack, but nothing came. Instead, he could only picture how furious Rudolf was for his glorious creation to have abandoned them. Or perhaps Rudolf hadn't even noticed yet.

Breathing in the scene below, Afis felt his stomach turn over inside but did not gag. *Something seems wrong, and yet something seems right. Am I destined to bring destruction to Lilligrav, a world so new to me? Or perhaps—* He paused, contemplating.

Ahead, a hidden deer trail cut through the beach grass, off into the somewhat far-off shadowy woods. *The Avro Woods,* he now remembered.

He glanced down at his arm, which glowed a faint red due to no moon in the sky. He hoped to be alone and out of sight soon – for the rest of his life.

It's either give up and rejoin Rudolf – or – find something out for myself, Afis decided. Pulling the barrel higher up on his shoulder, he jogged down toward the trail.

In the fresh morning light, Vic stood in grass reaching to his knees. Just behind him towered Antelope Rock – called such for its peculiar shape similar to a leaping antelope. *Well, a vague likeness,* he'd realized upon finding it. The stories said the Dark One's roam didn't reach past this landmass, meaning he wouldn't need to worry about running through the night.

But Vic didn't pause to embrace his success. Instead, he contemplated the sudden loss of connection to Snook from the middle of the night. He hadn't much of a chance then to stop and think about it – but now that he was past the Dark One's realm, he stopped to take a breath and consider.

The last he had sensed was of Snook's pain and terror – a vivid image of a man cracking a whip – and Vic had reached out, wanting to know if there was anything he could do. Snook's emotions were so strong that Vic himself had felt terrified, but he'd swallowed the fear down to keep himself from remembering Manno's death.

But then a sort of blackness had invaded both their minds, the string lost in it. Without a cord to grab hold of, there was no point in trying to send messages across. There was simply no connection.

Sitting down, Vic leaned against the cool surface of a boulder. His muscles screamed for recovery, and he winced at the sight of bruises and cuts from various plants. He fished out the strip of jerky and began munching on it. He hadn't eaten since leaving Drema, too focused on outrunning the Dark One, but his empty stomach churned in anger now that he'd finally stopped.

He inhaled and, standing again, stretched. Ahead to the north was the tip of the Upper Spring, with plenty of clear, cool water. *I can fill up there and perhaps hunt something for dinner,* Vic thought as he swallowed the last bite of jerky.

He also knew that to the south of the river was the village of Levar, where he could rest overnight. *Because if the stories aren't true, I doubt I can outrun the Dark One forever...*

Facing the direction of the river, Vic didn't notice a dark shape slide out of hiding as he jogged off. As silent as sleep, the figure slipped after him, keeping to the shadows.

"Feeling better, jerda?"

Feeling groggy, Snook opened an eye.

A blurry figure knelt over him. Speaking in a voice that reminded Snook of bluebells, the figure continued, "Ah, you're awake."

His vision focusing, Snook opened his other eye and raised his head. No longer in Drema, he was lying on his side in the Avro Woods, and he watched as the figure – a young man – applied herbs to his body, humming as he worked. There was something in the man's singing that rendered Snook's body numb, in a good way – a healing sort of numb.

Snook looked up from watching the stranger's hands work and instead gazed into his face, taking in his appearance. His short hair was blond, and he wore a green tunic with white pants, with a green vine-like design and strange lettering embroidered along the edges. Around his neck hung a half-moon amulet, with another strange shape etched in the middle.

Snook's nose wiggled in curiosity. Then something moved on the man's shoulder, and he wriggled his nose again. A falcon sat perched there, gazing at Snook with soft grey eyes.

Snook cocked his head, thinking, *It's clear he's a friend – or I'd be dead by now. But is he a healer too? My master spoke of such healers when the young master took ill, but I've never heard of one for a dog.*

And then there was the endless supply of magic that Snook sensed around the man, not quite sure how this was possible. Invisible but still felt, the magic seemed to weave around Snook and his healer, saturating him with peace. A quiet bark escaped his muzzle – a bark perhaps of gratitude and awe for this human above humans.

The man stopped singing, and the falcon looked down at Snook's side. "Well, that about does it, eh?" he murmured, leaning back on his heels. Where he'd applied herbs, Snook felt a deep cooling effect, like a refreshing spray of water, crystal clear and cold. The stranger smiled, setting down a bowl filled with green paste. It smelled sweet to Snook, and his nose wriggled faster.

All of a sudden, the falcon flew off the stranger's shoulder, but not before Snook caught sight of a small scroll tied to its foot.

"That should take care of you, jerda. Take care of yourself, now – we need you. Until we see you again." And in front of Snook's very eyes, the man faded away.

With a rumbling bark, he rolled off his side and onto his belly, ears perked and alert, head raised. *Where did he go? He simply disappeared!*

He glanced to his side. The paste must have vanished too, for there was not a trace of the green herb on his fur. Deep inside him, he still felt the coolness, and it spread throughout his veins. After a few tender licks to his paws, Snook feebly got to his feet, relishing in the feeling of being unchained after so long. His nerves must have been asleep, for they screamed with pain as he stood, but then the coolness took over and diluted the agony.

Ahead of him gurgled a small spring of water, nestled among the trees of the Avro Woods. Snook stepped over to it, pleased to discover none of his paws hurt with each step, and looked at his reflection. No marks. No singed fur. No blood. Nothing. As if no fire had ever happened in Drema.

He did so well — so why did he just disappear? I didn't even thank him! Snook thought.

With no physical indications of the fire, Snook instead tried to recall the night before, but the memories were a hazy blur: *Like a dream — or nightmare — that I can't quite recall...*

Throat dry, Snook lapped up as much water as his stomach could hold — a feeling he embraced with content. After shaking himself, he picked up his paws and trotted deeper into the woods, leaving Drema behind. He'd never left on his own before, for whenever he'd left the small yard of his master's, his young master went with him. Now he stood alone — again — in a strange, dark wood he'd never explored before. All around him rang out noises, and the trees stood tall and foreboding, shadows everywhere. Snook shivered, fur bristling, and then shied as something shrieked nearby. Out of nowhere flew an owl, missing Snook's muzzle by mere inches as it glided past on silent wings. A wind racked the trees, causing Snook to shiver again. *If only Vic were here; if only I weren't alone!* he thought.

There was the small twitter of sparrows, then the scampering of a field mouse, before whatever it was shrieked again — but much closer now. Snook laid his ears flat, growling. Then something scraped his hindquarters, and he bolted. Through the trees — their dark needles scratching him — he ran, dodging low branches and squeezing between tight spaces, afraid to stop and afraid to look back. Ahead, a small cave cut in the rocks beckoned him. He darted inside, curled up in the corner, and looked out into the shadowy trees. His breaths heavy, he watched, waited, but nothing appeared.

So, exhausted, he slept.

Her

When Snook awoke, the woods were no longer threatening and dark but soaked in sunlight, which illuminated the cave opening. Birds sang among the branches, a familiar and welcome sound. With a yawn, Snook stretched. Panting with newfound thirst while also aware of his empty stomach, he peered out of the cave, hoping to remedy both concerns at once.

A scratching sound caught his attention, and he glanced back into the deeper parts of the cave. It was barren other than for a handful of odd shapes strewn across the floor. Inching closer, Snook noticed they were clean and white. *They look an awful lot like bones...* He tensed as he heard another scratching sound. Turning, he caught sight of two green eyes glowing in a dark corner, opposite from where he'd slept. The eyes moved closer, taking on the shape of a tawny forest cat. The cat snarled, the fur on its back bristling.

Son of Kell, a mighty warrior, Snook reminded himself then lunged, rumbling a thundering bark. The cat swiped at him but missed, and Snook let his teeth secure onto its side, digging into its fur. A growl escaped from deep in Snook's throat as he held on.

With a yowl, the cat tried swiping at him. When that didn't work, the cat flipped over, also flinging Snook over, who landed in a heap, whining in pain. The healer's paste no longer cooled his veins, and pain returned to his muscles. Snook opened his eyes to glimpse the angry cat approaching, cracking the bones under its clawed paws.

Snook bared his teeth, growling, but the cat snarled back. Raising a paw, it swiped at him, raking its claws across his snout, making him jump to his feet to snap at the cat's face. With another yowl, it jumped back, fur raised. Snook advanced, growling, and the cat hissed. Then Snook slipped on the bones – the femur of a deer – and the crazed feline lunged, knocking him back against the cave wall. His head hit the stone, and he whined, vision spinning.

Helpless, he watched as the cat raised a claw to strike his muzzle. But just as the cat's paw collided with Snook's head, he felt a sharp shock travel through his body. It didn't hurt him, only startled him, but the cat experienced it, too – for it leaped back, yowling over and over in pain, tawny fur singed. Braced against the cave wall, to the left of the cave opening, the cat shrieked. Snook struggled up to his feet as his vision cleared. He lowered himself, hindquarters tightening, ready to lunge, when all of a sudden, a shout echoed in his mind, as if he had spoken: *Kierenata: sukrl kazam tuk!*

He saw a flash of orange, and then the cat disappeared into a pile of soft fur. Snook started, frozen in pre-lunge. *What—Vic?*

Vic's relief flooded the string connecting them: *Snook! You're alive!*

Guilt flashed through Snook for failing to reassure Vic he'd survived. *Yes…but—but what was that?*

It was another cuchel, Vic explained. *It causes whatever you're "aiming" at to vanish into a pile of fur, skin, scales, feathers, you get the idea.*

Snook blinked and straightened, cocked his head at the pile of fur. *But how did it come through me?* he asked.

With the word kierenata – "transfer" – I cast the spell and passed it to you through our bond, and then it formed in your mind. I read the basic spells before I left for my journey.

Snook sat down, cocked his head the other way, still observing the furs with skepticism

When I rediscovered our bond, it was hot with your pair. I used the first spell that came to mind because — well — I wasn't quite sure of the situation. Vic paused. *By the way, don't tell anyone about my book. As a peasant's son, I'm supposed to be unlearned in magic, considering since I'm not old enough for the Training Camp.*

Humans have so many rules! Of course, I won't tell — how could I anyway? Snook could feel Vic's laughter. *Thank you. For saving my life.*

What are friends for, after all?

He wagged his tail.

What happened, anyway? Vic asked.

A fire in Drema. It destroyed the village, I think. I don't quite know, Vic. I passed out somehow, and when I awoke, I was by the woods. Someone was healing my wounds, but he vanished.

A stranger? Vanished? Vic questioned.

A kind stranger, Snook added.

Well, I'm quite glad you're all right. I panicked when I lost the connection to you. I'm about four nights journey from Levar. Where are you, then?

The woods, Snook said simply.

The Avro Woods? Vic clarified.

I suppose so, if that's what your kind calls it.

Until I get there, take care of yourself. I can't use too many cuchels without draining my energy — and then I'd be in no shape to travel.

Snook understood. Cautious, he stepped around the furry pile then shook himself and trotted out of the cave into the sunlight.

Afis steadied his breath, raising his bow and aiming his crudely-made arrow. The yearling buck continued nibbling the forest grass, and Afis sucked in his breath, cleared his mind. There was the crinkling sound of something stepping on a leaf — another animal, he figured. The buck raised its spiked

head, but Afis had already released the arrow. It zipped through the air and just as the deer looked up, the whittled point collided with its side. Before Afis could blink, the buck dropped, dead.

Afis dumped his barrel, tossing his bow inside with his other arrows. He'd whittled them all himself, after realizing he needed something to hunt with other than his bare hands – which hadn't worked too well. He was pleasantly surprised at how easily hunting with the bow came to him. It was as if a switch in the back of his mind clicked on all of a sudden whenever he picked up the bow.

He began to devour the venison, letting his animalistic side take over. No one had taught him how to prepare his own food, for the Blood Bearers had always brought him "tributes," as they called it – platters of scrawny meats from the measly game they bred.

When he'd finished the deer, he buried the carcass and wiped the blood from his chin. Returning to his barrel, he strapped it once more to his back after pulling out his bow and another arrow. Silent as a shadow, he stalked the woods, arrow strung on his bow.

There was a noise ahead of him. Afis whipped around, pressing his back against a tree. Out of the trees appeared a massive golden dog, walking absentmindedly, as if interested in something Afis couldn't hear or see. He raised his bow, stretched the string, and lowered himself to the ground. Ducking behind the tree needles, he aimed, ready to release the arrow if need be.

But then the dog's nose wriggled, and Afis realized it had picked up his scent – or perhaps, rather, the scent of the blood on his hands. Ears perked, it sniffed until placing the scent. When the dog turned, Afis caught a look of sadness in its eyes. *Whatever does a dog have to be sad about?* he pondered.

All of a sudden, the dog tensed, and Afis realized it had now caught sight of his bow, the cruel tip of his arrow. The animal growled, bared its teeth, and Afis felt something he'd never experienced: fear.

If he doesn't fear me, am I the terrifying creature the Blood Bearers say I am?

Should I instead fear this dog? Unsure, Afis lowered his bow.

The dog growled once more before, all of a sudden, perking its ears and cocking its head.

Afis swallowed, pushing aside his strange fear for a more tactical approach: *Better to be friends than enemies.*

"Hey, boy," Afis said, clicking his tongue. "Hey, hey – what are you doing out here alone? Hey." The dog whined, and for a brief moment, Afis worried that his tone hadn't come across as friendly. So, he tried again, getting to his feet and extending a palm: "Hey there. Good boy, that's a good boy."

In response, the dog gave a thunderous bark – a sound that seemed to split the trees. Tongue dangling out, the dog rushed forward, straight at Afis.

"Hey! Whoa, boy, whoa!" *Run!*

Afis stumbled through the forest, dodging needles and branches, with the dog at his heels. Certain the beast would snap at him, Afis recalled what Rudolf had once said: "See their fangs? Those will rip you apart after the dog has barked its threat." *I may be the Bloodthirsty One, but this dog doesn't seem to care!*

Turning to glimpse his canine pursuer, to see if it had given up, Afis found himself falling. Pine needles ripped into his skin, and he landed with a thud onto his stomach. With a muttered curse, he pushed himself up, twisting onto his side.

The dog was at his feet now, sniffing them with curiousity. *If he wanted to kill me, he would have done it by now – right?* Afis thought, hoping to reassure himself.

Afis caught sight of his own torn knee, from where the blunt end of a tree branch had pieced his skin – the warm blood soaked through his pants. The dog looked up, tongue rolling out again, and trotted over to sit beside Afis' head, peering down at his face.

"Blast it. What do you want?" The dog cocked its head, and Afis took his chance to roll up his pants leg, revealing the bloodied knee. "Blast blast blast!"

He shrugged off the barrel, tossing his bow inside. Out of the corner of his eye, he saw the dog still sat staring at him, nose wiggling. "Are you just going to sit and stare, puppy?"

The dog barked again – sending a shudder through Afis – before trotting over to his leg. The dog began to lick the blood away, and Afis winced. "Hey, that kind of hurts, you know!"

Muttering to himself, his mood like a rain cloud, Afis glanced around. *What a wonderful first day. And now it's over,* he remarked, sarcastic. For at that moment, the woods fell into moonlight, and stars twinkled through the thick branches.

Pulling himself up, Afis winced then groaned. Bursts of pain skyrocketed up his leg, and he shook his head. *Guess I'll be spending the night here.*

"So, are you staying with me, then?"

The dog sniffed Afis' knee – no longer bloodied but clean, if covered in dog drool – and looked at him, head cocked. It whined.

"Guess so." Pulling his barrel closer, he rummaged through to find himself a wool blanket and a few pieces of beef.

The dog whined again at the sight of the food, coming over to sit beside Afis, its muzzle inches away from his palm.

Afis drew his hand away, stifling an instinctive growl. "Okay, okay, if you want to eat it, you have to do it *away* from my hand. Got it?"

The dog smacked its lips.

"Okay. There. Fetch," and Afis tossed some meat to his right. The dog bolted after it. Afis gobbled down the rest in silence. In seconds, the dog returned, watching his chewing jaw with a hungry look. With a grunt, Afis pushed the dog aside. "Go away."

The dog dropped to the ground, still whining. When Afis finished chewing, he got to his feet, shuffling off toward the trees to empty himself.

He could feel the dog's eyes on his back as he stood before a tree, and he grunted to himself, muttering a frustrated curse.

Returning, he took a seat beside the dog. "Okay, show's over. Stop staring."

The dog sneezed then placed its head between its paws, eyelids drooping. With a yawn, it opened its giant maw wide. Glimpsing the dog's sharp teeth, Afis, out of instinct, slid his tongue across his own hidden fangs. A satisfied smirk broke onto his face. *Perhaps...perhaps this dog and I are almost equal.*

Tucking himself in, Afis lay down on his side, closed his eyes, and let sleep envelope him.

In the middle of the Viper Plains, rocky terrain surrounding him, Vic stood still, reaching for some sort of connection: *Snook?! Snook!*

But there was nothing. Snook wasn't grasping their thread, only a silent other end. It was just like Vic's book had told him — as if a wall of quiet, a wall of blocking stone, had been erected. He knew, from reading his book, that it was temporary, and that Snook had done it on purpose. *But how? How did he catch on so quick? When I'm still learning myself! Who's the one learning magic: Snook or me? One thing is for sure — he is quite different from...well, "normal" dogs. Or perhaps I don't know what a normal dog is like.* He didn't know when Snook would lower the mental barrier, but he hoped it would be soon.

All around, ridges jutted from the ground, flat on top but steep along the side. While these ones were somewhat small, Vic knew the ridges would soon tower over him the closer he got to Levar, which was nestled at the heart of them.

In the back of his mind -- in *reality* – he heard the clatter of pebbles falling down the side of a ridge. Though Vic told himself it was a deer or other wild animal, the sound broke his concentration enough for his grip on the slippery mental touch to loosen and disappear.

He whirled around, bow and arrow at the ready. *Nothing. I knew it was a wild—*

Then she stepped from the shadows.

She seemed his age, perhaps a year or two younger, with raven-black hair that fell past her shoulders. Vic lowered his bow and, out of instinct, raised a hand to his own ebony hair, thinking: *If her hair were shorter…she'd be my twin!* Her thoughts seemed to be along similar lines – she had one eyebrow raised, her head tilted just a smidge to one side.

Moving closer to him, she straightened, and he took in her pose, her stance, her form. *Why, she walks like the daughter of a wealthy man – and yet she stands defiant like a solider. Out here in the Plains, wearing those clothes?* Her brown dress, with purple flowers lining the hem, was torn and covered in blood stains, scuffs from rocks and dirt.

Astonished, Vic looked her over again, loosening his grip on his bow. *Who is she?* he finally asked.

"Stref hombä," he uttered, and then he was inside her mind, prepared to search. He almost stumbled backward at the overwhelming force of her mind. No mental barriers were up, and yet just the feel of his own invisible hand probing her central base made *him* nauseous. *I suppose every Magic Master feels off-balance their first time in someone else's mind. At least, I hope so,* he added, as another wave of nausea overcame him.

As he groped through her mind, he sensed a large orb of knowledge at the core. And as he felt his way toward it, weak barriers sprung up before him. They were easy to knock down with a gentle poke of his reaching consciousness. A verse from his tome came to him: *barriers of the 'ones without practiced magic' are weak but still full of cuchel as everyone's core being is built upon magic.*

So why is Snook's block so strong? Vic again wondered.

At last, Vic found himself before the orb. Preparing for whatever lay ahead, he tensed. Then, hesitant, he reached out and embraced the core of her mind.

Images, words, and even senses flooded over him. He saw a girl –

like the one before him, but much younger – weeping over a burial casket. Another image took over. He saw the same girl – but now he was certain she was the same as the one before him. Her head bowed, she whispered: "Father, you gave me my name – Via Simonschild – but today, I seek your blessing to become a woman." A blurry image of a smiling man appeared, hands on her head, before vanishing. *So, her name is Via…how bizarre,* Vic thought. *We look like twins, and our names are eerily similar….*

Sweat covered Vic's body as he continued his search, and he knew his time was short. Before him, but not seen as he searched her mind, Via cried out in alarm and pain. Below him, he felt her pulling away. Vic hurried now, feeling her falling beneath him. Frantic, he searched the orb for valuable information. The image of Via fleeing away from a city on a bay horse shone before him. Tears clouded her eyes. *An…outcast?* he questioned.

But then the orb pulsated three times, and a tingle ran through Vic's every finger. A burst of prismatic light erupted from the orb and sprouted into the air. The light washed onto him, and yet he was left dry. *What is the meaning? Translucent light – signifying…goodness?*

Beneath him in her mental space, he began to sense her weakening. Snapping away from the orb – instantly he was filled with sorrow for this – he retreated from her mind. "Tjord dahla." Yet the magic tried to pull at him, begged him to keep using it. In shock, he doubled over, arms hugged across his chest and panted for air. He fell to his knees.

After almost an hour, he made himself more stable and glanced up at her. She was lying unconscious before him. Around them was only silence.

Vic took one last gasp for air and crawled over to her. He laid a hand across her forehead. Other than being sticky with sweat, she was cool to his touch. His hands moving in a flurry, he took off his bow, quiver, and pack. Dumping them beside him on the ground, he rummaged through his pack until retrieving a goat horn, brimming with water from the Upper Spring. He unplugged it and placed it to her lips, guiding it down her throat. Then he poured a little pool into his palm and splashed it onto her cheeks.

She awoke the moment the coolness touched her skin. As she uttered a sound of surprise, her eyes flew open, taking in her surroundings.

At last, they found Vic. He opened his mouth to explain but, all of a sudden, found himself with a dagger to his throat.

Via eyed him, her eyebrows furrowed. "What happened, boy?"

Boy?! Vic repeated. He hesitated, chewing his lip. "You fainted."

"I know that's not true," she said, pressing the knife closer.

Cautious, Vic reached for his bow, as he continued: "It's true. It was a reaction to my spell."

She studied him for a long moment before drawing back. "I haven't met someone who speaks the truth in a long time."

His fingers just grasping his drawstring, Vic paused. "I'm sorry?"

"Someone once explained the 'mind search' cuchel to me, but that was a long time ago." She sighed. "I should have had more barriers up."

Vic snatched his bow and raised it, but Via shook her head.

"You don't need that." Breathing out, she brushed back the hair clinging to her face. "I've been watching you—"

"You were *watching* me?" *How did I never notice?!*

"Yes," she replied, never flinching, never turning her gaze. But a hint of rose flushed her dirtied and tanned cheeks. "You passed my camp several times, and I watched to gauge if you were friend or foe. Then I followed you." She squinted. "And I saw you seemed to be in need of help."

He blinked. "Help?"

"You kept stopping to stand in the middle of the Plains. Only fools do that." She paused, tilted her head. "Who are you?"

"Vic. From Dugar."

"And I am Via, of Levar."

"I know."

"Right. Your cuchel." She turned away. "Why—why exactly did it cause me to faint?"

"It was my first time using it." He resisted the urge to tell her about

Snook – how it was not quite his first time, but that with Snook it was different. Instead, he said, "It didn't quite work the way I expected. I apologize for that."

Via had moved closer, listening in earnest. "Have you *studied* cuchels?"

Vic shook his head and realized her confusion. "I…learned them from my cousin," he lied. *But I can trust her,* he reminded himself.

She seemed to accept the false explanation. "What are you doing out here, anyway?"

"I'm headed to Drema, but because of some…well, unexpected incidents, I need to arrive sooner than planned."

"So, you need help after all," she observed as a small smile crossed her face. "I can get you there faster. But we'll have to take side roads around Levar."

"No. Main road is fine." *That's what it's for, after all,* he reasoned. *Besides, a night in Levar's inn would be a welcome change.*

Via shook her head. "It's too dangerous. Don't you know who rides there?"

Vic glared at her. "If you think I'm a runaway, think again – because I'm not. That's why we can take the main road through Levar."

She sighed, looking away. With a shrug, she murmured, "Fine."

Glancing over her shoulder, sweaty hair clinging to her neck, she whistled in the direction of a ridge. There was the sound of hooves, and then a massive black-colored stallion trotted into view, a rope in his mouth.

Vic's jaw dropped. The other end of the rope sat looped around the neck of a bay-colored stallion, his coat shining despite the harsh conditions. In his eyes sparked a flare of untamed restlessness. While the black stood still, the bay seemed restless, almost prancing in place.

Getting to her feet, Via went over to the two stallions, taking the rope out of the black's mouth and then turning to the bay. "Settle, boy. Did my disappearance anger you? There, there. Azeri took good care of you, I'm sure," she added as she wrapped an arm around the black stallion's neck.

Vic's heart jumped when she looked at him. "You do ride, yes?" she asked.

"Yes, but always alone," he confessed.

"Azeri and Zukav are trained to keep pace alongside each other," she reassured him. "You can ride Azeri," – she pointed to the black – "while I'll ride Zukav." When the latter shook his mane, Via added, "I should warn you: Zukav is very protective of me, so don't get too close. But Azeri is a very gentle giant. You'll be in good hands – I mean, hooves."

Vic took a deep breath. Back home, Zurze had a lease on a mare from the village stables for his longer travels, and Vic often exercised her in between, so he was familiar with horseback riding. But, even so, Azeri was huge compared to the mare. *I can do this. He's still just a horse,* Vic reassured himself. *It's the terrain I'm worried about,* he admitted, taking in the surrounding ridges, *which will soon be much, much taller...*

Mounting the black, Vic glanced at Via. She was also mounting – much quicker than him, of course – and when she caught his gaze, her eyes broke away, her cheeks dappled with a rosy pink. Each clicked to their steed, and the two horses broke into a steady lope, headed for the main road that broke out of the Viper Plains – like a snake escaping an overgrown skin.

I'll be with you even sooner now, Snook, Vic called out, hoping the dog still heard him despite the silence.

Via studied Vic with discretion as they rode, making sure to avoid catching his interest. She couldn't quite describe it, couldn't quite understand it – but she felt, somehow, drawn to Vic. *I—I can't understand how he looks so much like me,* she thought, fascinated. *If only—*

She gazed out at the main road in sight not far ahead. Like any child of Lilligrav, she knew the stories that spread from village to village. But unlike the far mountain villages' tales of the Dark One, the merchant villages told tales of weevil attacks – surprise attacks, often with no survivors. Besides that, Levar's inhabitants weren't the friendliest people a person could chance to meet.

Father. Unwanted tears from unwanted memories threatened her, and she brushed them away – without Vic's notice. *He may not think he's naïve, but I know better. Let's just hope we even make it to Levar.*

Swapping Stories

Their first day together had been full of awkward silence, so Vic decided to remedy that once they'd made camp for the night. After sharing a cooked hare for dinner, Vic cleared his throat. "I thought perhaps I could tell you more about myself?"

Via looked up at him quizzically. "...I suppose?"

He laughed, embarrassed. "I just thought it might help us to feel less like strangers together."

She shrugged. "If you'd like."

Just jump right in, he figured, so, with a nod, he began: "I live with my cousin Zurze in Dugar. Zurze is the village carpenter, just like his father before him. And just like my father was and his father before him. Brothers then cousins, together." He sighed. "I never knew my father; he left when I was a few years old. Zurze has never given me a direct explanation, but I've overheard the whispered gossip around town: my father was ashamed of me."

"Why?" Via questioned.

Vic felt relief at knowing she was listening, that he wasn't just talking to fill the air. "He was ashamed of his bastard son. He wasn't married to my mother, and she died in childbirth. So, when he could no longer bear the shame, he abandoned us. Just left one night." Vic pictured the deer figurine he'd left behind, the one his father had also left behind. "He said he was going to catch some—some special deer, but he never returned."

"I'm sorry," Via said. "Truly."

He shrugged. "Zurze raised me instead. If I'm being honest, I thought he *was* my father – that is, until I was old enough to understand."

"So, are you a carpenter?" she asked.

"No," he answered with a shake of his head. "I want to be a Magic Master."

"Can your cousin afford the Training Camp? Or is that why he taught you cuchels?"

He grimaced at the memory of his lie and hoped she hadn't noticed. "We've—we've been saving up. I'm sure Zurze would prefer that I follow in our family's footsteps, but I just know that I'm—I'm meant for more."

Via frowned. "But wait. How does a carpenter know cuchels?"

I've dug myself a hole, but I must keep digging, Vic realized. "The students of the Training Camp often practice in the Plains. Zurze overheard basic cuchels, so he passed them along to me." *At least, this time, it's a half-truth.*

Seeming to accept his answer, she said, "Your secret is safe with me. Like I said earlier, someone once explained the 'mind search' cuchel to me, so I know there are unconventional ways to learn magic." Her frown turned into a small smile. "I hope your dream is fulfilled someday."

"Thank you," Vic said, an unknown feeling surging through him. As if someone had finally seen him, without judging. *If only others were just as…accepting.*

Blushing, Via attended to the fire.

While he recalled where he'd left off, Vic drummed his fingers on his knee. "So, that's where I come from. I suppose next would be where I'm headed."

"You already told me: to Drema," Via interjected. "But you also mentioned some unexpected incidents." She tilted her head, curious.

"The one I'm searching for…he's on the move."

"How do you know?" she questioned. "Magic?"

This time, I can't lie. "Yes: I'm mentally connected to him. Moments before you and I met, he told me he was no longer in Drema."

"So, where is he?"

"Somewhere in the Avro Woods."

"We can still snake our way around Levar then."

Confused, Vic shook his head. "The fastest way would be through Levar. You *can* guide me through the city, yes?"

Via stared at the fire. Moments passed before she responded: "I can."

Good. "I must admit that, when I left Dugat," Vic continued, "I never expected to stumble upon my lookalike."

She locked eyes with him. "We are alike, aren't we?"

With a slow nod of his head, Vic murmured, "Do you think the spirits intended for us to meet?"

"They must have." They stared at each other in silence until Via cleared her throat. "I do have one question."

He waited.

"Everyone knows the stories, but they aren't as…prominent on this side of the island, due to weevil attacks being more of a threat than the Dark One himself. But on your side of the island…" She trailed off before taking a deep breath. "Is it true that the Dark One kills anyone before they can cross the Wilderness Mountains?"

For the first time since Antelope Rock, the nightmarish memory trickled its way to the back of his mind. Vic swallowed it back, feeling shaky. "Yes. He does."

"Why?"

"No one knows," Vic admitted. "The stories merely say that the Dark One stalks the Plains at the foot of the mountains, killing anyone before they can venture beyond."

"But why does he seek out our ntéhs?"

Manno, Vic whispered before he could stop himself. "The spirits foretold a ntéh will reunite the races, so it seems the Dark One opposes that."

Again, silence filled the space between them.

Vic almost jumped when Via prodded the dying fire. "I'll take the first watch. Get some sleep, though I must apologize if my questions have made it…difficult."

You have no idea, Vic mumbled, praying to the spirits to be allowed some rest.

The following night, after a hard day of riding, Vic and Via sat beside another dying fire. Surrounding them were countless ridges, but these were at least five times bigger than the ones Vic had first encountered. *No wonder our ancestors built their kingdom at the heart of these ridges,* Vic noted. *They're like a maze, nature's own fortress.*

He cupped his chin and reflected on his experience in Via's mind, especially the prismatic burst of light he wasn't sure about. He watched her as she stood, approached the horses, and calmed them with words, so that they would sleep in peace. Thoughts and questions pestered his mind – he couldn't stand being quiet anymore.

When she'd returned to the fire sometime later, Vic organized his thoughts and cleared his throat. "So, Via – what is *your* story? Why are you alone, with only two horses for companionship?"

She sighed. "I suppose you already know most of it, having seen my memories when you searched my mind." She looked to the stars and then back at the glowing embers. "I hail from Levar – born and raised inside its walls. It is the only city I have ever known."

And yet she wants to avoid the city? Vic questioned. *What kind of memories does she have there?*

"Not that I wasn't aware of the other villages – my father would enchant me with stories about them. He was a merchant, so he would tell me tales of his travels, the sights of the other villages. My mother was killed by the Blood Bearer dwarfs when I was a few years old. I can't recall much, just blurs from that night. My father hadn't returned from selling wares off in Armoth. I heard a scream and found my mother breathing her last. I—I've never known why they killed her. She…she wouldn't hurt anyone..

"Because of my mother's early death, my father was quite protective. Many women, old spinsters, offered to watch me by day, but he refused. Few in Levar are trustworthy, you see. It's—a horrible place."

She must despise me for insisting we go through the city – but that's the fastest way, isn't it? Vic thought.

"One person Father did trust: Kaio. He was, and is, the one person besides my father whom I trusted with my whole heart." Vic pointed to himself, curious, but Via shrugged. "I could never trust anyone as much as I trusted him."

She gave a little laugh. "It's hard to describe him, Vic. Well, most important: he was a Magic Master." Vic's eyes widened, and she nodded. "I think you would have liked him very much. Perhaps he could have taught you some cuchels that your cousin hasn't." She swallowed. "Kaio was a second father to me, yet it all ended too soon.

"One day, Father had to deliver some wares to an outcast living in the outskirts of the city. Kaio came along to entertain Father, and I was old enough to join them. Weevils attacked just outside the gates – far enough away for help. Zukav spooked" – she gestured to the bay behind her – "and so I was left to wait for their return in Levar, helpless."

She broke off, and when she began again, her voice was scratchy. "Father returned, bruised and exhausted – and alone. Kaio's mare had also bolted, not long after Zukav. She had disappeared into the Avro Woods, which weevils fear, so they did not pursue. I'm sure you can guess what follows: Kaio—Kaio didn't return, only his mare, without a rider. The soldiers took her, and I never saw her again – she was an old mare.

"With Kaio gone, fear filled the void created from Mother's death. Father—my father didn't speak from then on. I—I.." Her words failed her.

"You never trusted anyone again?" Vic put in.

With a small nod, Via paused. After a few moments, she raised her hand, wiping away at her eye with the back of her palm. "Almost a month later, my—father was killed."

"Your father?" Vic whispered.

She gave the smallest of nods.

"But how?"

"By an angry customer. Father gave him the wrong item, they said. I'll never know why the customer was so…hateful. But he unsheathed a knife and murdered my father. I arrived too late. Father died in another merchant's arms, but I saw him reach for me when I arrived. That was my goodbye."

She reached down, and when he saw her hand in the dying light again, she was grasping dry grass, which she tossed into the embers. Vic caught sight of the two silent horses behind her – Zukav half-asleep, restless, and Azeri a quiet watching shadow.

"But if your father died, how did you…" Vic let the sentence dangle: not a question, not a statement, just an unfinished thought.

So, she finished it for him: "Escape the customary auction to become an outcast?" She scoffed. "What an excellent question. Now you'll know everything, even if you're too afraid to ask."

Vic ran a hand through his hair, embarrassed. "I know auctions are more common among merchants, but we don't sell possessions in Dugar," he said. "The deceased's family instead gives them away. Children live with relatives or friends of the family." He looked at her. "But Dugar is small, and Levar is a huge city."

"As you know – as is customary – my father's possessions were sold off to the highest bidders. Everything. And who sat among his material possessions?" She raised her eyes, brimming with tears, to look right at him.

Vic swallowed, faltered in her gaze.

80

"Me. I'm *property*, Vic. Not the daughter of a merchant, but one of his possessions." Pausing, Via brushed her long ebony hair to the side, displaying the tattoo on her neck. It glittered in the light of the fire. "See? The merchant crest of my father. Forever marked as an *item*, not even as a human." She let her hair fall back, hiding the tattoo once more. "Perhaps where you come from, children have a better way of life after a father's death, but for me – the best scenario would be a merchant's mistress."

Upset, she shook her head then cleared her throat and lowered her head again. "So, everything was sold, and I stood next, to be followed by our animals. At least I am not considered livestock," she said with contempt. "A wealthy merchant I despised gave the highest bid. But somehow, Zukav knew what was happening." The stallion gave a nicker, and Vic heard him swishing his tail. "He broke free of his handler and charged at me, and out of instinct, I leaped onto his back. Azeri, being the gentle giant he is, didn't have any ropes – they believed they could trust him to stand still. But he got away, too, and followed us." As if on cue, Azeri nudged her shoulder with his nose, but Via ignored him.

"Many pursued us for months after, but we always eluded them. I had no choice but to learn how to survive. Living in the Plains isn't easy, but it's all I have now. And so, here I am: an outcast, a runaway, shunned by Levar, unknown to the rest of the world. With only my mother's stallion and my own to keep me company. For four years, the Plains have been our home."

She was silent, finished.

Guilt and shame weighed on Vic's shoulders. "So, you want to avoid Levar – avoid any possible contact?"

"The truth is: I haven't avoided Levar altogether. I've snuck in and out over the years when necessary. But always alone, never with another person." She tossed more dry grass on the embers. "I am not welcome there, Vic. I overheard some gossip once, whispers about me as if I were a curse." She brushed her hair out of her face. "You aren't naïve in everything, but you have certainly misjudged Levar."

Bowing his head in shame, Vic considered her words. After a pause, he spoke: "I do have one question."

She waited.

"How—how did you avoid the Dark One? Every child of Dugar is forbidden from staying in the Plains overnight, and yet you've lived here for four years."

Cautious, she looked around. "I've heard the stories, but the Dark One doesn't haunt our side of the Plains as much as he does yours. And I never go beyond Antelope Rock." She wrapped her arms around herself, whispering, "But sometimes I swear I hear voices, see things. The horses avoid certain areas at night. The closer to Levar, the safer I am – ironically."

Vic rubbed his chin with his thumb. "We should rest now. I can take first watch."

Glancing up at the horses, Vic was surprised to see their ears perked forward, as if something had disturbed them. He rose and strode over to where Zukav shifted, ground-tied, with faithful Azeri standing by. The stallions were watching the road headed toward Levar.

Following their gaze, Vic caught sight of five silent figures, silhouetted by moonlight, riding horses. The figures moved toward their camp, only a few gallops down the road. Two figures rode in front, two behind, and the last rider took up the back of the formation. The men searched the road, looking for – Vic knew – any helpless travelers. *Via was right,* he realized with dread.

She had chosen to camp near the bushes, among the shadows cast down by the looming ridges above. At that moment, Vic heard a quiet but audible *whoosh* and glanced over his shoulder to see Via had just put out their fire, using water from his goat horn.

"Now you see why we don't take the main road." Via didn't look at Vic as she spoke, but her words cut deep into him, and he regretted his stubborn decision earlier. *I could outrun them if they weren't riding, and I can't leave*

Via alone, he said, knowing her fate.

Turning back to the figures, he saw they were heading closer, eyes catching every single movement around them. *They're sure to see us. Think, Vic!* he shouted to himself.

Silence, ready to be broken, filled the night.

And then, all of a sudden, Zukav threw back his head to let out a shrill, wild neigh. His eyes blazed with wild passion as he half-reared, nostrils flaring and picking up the approaching horses' scents. Snorting in a crazy rage, he pranced in place, tossing his fiery head. Vic heard Via's harsh whisper: "Their mare is in heat; it's a trap!"

Vic gulped, a shiver running down his spine. After Via's story, he was quite positive these strangers weren't just on the hunt for thieves. *They're looking for anyone,* he realized.

He watched as the riders pulled back on their mounts' reins after hearing Zukav's scream. They all drew their swords, silver blades glinting in the moonlight. Vic crouched. *They haven't seen us yet, only heard Zukav. I just need to think*—but he spoke too soon. One of the riders in front shifted his eyes from a bent tree over to Zukav's pacing form. His eyes smiled with delight as he shouted over his shoulder, gesturing with his blade. In a split second, they urged their horses into a mad gallop, swords pointed ahead as they charged.

Vic's heart raced. Hearing Via moving, he whipped around, trembling, and saw her hurrying to prepare the stallions. "We have to flee – now!"

Via nodded. "Give me a moment. I'm used to this. These guys have been giving me trouble for seven nights now. It's that blasted mare."

Before Vic could respond, she was finished. "Here's the thing," she said, her voice blending with the approaching, drumming horses' hooves. "To get away, we have to head away from Levar and then loop around. Understood?"

Vic looked over his shoulder. The leader was nearing them: any minute he would be upon them. Two others tugged their horses out of a ditch, straining on the reins as they shied away. The last two were on the heels of their leader's mount. Facing Via again, Vic shouted as he mounted Azeri: "Whatever it takes!"

Via leapt onto Zukav's back, and the stallion broke into a gallop. Under him, Vic felt Azeri charge forward, right at the bay's tail.

Behind them came their armed pursuers.

Pursuit

With a jolt, Afis awoke and sat up. Some distant dream had startled him from sleep. Now, he glanced around him: it was dark – night – and the moon shone down on the woods in an eerie way.

With a groan, Afis rolled onto his side and looked down at the dog beside him. He and the dog – whom he'd named Thunder for his deafening bark – had been wandering the woods for two days now, hunting when they could, enjoying each other's silent company otherwise. Every dusk, they returned to the same small clearing to rest. Afis had been pleasantly surprised at the dog's hunting skills, and he'd had more than enough food the last few days, with few leftovers.

With a sound of curiosity, the dog raised his head and licked Afis' fingers. "You need to stop doing that, Thunder. It tickles." Thunder lost interest and went back to sleep with a yawn.

Still hot and sweaty from whatever dream had awoken him, Afis slid the blanket down to his legs. His bare chest glistened in the moonlight, and all of a sudden, he remembered his skin's glowing ability. *I'm lucky the moon's out tonight – otherwise, I'd be a living red beacon.* Still, he pulled the blanket back up, covering himself again. *The Blood Bearers must prefer to attack when there's no moon out, or they would have created me to glow every night,* he reasoned.

Afis pulled his barrel toward him, taking out one of the few strips of meat he had left. Thunder perked up again, having smelled the dried venison, and barked once – a sign Afis had learned meant hunger. Tossing a piece toward the dog, he turned to his own, gnawing at it, trying to recall his dream.

A low growl caught his attention – Afis had also learned this meant danger of some kind. "What is it, Thunder?" He followed the dog's gaze toward the trees but saw nothing. And yet, when he returned to his midnight snack, he heard a rustling from where Thunder had been watching. Heart skipping a beat, he sprang into action: with one motion, he grabbed his bow and nocked an arrow. "Who's there?" he shouted. "Show yourself! Or I'll set my dog on you!"

The rustling continued, and then a man's face appeared.

"What do you want?" Afis growled.

The stranger smiled, raising his hands. "Don't worry, lad, I won't hurt you. Like you, I'm searching for a midnight snack."

"Oh, yeah?" Afis tightened his grip on the bow. "What are you in the mood for – flesh?"

With a hearty laugh, the intruder shook his head. "There's a patch of berries nearby that I visit often when I'm hungry at night. They only appear by moonlight – Nightjuice Berries, they're called. Would you like some?"

Afis glanced at Thunder. To his surprise, the dog was no longer tense but had gotten to his feet, wagging his tail – a good sign, Afis had learned by now. The man noticed Thunder's new reaction, too, and with another laugh, nodded toward him. "See? Even your dog trusts me, and you can't argue with that!"

After a moment's hesitation, Afis lowered the bow and sighed. "You're right: I can't."

The intruder emerged from the trees, letting the moonlight outline his face. His hair was white as snow, but his eyes were young and twinkled as he came over to Afis, palm extended. "Go on, try the berries. You've never had anything as sweet."

Afis took a few and plopped them into his mouth. To his surprise, *he's right*.

"I told you, lad." The man turned to Thunder next. "How about you, boy?" the newcomer asked with a chuckle, bending over so his face was level with Thunder's muzzle. "These berries are for everyone." The dog gobbled some up before licking the man's face in appreciation. For the third time, their visitor laughed, and Afis smiled to himself. Taking a seat beside Afis, the man held out a hand toward Thunder, who trotted over and allowed himself to be petted. "He's your dog, then, lad?"

Afis shrugged. "Sort of. We more or less found each other and can't seem to get rid of one another."

"Aha!" The stranger laughed yet again. "Well, he looks a bit cold. There's a chill in these woods at night."

"Aye. But my blanket keeps me warm."

"And him?"

Afis started. "I—I.."

"What do you call him?"

"Thunder. For his bark."

"A good, strong name." The newcomer smiled and turned to look down at the content dog lying beside him. "Will you bark for me, Thunder?"

There was a pause as Thunder stared at the man before, all of a sudden, rumbling out a thunderous bark – one that made Afis cover up his ears with his hands. But the stranger was silent as he looked down at the dog.

And then the newcomer turned back to Afis, another smile on his lips. "Now, my good lad, you look like you could use some decent rest. Sleeping outside may be wonderful with the stars, but there's a chill as we've said. Perhaps you'd like to come and stay at my abode tonight? I'd be happy to offer you breakfast in the morning. One can only live on just venison for so long…I have warm bread at home."

Afis paused, considering: *The man's friendly enough, and Thunder likes him.*

My training would protect me if necessary, and I know that Thunder can take care of himself. I'll admit that sleeping out here on pine needles isn't the most comfortable. Picking up his barrel, Afis got to his feet and held out his hand to his new friend sitting below. "Lead the way."

Vic could feel his blood in his cheeks, the sweat dripping from his eyelashes. *We've got to outrun them! We've got to!* Somewhere behind him, he could hear the shouts of the armed riders, the pounding of hooves, the snorting breaths flaring out of the steeds' nostrils. "Got any ideas?" he shouted, praying Via could hear him.

Apparently, she could: "Yes – follow me!"

He glanced over just in time to see her turn Zukav toward a ridge, see the desperate stallion climb the rocky slope. This close to Levar, the ridges now towered above them, and he could tell Via was aiming for the flat top. *Like I said, it's the terrain I'm worried about – but we don't have much choice!* Vic reminded himself.

"Coming!" he shouted, yanking Azeri's mane to follow. Azeri leaped after Zukav, scaling the sloped ridge with ease. Higher and higher up the incline they raced, and he could sense the tumbling rocks slipping behind them, making their pursuers' journey upward a bit more difficult.

His heartbeat caught in his throat when he caught sight of a wide gap: the ridge they'd climbed ended abruptly, with another jutting out on the other side. *Spirits, help me,* he prayed. Just ahead of him, Via eased Zukav into a jump, and the bay soared over the gap to land on the next ridge.

"Okay, boy," Vic whispered into Azeri's ear as he leaned forward on the black's back. His hands shook as he grasped his mane tighter. "Go easy on the beginner." With an echoing neigh, Azeri threw himself forward and flew across the gap.

Vic let out a shaky cry: *It's like flying!*

Then Azeri landed, and Vic fell forward into the stallion's thick mane.

Straightening, he spit out a mouthful of horse hair. Azeri snorted and picked up speed, gaining on Zukav.

Vic glanced behind him to see the men urging their steeds to also take the leap, one at a time. He swallowed hard. *Just leave us alone already!* "Now what?!"

Via turned Zukav left, following along the path of the ridge. "Just keep riding – we're too high up to scramble down the ridge!"

Vic gulped. Guiding Azeri after Zukav, he noticed just how high up they were – the rocky Plains stretched out at least a falcon's dive below.

All of a sudden, up ahead of them, Via halted Zukav, and Vic felt Azeri below him skid to a stop. Zukav snorted, impatient and prancing, but Via turned her head and pointed behind them. "Look!"

Vic did: their determined pursuers were gaining upon them, but their mounts were foaming at the mouths.

"They're pushing their horses too hard," Via explained. "They're weak. Use magic."

"What?" Vic asked, turning back to her. *Did she just say—*

"Magic! Use it to slow them down!"

Vic gulped, gathered his energy, and then screamed: "Hireel zukav – leyef!"

The ridge below them trembled, and Zukav reared with a frightened neigh. And then a pillar of rock burst from the ridge, forming a wall between Vic and Via and their pursuers. They could hear the men cursing. A shaky breath escaping him, Vic drooped on Azeri's back, feeling light-headed. The word around him shifted, flashing a brilliant teal color for a brief moment.

"Vic!" Via cried, her voice echoing in his ears. "Are you all right?"

"The goat horn," he mumbled. "Pass me the goat horn." She pulled it out of his pack and passed it to him. He drank in a hurry, feeling the water clear his head. "It took too much energy," he said, wiping his arm across his sweaty brow. "Give me a moment to recover."

She turned Zukav's head. "You don't have much time," she said, nodding toward the rock column. Even with the echoing in his ears, Vic could make out the sounds of their pursuers turning around their horses, pebbles sliding as the stallions scrambled back down the ridge. "Vic?"

Straightening, he closed his eyes, sucked in his breath, and pinched the bridge of his nose between two fingers. Feeling his mind refocus, he nodded. "Okay. Let's go."

"Good." She nudged Zukav forward, toward the slope of the ridge. "They'll be expecting us to continue along the ridges. They'll ride up that next one and hope to block us ahead. But we'll go down the side." With a click of her tongue, she urged Zukav down the steep side. The bay stallion snorted, tossing his head as he slipped down the slope with caution.

Vic let out a whistle of breath then whispered to Azeri's perked ear: "My trust is in your hooves, boy." The black giant flared his nostrils, shook his mane, and trotted over to the slope to follow Zukav.

The stranger led them to a medium-sized hut leaning against a giant oak. With a crude bow, the man said, "Welcome to my humble abode. It's not much, but it's better than pine needles."

Afis laughed and followed his host inside, Thunder at his heels. Inside, as a cool breeze blew through the hut, Afis snuck a careful look around. To his relief, shafts of moonlight came streaming into the hut through holes in the woven rug, which served as a door flap. Afis turned back to his host and opened his mouth to speak.

But the man held up his hand. "Introductions later, my friend. For now, get yourself some decent sleep. You too, Thunder."

Thunder barked – a less rumbling sound. Afis shrugged, curled up in a corner beside the dog, and embraced the sleep that crept over him.

Their host smiled at Snook, who observed in curiosity.

As he draped a fur blanket over Afis, fast asleep, the man said to Snook: "For years, I've been searching, and now you are found. Your bark was true." Then he was gone, headed for his own bed in the next room.

Snook looked off toward the dark, where the man's figure had disappeared, pondering: *I'm found? Whatever does he mean?*

Earlier, after he'd barked for the stranger, Snook had sensed a strange spark within him, as if something in his soul had, at long last, awoken. He'd watched as the man searched into his eyes then felt a sort of calming fear — as if he should be afraid but, at the same time, that it was all right to be afraid.

And now, waiting for sleep to find him, Snook dug deep, trying to locate the spark again, hoping to understand.

Glancing over his shoulder, Vic let out his breath in relief, seeing no riders in sight. *We must have left them atop a ridge, as Via guessed,* he thought. Below him, Azeri tightened, picking up speed on the grassy terrain, and Zukav shrilled to his right. Vic looked over at Via, who was watching Zukav's ears.

"They're close," she said, her words almost inaudible over the stallions' hoofbeats. "Look at his ears." Vic did, seeing Zukav swivel his ears to the left.

All of a sudden, there was a shout above them: "There they are!" Vic looked up. On the rocky ridge above, a rider raced on his horse, matching Azeri and Zukav's beat.

"Whoa!" Vic said, and Azeri skidded to a halt. "They've found us."

Beside him, Via stopped Zukav, pulling back on his mane, and the stallion stamped a hoof. She glanced around before shouting, "Quick: follow me!" Spurring their horses, they galloped underneath an archway cut in the rock.

Via shifted on Zukav's back to glance behind her and caught sight of the four riders following. "Use your cuchels again, give us more time!"

Vic hesitated before choosing one: "Gäzarf!" Biting his lip, he glanced over his shoulder to see one of the riders lying on the ground, the riderless horse continuing its gallop, not even noticing its missing rider. *I wasn't strong enough: I only knocked off one rider!* he realized, kicking himself.

"Who are they?" he shouted to Via over the thunder of hooves. "Why are they so persistent?"

"I don't quite know." She leaned close to Zukav, urging him to go faster.

"But they've been giving you trouble for a week?"

"They're employed by the black market. They'll sell me as a concubine, I'm sure."

He swallowed, hard.

"They won't show any mercy to you either, Vic: you'd make a good servant for a rich merchant." Their two stallions flew over the rocky terrain, and she pointed ahead. "There. If we can reach that ridge up ahead, there's a place where we can duck down and hide!"

Their pursuers were above them, racing along the towering ridges overhead. Vic could hear them urging their horses to match Zukav and Azeri below. There was the sound of rock sliding, and Via yelled, "Look out, Vic!"

He glanced upward to see a shower of rocks hurtling down toward them. With a nudge of his heel, he guided Azeri closer to Zukav, as he leaned away to avoid the cascading rocks.

A rider appeared out of nowhere, soaring down from above, to land in front of them. He raced ahead of them before turning his horse around, coming to a halt in their path.

No! Vic thought, defeated. *We almost made it!*

Vic and Via skidded their mounts to a stop, and Zukav reared.

The rider reached for Zukav's rope and succeeded, just as his three companions guided their horses into a jump from above and trotted up to their leader. "You two," the leader said, sword drawn and Zukav's rope clasped in his other hand. "State your business here. Now."

Vic opened his mouth to speak, but Via cut him off: "We're passing through Levar, headed for Drema. We mistook you for weevils. I'm sure you know as well as we do that their attacks are quite common here."

The man squinted at her. "You look quite familiar, young lady."

Vic spoke now. "She's my sister, sir. We're twins."

The man kept his eyes trained on Via without blinking, and Vic was surprised when the man addressed him, even though he kept his gaze on Via. "And the purpose of your cuchels?"

"Self-defense, as we thought you were weevils. I pray your companion is uninjured and give him my sincere apologies." Vic could feel his heartbeat pounding in his ears, the adrenaline mixed with nausea. *Will they let us go? Or is Via right – again?*

The man finally looked at Vic for a moment before studying Via again. Then turning to his companions, the man paused before facing them again. "You two: move out. Now." The rope slid out of the armed man's hand, and Zukav yanked back, snorting and flinging lather.

Eyes still on the strangers, Vic leaned closer to Azeri, pressing his heel against the stallion's side, turning the horse around. After calming Zukav down, Via followed suit.

But the moment she had turned Zukav halfway, the leader pointed at her with a shout: "Aha, the tattoo! You are Via Simonschild: I knew it!" Before either Vic or Via could react, the leader reached out and seized Zukav's rope, causing the bay stallion to rear again. Azeri took a few steps back, and the other two men leaped off their mounts and rushed over, knocking Vic off the black giant.

"Let go of me! Via!" he shouted, as the men held him down by his arms, and Azeri reared. "No!"

Their leader yanked Zukav's rope, bringing the stallion closer, and then pulled at Via, who struggled, shouting. Her bay mount gave a bloodcurdling scream and reared again. The leader managed to drag Via from her steed and onto his own horse's back.

Vic fought against his handlers. "No!"

Holding Via to him, his arm around her chest, the leader unsheathed his sword again and cursed, saying, "Crazy horse." Vic realized his intent as he aimed his blow, right at Zukav's neck.

"NO!" Via screamed.

Without another thought, Vic pressed against his attackers before shouting, "Ir kazams yoi zukav!" His two oppressors flew backwards, ten feet at least, colliding with a ridge. Dazed, they lay on the ground, the outlines of their bodies impressed in the rock behind them.

Their leader glanced back, distracted from his task.

Taking advantage of the distraction he'd caused and the time he'd created, Vic pulled his bow off his back. In one motion, he'd strung an arrow and released it, just as the leader turned to look at him in fury. The arrow flew right past the leader's head. The man, eyes wide in surprise, dropped his sword to press a palm to his cheek. When he pulled his hand back, there was blood on his palm, smeared on his cheek where Vic's arrow had nicked him.

Zukav bolted up a ridge, Azeri following.

The leader's face hardened, eyes watching as Vic lowered his bow. Then he shouted a command to his men, who had gotten up from the ground, groaning. The other two men glanced at Vic but hesitated, wary of being outmatched. When their leader shouted at them again, they moved forward, drawing their swords.

Unafraid, Vic watched as they approached, waiting till they were standing on either side of their leader, who gazed at Vic with seething hatred. Then he threw up a hand, palm forward, as he shouted, "Shu surg tuk!" His eyelids drooped as the power left him, but he forced another cuchel from his lips: "Beu shu!" A bolt of lightning crashed through the sky, striking the ground right in front of the leader, whose horse spooked and reared. The leader cursed, fighting to regain control, but dropped the reins as Vic's spell continued.

Where the ray of lightning had collided with the ground, an orb of red energy bubbled forth. Like a stormy sea, its surface rippled with waves. The men slid around on the energy bubble, crying in alarm as electric shocks zapped them. The leader fought again to control his steed while holding onto

Via. Her face went pale as she stared down at the bubble of electric energy, at the two men attempting to escape the electrical shocks in vain, instead sliding about in desperation.

When the orb subsided, the two men scrambled toward their steeds, mounting. Despite their leader's shouted orders, they spurred their horses forward, vanishing into the night. The leader brought his stallion back to all four legs and cursed.

"Via! Duck!" Vic shouted, another arrow strung and aimed. She did as he bid, and he released. A split-second later, the arrow had found its mark in the leader's throat. The bandit glanced down, confused at the feeling of an arrow piercing through his flesh. Then he fell from his horse with a thud.

Swinging his bow onto his back, Vic gathered his strength again and took a deep breath. Shaking a bit, he moved forward and stooped over the dead body. "Beu," he whispered, and the man's remaining life energy washed over him, resupplying his mental core.

Fully recovered, Vic straightened and saw Via leading Zukav, her hands holding his head. He noticed Zukav's trembling gait, and the way the stallion tried to pull his head out of Via's grasp. "What's the matter with him?"

"He's afraid of lightning." She kissed Zukav's cheek.

Vic sighed. "I'm sorry about that, Zukav. I intended to startle them, not you."

"He'll be all right." Via lowered her gaze to the ground. "And thank you, Vic. I owe you my life – and Zukav's."

Embarrassed, Vic looked away, shrugging. After a long pause, he cleared his throat to say, "Shall we move on, then? I suppose we should try and reach Levar by dawn."

"Yes," Via agreed, and she mounted Zukav.

Vic whistled to bring Azeri over and then mounted. "And you're right: we should take the side roads to Levar."

She smiled, clicking to Zukav to urge the bay forward. Vic did the same, and they cantered their way around the ridges, sticking to shadows and avoiding the roads. Almost three hours later, the city of Levar loomed below them. From their vantage point atop a towering ridge, Vic and Via studied the illuminated city.

"Look like where you're from?" Via asked, her voice cutting the silent darkness.

Vic shook his head. "Much larger than home. Dugar's a mere pebble in comparison."

Via patted Zukav's neck as the impatient stallion stamped a hoof on the rocky ground, and a shower of pebbles slid down the ridge. "Levar's like a kingdom in itself."

"From up here, it's easy to imagine how our ancestors' kingdom looked," Vic mused. "Well, before the Mad King, that is."

"As a child, I used to daydream about such a kingdom. If the Mad King hadn't relocated to the abandoned elfin palace, perhaps Levar might've become a better city." Via sighed. "But the first governor of Levar built his mansion above the old castle ruins and, thus, buried our history."

"But the Storytellers keep the truths of our history alive," Vic interjected. "The Six can never erase that."

Via shook her head. "Not in Levar. Stories must be purchased, not given away." When Vic titled his head in confusion, she shrugged. "It's been that way since before I was born."

"Well," Vic coughed out, unsure what else to say. "How do we get in?"

"There." Vic followed Via's pointing finger with his gaze but couldn't tell what she was gesturing to. "It's too small to see from here, but that's the smallest gate, the back entrance, if you will. It's the least guarded, the special entrance for merchants coming back late at night." She nudged Zukav forward, guiding him down the ridge. "We'll have to loop around Levar, to avoid any lurking guards, and then curve back in. Just follow me."

Almost another hour later, they approached the gate, and Vic could feel the tension in Azeri's muscles. "Azeri remembers," he whispered, his voice slashing through the dark.

Via leaned forward to pat Zukav's gleaming neck. "So does Zukav."

Vic raised his eyes as the gate grew larger before them as they drew closer, until it rose like a giant above them. *Via said we're entering via Levar's smallest gate, but it's gigantic compared to the ones back home,* Vic noted. With a gentle tug on Zukav's mane, Via brought the bay stallion to a halt, and Vic stopped his black steed beside her. Silence hung like sharpened knives in the air.

Then Via did something Vic least expected: hooted like an owl. There was the sound of clinking chain mail, and a guard's helmeted head appeared above, staring down at them, holding a lantern in his hand. "What's the password?"

Via cleared her throat before speaking, throwing her words up to the guard for only him and Vic to hear: "King Armond."

His eyes wide, Vic stared at her, scandalized by her words. But the guard merely grunted and disappeared again. Then the outer gate lifted, and the inner wooden one swung open. Once through the gates, Vic waited till they were shutting behind him – the iron one creaking in the night – before letting the harsh words out: "*That's* the password? The Mad King?"

Via kept her eyes straight ahead. "Don't judge."

He shook his head in amazement as Azeri trod alongside Zukav. "How did you know it?"

"My father told me, once. And I've been quite the eavesdropper."

"I'm impressed." He glanced over his shoulder, but the guard was invisible, so high above. "And he didn't question you?"

"It's a firm belief that if you know the password, then you need not be questioned." She leaned toward him. "It's the cheating merchants who know it. They have the power here." With a sigh, she nudged Zukav toward a side street. "That's why my father was so disliked."

Vic nodded, knowing to keep silent.

Not long after, Via led them to a stable and dismounted. "We'll keep Zukav and Azeri here while we lodge elsewhere."

Vic dismounted, observing the small stable that smelled quite odd and the dilapidated hut beside it. "Where are we?"

"The tanner's."

Vic stared at her in complete disbelief. "You want to leave your horses *here?*"

She brushed Zukav off with one hand before picking up his rope. "It's the only way – they won't let me into the city stables." She shrugged then patted both her horses goodbye. "As long as we're back to get them by dawn, then we'll be fine. He's never up early – he's a drunk and lies in bed for as long as he can with those terrible hangovers." She laughed. "His wife hates him."

Still a little disbelieving, Vic glanced one last time at the tanner's hut. Via touched his shoulder. "Follow me."

He did, glancing warily around as they ducked through the quiet and dark city, keeping to side streets, feeling strange inside, like a thief in the night. After a long while, the city inn stood before them – five times larger than the one in Dugar. "Will they let us in?" Vic asked her as she spied out from their hiding place in an alleyway.

She shook her head. "No. They'd turn me in instead."

At the inn, two guards entered, shutting the door behind them. Through the windows, Vic could see men drinking and hoisting their mugs of beer, silhouetted by the lights inside. "So, what's the plan then?" he questioned.

"Tajern never rents the back room out – he always raises the price too high. We'll sneak in through the window in the back." She surveyed the area. "Just avoid being seen in the tavern light."

They snuck their way to the back of the inn, careful to avoid patches of frosted light by sticking to the shadows. Vic could hear the rowdy drunk talk of the men paired with the loud and off-key music being played.

Via stopped and pointed upward. "There's the window. No light. Good. I'll go first." She moved to a stationary shape; Vic realized it was an olive tree, with branches leading right up to the window. Deftly, she climbed the tree and then pulled herself across the branch closest to the window. Prying the window open with a handy stick, she ducked through.

Inside, the room was dusty and dark. A single elevated bed of furs sat against one wall; otherwise, the room was bare. Via turned as she heard Vic climbing through the window. He dusted himself off then surveyed his surroundings. She could see the confusion in his eyes.

"This is his most expensive room?" he asked, incredulous. "It's the same as any other."

"Indeed." She went over to the door, checking the lock. "You should realize by now, Vic, how selfish these people are."

Shaking his head, Vic shrugged off his outer tunic. Via glanced at him then ducked her head.

"You can have the bed," he offered, pulling off a thick wolf pelt, "and I'll take the floor." Without a word, she went to bed, her back to Vic.

He tucked himself under the fur before removing his inner tunic. Then, before falling asleep, he reflected on what he'd seen: *I never realized how…different my youth was, compared to some.*

Levar

Vic woke the next morning after feeling Via prodding him in his sleep. "What time is it?" he moaned.

"Hush," she whispered, leaning over him. "We snuck in, remember? It's almost dawn, and we must retrieve Zukav and Azeri before the tanner's wife wakes him. Come on."

In a rush, he slipped both of his tunics back on and got to his feet. Outside was windy, and Vic was afraid the olive tree would bend from the powerful gusts. But the trunk was thick, and he and Via made it safely to the ground. Passing the now-lightless windows of the inn, Vic noticed the tavern was not very full, a handful of men hunched over their kegs. He came to the door and stepped to move inside.

"Vic! What are you doing?!" Via's words were daggers through the crisp air.

"We'll need breakfast," he murmured. "Just a few moments, and I'll be back." Inside, he approached the counter. The man behind it cocked an eyebrow, a look of uncertainty flashing across his face. "I'll take whatever you can give me for a bronze piece," Vic said, displaying the coin as proof.

The man opened his mouth to say something then shook his head and turned away toward the kitchen. As he prepared the food, Vic stole a glance around the room. In the far corner, two guards, their armor almost invisible under their black cloaks, sat together, talking in low tones over their drinks. Vic's heart skipped a beat.

"'Ere ya are," the man said in a gruff tone, setting a small platter on the counter with a clink.

Vic observed the plate: a fist-sized roll and a small clay cup of some liquid. "No meat?"

The man shook his head. "Not for a bronze piece. But I can add some bacon for two bronze coins," he added with a wink.

Taking the bread, Vic shook his head. "No, this is fine. Keep the cup."

The man reached for the platter and turned away, his back to Vic. As Vic laid the bronze piece on the counter, he noticed the man dumping the liquid in a dog's bowl. *Guess I'm getting my first taste of Levar hospitality,* Vic observed.

Leaving the tavern, Vic stood outside in the biting wind and glanced around. Then he caught sight of Via hidden in an alleyway. Coming over to her, he tore the bread and gave her half. She took it with gratitude, swallowing it in one bite.

"Here: put this on." And then, from behind a crate, she produced two black cloaks.

Vic almost choked on his bread. "Where did you get those?"

"While you provided a distraction in there," with a nod toward the inn, "I snuck inside and managed to grab these from their hooks. We'll need them when we ride through Levar. Quick, put it on." She tucked herself inside hers.

Taking the other cloak from her, Vic raised his eyebrows. "The merchant's daughter is also a thief?"

She shrugged. "They're made from cheap material, allowing the merchant to overcharge. Whoever bought them isn't losing much." She started to lead the way down the alley.

With a small shake of his head, Vic fastened on the cloak before following.

Zukav was jubilant to see Via again, and she had to lay a hand on his nose to quiet him. Vic marveled at the fact that Azeri welcomed them without a sound and instead dropped Zukav's rope from his mouth into Via's outstretched hand. Once they'd mounted, Vic and Via nudged the horses down another side street. "Where's our exit?" he asked.

Via pulled up the hood of her cloak, obscuring her face. "The gate to the Avro Woods is just a bit north of the gate to Drema. So, we still need to take the main road through the merchants' stalls. The side streets won't get us there. Hence," she said, turning to him, "the hoods."

He pulled up his own hood to cover his head. "Via?"

On Zukav's back, she turned to look at him, the hood forming shadows on her face.

"What...what happens after that?"

"I offered to get you to Drema – now, the Avro Woods – faster. That was our agreement." She nudged Zukav toward another side street, and Vic followed on Azeri. "When you need me to leave, then I will."

He nodded, heart quickening in his chest. "I'll let you know." *But what if I enjoy your company?* he murmured.

Almost an hour later, she halted Zukav, and the stallion tossed his head, nostrils flaring. "Zukav knows where we are. Azeri does too," she added, pointing at the giant black's arched head. "Are you ready?"

Vic could hear the noise from the merchants' shouts, from the children running through the streets, from the dogs barking, from the occasional high-pitched whinny and clatter of hooves. *A busy city, indeed.* "I think so. Are you?"

With a sigh, she stroked Zukav's sweaty neck. "Ready as I'll ever be."

He swallowed hard as he watched her straighten, throw back her shoulders, and click Zukav forward. Following behind her, Vic turned the corner to find himself staring straight at the main road cutting through Levar, a busy sight before him.

All along the road were merchants at their stands, selling items among themselves and to others. Female servants sat outside the houses, weaving, cooking, any chores they could. Guard dogs lay under each stand, protecting their masters' belongings. Rich men's wives clustered around the stands selling fans, jewelry, or clothing. Throughout it all, a mass of people moved through the street, some dressed for the long travels ahead of them. *Perhaps someone is headed for Dugar,* and Vic felt a twinge of homesickness.

It was all a flurry of colors, of people, of money.

"Welcome to Levar," Via murmured as Vic guided Azeri alongside Zukav. The streets were so packed, however, that he sometimes had to steer Azeri behind her to squeeze through the crowd.

Awhile later, they passed an older woman sitting among woven mats. Her clothes were made from expensive fabric, with delicate embroidery. Vic was surprised to see such fine clothing on a crone with yellowed teeth protruding from bleeding gums. *She dresses like a queen yet looks like a soothsayer,* he remarked.

The woman looked up as they passed, reaching out toward the heavens. "Fortunes told! You, riding the black stallion, I will tell you what the spirits have to say about your future!"

Vic glanced over at Via, but she had shifted on Zukav's back, facing away from the woman. So, he rode past.

"You can trust Momma Harpy!" the woman shouted after him.

A small gap in the crowd formed, and Vic guided Azeri alongside Zukav. Via turned to look at him. "You cannot trust Momma Harpy," she said simply.

"Why not?" Vic glanced back at the woman, who had already turned to another potential customer passing by. "Because she's from Levar?"

"No." Via halted Zukav as a merchant on a stunning white stallion cut across them. "Momma Harpy tells fortunes as a ruse. Her true profession is running the city brothel, and my father was suspicious of her controlling the corrupt merchants through her prostitutes. I think he intended to expose her...but was killed before he could."

"You mean your father's death was no accident?" Vic stroked Azeri's neck, the stallion already sweaty from the midmorning suns.

"Well, of course not: the customer murdered him. But....I have good reason to believe it was a set-up, paid for, if you will."

"Why didn't you tell me?" Vic nudged Azeri forward once more, the crowd having parted enough for them to move through.

"I—I didn't know how much to tell you, then."

I just have to press further: "And now?"

"Now you know everything." And she turned away.

Vic sighed when he felt a tingle down his back. Glancing over his shoulder, he didn't notice anything amiss nor did he see anyone watching him. With a shrug, trying to calm his beating heart, he faced forward again. Via must have had the same feeling, for he caught her in the act of looking past, her face shadowed by the hood, hiding her emotions.

Hours later, Vic found an opening so as to let Azeri walk alongside Zukav. "How much longer?"

"About another two hours or so," she said, glancing at the sky.

Vic did also, noticing the two suns were close to passing each other on their paths to opposite rims of the island.

"It'll be past midday when we reach the gate," Via continued. "We're about halfway through Levar."

"Such a large city."

"A merchant kingdom," she said with a shrug.

He touched her arm. "Wait."

"What?" She whistled, and Zukav came to a halt.

"Let's water the horses. The continuous heat of both suns must have made them thirsty." With that, he dismounted and, placing one hand on Azeri's neck, led the giant stallion toward the city fountain. She followed suit, leading Zukav by his rope. As the horses plunged their muzzles into the cooling water, Vic and Via rested against the stones of the fountain wall. She watched her horses while he observed the people passing by.

Vic spoke up: "It's hot and past midday. Let me buy us something to eat."

She sighed and shook her head. "We don't want to risk anything."

"What do you mean?"

"You won't know how to deal with these men, while I cannot for fear of being recognized. It's happened before, and I almost didn't escape. We'll need to only drink water, no food. Do you have the horn?"

He nodded and dug it out of his pack. Filling it with water, he then took a long drink before offering it to Via. They finished it, and he refilled it.

"The horses are ready now," she said, picking up Zukav's rope. "Let's go."

Long after, Vic noticed a merchant ahead selling a fine collection of knives and daggers. *Zurze could use a good quality knife with an engraved hilt. After all, I owe him something for sneaking off on him like I did,* he decided, saying aloud: "Via, I need myself a dagger."

"Why?"

"To give someone as a gift…for letting me leave." Before she could speak, he added, "Will you help me in bargaining?"

There was a pause before she answered: "Fine."

He swallowed hard. *I know she doesn't want to, that she's afraid, but I've got to. It's for Zurze,* he convinced himself.

"How many coins do you have?" she asked. "Give me something to work with."

"One silver coin," he replied. *Truth is, I have six, but I want to save the other five, just to be safe; I might need them.* "He won't take bronze – even I know that."

Via sighed and glanced at the sky. "Even one silver coin is too little. But we'll try and convince him to take it."

Coming up alongside the merchant's stand, Vic halted Azeri. The merchant looked up in surprise, a sudden glint coming to his eyes in anticipation of their upcoming bargaining. "May I help you?" he asked – a little bald man with a long salt-and-pepper goatee.

"I'd like to buy that dagger," Vic said and pointed to the one of his choosing. He'd seen it as he'd approached the stand: a gorgeous knife with a hilt decorated with engravings of deer, rivers, and trees. A golden hilt and a blade of untainted silver.

The merchant glanced over at it and then stroked his goatee with one hand, the other resting on his large stomach. "Ten silver pieces."

Vic glanced at Via. She nodded. Turning back to the merchant, Vic set his face with determination. "Five."

"Five?" the merchant cried, incredulous. "Eight!"

Via had expected as much. No merchant in his right mind would stoop to his customer's demands – and in this case, demands of *half* of what the merchant had first declared – without some ruthless bargaining. *Except Father.* When Vic looked back at her, she nodded again and mouthed, "Keep going. Drive him," and made sure Vic had caught it before backing Zukav up two steps, giving her enough room to breathe. Her eyes pricked, so she raised a hand to wipe away sweat and, with discretion, tears. She would not think of Father again while in Levar, for fear of revealing herself.

Again, she glanced over her shoulder, feeling the same fear of being watched creep over her. She'd felt as if eyes were watching her for a few hours now, but then again, every time she'd been in Levar – during her father's time or after his death when she'd snuck in – she'd felt as if eyes were continuously on her. Today, her eyes caught nothing suspicious. But her heart did quicken at the sight of three city guards astride stallions. Their conversation appeared casual, but their very presence caused her to sweat. *I cannot be discovered because of Vic,* she reminded herself. *I cannot.* She'd avoided being caught the many other times she'd snuck in, but she was always alone. Or with one of her horses. Never with another human being.

Agitated noise from the merchant stand broke her thoughts. Moving Zukav alongside Azeri once more, she asked, "What's the trouble?"

"He's asking for three. I said two," Vic explained as the merchant gave a determined nod. He wiped a hand across his forehead. "I can't think with how hot my head his." Then he threw back his hood, and Via saw the sweat beads across his forehead sparkling in the sunlight.

She also caught sight of the strange behavior that came over the merchant. She had recognized him – a new merchant at the time of her father's death but already rising in prominence. His name was something like...*Fernando,* she remembered. Now Fernando's eyes were widening, so wide she wondered if they would pop out of his head. He opened his mouth to speak, but the words were stuck in his throat for he then clamped his mouth shut. A look of fear overtook him. Via glanced back at Vic, the pieces starting to come together.

Vic didn't seem to notice Fernando's startled appearance. "Where were we?"

"Take it," Fernando hissed. His voice was a sharp as the daggers he sold. "Take it for nothing and get out of here."

Confused, Vic paused for a moment then leaned forward to pluck the dagger off the display.

As he did, Via suppressed a grin and glanced over her shoulder, for another look at the guards just to be safe. To her horror, she saw Momma Harpy amid the crowd, near the guards. *She followed us. Why?* She didn't expect an answer. *But Momma Harpy isn't looking at me,* she realized. *She's looking at...*

Without turning, she knew: *She confuses Vic for me – thinking that I've cut my hair!*

To her growing horror, she watched as Momma Harpy sidled over to the guards, standing on tiptoe to whisper to one who leaned down toward her. Via recognized him as one of Momma Harpy's regulars, but then a memory struck her: he'd possessively kissed her without her consent before the auction. She remembered the gloating gleam in his eyes, despite her defiant glares.

Via's stomach dropped. Jabbing her finger in the direction of Vic, Momma Harpy flashed a disgusted but triumphant face. The guard straightened and barked something at his two companions. Then they drew their swords, kicked their stallions forward.

"Run, Vic!" Via screamed, turning Zukav in a hurry. "Put your hood up and run!"

Even more confused, Vic turned to look behind and caught sight of the oncoming guards. Clenching his new dagger between his teeth, he grunted at Azeri to move forward, and the giant black stallion did.

People dodged out of the way as the two horses hurtled down the street, and the riders focused on trying not to trample anyone in the crowd. Behind them came the guards, swords drawn as they shouted, "Make way! Stop, you on the black stallion!" Merchants yelled, dogs barked, horses screamed at the public auction stand, but Vic and Via paid them no heed.

"There!" she shouted, pointing. "There's the gate!" Vic could see it up ahead, high above the heads of the people entering and leaving.

Someone rolled wooden barrels out in front of them while trying to cross the main road. Zukav soared over them, and Vic urged Azeri to do the same. The giant stallion needed no convincing. For a split second, Vic flew through the air on the stallion's back. Then they landed, continuing to gallop forward, and again the people threw themselves out of the way, too shocked to do anything. Glancing over his shoulder, Vic saw the guards closing in, guiding their horses around the last barrel.

Then they were out of the gate, surrounded by the large mass of people. Hearing the guards' continued shouts, Vic and Via broke their horses free and urged them toward the Avro Woods, to the east of Levar. The ground darkened as the clouds merged together to become a giant grey sky. Then the raindrops came, followed by lightning. Vic could see Via's slight struggle to keep control of Zukav. The guards had fallen behind now, beyond two ridges.

All around them raged the storm; heavy raindrops fell in sheets, with crackling lightning followed by booming thunder. Vic almost couldn't see. Via's voice startled him: "There, there – hard to see, but it's the Avro Woods." He could make out the evergreen trees that formed a sweeping mass of darkness ahead. The powerful gusts of wind bent the trees as it howled. Azeri neighed upon entering the forest behind Zukav – a loud ringing neigh of relief. Once they were deep enough in the woods, Via dismounted to handle a shivering Zukav. "Sh, boy, sh. There, there, it's all right."

Vic slowed Azeri to a trot before halting him and dismounting. At long last, he took the dagger from his teeth, massaging his jaw, and stood beside Via with one hand on Azeri's neck. "Will he be all right?"

"As soon as we get him into shelter, yes. Azeri will calm him then." Already the black stallion was moving toward the bay, nickering before brushing his muzzle against Zukav's neck. The bay tossed his head.

"Outcasts live here in these woods," she said, catching her breath. "We should be able to find one of their huts soon and ask for shelter for the night. And then—" She paused, looked away.

Don't leave. Not yet. "Tomorrow isn't here yet," Vic said, a sinking feeling in the pit of his stomach. "Come on, let's find somewhere to sleep."

Though distant in dreamland, Afis caught the scent of meat, wafting into his nose, wetting his tongue. Already forgetting the dream, he surfaced from sleep to a midafternoon light filling the room.

"Ah, good morning, lad!" His host appeared, moving aside the door flap, letting more sunslight stream in. Afis blinked, still sleepy, his eyes adjusting to the light. "Or rather," his host added, with a chuckle, "I suppose it's a good afternoon!"

"I slept this whole time?" Afis asked, with a yawn.

"Aye. I thought both suns would awaken you, but you didn't even stir."

Afis smiled. Sliding the fur blanket off his legs, he got to his feet and walked over. "Can I help?"

The man grinned as he set up a large reed mat on the hut floor. "Thunder beat you to it." Confused, Afis raised an eyebrow then looked toward the door flap at the sound of a familiar bark. "Ah, that's him. The meat must be done."

Afis followed him out of the hut. Once his eyes adjusted to the outside light, he saw a fire crackling before him, controlled by a ring of wet rocks. A wooden tripod stood over the fire, from which three slabs of meat sizzled. Afis shut his mouth to keep the drool from spilling out.

Feeling his arm hairs bristling, Afis looked up. A breeze blew through the treetops, but he sensed its accelerating strength.

Their host removed the meat from the tripod and laid it on a giant wooden platter. "Come. Let us eat inside, away from the incoming storm. Both suns may be out now, but very soon they will be gone." Once back inside, the man laid the plate of meat on the mat. "Please, take a seat. I will be right back." He disappeared outside again.

Afis sat down at the mat, facing the door flap. Thunder plopped down beside him. "What do you think, Thunder? Do you think we deserve all this?" he asked, gesturing at the meat before them. The dog laid his head on Afis' knee, staring at the meat, nose quivering. Afis laughed. "I should have known – all you care about is the food!" Thunder whined while Afis stroked the dog's head. *It's not unlike the offerings the Blood Bearers bestowed upon me but this man—this man seems to do it for a different reason,* Afis thought.

Thunder licked his chops. Their host returned, with five biscuits in hand as he stepped through the flap. Afis could see the mighty trees bending in the wind, the sunslight gone, replaced with a grey light. "I was right," he said, placing the biscuits down on the mat. "A storm is coming – I can smell the rain." Thunder raised his head, nose quivering faster, and he gave a low whine. "But not to worry," the man continued with a wink. "There's magic around my hut. To keep it safe from harm."

Afis stopped chewing on a biscuit. "Magic?"

"Aye, lad." The man laid a slab of meat before Thunder, who began tearing it apart. He straightened then, looking Afis full in the eye. "I am Kaio, Master of Magic."

"What is this magic?" Afis asked, while thinking, *Magic....the Blood Bearers spoke of it, and yet I don't understand it.* He paused. *They said they used it to create me, but Kaio said he used it as protection from harm — so that must mean there is more to magic than the Blood Bearers' intent, for theirs* was *to harm.*

Kaio threw back his head and laughed. "What is this magic?" he repeated. With a chuckle, he flashed a mysterious smile at Afis. "Well, lad, let me show you."

And then the room changed — and all of a sudden, Afis sensed as if he was slightly rising off the ground. The bare dirt was transformed into a carpet of lush green grass, which spread across the room like a puddle of water. Along the walls, trees sprang up, rising higher and higher, until Afis could no longer see anything but trees around him. He spun around, head thrown back, mouth agape. It was a picturesque forest, like one he'd often dreamed about back on Glasiea with the Blood Bearers.

"This, lad," came a voice that cut through his observations. He looked to his right to see Kaio emerging from the trees, a grin on the man's face. "This, lad, is magic." Kaio opened wide his arms. "What do you think?"

Afis gave a short, incredulous laugh. "It's fantastic!"

Behind Afis came a rumbling bark, and he turned to see Thunder come bounding out of the thicket. Thunder stopped beside Afis, glanced at him with tongue hanging out, and then he shook himself — casting off ferns and brush. Kneeling beside the dog, Afis smiled when Thunder licked his face.

"Magic is why I knew our friend here is no ordinary dog, lad," said Kaio. Afis looked up as the man approached and put his hand on Thunder's head, between the golden ears.

"What do you mean?"

Kaio scratched Thunder's ear. "Normal animals cannot project thoughts, like you or I can. They do not speak internally, do not think like humans do. They instead act on instinct. The only information they retain are images – images of where they were born, images of their parents. They cannot retain words."

Afis cocked his head; Thunder licked his ear.

"But your Thunder – or rather, I should say Snook, for that is the name his first master gave him—"

Afis' jaw dropped as he stared at Snook. Moments passed before he admitted, "I never even considered that he'd had another name before I met him."

"You wouldn't have known unless you'd searched his mind, which would have shown you how unique he is," Kaio continued. "Snook can think like you and me. He can think in images, but he also thinks in *words*. As if he is speaking. In fact, he has been mind-speaking – a magical trick – with a young lad named Vic, who at this very moment is headed west from Dugar to find Snook."

When Snook whined in response, Afis noticed how the dog whipped his head in Kaio's direction, as if taken aback by his words.

"So, you see," Kaio said, finishing. "Our friend here is no ordinary animal."

Afis got back to his feet, staring at Snook, trying but afraid to understand what Kaio had said. "What does it all mean?" he asked.

Kaio chuckled. "In just a moment, you'll have your answer." And in the same moment that he'd finished speaking, a knock came from outside, and the woodland illusion vanished.

Reunited

Kaio looked over his shoulder. "Ah, right on time."

Afis shook his head, trying to clear his thoughts: *He was expecting this to happen? What all does Kaio know?* Curious and bewildered, he followed Kaio to the door flap, peering over his host's shoulder.

Outside in the pouring rain stood a young couple – both wearing soaked cloaks over their clothes. The young man had his hood lowered, but the young woman kept hers raised, avoiding eye contact as if shy.

Kaio observed them, but Afis noticed his subtle double take at the sight of the young man's face. *Does he recognize him?*

Panting for breath, the young man said, "Sirs, with the rain and all, my companion and I would like to spend the night in a dry shelter. Would you happen to have any room? I'll pay you in advance," and he pulled out a bronze coin from his money pouch.

Kaio waved it away. "That won't be necessary – my home is always open for free to those in need. Come inside, come inside! You're wet enough – come, dry off."

The young man moved to step inside. Realizing the young woman was not following, he turned. "Come on, there's room," Afis heard him say to her.

Shivering, she looked over her shoulder. In the shadowed forest, darkened by storm clouds, two large shapes shifted back and forth. "My horses need to be put up somewhere, Vic. Zukav won't stand the lightning without me."

"If they are loyal, my dear, they will stay nearby and find shelter in the trees," Kaio said, putting a hand on her shoulder.

She swallowed hard, glancing at his hand, and nodded.

"In fact, there's a small run-down shed not far from here. They'll find it." Kaio extended his other hand toward the main room, gesturing. "But please, come inside!"

The young woman sighed. Turning back to the horses, she kissed her hand then held it out toward them, whistling a low tune, to which the horses replied with echoing neighs. Turning back to the hut, she followed the young man inside.

Afis ducked ahead to offer them biscuits once they entered the main room of the hut. Snook hadn't moved, still laying in the same spot with his head between his paws. Afis thought he saw the same bewilderment that he felt echoed in the dog's eyes.

Gesturing for his new guests to sit, Kaio finished tying the door flap and then joined them, taking a seat next to Afis with the newcomers across the mat. "Meet my other guest, who also needed a place to stay. You don't mind some fellow guests, eh, lad?" he asked Afis, who shrugged. "Good. But before that, let's get acquainted," Kaio continued and winked at Afis, who blinked back in confusion.

Does he know something I—we don't? Figuring Kaio's wink was some sort of signal, Afis cleared his throat. "Um, well – my name is Afis. And you are?"

With a smile, the young man swallowed his biscuit. "My name is Vic."

A deep rumble filled the room. In a mighty stride, Snook crossed the mat and landed atop Vic, knocking him over. As Vic lay on the floor, startled, Snook's tongue flopped out of his mouth, and he began covering Vic's face in saliva.

"Hey!" Vic said, laughing, trying to push Snook away. But all he succeeded in doing was folding back the flaps of skin around his muzzle.

Mouth agape, Afis watched the scene, and then gawked at Kaio, who chuckled and winked back. *Aha – his name: Vic!* Afis thought, connecting the dots. *Kaio was expecting him this entire time – but how? And how, just how, did he by chance happen to come here, precisely where Thunder – er, I mean, Snook – was?*

"He's been waiting for you, Vic, lad," Kaio said, his tone cheerful. "How lucky the storm drove you right to us." Again, he winked in a mysterious way at Afis, who gaped back.

The dog had moved back to give room for Vic to sit up – but only to sit up. Once Vic had gotten off the floor, the giant dog was back to spreading his saliva across Vic's face.

"Pardon, sir?" said Vic, almost choking on dog spit as he spoke. "Stop, boy!" The dog did, dropping to the floor, head in Vic's lap. His imploring eyes watched him. Vic patted the dog between the ears and then repeated his question: "Pardon, sir?"

Kaio chuckled. "I see you have much to learn before you can become a Magic Master, young Vic."

Bewildered, Vic could only blink back. *What?!*

"However," Kaio continued, stroking his beard, "that shall be easy to remedy," and a smile danced on Kaio's lips.

Now it was Vic's turn to gape, and he glanced between Kaio and Afis; the latter just shrugged. "Sir, pardon my confusion," Vic managed to say, "but did you say 'Master'?"

"Aye, young Vic. But you do not wish to become a Magic Master?"

"Yes, sir, yes, I do. But how—"

Kaio brushed it aside. "All that will be explained later. For now, why not put your magic skills to use? Who is the dog beside you?"

With a shake of his head, Vic patted the dog again, and the creature whined. "I do not know, sir. He must be yours?"

"He is not mine," Kaio said with a chuckle. "Is he yours, Afis?"

Afis frowned. "No longer, I suppose."

"Good answer," Kaio said with a teasing wink. This time, Afis smiled back. Facing Vic again, Kaio motioned toward the dog. "Why not search his mind?"

Again, Vic shook his head. "But that's impossible, sir. Animals are not like humans."

He saw Via frown beside him, though her face remained obscured to the others by her hood. "Sometimes, animals are better than humans."

Vic turned to her. "I understand what you mean – but in terms of the mind, animals are not like us." He looked to Kaio, hoping to gauge the man's expression. "Animals do not retain all the information that we can with our mind."

"False." Kaio stroked his short beard. "They can retain images."

"Of their birthplaces, their parents – images of the world around them. But not of words. The dog's birthplace," Vic added, motioning toward the animal, "will not reveal who he is."

"Ah, but you can test his mind. Tell me, have you lost all connection with your friend, Snook?" Vic's eyes widened, and Kaio leaned back. "Kai, Vic, I know about that. Now, tell me, can you reach out to Snook?"

"I haven't been able to, but then again I haven't tried recently."

"Well, then," Kaio said, now leaning forward. "Try."

Vic squinted, reaching out toward the ribbon connecting him and Snook. It vibrated, pulsated – and tingled when he grasped it. *Snook?*

The reply was instantaneous: *Why mind-speak to me when I'm right here?*

Vic gasped, released the string, and looked down at the dog beside him. He was smiling, tongue hanging out, tail wagging. "Snook!"

In answer, the dog gave a rumbling bark.

Vic grinned. *I'm so glad I found you!*

As am I. Though you did take forever to figure it out, Snook teased.

Who is this Kaio? He knew all about us.

He said he's a Magic Master, Vic. He knew much more, too — more than he's told you thus far.

…how is that even possible? Vic asked, incredulous.

I'm not sure, Vic. But my sixth sense tells me we can trust him.

"Is he the one you're searching for, Vic?" Via asked, leaning toward them to offer her hand for Snook to sniff. Snook did then licked her. She moved to scratch under his chin. "You never mentioned he's a dog!" she teased. "He's so sweet!"

"How did *you* know, sir?" Vic asked.

Kaio smiled. "Please: call me Kaio. As for your question, I used the mind search cuchel. You have no usual dog there, Vic."

Vic grinned back. "I know." Then he cocked his head, frowning. "The question is: how? Why?"

"That *is* the question," Kaio agreed.

Vic nodded. "So, you are a Magic Master." Then his eyes widened, and he put a hand on Via's shoulder. "Kaio the Magic Master."

When he uttered the words, her heart skipped a beat. *Could it be? …yet the name Kaio is—is so common among men,* she told herself. *Perhaps even among Masters of Magic.*

Since arriving at the hut, she'd avoided direct eye contact and kept her hood up. The Avro Woods were populated with countless outcasts of Levar, like herself – but any of them could still have ties to someone in the city. Someone interested in locating her, even if she wasn't ready to be found. *Until I know it's safe,* she'd decided, *I must protect my identity.*

Gazing with discretion at the stranger across the mat, Via took in his face. *It's been almost five years since I've seen my second father…but surely, I would still recognize him. Or perhaps—perhaps I am still afraid to believe after all the heartbreak.*

119

Hope blossomed in her heart when she looked into his eyes. *He looks like my Kaio – but my Kaio was blond then. Has he aged so much since I last saw him?* Doubt surged through her. *Have I aged so much since I last saw him?*

Their host was smiling – but Afis caught the hint of confusion behind it. *Aha!* Afis mentally crowed when he realized that Kaio knew the cards were out of his hands now. *Something he doesn't know!*

But then, somber, he realized: *If I am to stay, I'll need to create some sort of backstory. I'm sure anyone would question why I know some things but not others. Even I do not know why.*

"Aye, lad: Kaio the Magic Master," Kaio repeated, adding a slow chuckle at the end.

I do know that voice! Via's heart skipped another beat, and she finally lowered her hood. "Kaio, it's—it's me."

When he looked at her, Via saw her own emotions echoed in his eyes: hesitation, hope, heartbreak. She knew they both wouldn't believe the truth without some sort of test. So, she whispered, "Elvas vieké avro betelyir zhan chinel, Via-Simonschild."[1]

A glassy look came over Kaio's eyes, and it was moments before he spoke. "Ké nyv viek kai, my dear, dear Via-Simonschild."[2]

Tears sprang from her eyes. "It *is* you," she whispered, and like the sound of a key unlocking a door after many tries, her heart was filled with joy. "It's you."

His eyes also welling up with tears, Kaio nodded. "It's me, Via, it's me." He opened his arms. "You're all grown up, and you've come home."

---

[1] Elves are not more beautiful than you, Via-Simonschild.

[2] And this is true, my dear, dear Via-Simonschild.

Ignoring the crumbs on the mat, Via leaned across, almost falling into Kaio's embrace. "I took you for dead! Your mare—she returned—no rider—"

Her second father stroked Via's hair as the sobs racked her body. "I fell and lost consciousness. It was months before I opened my eyes. I then decided to repay the outcasts' kind treatment by serving as their healer. But I never once forgot you – I would come looking for you, but you were gone."

Via sniffled and wiped her eyes with the back of her hand. "Father died, and I had to escape."

Touching her cheek, Kaio caught his breath. "Thank the spirits above. I could never live and know you'd been a harem girl."

"Zukav and Azeri saved me. But you came looking for me?"

"Of course – and to invite you to come live with me, both you and your father. I did discover his death, but I never discovered your whereabouts. I even searched all of the Avro Woods, the entire outcast camp here."

"I survived on the Plains," Via whispered.

"Oh, Via," Kaio murmured. "I am so sorry. If I had known…" He shook his head. "But none of the merchants would speak to me about your disappearance. All fled at the mere mention of your name. I suppose they considered you terrible luck, eh?"

Through her tears, Via let out a short laugh. "Of course they did, but little did they know I still went in and out of Levar."

With a slow shake of his head, Kaio ticked his tongue against his teeth. "And to think we never saw each other."

She brushed the tears from his eyes with her thumb. "But now we've found each other."

"Kai," Kaio said, smiling. "And I won't ever lose you again, dear Via. Never again."

Vic awoke to the sound of music. He sat up from his makeshift bed and looked around the room: *Where is everyone?* Stretching, he got to his feet and, still groggy, followed the music.

Afis stood beating a drum in the morning light as Via swung round and round, dancing. She seemed to be hovering over the ground, her feet never touching, a feather in the air. From her lips came the sweetest sounds as she sang along to the rhythm, and Vic recognized a few lines from the books of old.

Kaio leaned against a birch tree with Snook at his feet. He caught sight of Vic at the door flap and motioned him over. Vic stood with him awhile, adjusting to the morning air, watching Via dancing to the drumbeats, when Kaio turned to him. "How would you like me to teach you cuchels?" their host asked. "You have the basic training, but I can improve you still."

"Who told you I wanted to become a Magic Master?" Vic questioned, still confused over the man's seemingly all-knowing power.

Chuckling, Kaio nodded toward Via. "A little bird told me. So, what will it be, lad?"

Still confused, considering he somehow knew before reuniting with Via, but he grinned. "I'd love it if you'd teach me, but won't we be a bother?"

Kaio laughed so loud that Afis paused to look at them. "Of course not, lad! As I said before, my home is always open. I wouldn't have offered if I didn't mean it."

"What about the others?" Vic asked, watching Via resume her dancing once Afis began drumming again.

"They have already decided to stay. Via is like a daughter to me, and Afis has nowhere to go – and with no memory of home. At breakfast, he confessed to us that fishermen found him, stranded and confused, on Glasiea. Seems he has amnesia so until his mind heals, he is welcome to stay." Kaio faced Vic, serious now. "That leaves you and Snook. Your decision is to stay or depart." He paused. "So. What will it be, Vic?"

What do you think? he asked Snook.

I'm not in a rush to leave, Snook replied. *Besides, perhaps we should learn more about Kaio and what he knows.*

Vic returned Kaio's gaze. "We'll stay for at a full moon cycle then be on our way." He grinned. "No one teaches magic in Dugar. I'm excited to have someone to discuss cuchels with."

With a smile, Kaio patted Vic's shoulder. "Good, good! We'll be glad for your company, and I'll be quite glad to discuss cuchels with you, too."

A new voice pierced the woods: "Kaio!" They all looked up, stopping their merriment, to glimpse a plump woman running toward them.

Kaio's smile widened. "Marsha, my good woman, what brings you here today?"

Marsha came to a stop in front of him, breathing hard, doubled over. "My Jalea has a terrible cough. I was hoping you had a powder to cure her. She deserves it, Kaio: she's such a good girl."

"You're in luck, Marsha, because I have a powder that can help. You look hot. Were you baking?"

The woman smiled, and two dimples appeared on her cheeks. "Indeed, I was, Kaio. My famous biscuits were in the oven when, when... oh."

Kaio motioned Afis and Via over. "Take Marsha to the shade and entertain her. Vic, come with me. Your first lesson begins today."

In Kaio's bedroom, Vic looked around in amazement. Two bookshelves lined the far wall. One was packed with books – from thick tomes to thin pamphlets. The second bookshelf was lined with various items. Drying leaves. Sketches on parchment stuffed between two clay bowls. A dozen or so glass bottles – about half filled with bubbling brew. Standing in front of the bookshelves, Vic shifted to see different parts of Kaio's eclectic collection scattered about the room. "I didn't know you had an entire collection of magical stuff here." Vic laughed to himself. "But then again, what did I expect?"

Kaio smiled. "I'm sure you'll have a collection as great one day. But pay attention as today is lesson number one."

Vic focused on Kaio – somehow resisting the urge to continue gaping at the magical collection.

Kaio was leaning over a stone bowl, and Vic recognized some of the strange markings along its rim from his tome. *But I can't let him know I recognize them, nothing beyond the basics. I don't know how he might react,* he reminded himself. *He taught Via about cuchels, but she was the daughter of a wealthy merchant back then. Whereas I am the son of a poor carpenter.*

"Elfin words," Kaio said, catching sight of Vic studying the marks.

Peering closer, Vic noticed that Kaio was crushing roots with a rock. Underneath, a pile of crumpled leaves lay scattered on the bottom of the bowl. "How will these two items heal Jalea?"

"The root comes from an evergreen tree, perfect for healing coughs. The leaves? They add a sweet taste. For children, the sweetness hides the otherwise bitterness of the roots. Adults shouldn't mind, but I have begun adding leaves to their medicines, too."

Kaio rummaged through the shelves before finding a piece of deerskin and placing the power inside, rolled it up with a sliver of twine. "It may not be dahlas, Vic, but even a simple healer's work is connected to the realm of magic. For it just shows that everything around us is connected, like an entire web, and we can tap into a small part of it." He moved toward the hanging rug that separated his bedroom from the main room. "Remember these words, Vic: even the simplest things can hold the greatest power. Think of the word 'beu.' All that energy! Or in our case, these simple natural ingredients. Evergreen root will cure a child. That cuchel will cure a man from overusing magic."

Taking a deep breath, Vic followed Kaio back outside and thought, *I've got a lot to learn.*

Vic yawned. "When you asked me yesterday about taking lessons, I didn't realize it would be quite so early." *And despite not seeing his face, I know he's smiling.* Earlier, Kaio had shaken Vic awake and said that lesson two – medicine and some cuchel techniques – would be in five minutes. Vic had rushed awake, but once outside, he'd realized both suns were still rising from the east and the west.

Kaio looked over his shoulder. "But just look at that sunrise," and he swept his hand across the horizon. The two stopped, watching in awe as tendrils of light kissed the awakening world. They stood on a small hill, and a slight breeze zipped by. A shiver running down his back, Vic hugged his wool jacket closer.

"Aha," Kaio said, his tone eager. "Come over here, Vic." Kaio stood among a patch of flowers, and he plucked one to show Vic. "Describe this flower to me. I want you to discover your own way of recognizing it."

As bid, Vic studied the plant before answering: "I see the color red; I smell the intense fragrance; and I can sense its blooming life."

Kaio nodded in approval. "Good. You're already using more than one of your senses to identify it – and I am quite pleased to hear you've tapped into the magical side of things."

"Well, I was going more off of how full in bloom it seems to be," Vic admitted. "Was I wrong?"

His mentor laughed. "You have not reached the experience needed to see the strings of magic in the air." Vic gaped, and Kaio winked in a mysterious way. "Kai, lad, I'm watching the threads whirling through the air around me. You'll get there. One day."

Kaio held the flower higher. "But, Vic, I'm sure that you can sense the pulsating energy emitting from the flower. It's how the bees find it – for even the animals are in tune with the most basic traces of magic. And like a bee, you also noticed its smell. But unlike a bee, you can see its color." Kaio traced the blossom's petals, adding: "This flower is called Ruverb, and it's perfect for healing an open wound. All one has to do is mix the crushed roots with water – after bandaging the wound first!"

Vic grinned.

Kaio plucked another bloom. "This, Dertic. We're lucky to find one. They're quite rare: this being the third one I've seen in my lifetime. If you live to see four, I shall consider you quite accomplished," and he chuckled. Passing the flower to Vic, Kaio added, "Ruverb is red; Dertic is not. What other differences?"

Vic shook his head. "Not much, except that it's white and blue."

Stroking his chin, Kaio prodded him further: "No other differences?"

"Well, I realize now that this one has no smell."

Kaio turned the flower over. "And the leaves are pointed down here, forming a nest for the blossom, one might say. It's important to examine all the details, Vic – in some cases, it could mean life or death when determining the difference between a poisonous and non-poisonous flower."

"Well," Vic said, "Dertic must be safe because its name means 'to cure,' no?"

Kaio looked hard at Vic, who felt scrutinized and uncomfortable. *I mustn't let him know my secrets,* he told himself. *He may live among the outcasts, but he could still alert the Six Tines. After all, I'm not old enough yet to attend the Camp, even if I could afford to.*

"Excellent observation," Kaio answered. "It does indeed translate as 'to cure' – a headache, to be precise. Use the roots, which you may keep, mixed in with your daily meal."

Vic accepted the handful of roots.

"Now, sit," and Kaio patted the earth beside him. "How long have you studied cuchels?"

"For a few…months," Vic lied.

"And just how many do you feel comfortable with? Say, if I asked you to cast a cuchel this instant, how many come to mind?"

Vic paused. "About four. But I know more; they're just farther back in my mind."

Again, Kaio gazed hard at Vic. "Where did you learn these cuchels? It's been years, but last I heard, the Training Camp only supported the sons of richer men."

How does he know so much about me? "My—my cousin. In secret."

Kaio stroked his beard. "Vic. Your cousin taught you many things, but I sense magic was not one of them."

How—how?! Vic panicked.

"You can trust me, lad," Kaio continued. "is meant for anyone to use, but society has deemed it accessible only to those with money and power. I merely want to understand how you found a way around the stigma."

I can't continue lying. He somehow knows too much. He swallowed hard. "I—I don't understand how…" He shook his head. "I lied to Via about my cousin. In truth, my cousin gave me a book, a family heirloom that my father wanted me to have. I—I can show it to you."

Kaio waited.

Still hesitating, Vic removed his pack, took out his book, and slid it over to Kaio. His thoughts were on fire: *What if—what if he's upset that I never went to the Training Camp? What if the Six Tines find out? What if—*

Vic watched as Kaio's eyes darted across the pages he flipped open. Then all of a sudden, Kaio shut the book with a thud. "Breakfast is waiting. Come."

Getting to his feet, Vic reached for his tome. But Kaio moved it out of his reach. "I'm sorry, Vic, but I must examine your book before I can return it to you. There are just a few things I need to check."

What's wrong with my book? Vic worried.

A few days later, Kaio called Vic over, who came running. "Come, lad.

Today's lesson involves swordplay."

"But what do swords have to do with cuchels?" Vic asked. As of late, Kaio's lessons had drifted away from what Vic considered the realm of magic. It had started with a lesson on mental bonding with Snook and then hunting together. Vic hadn't thought anything of it until the following morning when Kaio announced they would learn how to trap animals.

"Nothing, really," his mentor responded. "However, if any injuries occur, I shall be glad to help you with the healing cuchel – one of the most dangerous of all."

With the hint of a grin, Vic turned back to the others – heading off to a picnic – and shouted his farewells. Then he and Kaio disappeared into a different part of the woods.

Coming upon a brook, Kaio gestured to the water. "Get yourself a drink, Vic. Our sparring will wear you down, I can guarantee."

I doubt that. Vic squatted and cupping his hands with clear water, gulped it down. All of a sudden, out of the corner of his eye, he saw something come flying at him and land, splashing, in the brook. *Must be my "sword,"* he said, picking up the stick.

"Part of sword fighting is anticipating your opponent's next move," came a voice behind him. Vic spun around, stick at the ready, but found himself knocked to the ground – Kaio having whipped his stick into his knees. From where he lay on the ground, gazing into the bright blue sky, Vic blinked in surprise. "I can see precisely what you need to learn," said Kaio, leaning over him, hand extended. Vic reached for it, but Kaio retracted and pressed his stick against his chest. "And never trust your enemy. Today, Vic, I pose as a threat."

With a groan, his protégé nodded. "Okay, okay. I understand." He held up his arms. "Can I get up and we start over – properly?"

There was a long pause before Kaio smiled, his green eyes sparkling with amusement. "Kai, lad."

Once back on his feet, Vic braced himself for a strike. "So. Learn to anticipate my opponent's next move, you said?"

"Learn to sense it as a fighter but also as a wielder of magic. Close your eyes."

Vic did so, though a bit reluctant, gripping his tree branch tighter. "Now what?"

"Can you sense where I am?" To Vic's surprise, Kaio's voice seemed to be coming from another location. He listened, straining. Then came the sound of Kaio's branch whizzing through the air, and he responded out of instinct, holding out his stick to counterstrike. "That's a start."

Afis growled as a bluebird perched on a branch near him, and with a flutter of wings, the intruder was gone. Leaning back, he sighed: *It's been several days, and I still don't feel any less unsure than when I left the island.*

In the distance, he could hear Via humming as she prepared fish for their lunch. Snook would still be lying beside her, probably drooling over the smell. So long as he could hear her, she would be safe – and she was used to him needing to take a walk to clear his mind. With Kaio mentoring Vic every single day, Via and Afis had spent plenty of time together. He wasn't quite happy about it, as he considered himself more of a loner – and yet at the same time, he'd found himself somewhat enjoying her companionship. Until he needed space. She'd never questioned him.

And now, he sat high up in an oak tree, back against the thick trunk, watching the breeze tickle the flowers on the forest floor. *I don't know why I get these…moods. Perhaps it's something of Glasiea left in me.* He groaned, tossing away a stick he'd been whittling. *The island. I can't get it out of my head! There must be more of life than what the Blood Bearers lived for – and yet I still can't rid myself of the idea that maybe…maybe that's all I'm cut out for.* With an angry snarl, he tore another branch off the tree and began whittling it, cursing under his breath. *When am I going to figure out what more there is to my life?!*

Before he could blink, a chill crept down his arms, sending his

Bloodthirsty hairs on end. Pupils turning to slits, Afis raised his head and sniffed — a familiar scent creeping into his nostrils. There was a flurry of wings, and then two deer came bounding out of the nearby thicket. Afis straightened, straining to see through the trees. Among the green, he caught sight of red: hot flames burning the forest to the ground. *Fire!* And he froze, the tormenting memory flooding his mind.

Bronté

Via gutted the fish she'd caught, smiling at the thought of the delicious lunch they'd eat once Afis returned. When the two of them had first spent time together, she'd been confused, a little hurt even, by Afis' wandering. But now she'd learned his mood swings weren't because of her. *He just needs space to think, to recall what he's forgotten,* she told herself. *And anyway, I'm used to being alone, like on the Plains.*

"Well, not quite alone: I have you, after all," Via said aloud, looking over at Snook. She laughed at the sight of his drooling mouth. "You'll get a bite, too." Snook wagged his tail and opened his mouth to bark – but Via jumped when he howled instead. "What's wrong?" Via asked, but then her senses kicked in: *Something's off – I can feel it the same way I did every day on the Plains.*

As if hearing her thoughts, wildlife came rushing out of the trees – deer, fox, grouse, rabbit – and went splashing through the tiny creek. Via turned to find herself staring at grey smoke and red flames.

Getting to her feet, Via glanced at Snook. He was trembling, eyes wide as he stared at the approaching flames. "Run, Snook!" she shouted, shaking him. "Find Kaio – and Vic!" With another howl, the dog leaped to his feet and raced away.

Via went to follow when the creek caught her eye – as well as the pail carrying the bread and cheese from Marsha. *I must try to douse the flames – I can't stand by and let the forest burn!* she thought, and dumping the pail's contents, she rushed to the creek.

With a grin, Vic braced himself for the swing of his stick that he hoped would give him the upper hand – when a deafening shout echoed in his mind: *VIC!* Dropping to his knees in shock, he cradled his head, rocking back and forth. The intensity behind Snook's voice overpowered him, the string connecting them vibrating with determination.

"Vic?" came Kaio's distant voice, the touch of his distant hand.

It seemed Vic was straddling the line between both worlds. In the physical world, Vic faintly heard Snook's rumbling bark, sensing a scuffle between the giant dog and Kaio – but in the mental world, he was overcome with a string of information, images, emotions. But most important, Snook projected—

"Via!" Vic shouted, at the sight of her lost in the flames. He stumbled to his feet, found Snook licking his hands.

Come, Vic! We must save her – and the forest! It's not safe here! the dog yelped, and Vic knew Snook's intense emotions stemmed from having watched Drema burn.

Vic pointed to the creek, shouting to Kaio: "There's a fire, so we must bring as much water as we can to douse it!"

Kaio placed his hand on Vic's shoulder. "Buckets and pails won't do, lad. It's time for cuchels."

Catching his breath, Vic nodded and then winced as Snook bit his pant leg, tugging.

Come on, Vic! the dog demanded.

"Show us the way, Snook," Vic said, before he and Kaio rushed to keep up.

The three of them could feel the flames before seeing them – but when they did, the sight almost took Vic's breath away in shock. Like dæmons, the flames leapt from the treetops to the sky, surrounded by dark smoke. Various wildlife circled about in confusion, some driven back into the flames. Kaio held out his arm to stop Vic. "Close enough, lad. We're lucky. The flames are driving southeast, away from the outcasts' camp. But stand behind me, Vic, and control Snook, please."

Standing behind Kaio, Vic watched as the Magic Master faced the fire and took a deep breath. *I get to see him perform real dahlas and cuchels – stronger than any of mine!* he said, excited, to Snook.

At his side, Snook whined, ears perked. *I can't smell anything but smoke – how do we know if she's out of the flames?* he asked.

Via's smart, Vic replied, sending reassurance across their bond. *She must have followed you and gone to Kaio's hut.*

Let's hope so. And Snook whined again.

In front of them, Kaio raised his arms toward the sky, and Vic looked up to see a black storm cloud forming. There was a loud rumble before it loosened, releasing a giant sheet of rain. As the raindrops hit the flames, a crackle filled the forest, and the flames shrunk, leaving behind crisp, burnt tree trunks. And then the storm cloud was gone, replaced with a clear sky and two bright suns.

Vic came up behind Kaio, placing a hand on his mentor's shoulder. "That was incredible. You called a storm cloud out of the air!"

Kaio laughed. "That was nothing, lad. You'll realize the true potential of cuchels someday – and a mere rain cloud will be like a simple ant hill." With a sigh, Kaio turned to face him. "But enough about cuchels, Vic. The fire is out, but its impact is not lost on the forest. And we must ensure that Afis and Via are safe. Ask Snook if he saw them leave the flames."

"He didn't. And he couldn't smell anything through the smoke."

With a nod, Kaio moved to step away. "We must find them, then."

"Wait." At the sound of Vic's voice, Kaio turned back. "Why did you choose a storm cloud? Why not, perhaps, a wave of water?" Vic questioned.

"Simple." Kaio looked to the east. "The coast is too far away to draw water from. Creating a massive, controlled wave of water would be too much energy from one Magic Master – a fatal cuchel, even. If I had three more Masters helping, perhaps it would have worked." Kaio looked Vic straight in the eye. "Don't overestimate yourself, Vic. A cuchel out of your league – a strong cuchel when you're weak, even – could be fatal."

Vic swallowed, recalling the weakness he'd felt after searching Via's mind. *But how do I know my limit?*

"Now come, lad. Let's find the others."

Vic stepped around a dead stag, swatting away the flies. "Snook!"

I'm not far ahead of you, Vic.

Any luck finding a scent? he asked.

Ahead came a rumbling bark. *None yet.*

Vic sighed, scanning the trees ahead for any sign of movement. Something tickled the back of his mind – a notion that he couldn't quite scratch away: *How is that, as large as the flames were, the impacted area of the forest is so…small? Almost as if the flames were contained – but how? I'll have to discuss it with Kaio.* Behind him stood the erect skeletons of trees. Ahead stretched the green untouched forest. *Afis and Via must be somewhere in there. Kaio would have alerted us by now if they'd returned to the hut.*

A scratching sound caught his attention, and he turned to see Afis emerging from the thicket. *Snook! It's Afis!* he called out, and the dog's distant rumble answered him. "Afis! Thank the spirits – we've been looking for hours—" Raising his head, Afis stepped into the light, and Vic caught sight of a limp form in his arms. *Via!*

Back at the hut, Via lay unmoving, hooked in Kaio's arm as he examined her. Kaio laid his ear to her throat, and his lips moved, forming cuchels beyond Vic's knowledge.

Somehow, Afis emerged unharmed from the fire, yet Via is still unconscious. Vic glanced down at her calves, where Kaio had already applied a salve to soothe her burns. *But I'm sure Kaio will be able to wake her through his healing.*

Snook reached across their bond: *My sixth sense worries me, for I feel, somehow, as if Via is not only burned. It's as if…something unknown is at fault here.*

More than just the fire? Vic prodded.

I—I don't know, Snook admitted. *Perhaps I am still too…tormented by fire.*

Vic leaned forward, about to speak, when he felt Afis' hand on his shoulder. He glanced back to see him shaking his head, a firm expression on his face. Vic swallowed and nodded.

Several minutes later, Kaio raised his head and murmured, "Tjord dahlas."

Kaio told me his magic would help him assess the cause of Via's unconsciousness, like a healer's version of the mind search cuchel. Vic chewed his lips, anxious for Kaio to speak again. *Using the undo cuchel must mean he found an answer.*

After a long pause, Kaio murmured, "I have cared for many sick and dying people all my life: outcasts, the rich merchants, even Levar's governor once. Yet I've never seen a case like Via's. It's as if…as if there's magic hiding under her unconsciousness. We must pray to the spirits that she'll make it."

Vic cut in without hesitation: "You must save her, Kaio. You're a healer – and a Magic Master too! Please!"

Kaio sighed. "I will try, Vic, but even the herbs I know of – the best healing herbs – those, I fear, may not save her. The magic I sense underneath unnerves me. I don't think…" He stuttered, as if the words were hard to produce. "I don't know if I can save her," he finished, his voice quiet.

No! "There must be something we can do," pleaded Vic. "Think,

135

Kaio. We cannot let her die."

His mentor sighed, brushed Via's hair off her face. "The best we can do – and we *will* do – is keep her in my room. There, I can tend to her and keep an eye on her. I cannot have the two of you interfering – her healing will require most of my concentration, and I must not be distracted. Is that quite clear?" Beside him, Vic nodded; farther behind, Afis also nodded, less enthusiastic. "Good." Then Kaio sighed. "But if she—if she—"

Vic placed a hand on Kaio's arm. "She won't. I know you won't let her, Kaio."

The following day, Kaio interrupted Vic and Afis whittling arrows in the main room. "Lads, every fortnight I'm due to visit an outcast with the crimson cough – so I must leave Via for the day."

"How is she doing, Kaio?" Vic asked.

He paused on his way out. "Her coma still persists. But I do what I can, Vic, and pray the herbs will heal her." He turned to Afis. "Don't forget about the venison you hung up in the back hut, Afis."

Afis jumped to his feet. "I almost did!" Following behind Kaio, he ducked around the hut to the smaller one behind – a simple one-roomed hut used to store provisions and dry healing herbs. Standing in the doorway, he allowed the various scents to fill his nostrils before heading to the venison in the back – from a deer he'd caught just the past day. Reaching for the meat, absorbed in thinking about the herbs Kaio had shown him to use for flavoring it, Afis flinched at the sight of his arm, glowing a faint red in the dark shadows of the hut. *Just another reminder of who I really am,* he murmured to himself.

But then Afis' heart leapt to his throat at the sound of a growl. He spun on his heel to see two eyes shining in the dark: *Snook.* His instincts kicked in, and Afis crouched, hissing, but Snook snarled back. *I mustn't let him warn the others,* Afis decided. *My past is my secret, and I won't have a stupid dog spoiling it.*

Pupils forming into slits, Afis felt a powerful force overcome him – a force that filled him with a fury, driving his arm hairs on end. He bared his teeth, quite aware of their sharpness, and pounced. With a ferocious bark, Snook chomped down on his arm. His grip filled Afis with a rage he'd never experienced before. His vision flashed red, and he pictured himself drinking the dog's blood. He yowled and clawed at Snook's side, causing him to back up, whining.

Then the dog growled and bolted out the doorway. *Coward!* Afis shouted and followed. Emerging into the sunlight, Afis found Snook in a defensive stance. He approached, snarling, while Snook backed up, matching Afis' pace.

And just as Afis prepared to lunge again, a heavy object collided with the back of his skull. "You seem to have forgotten our bond, Afis – and Snook's told me everything," came Vic's voice, as the darkness overcame Afis' vision.

So. I really am the Bloodthirsty One.

Like being called out of a dream, Via drifted awake. Blinking, she coughed, her throat sore. *Where—where am I? Why is it so dark?* She tried to sit up, but the fierce pain burning through her legs overwhelmed her. With a cry, she paused, took in the sensation.

"Slowly, slowly. You wouldn't want to split open the wound after I just healed it."

Via turned, startled at the sound of a stranger's voice, and peered into the darkness. She caught sight of him, in the corner. He was a young man, with tousled blond hair. His back was to her, and his bent-over pose suggested he was preoccupied with something. After a moment, he stood and approached her. Over his right hand hovered a strange globe of light and in its glow, Via caught sight of the blue half-moon amulet he wore around his neck. As he sat beside her, her words formed: "Who are you?"

With a chuckle, he bowed. "I apologize for my manners. My name is Bronté. I have come to help you, Via."

"How—how do you know my name?"

With a small sigh, Bronté turned and set the hovering light above a stick – above which it hovered as well, wavering. Facing Via again, Bronté murmured, "Elfin healing light. Just one of the many resources of my kind."

Via caught her breath. "Your—your kind?"

He titled his head. Behind the wisps of blond hair, she caught a glimpse of pointed ears before a strange haze covered them. "You're an elf!" she whispered then winced at the pain rushing up her legs. Before she could breathe again, Bronté reacted by placing his hands on her calves. He applied an ointment, which filled her entire being with a strange sense of peace, something deeper than just healing her pain, almost as if calming her soul. When she relaxed, he stopped and resumed his seat beside her. She smiled. "Thank you."

She lowered her head, considering her next words. *Kaio always said that elves are tasked with guarding the secrets of Lilligrav. If Bronté says he's come to help me, then it must be for something important.* "You say that you've come to help me?"

His eyes were serious when he said, "Look," and pointed to the far wall.

Via tilted her head, eyes glued on Bronté, when a flickering light caught the corner of her eye, and she turned, gasping at the sight.

Vic appeared, a sword raised above his head, and charged. His sword clashed with another, dipped in blood. Over and over, the blades struck, the sound ringing through the silent darkness.

Why does it show Vic if I need help? she wondered.

She was startled to hear a voice echo in her mind: *You will have to help him.* Via glanced at Bronté, but he had his eyes on the scene. So, she turned to watch it again.

Vic knelt on the ground now, beaten. A gash in his arm bled as another wound, hidden under his mail and tunic, gushed out blood down his legs. All of a sudden, a stranger appeared above him – a stranger whose long, brown hair with black highlights billowed in the wind. The stranger raised his hands above his head, lightning sparking at his knuckles, as he shouted, "Vic, taste the shriek of death! Die worthy enough for your weeping dragon!" He lifted his hand, casting a shadow over his eyes. The air crackling around him, he cried, "Shą vejvő hové!" A scream filled the air. Then the vision faded away.

Via turned away, sick at heart, overwhelmed by the weight she now carried. *Why me, spirits?* she prayed. *Why must I hold onto this secret: knowing Vic's fate but unable to share it with anyone?*

Beside her, Bronté sighed. "It may seem like a curse, but becoming a visionary is also a gift. You were to be prepared for the danger the future brings. Remember: you must know all to see all." He paused. "Your instincts will know which visions you can share with others, but many – such as this one – are only for you."

She squeezed her eyes shut, shook her head. "Isn't there any way to stop the vision from happening?"

He touched her face, tucked the hair behind her ear. "Alas, no. The spirits have chosen."

A white light flashed, and she looked up to see Bronté had vanished. Struggling, wincing, Via stood and approached the wall. She pressed her forehead and hands against it and shut her eyes, trying to force the vision away. *Please, spirits, please.*

Afis struggled against his bonds as Snook growled, watching. "You're going to tell me every single thing – the truth – about you, Afis," Vic said, pointing a dagger at him. "And if I think there's a shred of falsehood, I'll tell Snook to lunge."

Tied to a tree, Afis pressed his head against the bark, looking high into the canopy. After a long pause, he looked at Vic and nodded.

Watch him carefully, Vic instructed.

Snook growled again. *Aye, Vic.*

Approaching Afis, Vic cut the gag, which Afis spat out with a snarl. "Speak," Vic repeated, knife to Afis' chest.

With a glare, Afis frowned before rolling his eyes. "Fine. You want to know everything? I'll tell you everything. I'm going to die anyway."

In response, Snook growled, shoulders rolling in anticipation.

"I don't have amnesia, but I do come from Glasiea," Afis admitted. "I created a backstory so as to explain why I do and do not know certain things."

"Then tell me the truth of your origins."

"I'm not like you," Afis said, the words forced. "I'm not human, as Snook has discovered. I was created – I am the product of your world's magic."

"Who created you?"

"The Blood Bearers."

Of course! After the Blood Bearer dwarfs disappeared off the coast, they must have set up camp on Glasiea. And yet— Vic touched the tip of his dagger to Afis' throat. "You're lying. There's no way a bunch of dwarfs could have created you."

"Dwarfs?!" Afis laughed. "The blackbeard dwarfs tag along out of sheer boredom. The real Blood Bearers are humans like you – though the dwarfs do seem to outnumber them."

But all the stories – only dwarfs are mentioned, Vic said, confused.

Snook whined. *Perhaps there is more to the Blood Bearers than the stories say.*

"How—how many are there?" Vic asked.

Afis shrugged. "Dwarfs – perhaps a hundred. Only about fifty men. They created me – Afis the Bloodthirsty One – to help raid Lilligrav. Or at least, that was *their* intent."

Vic studied him. "It that your intent?"

Turning, Afis spat on the ground. "I don't know what I want, Vic. Unlike you, I have no past to compare to. Instead, I have what I've been trained and what I've discovered for myself." He lowered his gaze. "But I do know that I never meant to hurt Via."

"Explain," said Vic, teeth gritted.

"When we were on that picnic, I—" Here Afis paused, hung his head. "I left Via. I needed to clear my head. But when I saw the flames, I froze. It reminded me too much of Drema."

At the name, Snook perked, snarled. *He knows about Drema.*

You told me the Blood Bearers were involved, Vic said. *He must have been part of the attack.* "What about Drema?" Vic demanded.

"The Blood Bearers set fire to it. But I wasn't there," Afis added in haste when Vic drew his dagger closer. "I abandoned the ship during the raid and swam ashore – to the Avro Woods. But I saw the aftermath, Vic, and I couldn't stomach it. When I saw the fire burning down the trees, I froze." His face twisted, and Vic thought he saw tears in the corner of his eyes. "I should have come back and rushed Via out of harm's way, but by the time I snapped out it, there was too much smoke to see."

"So how did you find her? You're the one who brought her to Snook and I."

Afis sighed. "I found her in the creek after forcing my way through the flames. She was trying to douse the flames, Vic – Marsha's pail was in her hands. But the smoke must have overwhelmed her." He held Vic's gaze. "But I swear to you, Vic: she was already passed out when I found her. I swear to you."

Straightening, Vic considered. *Do you believe him?*

He's been lying to us, Vic – this entire time, he lied when we trusted him.

You spent several nights with him – did you ever see his skin glowing then?

Never. Snook growled. *He covered himself with a blanket every night.*

Vic squatted in front of Afis. "There is one way to prove to myself if your story is true." For a split second, Vic caught fear crossing Afis' eyes.

"What do you mean?"

"I'm going to search your mind. Stref hombä." And in a blink, Vic found himself inside Afis' mind. Below, he sensed Afis squirming, fighting the unfamiliar touch inside him, but Vic pushed through. He found Afis' mental being wide open without a barrier in sight, and approaching the orb at the core, Vic brushed it with his fingers. A scene unfolded in front of him: *Burning. Death. Heartbreak. And then the unknown: the dark, intense shadow of the Avro Woods. Below, the burning corpse of Drema.* Rippling underneath the memory were the regret and conflicting loyalties Afis had experienced – and upon sensing them, Vic felt relief. *He isn't lying, Snook,* he called out. Pressing further, Vic stumbled upon the memory of the Avro Woods fire. He saw Afis freezing at the sight, and then he saw him scooping up Via's limp body out of the brook.

Vic dropped his touch and stood, causing a tremor through Afis' body. Unlike last time, Vic didn't faint – but he did drop to his knees, as Snook licked his face. *Vic?*

I just—too much— "You speak the truth," Vic said once the lightheadedness had passed. He sensed Snook relaxing beside him.

Of course I speak the truth, Afis scoffed to himself. "Snook stumbled upon the one deceit I have. Why hide any longer?" Afis shrugged. "You're going to kill me anyway." *That's what the Blood Bearers would do.*

Vic seemed to ignore that last bit: "If you didn't lie about Drema, and if you saved Via's life, there's one thing left to know: why attack Snook?"

"When I first saw Snook, I was afraid of him," Afis said, cursing. "I'd never had someone chase *me,* and I panicked. But today, seeing Snook..." He trailed off, looked up at the sky.

Meanwhile, his mind was buzzing: *What* was *that rage that took over me? Were the Blood Bearers right all along?* His heart sunk with dread as he pictured Rudolf's gloating face. *Do I have a—a Bloodthirsty side?*

Swallowing back his uncertainty, Afis closed his eyes to avoid Vic's watchful gaze. "Today, something else came over me. I'd never felt like the Bloodthirsty One until that moment – and looking back, it frightens me." He cursed again. "Maybe I am what the Blood Bearers conceived."

He waited for Vic's response but was startled to feel his bonds loosen, Vic having cut them. He looked down at his now-freed hands and then up at Vic, who studied him, head cocked.

"A monster wouldn't save a girl he's known for less than a full moon cycle."

Afis let Vic's words sink in before nodding. "Perhaps you're…" He got to his feet. "So now what? You're going to tell Kaio?"

Vic shook his head. "Your secret is safe with Snook and me." Both jumped when Snook howled and turned, running back to the hut. Vic's eyes widened, incredulous, as he looked back at Afis. "It's Via."

Huddled in her blanket, Via sat by the wall, one shoulder pressed into it, head lowered in sleep. The touch of Snook's tongue on her cheek opened her eyes, and she forced a smile at the sight of Afis and Vic's agape mouths.

"Would one of you mind getting me some water?" she coughed out, and scrambling, Afis disappeared to do as she asked.

Vic stooped down, offering a hand in assistance. Before grasping it, Via locked eyes with him – and a burst of ice chilled her veins, her heart dropping into her stomach. Her first vision echoed in her ears, and Via swallowed back the panic, the urge to tell Vic about the awful things she'd seen. But, unable to speak, it was as if her tongue had become frozen in her mouth.

Dread filled her upon realizing Vic hadn't even noticed her inner turmoil. Outwardly, she knew, nothing had changed – but within, she felt incredibly alone.

This gift truly is a curse.

The Book

Two days later, Vic awoke to bird song, and he felt Snook shift, restless, beside him. *You told Kaio we'd be on our way after a full moon cycle,* the dog reminded him. *Today is the day, Vic, for a fresh moon rises tonight.*

Rubbing his face with a hand, Vic sighed. *I know. But Kaio still has my book, and I'm not leaving without it.*

"Good morning," Afis called from the other side of the room. "Come have breakfast."

Vic shuffled over to join him. "Where's Via?"

Afis jabbed his thumb toward the bedroom. "With Kaio."

Vic leapt to his feet, stuffing a biscuit into his mouth. "Thanks for the reminder. I'm to run an errand for him today." And then, with Snook at his heels, he dashed outside.

And why didn't you complete your task yesterday? Snook questioned.

I was so exhausted after helping Kaio attend to all of those outcasts yesterday. But he gave me specific instructions to find a certain herb for him — he won't tell me what for. Race you?

Snook rumbled. *You'll lose!*

Indeed, Snook beat Vic, twice — both to the patch of flowers and

145

back to the hut. At the door flap, Snook circled and stretched out in the sunslight.

Don't you want to come inside? Vic asked

Not yet, Snook projected, panting. *Both suns feel too good to rush inside quite yet.*

Back inside, Vic chuckled at the sight of Afis still consuming biscuits. "You've got the appetite of a bloody lion, you know."

Afis glanced over at him. "I'm not sure what that is but thank you."

Laughing, Vic stopped when he came upon the rug separating Kaio's room from the main room. *Why does he have it closed?* he wondered and moved to push it aside when he heard voices.

"But Via, it was so soon."

He sounds frustrated, Vic noted.

"But I healed all the same. Is that not most important, Kaio?"

She sounds angry, Vic also noted.

"Something must have happened, Via. Why won't you tell me?" There was a pause, and Vic caught his breath. "Via, you're like a daughter to me – you know that. I would never ever harm you. You can tell me."

Again, she paused – but then her words were quiet: "Kaio. Nothing happened. I woke up, that's all. Your magic must have worked."

"No. My herbs and magic were not as strong as the m—" Kaio sighed. "When I first held you after the fire, I sensed a strong magic under your...sickness. Yet you heal a mere day later and expect me to believe nothing happened?"

Vic held his breath. *Perhaps I shouldn't be here. And yet...*

When Via spoke, her tone was strong and firm. "Yes."

"Then I must believe you," Kaio conceded, with a sigh.

As Vic let out his breath, Via brushed past him through the door flap, catching him off guard. A look of surprise crossed her face as she said, "Good morning, Vic. Excuse me. Do you suppose there's any breakfast left?"

Feeling awkward, Vic laughed. "Afis was chowing down on the biscuits a moment ago. Pray to the spirits he left one for you." She darted past him, calling Afis' name.

Exhaling, he moved into Kaio's room. Kaio sat wrapped in an albino goat fur. As if in exasperation, his head was in his hands, elbow propped on his knee. At the sound of his pupil's entrance, he raised his head. "Vic," his mentor said with a sigh. He threw his head back, laid it against the wall, and the hut creaked. His mouth moved, but Vic didn't catch the words.

Clearing his throat, Vic rubbed the back of his neck, raising the plant in his fist. "I found the, uh, plant, Kaio."

Kaio didn't move his head. "You did?" he asked in a flat tone, his eyes trained on the ceiling.

"Here." Vic laid the plant on a pair of books.

Kaio closed his eyes and groaned.

Vic stepped backwards but stopped when he felt the rug against his back. He held his breath, glancing to his right. *My book.* Kaio had it set upon a pedestal, in the middle of the room. To Vic, the book seemed to glow. *I've missed it* – he said, straining. *Just a look.* He slid to the side, eyes on Kaio. In that moment, his mentor looked his age, hunched over. *He's sleeping. If I'm quiet…* His fingers graced the cover, reaching to flip the tome open.

"No!" Kaio's voice boomed. Vic flinched back, startled. *He's never been…angry at me.* Vic spun around. Kaio towered before him, the fur curled around his feet. Twitching, a hand formed a fist, relaxed, then made a fist again. "Vic."

With a gulp, Vic said, "Just a look, Kaio? It is mine, after all."

His eyes on him, Kaio sighed. "No. I must keep that away from you for now."

"Why?!"

"Don't yell, Vic. Peace. If you open that book now, you… Your very life will be threatened. I'm protecting you, lad."

"Kaio," Vic demanded, confused. "Make sense, for once. How is that book threatening me?"

"It's not the book. It's the very one wanting you…and Snook."

"Who?" *He's insane!*

"Him." Kaio groaned, shutting his eyes for a brief moment. "Stop, Vic! This is for your own good, I promise you."

Vic thrust himself past Kaio, but at the rug, he turned back, fuming. "You can't keep it from me forever."

"That I won't. I only—" There was a strange pinging sound from a far corner of the room, but when Kaio raised his hand, the sound stopped within a moment. "I only need keep it awhile longer to see what I must protect you from. The Cursed One is too dangerous."

The Dark One?! "Kaio, don't be ridiculous. What would the Dark One want with a simple book?"

His mentor sighed, reached out toward Vic. "More than you could possibly know, lad."

Gritting his teeth, Vic stormed out, almost bumping into Afis and Via. Afis smiled in an awkward way; Via shook her head: "Don't stress him, Vic."

"Leave me be." And he pushed past them, joining Snook outside. *Who in all of Lilligrav is he talking about?!*

Snook leapt to his paws. *Did you tell him we're leaving?*

Vic shook his head, hugging himself and glancing back. *Not until I get my book back.*

Vic stumbled through the evergreen trees, feeling the needles scrape his bare arms. Laughing, he glanced over his shoulder, searching for Snook. *You'll never catch me!*

Watch me!

Vic laughed harder and forced aside the branches ahead. He was just about to pass a large oak tree – *Almost to the border of the forest* – when he almost rammed into the trunk as Snook forced himself into Vic's mind: *Did Kaio say anything about danger?*

Ouch! Tree bark hurts when you bump into it. Don't burst into my mind like that without warning! Vic reprimanded.

Did he or did he not? Snook pressed.

Vic rolled his eyes, feeling the morning's frustration return. *I really don't care, Snook.*

With that, Snook's golden form leaped from the trees and knocked Vic over. Both human and dog rolled about the Avro Woods floor. Once Vic stopped rolling from the impact, he groaned, struggling to his feet. He swayed, demanding: *What in all of Lilligrav was that for?!*

Snook didn't answer. Vic caught sight of him lying on the ground, facing a tree and licking his paws.

You deserve it, he snapped. Clutching his chest, Vic turned for Kaio's hut, groaning from the pain. But something pulled him back. He glanced over his shoulder to see Snook tugging on his outer tunic, the dog's upper lip curled back. "What are you doing?" Vic demanded, too frustrated to project his thoughts.

No, Vic. Stay here, Snook insisted.

His frustration stretching thin, Vic raised a hand to slap Snook away when the sound of pounding hoofs distracted him. They grew louder, and he dropped to his hands and knees. "You were right," he muttered.

Of course I am.

With stealth, Vic slunk to the closest tree – ignoring Snook's warning growl – and, cautious, peeked around the trunk, hidden by needles. *Snook!* he called. *Come see!*

Snook crawled over, sniffing. *Big danger.*

You're right: but look at them! Three muscular men rode their horses at a steady trot through the clearing. Two of them – the riders at the back – sang a rowdy song, their voices slurring in a way that reminded Vic of the tavern. The rider at the front didn't say a word, focused on what lay ahead

149

and guiding his horse. *He's the leader, Snook.*

Of course he is.

Vic caught the glare on the trio's leader face as a hut came into view. *Kaio's hut!* he realized.

Snook growled. *I tried to tell you. What do we do?*

Vic paused then shrugged. *What can we do? They're all armed. All I have is my magic – but my limited knowledge of spells wouldn't be too impressive. Besides, even if I knocked them off their saddles, we'd be outnumbered in a confrontation. They're between us and the hut, meaning we can't warn the others.*

He and Snook crept closer, keeping to the shadows. *If it gets out of hand, we'll jump in,* Snook decided, and Vic sent agreement across their bond.

The riders halted their horses. Dismounting, they dropped the ropes at the foot of an oak tree and approached the hut. Raising a sinewy arm, the leader knocked on the slab of wood beside the door flap. Vic bit his lip and projected: *If they break in, we scare the horses and confront them.* Snook's shoulders rolled with anticipation.

There was a scuffle of muffled footsteps and then Kaio pushed aside the flap. He stepped out into the light, squinting at the men. After a brief pause, Kaio's mouth moved. One word. *I can't hear them,* Vic admitted.

Neither can I – they're speaking under their breaths. We must watch for the signs.

The strangers must have spoken, but Vic couldn't be sure as he could only see their backs. But Kaio continued speaking. All of a sudden, one of the larger men dropped his hand to his sword hilt. Kaio didn't seem to notice, continuing to block the entrance. The leader's shoulders moved as he grunted – just audible enough for Vic's ears to catch the sound. Then he tried to force his way past, but Kaio refused, strong as a boulder.

Vic gritted his teeth, clenching his hands into fists. *What do you think they want?*

Something that Kaio doesn't want them to do, Snook said.

The leader backed up. Without flinching, he stared Kaio down. Vic could feel the heat of his stare even from where he stood. The same man drew his sword and raised it above his head. *Now!* Vic shouted.

Snook rippled. *With pleasure!*

Just as they were about to leap from the trees to Kaio's defense, the leader reached out and grabbed his accomplice's arm, stopping him. He made no sound but jerked his head to the right. Kaio's eyes glittered, and a small smile spread across his face. The man with the sword swore and slipped the blade across Kaio's leg, just under the knee. Kaio grimaced in pain. *They're slicing the bone! They'll kill him!*

No, Vic. Something is off — but in our favor, Snook said. *My sixth sense tells me that Kaio will be all right. But stay on guard, just in case.*

Then the man jerked his hand back, yanking the sword out of Kaio's leg, and knocked the hilt against his head. With a groan on his lips, Kaio crumpled against the hut. Blood darkened his pants. The leader's shoulders tightened, and he spun on his heel and marched back to the horses. After a pause, the other two followed, glancing at the door flap partially covering Kaio.

Vic whipped around, pressing his sweating back into the trunk of the tree. Snook slunk back into the shadows, sniffing. As the riders walked their horses past the trees, Vic caught their conversation: "Why didn't you let me kill him, Tierm?"

"Because, Shaak," the one called Tierm snarled in reply, "he's a Magic Master. Didn't you see the gleam in his eyes? Even if we had killed him with one blow, who knows what cuchel he could have muttered on his dying breath. We *all* could have died. Or his Yror would haunt us. It was too dangerous a risk."

A third voice spoke up: "But why didn't we go in — Shaak knocked him out, after all."

Tierm chuckled. "Didn't you hear him say that he'd hidden it where no one could find it? But don't you fret: we'll get what we want. You can bet your life on that."

Vic cringed. Chewing his lip, he peered around the tree trunk.

"But you're a Magic Master, too, Tierm," Shaak said.

"Will you be quiet about that?!" Tierm demanded, casting a venomous glance through the forest. "Having a magic battle? In these parts? We'd gain the attention of the entire outcast population, maybe even Levar. Besides, someone stronger is aiding that fool. I'm not risking my identity becoming known so soon. Trust me, Shaak, when I say that I shall get what I want — what we all want."

As Tierm turned away, Shaak fiddled with the reins, his eyes downcast. The third man reached out, patting Shaak's arm. Glancing over, Shaak caught the expression on his companion's face and grinned. Both men broke into their rowdy song once more; Tierm growled and covered one ear.

Snook only relaxed once the horses faded from sight, the song growing more and more distant. *Keep close to Kaio, Vic. Danger is following us...for some reason.*

Vic ignored him. *Where in all of Lilligrav are Via and Afis?*

I...don't...know.

Are they gone? Out of earshot?

Snook sniffed the air. *Yes.*

Stay with Kaio, Snook. Vic scrambled out of the trees. "Via! Afis!" He circled the hut and stopped at the back. Cupping his hands around his mouth, he yelled louder: "Via! Afis!"

She came stepping out of the trees. "Yes, Vic? We were visiting Azeri and Zukav."

"Kaio needs help."

Afis followed behind Via. "Kaio? What happened?"

"I'll tell you later, but right now—"

Vic! Snook interrupted.

"Were the horses glad to see you?" All three turned at the sound of Kaio's voice, as he appeared around the corner of the hut. Snook bounded after him, eyes wide, ears alert.

Vic glared at Snook. *What happened?!*

I went up to him, Snook explained, *but he opened his eyes and walked away. I tried to stop him, but he just kept walking. How, Vic?*

A healing spell — I assume — but it must have been quite strong for a wound that painful. Vic felt Via's eyes on him, and he ducked his head. "They were thrilled," he heard her say to Kaio, though her eyes burned through Vic's back. "If you don't mind, we'd like to go back."

"Of course. Dinner will be at dusk — a fine goose that Snook wrangled the other night."

Vic glanced up at the sound of them retreating into the woods, lost to the shadows. Squatting to Snook's level, he found himself unable to look Kaio in the eye. "All's well, lad," his mentor said. "Don't fret." But when Kaio walked away, Vic noticed the slight limp in his left leg.

That evening, while Via was saying goodnight to her horses, Vic waited until Afis started to doze off before tiptoeing toward Kaio's room. They'd all eaten supper together outside in the warm air, but Kaio had retired to his room as soon as he'd finished his meal.

He almost jumped out of his skin when he felt Snook's nose press against the back of his leg. *What are you doing?* the dog asked.

I'm still not convinced that Kaio is as healed as he seems. I want to know why he left supper while we were still eating. He peered around the rug, careful to avoid being seen, but Kaio was out of sight. Then Vic's heart dropped: *My book is gone!*

Gone?

It was on the pedestal this morning, but now it stands empty!

Snook sniffed the air. *I don't smell your book, but I do smell Kaio.*

In the same moment, Vic heard the strange pinging sound — the same that he'd heard earlier in the morning. He pulled the rug back another inch then quickly dropped it. *He's at the mirror! I can't risk him seeing me in the reflection.*

He paused, looking down at Snook. *Your better hearing is beneficial: I can listen through our bond.*

Snook trotted past Vic and sat down in front of the rug. His ear twitched then their string vibrated with words:

"I will live, purra to your healing cuchel," Kaio was saying, his voice no more than a whisper. *"The Cursed One sent the first of his warnings today, having somehow corrupted them into seeking out the young Xaniera's book. But I looked through it, cover to cover. It's harmless."* He paused. *"I fear they will not be the last. Have you seen any others, Fierelä'va?"*

Another voice responded, but Vic couldn't understand the words. They seemed almost…elfin, Vic realized with an audible gasp before covering his mouth in a hurry.

To Vic's relief, Kaio didn't seem to hear for he spoke again: "I've been able to protect it and our location through cloaking cuchels, but somehow the Cursed One still knew. I haven't given it back to the young Xaniera for fear of him being tracked."

More elfin.

"He's not ready. I need more time to mentor him."

The elfin reply was firm.

"The spirits have spoken." Kaio sighed. *"I understand, Fierelä'va."*

Snook broke the connection to flick an ear backward. *Via's back from visiting her horses.*

Before she entered the main room, Vic and Snook were already back in their bedtime spots, pretending to be asleep while Via tucked herself into her own spot. But despite his eyes being closed, Vic stared at Snook through their mental bond. *Who was Kaio talking to?!*

The Real Quest

The following day, after finishing his lesson with Kaio, Vic decided to spend the short bit of time before supper wrestling over a stick with Snook. *We both already know you'll lose!* the dog boasted, unrelenting in his grip.

But then a quiet voice called his name, and he looked up to see Via watching them. Her eyes seemed almost glazed over, which sent a chill down Vic's spine. "Could I talk to you for a minute?" she asked, rubbing her arm with her right hand.

He pushed at the stick, surrendering it to Snook. The dog rumbled in the back of his throat and began gnawing away. Coming over to her, Vic wiped his hand across his brow. "You look like you've seen a Yror," he said, trying to joke, but no humor flashed across her face. "You haven't seen a Yror, have you?" he asked, his tone serious now.

She took a deep breath. "Last night, I had a terrifying dream. Of you; of us. I think—I think it was a vision."

His eyes widened as he staggered backwards. "That's impossible." He caught the offended look that crossed her face. *I've upset her. But all I did was speak the truth: it's quite impossible.* So, he laughed, shrugged. "I'm sorry. But to have visions, you must be granted one by the elves. No other race can pass on that gift to us."

Her face paled, and she stared at him, wide-eyed.

"What?"

She shook her head. "Nothing. I'm sorry." Lowering her gaze, she paused. "I do remember Kaio telling me that as a little girl. But still, I can't shake the feeling that my dream was too vivid to be like any other."

Maybe she was granted a vision another way? Snook suggested.

Impossible, Vic repeated. *Like I said, the elves must grant the spirits' gift to humans. Kaio gave me an entire lesson on visions the other day.*

Still. Listen to what she has to tell you. My sixth sense is tingling.

"Go on," Vic urged.

"At first, I saw a tall, steep mountain. We – you and I – were trying to climb it. But what I noticed was the face of the mountain: covered in blood, skeletons, and jagged rocks. You and I laughed – yet it sounded hollow. And then, I lost my grip on a rock, and I began to fall. You reached for me, and I held on for a while but then—then I fell." She squeezed her eyes shut. "It was too late, and I woke up in a sweat." She trembled, Vic noted, as if reliving the experience.

Vic knelt, traced his finger in the dirt. "Kaio taught me about visions several days ago – after your coma. How visionaries are even more important than Magic Masters since the former have a direct connection to the spirits. But that, because their blessed gift is so powerful, it is difficult on the body and mind." He paused. "At least for humans. Elves have magic in their blood, so visions are easier for them to endure."

She gulped, a tremor running through her body. "But what does it mean, Vic?"

He stood, placing a hand on her shoulder. "I don't know. Kaio explained the meaning behind some visions, but your dream is beyond my training." He whistled for Snook. "So. Let's ask Kaio."

After Via finished describing her dream, Kaio leaned back, stroking his beard.

Via and Vic stood across from him, with the latter forcing himself to keep his eyes on Kaio. When they'd first entered the bedroom, Vic had noticed the pedestal and his book were both gone – and it took all his might not to search the room. *Last night, the pedestal stood empty,* he remembered, *but now it's gone entirely.*

Vic watched as Kaio pondered Via's words, catching a skeptical look in his mentor's eyes. *He agrees with me – it can't be a vision,* he thought. But Kaio's next words shocked him: "You are correct, Via. You have been granted a vision, and it's just the sign I've been waiting for."

Vic straightened. *Sign?* he repeated.

Kaio leaned closer, his voice lowered. "Listen to me: Via's vision signals that it is time for your journey to begin. Take Afis with you; he has nowhere else to go. As your friend, he will aid you."

"We have a quest?" Vic asked, confused. *My quest was to rescue Snook. Now I have another?* His mind went back to the conversation he and Snook had overheard: *Is this quest what they were discussing?*

"Indeed," his mentor confirmed. "I'd hoped to have more time to prepare you, but the spirits often have other plans."

"Prepare us?" Via repeated. "Won't you be coming with us, Kaio?"

Kaio paused then shook his head. "Alas, I cannot: the outcasts need me here."

Her face fell, so Vic bit his tongue: *She's too heartbroken for me to ask further.*

"But you'll have each other, along with all the lessons I've taught you." Kaio stood, motioning to the bed. "Sit. You'll need provisions for the journey." While they made themselves comfortable among the furs, he disappeared among his belongings; when he returned to them, his arms were full. "First, something similar for the you both." And he laid two scabbards at their feet.

Catching his breath, Vic pulled out his sword, and the silver flashed in the candlelight. His blade had a black hilt with a fierce dragon wrapped around. He flashed a proud smile. "I'll put your swordplay training to good use, Kaio. Purra."

Via unsheathed hers, less enthused. Hers was a deep violet, with a silver vine and budding flowers inscribed into the blade. The hilt was black as well but encrusted with lavender quartz. "Purra, Kaio," she murmured.

"Who did these belong to, Kaio?" Vic asked. "Surely not from an outcast who repaid you for healing powers?"

His mentor paused, bent over as he scrummaged through the pile. "They belonged to King Ecrovï – ruler of the dwarf clan Fũegarr."

Vic's jaw dropped. "But the dwarfs disappeared centuries ago!"

"Kai," his mentor agreed, nodding in a distracted way. "But these swords didn't, and now, knowing their history, treat them well." Kaio presented them with a steel club. "Give this to Afis. Tell him it belonged to a dwarf of the clan Bläncha – a dwarf who overcame a dark past. Perhaps some history will help Afis discover something about himself."

Via glanced quizzically at Vic, who shrugged.

She turned at the sound of her name, to find Kaio reaching for her. She grasped his hand, feeling her heart welling up inside her. "My dear child," Kaio continued, voice breaking. "I've loved you since I first saw you. You are the daughter I never had, the family I've never known. It breaks my heart knowing that you must go, but the spirits have called you. As their servant, I cannot choose to be selfish by disobeying them. But to remember me, take a small keepsake, one I created for you many, many years ago. How I wish our paths had crossed at Levar, my love: I would have brought you home."

With tears streaming down her face, Via cradled his gift in her palms. It was a cube of glass, with the form of a rearing horse suspended inside. The prism dangled from a leather cord, which Via realized she could tie around her neck. "What is it?" she asked, once her words could overpower the tears.

"It is called an imalre – 'image' in the elfin tongue. It's a legendary process known kept secret by the elves. Do not ask me, please," he added, holding up an open palm, "how I received the skill. The knowledge will come later. For now, know that it was created with magic – magic used to form an image inside the prism. But one last thing for you, lass."

Via took a glass flask from his hands. It was filled with a sweet-smelling powder, ground up into flecks. "What is it?" she asked again.

Kaio beamed. "*That* took me many years to find. Inside are the leaves of the Pllatæ Ralas tuk. Adding water to the powder and sprinkling it over the ground creates an inexorable ring of fire. Please save it for when you're in dire need."

She forced a smile. "Purra, Kaio. It's unfair that the spirits wish us to be torn apart after being reunited at long last!" She fell into his embrace, the sobs racking her body, and Kaio tightened his arms around her.

"It's quite unfortunate, but the spirits must be obeyed," Kaio whispered, stroking her hair. Several minutes passed before Kaio held Via's chin in his hand, brushing her tears with his thumb. "I shall cherish this blessed moon cycle for the rest of my days, Via, because it was the month that I found you again. But you have a journey to make, child, and with that imalre, I travel with you." She nodded, sobbing, and he kissed her forehead. "Spirits' blessing upon you and may good luck follow."

She stepped away, took a deep breath. "Azeri and Zukav need attending to. And," she added, with a shaky smile, "someone must tell Afis, anyway." And then, with one last kiss on Kaio's cheek, she left the room.

Waiting outside the hut, Snook perked his ears at the sound of approaching footsteps. *Vic?* he called out, raising his head – but instead, Via appeared, pushing the door flap aside to brush past him. And although she didn't acknowledge Snook's presence, he couldn't help but notice, on her cheeks, the tears shining like crystals in the fading sunlight. Concerned, he whined, but she disappeared among the woods. *What did Kaio tell her?* Snook questioned. *What did her vision mean?*

Ever since Via had approached them earlier, his sixth sense had ignited, burning like a fire within him. Well, truth be told, it had started tingling when he'd first barked for Kaio, all those nights ago. He'd learned to somewhat tune it out since then, aside from when the tingle turned into an itch – but today, he found he couldn't ignore it at all. *Almost as if Via's vision mustn't be ignored*....and he wondered again what Kaio had told her.

Or what he's telling Vic. He looked back at the hut, but there was nothing. Vic wasn't grasping their thread, only a silent other end. It was as if a wall of quiet, a wall of blocking stone, had been erected. Snook knew this barrier was temporary, and that Vic had done it on purpose, for he'd done the same in the past. *I don't even remember* how *I did it, but I'm sure Vic learned through his book or Kaio.*

Scratching at an itch behind his ear, Snook considered: *I could eavesdrop...but that feels like betraying our bond. Vic will tell me once he's ready.* Bored, he yawned. *I hope that's soon.*

Kaio took a deep breath and then faced Vic, still huddled among the furs. "The time has come, Vic."

"My book?"

"Kai." A cuchel formed on Kaio's lips, and then the tome manifested itself into the air. "I apologize for the delay in returning it, but I had to be absolutely sure your book wasn't anything more than a family heirloom."

I could have told him that, Vic thought, annoyed. "More than?"

"You have enemies, lad. And for some reason, they seek your book."

"Why?"

Kaio shrugged. "It's nothing more than a family heirloom."

Realizing Kaio didn't intend to explain further, Vic switched topics: "Are you disappointed that I learned cuchels outside of the Training Camp?"

"Of course not." Kaio frowned. "If I believed in only learning cuchels per society's expected path, I wouldn't have mentored you. But I had to prepare you, for I am not able to join you on your journey."

"Why not, Kaio? I'm sure the outcasts can find another healer."

But his mentor merely replied, "The spirits have spoken." Kaio sighed. "There is much you do not know, Vic, but likewise, there is much I cannot tell you, for fear of your enemies searching your minds. For that same reason, your quest must unfold in pieces, like a puzzle. This guarantees that, if something were to happen, your enemies won't be able to discover the full picture. You must trust me when I say that we have your best interests at heart. Do you understand?"

Though he nodded, Vic caught Kaio's use of the plural: *We?*

"But now, you must trust in yourself, your friends, and most important of all, Snook."

Vic titled his head. "What exactly are we getting ourselves into, Kaio?"

Kaio grasped the book. "A valid question, and I'm glad you asked. Alas, I cannot say. The spirits love to say only what is necessary – and often, it is minimal information that is necessary."

Rising, Vic reached for the book, but Kaio passed him another item instead. "This pouch is made from unicorn fur," he said, as Vic stroked the delicate white hairs. "Don't ask me how I got it. I'm not sure if you even need it at all, but someone will instruct you what to do if *and when* you do. Until then, leave it unopened."

Vic's heart leapt when Kaio handed over his book. "There is not time for me to explain all I know about your tome. Therefore, inside you shall find a letter detailing more. Much more would I have taught you, Vic, if the spirits had granted us more time." Again, Vic heard the strange pinging sound, and Kaio gestured, silencing the air. "I'm forgetting. But soon, you shall know." With a mysterious smile, Kaio leaned forward, cupping Vic's ear with one hand. "Go to the one with great knowledge in Armoth. He'll provide you with the next step."

Armoth? Vic repeated. *And who?*

"Kneel, Vic, for my blessing." Vic did, and Kaio placed his palms on Vic's bowed head. As Kaio droned ancient words, Vic sensed his mental being surge with energy and sharpen with focus. And then he felt Kaio pull him to his feet and into an embrace. "Goodbye, Twq'nmu," his mentor whispered, voice cracking. "Purra for reminding me of a life I once led."

Kaio's Letter

Grimacing, Vic shifted his weight on Azeri's back. *I'm bruised and sore from Kaio's training, which isn't a comfortable return to horseback riding,* he thought.

Via looked over and laughed. "You're out of practice, Vic." She rode Zukav alongside Azeri, with Afis sitting behind her.

He groaned. "You're right: I am. We should have taken the horses for runs more often."

"Afis and I did," she said, laughing again. "You were far too busy with Kaio." She faltered, swallowing. "I miss him already."

Vic maneuvered Azeri around the base of a ridge. "I do, too."

"Even I miss him," Afis joined in. "He was the first friend I'd ever known."

Patting Afis' thigh, Via smiled. "Well, now you have two new friends – three, if you count Snook." At the mention of his name, Snook rumbled from where he trotted ahead.

Afis cracked a smile. "I suppose I do."

Both suns beat down on their backs as they rode, and Vic felt the sweat pooling under his tunics. All around them towered the rocky ridges Vic remembered from his earlier journey with Via. But now, knowing what the roads might hold, he let Via lead the way – and to the north of Levar, snaking around the city, she went.

Ahead, one ridge arched over the beaten path, creating a tunnel. On the other side, Vic could see the path curving around another, blocking their view of what lay ahead.

Snook paused a few paces from the tunnel and froze, tensing. Vic felt Azeri tighten beneath him and glanced over to see Zukav tossing his head. "What do you think?" he whispered to Via. She was about to speak when Snook's voice broke into his mind: *Travelers! But I don't like the scent, Vic...* In a blink, Vic turned Azeri to a far ridge and dismounted.

Via followed, stroking Zukav's neck. As she touched the ground, she spoke in a hushed tone: "Zukav senses a strange stallion. I assume Snook is wary of the scent as well?"

Vic had only just nodded his head when Snook appeared around the rock formation, saying, *They're not far, Vic.* Then Snook projected into Vic's mind, and he could hear the hoofbeats approaching at a steady trot. Beside him, Zukav bristled, pawing the dirt. Via gave two pats to Azeri's rump. With a nicker, the giant black stallion stretched out his neck, bit down on Zukav's rope, and led the bay stallion away, disappearing beyond far ridges. Gesturing to the others, Via led the way up the back of the ridge. Just as Snook finished scaling the edge, riders appeared out of the tunnel. *Weevils!* the dog confirmed.

The riders looked human except for one difference: dark blue skin. There were four of them atop rugged-looking horses, riding in a diamond formation with one in front leading. All of the weevils were bald, their scalps dotted with various dark patterns etched on their skin. "What are those?" whispered Afis, his voice loud enough for only Vic and Via to hear.

"Weevils," answered Via. "Every child of Lilligrav knows the stories of their attacks while prowling the ridges for travelers. But seeing them so far northeast is quite...strange. Which means we'll have to be even more cautious getting around Levar."

Vic tried to nod, but his chin hit the ridge rock. His heart skipped a beat as a large pebble broke loose from the impact of his chin and toppled down the ridge.

Spooked, the weevils' horses snorted and sidestepped, but not in unison. They knocked into each other, some seeming to lose their footing. The commander's roan reared and opened his spitting mouth to scream, but his rider leaned forward to slap his hand across the stallion's snout. The roan snorted in surprise and crashed back to the earth. As the weevil leader grunted to his companions, the three above rolled over, out of sight, holding their breath. It seemed ages to them before the hoofbeats picked up again and faded away.

Afis moved to sit up, but Vic pushed on his arm. "Wait," he hissed. "Just to be safe."

After what seemed like an eternity, Snook lifted his head, saying: *They're gone, Vic. Their scent has faded.*

"All clear." Vic began the descent down the ridge. "I'll admit, despite living in a village close to the weevil fortress, I've never seen one alive."

"I also haven't seen many," Via said, climbing down next. "They're quite elusive." Once back on the ground, she whistled. "Nevertheless, we'll make sure to curve even farther north." Hearing her whistle, Azeri appeared, leading Zukav, and they mounted again, turning the horses toward northern ridges.

Both suns beat down on the Viper Plains. Dry weeds shifted in the slight breeze, and sugar grass filled the air with a sweet scent that was almost unbearable. Grasshoppers buzzed through the air, and a dark shadow passed overhead — a bare-necked vulture circling above. A lean wild dog raised its head from slumber, shook itself, and trotted away in search of a new meal. A blue-green lizard scampered down from sunbathing on a rock as two horses trod through the Plains, followed by a golden dog.

Vic's fingers caught in Azeri's mane as he patted the stallion's hot and sweaty neck. "Looks like a good place to rest the horses." He swung a leg over and dismounted. Azeri landed with a thud on the ground, shifted, and rolled back and forth in the dirt. Zukav joined him after Via and Afis dismounted.

"We mustn't rest here for too long," Via said. "The father north our camp, the safer we'll be. But while we're here, should we find more food?"

Vic slipped off his pack and looked inside. "You're right: already we have very little left from the provisions that Kaio supplied us with." He eyed Afis, who shrugged. "We know someone with the appetite of a bloody lion, after all."

Via laughed. "We're in the Plains now, so we have plenty of food available, either to hunt or to gather. Kaio didn't want to weigh you down, Vic."

Vic nodded and inhaled. "I smell sugar grass, so let's gather some to dry for later."

"But we'll need to burn it before we can harvest it." Via pointed to a clump of flowers. "Clover is a great source of energy."

"But sweet, sweet sugar grass—" Vic broke off to sniff the air.

She shook her head. "Vic, who survived life in the Plains?"

He rubbed the back of his neck in embarrassment, murmuring, "You did."

"Exactly." Her tone was firm. "So, it only makes sense that I must ensure we all survive the Plains together. Trust me. Clover is much less of a hassle." She gestured to the horses, who had rolled over onto their bellies. "Watch the boys. I know what I'm doing and won't be long."

Azeri and Zukav staggered to their hoofs, nipping at each other in a playful way. "Do we brush the dirt off?" Afis asked with a grimace.

Vic shook his head. "No, it protects them from insects." He pointed to their rumps. "Though you're more than welcome to brush their tails."

The grass brushed against Via's legs as she passed, and she smiled to herself. *I can't believe I'm saying this, but I've missed the Plains. As much as my heart yearned for Kaio all these years, my soul ached for the freedom I gave myself here.*

There was a flurry of dirt and feathers beside her ankle, and Via stepped back in surprise. Two beady eyes stared unblinking back at her from the darkness of a hole in the dirt. *A field owl. How I do not miss them.* Stepping over the owl's home, she came to the patch of clover. With impish heads adorned with purple hair, the flowers danced in the breeze. A mossy boulder shaded half the clump, and Via pressed her back against the cool stone, collapsing to her knees.

And then she heard the rattling.

Tensing, Via froze, sweat beading on the back of her neck. Without moving, she glanced sideways. Not far from her right elbow, a viper lay coiled in the Plains grass. Its black scales formed a pattern of diamonds…diamonds of death. Its red tongue flicked in and out, testing the air and then tasting her. Tail raised, the viper shook its rattles, and the loose scales scraped against each other.

Via wanted to cry out, but her throat was dry. *How did I not see the viper?!*

Tugging their fingers through the stallions' manes, Vic and Afis muttered curses under their breath. "They haven't had a thorough brushing in weeks," Vic complained.

"Don't whine too much – Azeri's is much thicker than Zukav's," Afis replied. At the sound of his name, Azeri flicked an ear back as he continued to graze.

Beside him, an impatient Zukav pranced, but Vic kept a steady grip on the bay's rope. He watched Zukav's head, however, knowing full well that the stallion could snap at him without a warning. At his feet, Snook lay stretched out, sunsbathing. But then he twitched, sat up in a blink, and growled.

Cursing louder, Afis tried to control Azeri as the giant stallion threw back his head and reared. Zukav tugged at the rope, snapping at Vic's elbow. "What's gotten into them?" Vic said above Zukav's screaming.

Afis spat on the ground. "How in all of Lilligrav do I know?!"

Snook, what's happening?

Danger! Snook barked, his nose wriggling. *Via!*

Glancing in her direction, Vic squinted. He saw her pressed against a boulder, her entire body tense, and he felt his own body tighten. *What's wrong? I can't see anything, but I sense it.*

Listen, and Snook projected a sound — a sound Snook himself was hearing — the sound of death: a viper's rattle.

"Snake!" Vic turned to Afis, whose eyes widened. "One move, and Via *won't* wake up this time!" Dropping Zukav's rope, Vic broke into a run toward Via, scooping up stones. "Don't move, Via!"

A blur of fur passed Vic. Snarling, Snook reached the viper first, circling it. The snake hissed, lashing out. At the last minute, Snook darted a step away, the viper's fangs just missing his hind leg.

Snook! Vic shouted.

Get Via! Snook commanded. *I'll take care of the viper.*

Dropping his stones, Vic reached over the boulder and grabbed Via's shoulders. Straining, he pulled her over, and once on the other side, she released the breath she'd been holding. Both jumped at the sound of Zukav's scream as the bay streaked past them.

Snook growled deep in his throat, jumping at the viper. The serpent curled around the dog's stomach, sliding toward his throat. Zukav reared, tossed his head, and crashed to the ground. His hooves cracked the viper's rattle, and it turned its head, hissing. In a blink, Snook pressed a paw against the back of the viper's hood, forcing it into the dirt. The snake wriggled as it tried to pull away. But it was Snook who leaped out of the way as Zukav trampled the serpent, hooves dancing in the sand. Within moments, what remained of the viper were pieces of flesh and scales. The vulture swooped in, landed beside the torn-up carcass, and bobbed down its head, beak open.

Pulling away from Vic, Via rushed to Snook and threw her arms around the dog's neck, burying her face in his fur, tears streaming down her face. "You good, good dog. Good boy, Snook. Thank you—you—you crazy dog! You could have been killed!" She broke off in a sob.

Snook licked her cheek, glancing at Vic. *Please help me, Vic.*

Vic pried her off Snook, and she let out a shaky breath. "I'm sorry— I should have seen the snake sooner, but I—"

Vic shook his head. "Don't apologize. I'm just glad no one's injured."

She turned back to Snook, who was lying down, panting in the sunlight. "Are you hurt, Snook? You crazy, crazy dog!"

Grinning, Snook barked. "He's fine," Vic said with a laugh.

A snort behind them caught their attention, and they turned. Azeri stood waiting, with Afis still caught with his fingers in the stallion's mane. Via began laughing when Zukav trotted behind her and nudged her back with his forehead. "You're crazy, too!" Via said, throwing her arms around Zukav's neck. "But then again, how many vipers have you saved me from?" Zukav nickered, and Azeri whinnied back.

Catching the expression on Afis' face, Vic cocked his head. "Anything wrong, Afis?"

Afis shrugged. "So…what exactly happened?"

Hours later, Via chose the spot for their camp. She'd tasked Afis with building a ring of stones while she attended to her stallions. That left Vic and Snook to search for twigs and sticks. "Not too green," she'd reminded Vic, "or they won't burn." So, after some playtime – *I am a dog, after all,* Snook had told Vic — they'd returned with an armful. Snook had saved his favorite, however, and held it in his mouth as he sat beside Vic.

"Use magic," Via instructed. "It'll be faster than waiting for a spark."

Vic grinned, saying "Ralas," and the wood ignited.

Snook's stick fell to the ground, and Vic reached for it, intending to play. Until he caught sight of Snook's expression: staring, as if lost, into the flames. *Snook, what's wrong?*

The dog's nose twitched. *The fire.*

For a moment, Vic felt a twinge of guilt: *I promise it's safe, considering I used magic to control it.*

I know that; it's just— Snook whimpered, and Vic waited for him to find the words. After a pause, Snook began again: *I've known fire all my life, especially in winter. But ever since Drema was attacked, I feel that my sixth sense — no, my soul— has been drawn to the flames. Like something is pulling me in, and I can't look away.* He looked at Vic with pleading eyes. *What does that mean?*

Vic scratched Snook's head between his ears. *I don't know. Perhaps your mind is trying to recall the attack. You told me once that the memories were hazy.*

That is true, Snook admitted.

Perhaps your mind believes that if you stare into the flames, Vic continued, *those memories will come back to you.*

"What are you two talking about?" Via asked, startling him.

Embarrassed, Vic rubbed the back of his neck. "You could tell?"

She laughed. "Your unwavering eye contact gave it away."

"We'll have to work on that," Vic admitted. "We can't risk giving ourselves away so easily."

"Why not?" Afis cut in.

Vic offered Snook his stick, and content, the dog began gnawing away. "We don't want to attract the wrong kind of attention. We have no idea what kind of quest Kaio has given us."

"What is our 'quest,' anyway?" Afis frowned. "Via offered it as an explanation as to why we left Kaio's, but I still don't understand."

"Kaio didn't tell us much," Vic explained with a small shrug. "He directed me to Armoth, but that was all he said."

"Well, we won't be getting to Armoth tonight or tomorrow," Via interrupted. "So, let's focus on supper and sleep. Who wants first watch?"

Vic enjoyed the sunrise during his watch. He hadn't argued when Afis had wanted the midnight shift – he was far too used to Kaio forcing him up early.

Speaking of Kaio… At his feet lay his pack. Inside the pack lay his book. Tucked inside the cover, the letter. *It's been at the back of my mind since we left,* Vic said to himself.

He glanced over at Snook, curled near his knees. The dog kicked a leg in sleep, tail winding through the grass.

With a smile, Vic shrugged off his blanket, picked up his pack, and headed off for the boulder where Via had encountered the viper. Sitting upon the cold stone, feeling both rising suns warming him, Vic traced the crystals set into the leather cover, as the prisms caught the newborn light. *As much as I respect Kaio, he had no right to keep my book from me. But now it's mine again. And I will learn more than ever!* he proclaimed.

Kaio's letter lay between the front cover and the title page. Vic removed it, unfolded it – and began to read…

Dear lad, faithful Vic,

I write these words because I fear it is not safe to tell you the truth. Even at this moment, I am being watched, but I have done my best to protect you and the others. Now you must protect your book. Do not lose it, Vic.

I will tell you its backstory – or, at least, what I know of it.

Your tome was written by an elf, who desired to make cuchels more accessible to humans, hence the translations. For yes, there existed a time before the Training Camp when man had no access to magic. I have never learned the elf's name, but perhaps one day, you will. When the elf passed on, the book he'd written was stolen, although the proper term is "smuggled." The smuggler was Flynn Hemonia-nama, one of your great ancestors.

Never let this book out of your sight, Vic, I beg of you. As I warned you, men seek you to drive their blades through your heart. Alas, some men are pleased by blood. In fact, several days after Via awoke (tell her I never doubted her), three men arrived at my hut. They ordered your book to be handed over. I disagreed, and I paid the painful price. I don't know why HE has spread word about your possession, but you must be on guard, Vic. I was able to protect the tome through ancient magic, but it is beyond your strength.

Therefore, you must protect it through sword and stealth. Show no one the tome, unless they have your complete and utter trust. As of now, the only people who qualify should be Via and Afis. Kai, you can trust Afis. He may not be everything he pretends to be, but guide him, Vic: for he is still like a newborn, with no one else to turn to.

And Snook. Of course, Snook. He perhaps is the only one you truly trust. And rightly so. But the answers shall come in time, Vic.

Your book is being searched for, and any chance given to your enemies is sure to be used with vile intentions. Lilligrav is a much darker place than the stories say.

Before you close my letter, turn to page eighty for a priceless treasure I entrust to you. Find its owner. He will help you, in more ways than one.

In Armoth, the one with great knowledge knows the way. I apologize for the riddles, but valuable information must be kept safe.
Goodbye and sincerely,
Kaio Tamno-nama

Kaio stood before her, a bittersweet smile on his face. She wanted to run to him — but it seemed, all of a sudden, that her feet were glued to the ground. She glanced down, straining, but her legs wouldn't budge. So, she looked at Kaio again and opened her mouth to call his name — but there was no sound. It was as if she'd forgotten how to speak, how to make any sort of noise. Kaio was starting to fade away now, and she could feel the weight of her heart as it sank deep into her soul, the painful desperation eating her alive. But then Kaio disappeared, and a four-legged creature ran past, a mere blur, but she knew.

Via gasped as her eyes flew open. She could hear her heartbeat pounding in her skull, and then the tears came, flooding her face. But like in her vision, she couldn't move, so she just lay there, wracked with silent sobs and praying to the spirits: *Take it all back, please. He's all I have left.*

At long last, the spirits' grip on her subsided, and Via, once able to move her arms, hugged herself. She rolled onto her side and curled up tight, shivering, but the vision offered her no warmth. *I only just found him again, but now I've lost him forever.*

Vic refolded the letter, fingers gliding along the parchment as he felt Kaio's written words sink into him: *There is so much that he said and yet so much that he didn't answer. Why? What does he know?*

Flipping to page eighty, he discovered another folded piece of paper. *Another letter?* He unfolded it in haste to discover a leather bookmark. Confused, Vic picked it up for a closer look. But then his jaw dropped, for the bookmark was lined with tiny diamonds that sparkled in the light. Vic also marveled at the detailed painting, depicting a unicorn in a bed of lush green grass while a dragon's silhouette flew across a bright blue sky. *Someone paid a lot of money for this, and someone very talented created it.*

Gazing at the painted unicorn, Vic brushed his chest, where the pouch of unicorn fur hung underneath his inner tunic. He considered it the most important item Kaio had given him – because of his mentor's severe warning – so had kept it hidden and close to his heart. *First a pouch of unicorn fur,* Vic mused, *and now a bookmark with a unicorn. Is there a connection?*

He turned the bookmark over. Inscribed across the back, in delicate calligraphy, was a name: *Hopacias?* Vic questioned, for it was completely unknown to him, not from any legends or stories that he knew.

Vic almost jumped out of his skin at the touch of Snook's nose on the back of his leg, and the bookmark dropped from his hands. *You've got to stop doing that!*

In reply, the dog sent an image of Via waking up.

He saw her approaching, a snoring Afis still curled up by the drowned

173

fire. Keeping his eyes on her, he swept the bookmark into his tome, which he shut and lowered out of her sight. As she came up beside him, he caught sight of the deep sadness in her eyes, almost hidden by her disordered hair. "Via? What's happened?"

She collapsed to the ground beside him, clutching his knees. "Vic, it happened again. Another vision while I slept. I must tell you; it's urgent."

Snook sat on his haunches with a whine: *I sense the sadness behind her vision, Vic.*

Then it must not be good news, Vic replied with dread. "Go on."

"I saw Kaio and—and his Yror, Vic." She began to cry. "He's gone."

Despite his heart twisting, Vic recalled tradition. "May his Yror avenge his death."

"Etta lilli espe," she whispered, swallowing the tears. A small howl escaped Snook's maw as he laid his head on Via's shoulder. She smiled, reached up, and stroked his head. "Purra, Snook."

"He was a good man, Via," Vic said, adding: "And may someday soon his spirit return to the afterlife."

She sighed, shaking. "The father that I thought I'd lost and then found is gone, Vic." She glanced back at Afis, looked at Vic. "Now all I have is the two of you, Afis, and my stallions."

Vic placed a hand on her shoulder. "And all we know at this moment is to go to Armoth."

"But, Vic, what are we supposed to find there?"

With a shrug, Vic let his hand drop to touch the cover of his tome. "An answer."

Mind Games

Afis exhaled, trying to control the onset of another one of his moods as Via and Vic continued chatting. *They've been discussing these things called dreams for...how exactly does time work?* Another wave of frustration crashed over him. *There's so much I don't understand, and yet they make it seem so simple. Like that...viper yesterday.*

All of a sudden, Afis realized the burning feeling of Vic's stare and with a little effort, he glanced up to catch Vic's eye. "Anything the matter, Afis?" Vic cocked his head, raising his eyebrows.

"Nothing," he mumbled back. Something flashed through him, a feeling he didn't recognize. As if he was upset for being caught pondering.

Via patted Afis' knee. "You've been quiet the entire morning. I remember how when we wandered the Avro Woods together, whenever you got quiet, it meant you were thinking something over. But now, you don't get to wander away."

Again, a flash of emotion, and Afis muttered a curse.

"So." Via twisted on Zukav's back, smiled up at Afis. "What's on your mind? We've got a long ride ahead of us, anyway."

Afis growled. "Fine." Dropping his gaze, he pointed one arm to the sky. "What are those?"

Via glanced up. "The clouds?"

"I suppose so," and Afis shrugged.

Vic grinned. "Afis, don't be afraid to ask questions. That's what my cousin Zurze always told me."

Via tilted her head. "The same cousin who taught you magic?"

Vic nodded despite the guilt: *She still believes my lie.* So, he added, "Of course, Kaio often told me the same thing."

Though Via smiled softly in response, Vic still caught the sadness behind her expression. Again, guilt washed over him: *Too soon, idiot. She only just told you last night.*

Don't be so hard on yourself, Snook cut in. *We are all still adjusting to the loss of Kaio.*

But Via most of all, Vic noted.

Vic returned to their previous topic by gesturing to the world around them. "We've got an entire island to introduce you to, Afis. Any other questions we can answer?"

"Wait a minute," Via interrupted. She twisted again to look at Afis behind her. "How is it that you forgot about clouds?"

Afis froze, his mind empty all of a sudden.

He was relieved when Vic spoke up instead: "The amnesia. It's a bizarre concept: to forget simple things like clouds but simultaneously remember advanced archery techniques." Vic nodded to Afis, who shot him a grateful look. "But we're here to help you readjust, Afis."

If I can keep my Bloodthirsty side at bay, Via will never need to know the truth about me. Afis sighed under his breath. *Easier said than done.*

They spent the next few hours teaching Afis until he pointed far ahead. "What is that?"

Via brought her steed to a halt, and beside them, Vic did the same.

"That's Zukav Ridge, Afis," Via said. "The northern-most ridge of Lilligrav. I've never seen it in person." She dismounted and started weaving through the tall grass.

As he dismounted, Afis pointed at her horse. "Zukav Ridge – like him?"

"Aye," Vic replied. "In the elfin language, 'zukav' translates as 'dirt' or 'ground.' Therefore, the ledge is named, well, for coming out of the ground." He laughed. "Humans are quite original when naming things, Afis."

The ridge protruded from the ground at an angle, pointing toward the western sky. "Legends say," Via began, as the other two came up beside her, "that as both suns disappear, the ledge points directly to the western fading sun." She turned to face them. "Shall we discover tonight if it's true?"

"I suppose the ledge will provide an excellent place for camp." All of a sudden, Vic sensed Afis had disappeared and looked around. "Where's Afis?"

"Over here," he called from the other side of the ledge. Via and Vic exchanged grins before looping around to join him. He knelt before a plant at the base of the ledge, head tilted, one hand outstretched.

As she turned the corner, Via cried out: "Afis, don't touch that!"

Startled, he drew his palm back, glancing up at her. "Why not?"

"Because your hands will be covered with blood," Vic replied, nodding toward the plant. It was tall, with bare red branches. "The story goes that, many centuries ago, a greenbeard dwarf nurtured a dying plant back to health. But he was attacked by bandits, and the blood of the dwarf seeped into the Plains. By some sort of miracle, the plant absorbed its caretaker's blood, and it sprouted to the height of the bandits' chins." He knelt beside Afis, pointed to the crimson red branches. "And when one touches it, the dwarf's blood passes along."

"It's said that the dwarfs know of the plant's healing powers," Via put in. "No human dares to touch it. And neither should you, Afis."

Though, since he's not human, it's possible that Afis is immune to the plant's mark, Vic mused but when Afis locked eyes with him, he could tell they both knew it wasn't worth the risk.

So, instead, Afis asked, "But when the dwarfs harvest the plant, do they not find their hands stained?"

Vic shook his head. "Incredibly, no. They are the sole race unaffected. And thus, its name: Flïnaro Tereuk tuk – or the Wound of Tears."

"Your people must have so many stories," Afis said with a shake of his head. "How do you keep them apart?"

Both Vic and Via grinned. "Sometimes they do blend together!" Via replied, laughing.

Vic shaded his eyes as he calculated the position of each sun. "It'll be suppertime somewhat soon. Afis, perhaps you could take Snook to fetch some fresh kill." He pointed to the north. "I see a patch of underbrush not far off. There's bound to be something there."

At long last, something fun! came Snook's voice, followed by a rumbling bark.

The three turned to see the dog weaving between the two stallions as they trotted over, Zukav tossing his head. "They're hungry, too," Via said, giggling and taking Zukav's muzzle between her cupped hands. "And they're much more impatient." She led them to the shade cast by the ridge.

Vic, why don't we go hunting together? Snook asked, scratching an itch behind his ear.

Vic knelt beside him, rubbed his muzzle. *The two of you have hunted together before,* he said, *and I have some things to teach Via.*

Via? Snook repeated.

Kaio gave both her and me swords. He taught me, and I suppose that means I must teach her, Vic explained. *It's never too early to start. The closer we get to my side of the Plains, the closer we are to the Dark One. We'll need all the protection we can get.*

Afis came up beside them, bow in hand. He hoisted his quiver higher up on his shoulder – a quiver that Kaio had taught him how to make. "Is Snook ready?" Leaping to all four paws, Snook gave another rumbling bark and loped off, Afis following.

"Why didn't you go with them, Vic?" Via asked, coming up behind him. "I don't need help gathering dry grass to prepare a fire for their kill."

He turned to her with his sword drawn. "How about I teach you a few tricks for that sword of yours?" he asked, nodding his head toward her own scabbard.

She hesitated. "I…I don't know, Vic."

"What's wrong?"

"Ever since I found myself alone on the Plains, I've had to defend myself. But that never involved killing anyone, not when I could outsmart them instead." She tucked some strands of ebony hair behind her ear, biting the inside of her lip while she considered her next words. "When Kaio gave us our swords, I felt…something in the pit of my stomach – something I can't quite explain."

Vic smiled in sympathy. "Via, when Kaio gave us our swords, he intended them as means of keeping ourselves safe. The last thing either of us wants is to kill someone. But, as Kaio taught me, it therefore follows that I must teach you."

With a sigh, she drew her sword. "I suppose you're right. What's first?"

Almost a half hour later, after teaching Via basic techniques, Vic found himself well-matched. "It seems I underestimated your skill level," he admitted between blows. "I suppose having to defend oneself all these years comes in handy?"

She shrugged. "Zukav and Azeri allowed for quick escapes. But sometimes, yes, I would find myself in close combat with a stranger." Vic saw an opening, and in a blink, Via lay among the long grass, with his sword pointed at her chest. "Yield," she murmured, and he drew back, allowing her to stand. "Kaio taught you well. Or were you always skilled with a sword?"

Running a hand through his hair, Vic laughed. "No, I've never picked up a blade in my life. But I often sparred with sticks, so I guess I'm a quick learner." He grinned. "Though Kaio gave me many, many bruises."

She winced and sheathed her sword. "That's enough for today. Both suns will set soon, and Afis should be returning with a fresh kill. We'll need to be ready with a fire."

Sheathing his sword also, Vic followed her back to the grazing horses. She knelt, plucking grass from the dirt to clear the area. He began collecting twigs and asked, "Via?"

She looked over at him, smiling.

"Let's try that flask Kaio gave you, shall we?"

Biting her lip, Via considered. "I suppose. But not much: we may need it again." The two of them wandered over to where Vic had laid his pack under the peak of Zukav Ridge. As Vic dug through his pack for the flask, Via fingered his bow then remarked: "I'm back on the Plains with my stallions, and you're back in the Plains with your bow. Yet I haven't seen you touch this since the day we arrived at the Avro Woods." She looked at him. "I know you can hunt well with it – after all, you caught our meals during our days riding to Levar. Why didn't you have Snook hunt with you?"

Vic chuckled. "Snook asked me the same thing." Retrieving the flask, he stood beside her, brushing his palm against the feathery ends of his arrows. "Afis and Snook have already hunted together, so I figured they'd make a good team. Besides, I had swordplay to teach you. It does feel strange not hunting anymore, however."

"Who says you can't?" she asked.

He considered her words when movement caught his eye. At the base of Zukav Ridge walked a pair of grouse, hunting for grains. Vic nocked an arrow and raised his bow. He sensed Via stepping back, careful not to disturb the birds. In the moments before releasing the arrow, Vic embraced the familiar feel of his bow in his hands once more: *How I've missed this.*

And then, everything went spiraling downward. In the back of his mind, Vic felt the sensation of burning – and a momentary flashing light. Before he could delve deeper into the recesses of his mental core, a gnawing pain ignited in the pit of his stomach. He dropped his bow, pressed his arm against himself, groaning.

"Vic?" came Via's distant words, echoing, pounding in his ears.

The pain increased and, at his touch, spread like flames. His arms froze, his legs turned to jelly, and his head spun. In his chest, his heart pounded so fast, it burned in his mind. As all the sensations crushed against him, knocking him flat on the ground, a blinding memory enveloped him: *The black void!* Desperate, he turned with force to Via, gasping: "Tear my tunic!" With each word, his throat tightened, and his lungs constricted.

"Vic!" she cried, and she shook her head, a confused and concerned look in her eye. "Vic, what's wrong?"

"Just do it," he managed, and as the pain enflamed further, he gritted his teeth.

After a moment's hesitation, she ripped his outer tunic, and Vic winced, feeling helpless. "Is there any…black void?" he choked out.

"No," and he could sense her utter confusion.

You're cleverer than I anticipated, Vic. This will be such fun.

The voice sent ice through Vic's veins. *Who—Who are you?*

If you recognize my signature spell, then you know my name.

The Dark One?! The memory that Vic had locked inside himself flooded back to his mind, and he squeezed his eyes shut, trying to block it again.

But it's too soon, young Xaniera. Much too soon. Don't forget me.

At the words, Vic's pain vanished, and he sat up, gasping for breath.

"Vic, what in all of Lilligrav—"

He put a hand to her lips, and a stinging sensation coursed through his arm. *Is it returning?* and he looked over at her. Via was blushing, looking at his fingers pressed against her mouth. Vic drew back, stuttering: "I'm sorry, I—I…" He sighed, shook his head. "I felt like I was burning alive, Via. But whatever it was, it's gone now."

181

"Vic, you're not making any sense. How—"

I have far more pressing matters to think about, Via. "I'm fine." Gulping, he opened his eyes. "Shall we find out if your fire flask works?"

She sat beside him, mouth agape in horrified bewilderment. Moments passed before she managed to speak, but it took everything in her to get the word out of her mouth: "Vic?!"

Getting to his feet, he walked back to the horses. "Enough." *The Dark One is after me? I'm not a ntéh, not yet at least.* Then, even more confused, he recalled the Dark One's strange choice of elfin: *He called me "Xaniera" – but owner of what? My book? Snook?*

"For the last time, Snook, what's wrong with this patch of underbrush?" Afis demanded, but Snook only whimpered in return. Groaning, Afis threw back his head and rolled his eyes. He and Snook had tracked and shot down three grouse thus far, but when they'd approached this final thicket, the dog had frozen, refusing to enter. Three times, Afis had pleaded with him, and three times, he hadn't budged. "There must be something in there we can catch, Snook. Just flush it out."

With another whine, Snook dropped to the ground, head between his paws. Afis was about to yell when he heard a voice. *What—what was that?* He looked back over at Snook, who had leaped back to all fours. "You heard it, too?" The dog growled, his teeth bared.

Well. It's too strange to not investigate. After stringing their catch up on a small tree, Afis cracked his neck and ducked between the thick branches. "Coming?"

Snook paused, ears perked. He'd been trying to reach Vic, but their connection was cloudy. *Something's strange about this…thicket, but I can't leave Afis alone,* he knew. So, within minutes, Snook found himself crawling through the underbrush. His nose quivered, both in curiosity and confusion: *How is this thicket larger on the inside? I knew something was strange about it… If only Vic were here. He'd know.*

But then Afis came into view just ahead. "Look," he hissed, laying on his stomach and looking through a gap in the thorns.

Snook could smell them before he could even see them, and a low growl escaped his throat. *Big danger!*

In a cleared area, the underbrush was alive with blends of crimson and brown, for each man wore these colors: crimson tunics, dusty brown jackets, and cocoa-brown pants. Several sat cross-legged in a semicircle, discussing war techniques while sharpening spears, daggers and swords. Flashbacks raced through Afis' mind, and he winced. *I've seen all these preparations before.*

Toward the center of the thinned brush, a ring of men stood looking at a map on the ground. One, in a silvery helmet, pierced the map with his dagger, grunting. At the head of the ring of men stood one with his hand on his hilt. He leaned forward to inspect while the others held their collective breath. *He's the leader,* Afis realized before admitting, *He's much more of a leader than Rudolf ever was.*

Another man moved forward, squinting at the spot, before shrugging and tapping the knife with his foot. Lips moving in speech, he turned to the leader, whose face flushed an angry purple. He unsheathed his blue sword, pointed it at the man before him, and hissed, "Beu durkva!" The other man fell backward, and the map crinkled under his limp form. The others fell silent, before the one in the silver helmet pushed the dead body off the map.

Afis felt his Bloodthirsty side rushing through him, and to clear himself of the daze, he looked away. As the red glare faded, he began calculating each man's strength and number of weapons – something the Blood Bearers had taught him.

He gasped when he recognized one of the men right away: *Rudolf! How did he...? I don't believe it! Is he attacking Armoth with these men?* Scanning them, Afis searched for other familiar members. He counted five men and seven dwarfs. *Ridiculous. Why would he select so few? Unless…he has more hiding out somewhere else.* He swallowed, hard. *We need to watch ourselves even closer than before. Who knows where Rudolf has planted his spies?* He also noticed that Brandi was nowhere to be found.

Turning back to Snook, he gestured behind them, signaling it was time to go. The two crawled backwards until the thorns parted enough for them to duck through. Bursting through the thicket, Afis reached for their earlier kill – then froze at the sight of a Blood Bearer scout. The young boy stood beside the thicket, holding the three grouse, blinking at Afis in surprise. "Just hand them back over," Afis said, extending an open hand. Instead, the scout dropped the grouse, flushed out a horn, and blew – but before he could blow again, Afis leaped forward, knocking the boy to the ground and pinning him. "Run, Snook!"

Rumbling a bark in response, the dog bounded away through the tall grass.

"Now, listen here, boy," Afis growled, and the scout stopped squirming. "Your fellow Blood Bearers are going to be out here in any moment, but before that happens, you're going to answer one question for me: Who leads you?"

The scout glared back. "Tierm." *So. Rudolf lost to another man.*

He could hear the clanging of chainmail, the rising of voices, and the singing of swords as the men drew closer, rushing out of the thicket. Afis set his jaw, analyzing the situation – just as the Blood Bearers had taught him. *And yet now, I use their tactics against them. If only Rudolf knew…*

Grabbing the scout by the shoulders, Afis lifted him into the air, then drew the boy's dagger out of his boot, and pressed the blade against the boy's neck. "If you know what's best for you, you'll run. If you turn around, my arrow will find your forehead." The scout swallowed, nodded. Afis dropped him. "Run," he hissed, and the scout obeyed.

By now, the men were close enough that Afis could almost hear their breath – tainted with blood and drink. He scooped up the grouse and jogged a pace away, before dropping to one knee and nocking double arrows. The men burst from the thicket, swords drawn, searching. Exhaling, Afis closed his eyes and released his arrows. One hit a man at the front; the other struck a dwarf, right in the forehead. With a unified shout, the men pushed aside their fallen comrades and raced toward Afis. He nocked and released two more arrows before turning and speeding away, the enemy not far behind.

Vic squatted in the sandy dirt, poking at a shed viper skin with a stick. Now and then, he stole glances at Via, but she never returned his gaze and instead kept her back to him as she attended the fire.

He sighed and rubbed his temples. His thoughts were overlapping so much, it was hard to detangle them, to comprehend: *What does it mean? Did Kaio know? He seemed to. What do I do? I can't tell the others. I must keep it to myself. And for now, I must try and block it from Snook.*

As if Snook had sensed something, the dog's voice leaped into Vic's mind: *Vic, hurry! We are all in danger!* Before Vic could ask, a projected image entered his mind: a burning village. He knew it must be a serious threat if Snook was sending his darkest memory.

Vic stood without hesitation, grabbed his pack and bow, and untied Zukav. Via came up beside him, but Vic turned to the fire. Holding up his hand, he whispered, "Tjord ralas," and then crushed out the embers and smoldering twigs.

"If you think I'll waste the flask again—" Via reprimanded.

"We need to go."

She calmed a prancing Zukav while Vic mounted Azeri. To her surprise, he stabbed his heel into Azeri's side, sending him into a startled gallop. She shook her head and mounted then urged Zukav to follow; the bay leaped forward. "What's going on?" she asked when the horses matched stride for stride.

"Snook and Afis are in danger."

Both horses cleared a barrier of boulders and weeds. "Danger?" Via repeated.

"He didn't elaborate. But it's an emergency." Vic and Via brought the two stallions to a halt as Snook appeared cresting a hill. *What's happened?* Vic called out.

Stay there! the dog instructed. *Prepare your arrows, Vic.*

Where's Afis?

He's coming.

To Vic's surprise, instead of joining the two on horseback, Snook circled back and lay at the base of the hill, ears perked. "Someone's coming," Vic whispered, drawing his bow.

Afis appeared at the top of the hill, running hard, almost out of breath, three grouse dangling over his shoulder. Not far behind, men appeared running just as hard – each armed with a sword or dagger. Via gasped at the sight of blackbeard dwarfs racing alongside.

Snook, you'll be crushed!

Trust me, the dog replied, his tone firm.

Whatever the two of you did, we have some cleaning up to do!

Via swallowed hard beside him. "So much for not killing people."

With a slow nod of his head, Vic aimed. "Only if necessary."

Snook twitched his ears, sidling closer to the ground. He flinched at the sound of arrows whizzing over his head. *How many did you hit?* he asked.

Three. But I have more arrows, Vic reassured him.

Wait for me. Snook laid his ears flat as Afis passed him.

"Where's Snook?" Afis shouted, approaching the stallions. Vic nodded toward the grass. Afis leaped atop Zukav, behind Via, and nocked another arrow. "I don't see him."

As the men came down the side of the hill, Snook rumbled and leaped into the air. The men paused – most startled, some frightened at the sight of the giant dog's fangs. Vic's arrow hit the closest man, who had brandished his sword at Snook. As the man fell, Snook snarled and lunged, bringing the next man down by the throat. Hearing Vic's and Afis' arrows bringing down the men in front of the line, Snook released his prey and growled at the others, tensing, ready to pounce again. The enemy stepped back. Vic whistled, and Snook turned, loping toward them.

But he felt the ground shaking, perked his ears, and stopped, barking an alert. *Listen, Vic!* A chorus of hooves sounded through the Plains, and Snook twitched his nose and swiveled his ears, trying to place the sound. Zukav snuffed the air and then screamed. *Horses!* Snook realized just as a herd of them appeared from the north.

Vic turned his head to see and cursed: "Blast! From a distance, they looked like mere antelope."

"I should have killed the scout," Afis growled, cursing. He released another arrow.

Pausing, Vic reflected: *Is he keeping his Bloodthirsty side under control? Or should I be worried?*

I didn't sense anything concerning, Snook responded. *We must trust in him.*

"Let's go," Via said, taking charge. "We'll need a head start more than ever now." She nudged Zukav to the southwest, and Vic followed suit.

They're mounting, Vic. Snook caught up and raced alongside Zukav. *Use magic to slow them down.*

Vic hesitated before shouting, "Shu surg tuk!" The air crackled as the lightning struck, but no shouts of fear or pain echoed behind them.

Their leader redirected the bolt with his own cuchel! Snook told him.

His hands trembling, Vic let out a shaky breath and closed his eyes. *Relax...Shilek.* In a blink, his entire body felt at peace, energized with deep relaxation, and the potential cuchels rippled through his mind. Words passed across his vision – but he held back: *Nothing too powerful. I can't afford to faint like before. What was the one Kaio said?* And then the words returned to him: "Elisdh!" His eyelids fluttered, and he felt his muscles weaken. *Snook, replenish me with some of your energy.*

Gladly. Beu.

Behind them came a loud cry as their adversaries encountered the crackling force field Vic had summoned. Afis twisted on Zukav's back and saw that one man had made it past the force field – but then the leader shot a sizzling ray of light from his spear to demolish it. Jumping from Zukav's back, Afis nocked an arrow and released. It pierced the lone rider's forehead, and as he fell backwards, his skittish horse trembled then bucked, knocking him off. Afis let out his breath and leaped onto the chestnut-colored stallion as it raced past him. "Don't worry about getting me a horse at Armoth!" he shouted. "This one will do!"

Via glanced over her shoulder and gasped. "He's a beauty!"

Afis tucked his bow across his back and leaned into his stallion's mane, as Via had taught him. For the first time, he felt a new sensation surging through his veins. But then a darkness flooded his thoughts: *Is my killing today any different than the killing the Blood Bearers uphold?*

"The men broke through your magic, Vic," Afis called out. "Try another!"

Vic glanced over his shoulder, locking eyes with a young man at the front of the enemy formation. He pictured his chosen victim's steed as he pointed and shouted, "Sukrl kazam tuk!" Vic looked ahead again as a bright orange light lit up the corners of their eyes.

How do you feel, Vic? Snook asked while remembering his forest cat encounter. *Last time you used that spell, you said it weakened you.*

Vic's voice was faint, distant: *I need a moment to recover. Your energy helped, but the pressure...it drains me.*

Hang in there, Vic. I think you might just get your rest. Ears swiveling, Snook turned, sharp and abrupt, then braced himself in the grass. With his tail stiff and upright, he growled, bared his teeth, and released a thunderous and triumphant bark.

Via turned Zukav's head as he snorted, lather foaming at his mouth; he trotted in place, anxious to continue moving. She peered past Snook. "They're leaving!" she exclaimed.

Her raised voice startled Afis' stallion into rearing, over and over. Heart pounding in his ears, Afis clung to the chestnut for dear life, watching as the ground grew closer and then distant from his face, over and over. Out of the corner of his eye, he saw Via dismounting and rushing toward him. She spoke in soothing tones to the stallion, reaching for his nose and guiding him to the ground.

"Are you all right, Afis?" she asked, peering around the horse's head.

Shaking, Afis dismounted, dropped to his knees, and vomited. "Better."

Vic chuckled, coming up beside them, still on Azeri. "Seems like your stallion is a little on the skittish side."

Stroking the horse's nose, Via smiled. "But with my help, you'll be able to control him in no time at all." She offered her hand to Afis. "Ready?"

He glanced up. "For what?"

Shading his eyes, Vic squinted toward their pursuers. "They may be retreating, but we need to keep a safe distance ahead. We ride until dusk."

"Just a few more hours," Via reassured Afis. "You can do it. Keep your stallion at a steady pace alongside Zukav, and I'll guide you."

As they rode, Snook panted alongside Azeri. *Vic: my instincts went on fire as we hunted, Afis and I. I knew danger was close. But I couldn't reach you.*

I was…distracted, Vic admitted.

I can feel the hesitation in your tone, Vic. What happened?

Nothing. Vic changed the subject: *I must say, you have a keen skill of sensing danger.*

You didn't see him, but their leader – I recognized him, Vic.

Vic raised an eyebrow. *From where? Drema?*

No, from…the one who attacked Kaio! Snook projected their shared memory. *It was him. What was his name?*

A chill went down Vic's spine. *Tierm.* In response, Vic sensed Snook tightening as he ran. *Are you certain?* Vic prodded.

Yes. Don't tell the others.

Placing a hand on Zukav's neck, Via felt how warm his hide was from both suns. She brought him to a halt, circled back. "Vic, both suns are almost set, and the horses are exhausted." Her stomach growled. "Besides, we're overdue for lunch."

Trotting over to her on Azeri, Vic nodded. "And you've found the perfect spot: this spring provides an excellent way to water the stallions."

Afis felt nauseous again but managed to speak: "I thought you told me around the fire the other night that...there are only three rivers in the Plains and one by Armoth. Which one have we found?"

Dismounting, Vic led Azeri to the spring and shrugged off his pack, massaging his shoulders with a satisfied sigh. "None. As I told you at the fire, the Upper and Lower Springs, Whirlpool River and Bear Claw River are our main sources of water in Lilligrav. But there are countless lesser springs, like here, that provide us hydration. Then there's the oasis Polaski is built upon. That was the main source for Whispering Sands wanderers."

"Whispering Sands?"

"A semi-desert at the foot of the Wilderness Mountains." He dismissed Afis' puzzled expression with a wave of his hand. "Enough geography. I'm tired."

Splashing water on her face, Via glanced at Afis. "You can dismount now, you know."

Afis shrugged. "I don't think I can."

She laughed. "Are you afraid, or are you unable to?"

"He might run. And my legs burn like fire."

Kissing the chestnut's nose, Via smiled. "He won't run. Besides, Azeri wouldn't let him." Helping Afis down, she nodded toward their new four-legged recruit. "What will you name him?"

As he dismounted, Afis groaned, rubbed his legs. "Fire."

"Ralas," Via muttered.

"What?"

"The elfin word for 'fire' is ralas," Vic explained, glancing over, sitting down on a protruding stone. "It's customary to use ancient language for nomenclature."

Afis gaped.

"He means: we often name things with elfin words," Via said with a laugh.

Massaging his legs with water, Afis winced. "Ralas it is." He scooped up the grouse hanging over his shoulder and passed them to Via. "Since we're both starving…"

She grinned. "I wondered if your hunt was successful – aside from discovering we have enemies, as Kaio said." She looked at Vic. "These feathers will provide for your next batch of arrows."

"Kai," and Vic laid his head against the stone. "But first, we rest."

Voice in the Wind

Afis watched as the world awoke at the touch of both suns' rays. Beyond the crest of the hill, he caught sight of a sleepy wild dog raising its head, snuffling the wind, and then shaking its mane of fur. High above, he heard the cry of a falcon, cresting through the dawning light. By the spring, the three stallions stood together, dreaming. Zukav's head rested against Azeri's back, and Afis' new stallion – Ralas – snorted in his sleep. Their colors blended together in a cheerful, pleasant way as the sunslight reached across their withers, tickling them into swishing their tails.

Despite himself, Afis smiled. *Curse the Blood Bearers for wanting to taint this.* But then he was filled with the familiar anger and frustration. Breathing in deep, he picked up his bow and stepped around Vic's sleeping form.

Via awoke at the sound of Afis rummaging through Vic's quiver for arrows. Rubbing her eyes, she propped herself up on her elbow. "Afis?"

He knelt beside her. "I'm going hunting. We'll need breakfast." *After all, we didn't leave any leftovers last night,* he thought, recalling how starving they'd been. *But lucky for us, I caught those three grouse before discovering the Blood Bearers.*

She yawned. "I'll keep watch and start a fire. Bring back something big – so we can save the extra meat for later."

Afis grinned. "Done."

As the antelope doe lowered her head to drink from the spring, Afis released his arrow, hitting her side. The doe crumpled to the ground, and Afis leaped to his feet. With one blow, he crushed the creature's skull with his club. Unsheathing Vic's dagger, Afis began to dissect it, shredding the hide from the meat, not wanting to drag the doe and leave behind a trail of blood. *Not with Tierm and the Blood Bearers also in the Plains. We can't risk leading them straight to our camp. And besides,* he figured, *the spring is right here to make cleaning up easier.*

His hands became soaked in blood, but he didn't mind the smell. He kept his mind on his work, stifling the Bloodthirsty thoughts trying to break into his mind: *There's nothing monstrous about what I'm doing – merely a method of survival.* When he had all the meat strung on a branch he'd grabbed earlier, he dipped his hands in the spring water, watching the blood vanish from his skin. It swirled through the water, darkening it, and Afis sighed. *I didn't even blink yesterday when I released those arrows. What difference is there between the blood yesterday and the blood the Blood Bearers shed at Drema?*

He'd followed the spring eastward, searching for its source. When he'd found it – a rippling pool coming from underground – he waited, hiding among the grass, knowing his prey would come to hydrate for the day. When the doe had appeared, he'd caught his breath, unsure if he could take down something so large. *And yet I took down several men yesterday. Vic said it was self-defense – that we were protecting ourselves – and yet, somehow, I still can't shake the thought that I haven't escaped the destiny the Blood Bearers intended for me.*

A distant sound broke through his thoughts, and he tensed. *Was that...a horse nickering?* Ducking back among the grasses, he draped the venison over his shoulder and nocked another arrow, listening. Only a wind ran through the grass, making a soft whistling sound. But then: a horse's whinny and muffled hoofbeats. After several minutes, he caught sight of four grey legs plodding past him – and two legs walking alongside. Jumping to his feet, Afis aimed, startling the stranger, who stopped. Taking in the boy's height, Afis could tell he was younger than either Vic or Via, with blond hair and olive-green eyes. "Who are you?" Afis growled, something itching at the back of his mind: *He looks...somewhat familiar.*

With open hands, the boy backed up into his grey horse. "I only came to water my mare."

"Who are you?" Afis repeated.

"Alnitak," came the hesitant reply.

"Water your horse, but then you come with me."

Vic tugged hard on the stick, but Snook kept his firm grip on the other end: *We've gathered enough — let's have some fun!* The two of them had left camp in search of twigs for arrows, but now Snook was ready to play. With a laugh, Vic pulled again, but now Snook dropped the stick and growled: *Look.*

Turning, Vic saw Afis approaching. Across his shoulders, Afis carried a branch strung with fresh meat — but Vic's attention was on the young boy walking in front of Afis. His eyes wide with fear, the boy moved with stiff steps while a grey horse followed behind them.

Snook's fur stood on end, and he growled again: *Something burns in me at the sight of that human boy.*

Hold your bark, for now. Vic walked over, a tense Snook at his heels. "What's going on, Afis?" he asked. His heart thudded in his chest: *Why does Afis have my hunting knife pressed against the boy's back?*

It's clear he does not trust him, Snook replied.

"He came upon me at the spring." Dropping the knife, Afis gripped the boy's arm and dragged him to Vic. The boy cried out, and his horse sidestepped, whinnying.

"Careful there, Afis!" Vic warned while Afis dropped the boy at his feet.

"Search him." When Vic looked at him with a blank expression, Afis growled. "As you did me."

I haven't seen him like this for many days, Vic thought, concerned. *Why is he being so rough? The boy is just a child!*

Afis has a strong ability to sense danger, Snook reminded Vic, *as I do. You're right to trust him. Search the boy's mind.*

Vic squatted and put a hand on his shoulder. Shaking his blond hair out of his eyes, the boy looked up at Vic in hesitation. "Please, sir—"

"Hush." And Vic closed his eyes, straining his consciousness. "Stref hombä." The boy didn't put up a fight, meaning Vic could enter his mental core with ease. He discovered the boy's name – but mere seconds later, when he dug deeper, Alnitak, all of a sudden, raised barriers and redirected his roving consciousness. *Suspicious…what does he have to hide?* Vic wondered. *And who taught him such skilled mental tactics?* Alnitak continued to evade the spell, so Vic eventually gave up. He released the boy's mind by muttering, "Tjord dahla." Feeling his head spin, he staggered, and Snook appeared at his side, supporting him by slipping between his arm and body, hoisting him back up. Vic breathed in deep, feeling his senses return.

Afis stood above them, looking at him in expectation.

"Alnitak, is it?" Vic asked, and the boy nodded. "I suppose you're hungry. Afis has caught us a bountiful supply of meat. Have breakfast with us."

You trust him? Snook pressed.

Not quite. Keep an eye on him for me.

Snook sent the image of a creature shivering in fear. *Gladly.*

"Our camp isn't far," Vic continued, helping Alnitak to his feet. "My name is Vic, and my dog is called Snook."

Snook bared his teeth, and Alnitak took a step back. "And my mare is named Betel," he said.

Vic grinned. "I know someone who will love to meet her," and he winked at a bewildered Afis.

As Vic had suspected, Via greeted Alnitak with a warm welcome, even ensuring he served himself a larger piece of venison, he noticed. She'd then gushed over how well-bred and mannered the grey mare, Betel, was. Alnitak, likewise, had attached to Via right away, looking up to her with shy smiles. After a while, Vic looked away – an unfamiliar feeling warming his chest. *She's only talking with him, being hospitable. Am I really feeling...jealous?*

He raised his head at the sound of Afis clearing his throat. Afis sat across the dying fire, his eyes darting from Vic to Alnitak and back then mouthed some words. Vic shook his head. *Not now, Afis.*

He coughed in an awkward way after Via caught the motion of his head, the frustration in his eyes. Watching Vic out of the corner of her eye, she turned back to Alnitak and offered to introduce his mare to her stallions – "but we'll need to keep an eye on Zukav around her; he's desperate for a mate."

When she led Alnitak and Betel to the other horses, Vic tended to the embers, muttering directly to Afis, "You have questions?"

"Of course I have questions!" Afis said, his tone sharp. "What did you see when you searched him?"

"I saw nothing suspicious." *Well, I didn't see much at all, if I'm being honest.*

Afis leaned back, crossed his arms. "So. You trust him."

"I didn't say that." *How do I know if I can trust him? His mind's barriers were intentional, not weak like I'd expect from a child.*

"You invited him to breakfast! Via let him take the biggest cut – and I'm the one who hunted the doe!" He cursed.

Vic ran a hand along Snook's back, feeling the dog's fur prickle under his touch. "He pushed me out of certain areas of his mind. So, I asked Snook to watch him."

And I won't take my eyes off him, the dog insisted.

197

Afis looked toward Alnitak, who stood with Via, still with the horses. "Something about the boy doesn't sit well with me."

"You're still on edge from the attack yesterday." Snook growled, so as reassurance, Vic added, "But as you should be."

Afis grumbled something under his breath.

"Speaking of…" Vic paused. "I need to know that you're keeping your Bloodthirsty side under control."

"Don't worry about me. I'm fine. Our concern lies with Alnitak."

"I invited him to our camp because it's dangerous to be alone on the Plains. I learned that the hard way." He looked up as Via led Alnitak back over. "Time to find out *why* he's alone on the Plains."

"Alnitak is en route to Polaski," Via explained once closer. "Soldiers attacked his family's farm." She looked at Alnitak, gesturing for him to continue: "Tell them what you told me just now, with the horses."

"My uncle lives in Polaski," Alnitak said, rubbing his arm. "I've no other family."

"Couldn't he come with us, Vic?" she asked, taking a seat beside him.

Vic blinked. "Come with us?" he repeated.

"Of course. We may be headed to Armoth, but we both know a boy Alnitak's age doesn't deserve to survive the Plains alone." Vic could hear the break in her voice, could see the quick flash of pain in her eyes.

She pities him, he realized.

Snook cut in: *Why?*

She grew up alone on the Plains, and it was difficult for her. She doesn't want the same hardship for him. "You don't mind stopping at Armoth first, do you?" Vic asked aloud, looking Alnitak straight in the eye.

Alnitak broke into a huge grin: "Not at all! Oh, thank you so much!"

And I'll watch him every step of the way, Snook reassured Vic.

"Your family farm was attacked?" asked Afis, and all of them looked at him in surprise. He'd been quiet during the entire exchange – so quiet that they'd almost forgotten his presence. But across the fire he sat, whittling the sticks Vic had collected into arrows.

"Y—yes," Alnitak stuttered. "The soldiers burned it to the ground."

Running his thumb along the smooth wood, Afis whistled. "And where is your family's farm?"

"The farmland is outside Drema's walls, but we live inside the gate." He paused to take the goat horn of water from Via and sipped. "The governor of Levar ordered an attack on Drema. I'll never forget the sight of the soldiers, marching in with torches—"

"Wait a minute." Afis stopped whittling, raising an eyebrow as he stared Alnitak down. "The soldiers burned Drema to the ground?"

"Y—Yes."

"How long ago?" Afis gestured for the horn and then chugged the rest of the water, never taking his eyes off Alnitak.

Alnitak coughed under Afis' stare. "The days blend together. Perhaps…a few months ago?"

Afis flicked a piece of wood off his new arrow. "Interesting." He got to his feet and rolled his neck. "I'll be back," and after tossing the empty horn to Vic, he wandered off to relieve himself.

I agree with Afis: the boy's story is interesting, Snook cut in and through their bond, Vic noticed the dog's bristling anger was cooled with curiosity. Sensing Vic's touch, Snook cocked his head and whimpered.

What do you mean? Vic asked.

His story. My story. What do you think?

Vic was still confused: *Your…story?*

Afis confirmed that the Blood Bearers burned Drema, and Snook projected their shared memory. *That is also my story. But Alnitak says soldiers were behind the attack.*

I'm following, Vic said.

Our stories are too coincidental to not notice. He says he has forgotten, but a few months sounds about right. It must—You haven't answered, Snook realized.

…I have no answer.

Snook licked his paws, wary eyes on Alnitak.

"I'm sorry," Alnitak was saying, as Via patted his shoulder in sympathy. "It still brings back...I'll never forget the sight of Drema burning down. I pray to the spirits every day and night that my sisters escaped too."

"Is that why you've stayed on the Plains for so long?" Vic cut in. "Why you didn't head for Polaski sooner?"

Alnitak looked at his feet and shrugged.

You must find all of this suspicious, Snook remarked.

Vic didn't respond. Seeing Afis returning, Vic instead cleared his throat and got to his feet. "We should get moving. Both suns are close to meeting halfway across the sky, and we want to arrive at Armoth before supper. I'll pack up our camp if you'll prepare the horses, Via."

She smiled. "Come with me, Alnitak."

When the two had left, Afis came up beside Vic and dumped seven new arrows into Vic's quiver. "Now what do you think?"

"About what?"

"About Alnitak," Afis said in frustration. "I told you the Blood Bearers burned Drema to the ground. So how could soldiers burn it again?"

Vic shrugged and looked up to the sky. A duck glided overhead, most likely headed for the same place as the humans below: Armoth, or rather, Bear Claw Lake. "Keep a close eye on him."

"Understood."

"Report anything strange to me. I already have Snook watching him, but I'll appreciate your input as well."

"Can't I just take care of any...situations?"

Vic took a deep breath. "I've seen how violent you can get, Afis. We'd better leave it to my magic."

Afis growled. "Fine."

"Come!" Via called, waving them over. "The horses are ready!"

Vic approached Azeri and tilted his head when he noticed how nervous the stallion appeared: *He's pacing, but that's Zukav's instinct. Azeri is always so silent and still. Does he sense something?* Mounting, Vic urged Azeri forward. He whistled, and Snook padded up, having disappeared to chase a hare through the grasses.

The dog's ears were low, his eyes wide. *I sense danger. Nature's danger.*

Nature?

Yes, Vic.

There are no storm clouds.

All the same, I sense it.

Vic glanced over as Via trotted up beside him on Zukav. "You seemed distant during Alnitak's story." She stroked Zukav's neck. "Why?"

Looking over his shoulder, he noticed Alnitak rode directly behind him while Afis, watching the boy, took up the rear. Catching Vic's eye, Alnitak blushed, mumbled an apology, and looked away. *I must be careful,* Vic told himself. *He intends to eavesdrop.* "*You* seemed intrigued," he said, turning back to Via.

Via shrugged. "Perhaps. But were you doubtful? That's what I meant."

He lowered his voice. "Does it matter? Does your pity toward him really extend to how I feel?"

A spark of anger flashed in her eyes, and she frowned. "I know firsthand how brutal the Plains can be for a child. I won't let another suffer the same fate."

Now Vic shrugged. "We'll escort him as far as our quest allows."

He saw her straighten, almost bristling. "It doesn't take a fool to notice how you and Snook – *your* dog – act strangely around the boy."

She's not wrong, he directed to Snook.

But Snook's response was sharp: *Yet you and I may have different reasons as to why we do.*

"Just—" She paused, and Vic could tell she was choosing her words carefully. "Just remember that not all of us led the life you had growing up, Vic." He opened his mouth to speak, but she had slowed Zukav down, so that Vic rode alone in the lead.

Vic gritted his teeth. *She treats him like a younger brother. For some reason, it unnerves me.*

Jealous? Snook teased.

Shut up.

A breeze zipped past him. The Plains' weeds trembled and bent low to the ground. Vic shivered but peered closer, as the grass began to whip around, and the wind howled like a drunken soldier. He glanced up at the sky, still shivering. As Snook whined – the sound echoing deep in Vic's mind – he saw several clouds had appeared and blocked out both suns. All of a sudden, the gale blew so hard, it almost knocked him off Azeri. Trying to steady himself on the black stallion's back, Vic twisted to see the others. They were no better. The wind blew the horses' manes into their riders' eyes, blinding them to what lay ahead. The sudden and steady gale pushed against the riders and made them bend low over their steeds' necks. A rumble sounded not too far off.

"Windstorm!" Via shouted into the growing tumult, trying to raise her eyes to Vic.

He tried to respond, but the wind whacked his face into Azeri's neck. An evil cackle rumbled around him, pounding into his mind. *Did you hear that?!*

Snook whined; his mind was blocked.

The Plains' grasses tried to avoid the storm but in time gave in, bending their withering heads to the ground. The trees scattered throughout the Plains shook their leaves, unable to withstand the onslaught. Wildlife skittered into holes to avoid the wind's rage. Azeri lowered his great head and moved toward Armoth. Zukav strained forward, ears flat, and snorted in surprise. Betel nickered and stumbled several times, though she never fell. Ralas shied from every leaf blowing through the wind.

"Vic! We should take cover!" Via called out.

"We can't! Just a little bit longer – to Armoth!" Vic bit his lip and urged Azeri on.

Go back, Vic! a voice thundered in the wind.

Vic jumped, his skin crawling, and he tried to look around, but the gale pinned his face to Azeri's mane. *Snook, was that you?* But the string was cold, distant. *I swear I heard a voice!* "What did you say, Afis?" Vic shouted.

Afis' reply came from far away: "I didn't say anything!"

"It's the wind, Vic!" Via choked out then pointed feebly. "Those trees will be good shelter from the storm. We can wait it out there!"

You'll never make it, Vic. Turn back now.

Who are you?

Oh, don't tell me you've forgotten me already.

Vic panted for air, eyes widening, heart pounding in his ears. *The Dark One!* "That! Did none of you hear that?!"

"What the hell are you talking about, Vic?!" Afis shouted, irritated. "There is nothing but the bloody wind, which you are forcing us to endure!"

Shaking, Vic gestured to Via. "Lead us to the trees, Via!"

"Finally," she muttered, turning Zukav's head, as Alnitak and Afis followed suit.

Mere trees won't protect you from my powers, Vic. If you choose to continue your foolish quest, I shall torment you until you fail in the end. But leave now, and you won't hear me again.

I can't stop now. Kaio is counting on me. But his mind was filled with the memory of Manno writhing in agony – and an evil chuckle echoed deep in his mind.

You and I both know Kaio is dead. So, are you willing to sacrifice your life and your friends' as well?

"Vic, wait, what are you doing – turn Azeri's head!" came Via's distant voice. He knew she'd realized he hadn't followed, that he sat frozen on an immobile Azeri as the giant black stallion bowed his head to the wind.

Vic? Snook spoke up for the first time since the storm had begun.

203

Snook, I can't—He said—Help me— Vic grasped Azeri's mane as his fingers became numb. Above him, the sky loosened with hailstones, which pelted the ground without mercy as the wind continued to howl.

See my powers, Vic? the taunting voice screamed. **Cursed or not, I still wield control over Nature herself. You've no choice but to heed my warning and turn back!** As this last threat died away, a fist-sized hailstone struck the back of Vic's head, knocking him out. He toppled off Azeri.

Blackness.

When Vic regained consciousness, he found himself lying among the grasses of the Plains with his back against a tree trunk. He winced, feeling something bound tight around his head. Reaching up with his hand, he deduced it to be a bandage made from cloth. He glanced down and noticed his outer tunic was torn, a piece missing.

A muffled yawn came from his right. Snook's head rose from the crook of his arm. With another yawn, Snook displayed his sharp teeth, followed by his pink tongue as it rolled out of his mouth. Vic smiled as the dog licked his arm.

"Morning, Vic," came Via's voice, and he looked up. She was tending to a small fire but glanced over her shoulder at him. The five horses grazed nearby.

Vic groaned. "What happened?"

With a smile, she moved to sit beside him. "A hailstone hit the back of your head, and you blacked out. We dragged you to the trees and waited the windstorm out with the horses protecting us from the gusts. You were out all night. Afis and Alnitak have gone off hunting." Snook barked, and Via smiled while tilting her head at him. "Snook lay beside you all night and morning. He's a faithful dog." Then she laughed. "As if you didn't already know that." Snook nuzzled his head against Vic's chest, and he scratched the dog's ear in appreciation.

Via reached for Vic's head, but he drew back, shaking his head, until she pointed out: "It was a nasty bruise, Vic. That's the third bandage I bound around your head – it might be time to inspect again and rebandage you."

With a groan, Vic closed his eyes. "I dread to see the bruise."

"Then don't. Well, you can't anyway: it's on the back of your head, after all."

He sighed. "I want to feel it." *I already know what he's capable of. This won't be any sort of consolation. But still…*

"Well, then, be careful when you touch it," Via said, untying the knot, "as you might black out again." With careful fingers, she unwrapped the bandage. Supporting Vic's head by cradling it in her arm, she grasped his hand and guided it to the wound. Sucking in his breath, Vic winced – eyes shut – as his fingers brushed against the bruise. It felt as large as his fist, and he imagined it was an ugly blue-purple color.

"Is it bad?"

Via shook her head, ripping some cloth off the bottom of her dress. "Just large and dark-colored, but not as bad as it could be. If you keep the bandage on throughout the day, it should heal well."

She whistled while wrapping the cloth around his head, and Vic tried to keep himself from watching her lips move. And yet, he couldn't help himself – and the strangest feeling surged through him. Vic couldn't quite describe it, couldn't quite understand it – but he felt, yet again, drawn to Via. *What does it mean, though? Is it just our destinies intertwined?*

When finished, she brushed back stray strands of his hair. "Is it too tight? That was my biggest worry when you were unconscious."

"No, it's fine." He waited, thinking. "Any chance we could leave it off?"

"And risk infecting the wound?" She shook her head. "Don't be ridiculous, Vic."

"When we reach Armoth later today, we might get questions. We don't want to raise suspicions."

He could tell by the conflict in her eyes that she knew he was right. But then she sighed. "Then we'll take it off when we near the gates."

"Agreed."

She half-smiled before standing up, leaving Vic to sit back up of his own accord. "Want some lunch?" she asked. In response, his stomach growled, and she laughed. "I saved the last of yesterday's venison for you."

Grateful, Vic accepted his food and turned at the sound of Snook's whining. He had laid his head on Vic's chest, looking up at him with large, sad eyes. Vic muttered under his breath. *Are you honestly begging right now?*

Snook grinned, his tongue rolling out again. *I already ate mine, but if you're willing to share...* Breaking off a chunk, Vic passed it down, and Snook licked it up. *Now,* the dog continued, *about this voice. Afis thinks you might be a little crazy.*

Vic rolled his eyes, frustrated. *I'm not crazy.*

I never said you were, Vic. But no one else heard it.

Well, I did. He paused, recalling a memory and projecting it across their thread. *And it wasn't the first time.*

Snook perked up, ears alert. *You never told me before.*

I didn't want to worry you, but now that it's happened again...I have no choice. I need someone to discuss it with, Vic admitted.

Who was it?

The Dark One.

Snook growled, a soft sound so as to not alarm Via. *I heard the stories my old master told my young master to keep him inside the gates at night.*

They're true. I grew up on the stories as well. Vic sighed. *Snook, the Dark One told me to turn around.*

As in, abandon our quest?

Yes.

Snook looked at him, head cocked. *Well, are you?*

All the memories Vic had of the Dark One rolled back into his mind, but he kept them from Snook. *A man I looked up to once said that to be a ntéh, you must risk something. To rescue you, I risked the safety of my home with my uncle. And for Kaio, I'm going to risk the Dark One.*

It's very...risky, Vic.

Trust me. It doesn't exactly sit well with my stomach. He glanced at Via stringing feathers to the arrows Afis had whittled. *I need a distraction,* so he said aloud, "Did you ever know any boys, Via?" Teasing, he winked, aware of the unknown feeling surging through him again.

She glanced at him, confused. "Of course. Merchants and soldiers...Storytellers from around the city fire..."

"No, no!" He laughed. "Boys your age!"

Blushing, she brushed some hair behind her ear. "I was too young then, Vic, and there's most definitely a shortage of boys in the Viper Plains. But I knew a few. Sons of fellow merchants. They used to tease me when they played." She grimaced, and Vic wondered why.

Vic slid the last of his venison to Snook, who gobbled it up. "As I discovered for myself, Levar is much different than Dugar. Were you ever betrothed? Or do merchants not hire matchmakers for their heirs?"

She avoided his gaze, mumbling, "Why the sudden interest in boys?" Pausing, she drew a line in the dirt with her fingernail. "They are unimportant, so I cannot understand where this is coming from. Did that hailstone strike you a little too hard?"

"Pure curiosity, I swear. You take in Alnitak like a brother, which intrigued me."

"I told you, I see pieces of myself in him." She kept her eyes downcast. "I was never betrothed. Father didn't believe in matchmaking – but yes, many merchants do to combine houses. It's good for business."

"So, it seems that Afis and I are your first male companions."

"I suppose I could say the same about myself," she replied, raising her head to meet his gaze. "I am *your* first female companion, am I not?"

Vic blushed.

She smiled in a teasing way. "What about you, then: girls?"

He shrugged. "None of the village girls ever took my fancy. I don't have time for all that courting and marriage stuff, anyway."

She stared off into the distance. "I'm sure when you return home, you may think differently."

Vic watched her, wondering. He took in her face, her pink cheeks, and her red lips. His gaze wandered over her tan skin, and he realized she was not like any girl he'd known back home. *All of them come from good homes and good families. Via's the only one I've met who's had to fend for herself. Perhaps that's all I'm feeling: admiration.*

Via stood. "Well, *that* was an interesting conversation. Shall we discuss career choices next?"

He opened his mouth to joke back but was interrupted by Afis' shout as he and Alnitak appeared over the crest of a hill. Snook bounded over to them, avoiding Alnitak but greeting Afis, who patted him on the head. Coming up to Vic, Afis grinned. "Ah, the fighter has awakened! What a bruise, Vic. Let's hope it heals soon." He dumped his bow and quiver beside Vic's. "No luck today. Seems the windstorm drove much of the wildlife out of sight."

"Armoth is a mere half-day journey," Vic said. "We should be able to get food there."

A Scroll

Their four horses, sweaty from both blazing suns, loped toward Armoth. Not too long ago, Vic had removed his head bandage, knowing that they'd reach Armoth before suppertime. He could feel Via's eyes on him, worried about any infection – *but a head bandage would pose too many unanswered questions,* Vic reminded himself, *which we cannot risk. Thank the spirits my dark hair hides the bruise well.*

Behind Via rode Alnitak with Afis taking up the rear. But Vic dared not glance over his shoulder, in case Via should catch the knowing look between him and Afis: *She still doesn't understand our suspicions...perhaps she never will.*

When a fat wild dog passed their path, Vic had laughed at the sight of the creature's swollen belly swaying from side to side, which reminded him of Zurze after dinner. But Snook had growled and chased the wild dog off. That *takes care of that,* the dog said.

It didn't hurt us. You could have left it be.

Snook growled again from his position beside Azeri. *I always trust my instinct more than sight,* as he projected an image of Alnitak riding Betel behind them.

Vic sighed.

So, remind me: who do we seek in Armoth? Snook asked.

Kristoff, the Storyteller.

Why the Storyteller?

My cousin Zurze once told me that Kristofer was the wisest Storyteller he'd met, Vic explained. *Whenever he traveled, he tried to make time to visit him because of how wondrous his stories were. Kaio said to find someone with great knowledge in Armoth. Who else but Kristofer could it be?*

Let's hope he has some answers, then.

Before long, they reached the multitude of travelers swarming together to make their way through the massive gates of Armoth. While they merged their way into the throng, Vic shifted on Azeri's back. "Why are the gates open, Via? Where are the guards letting us in?"

Via pulled back on Zukav's mane to keep him from stepping on a running child; the closer they got to the gate, the tighter the crowd around them became. "Most are stationed on the ground instead of above. It's market day, so all the merchants are entering to sell or trade goods. Might as well keep them open for the other travelers too. But trust me, there are more hidden among the town." She looked up and pointed. "And see, there's another."

He followed her finger. The guard was dressed in a brown hood and stood peering down at the flood of people entering. "I didn't notice him before," Vic admitted.

"Their aim is to blend in," Via explained. "He doesn't have to do much, so he sits back. The guards on the ground keep the crowd under control."

As they passed through the gates, delicious smells wafted toward them, and overwhelming sounds erupted in their ears. Sight followed soon after: countless stands lining the main road. Everywhere around them, merchants cried out, trying to promote their goods. Zukav snorted, backing up, as one man thrust a creamy cake under Via's nose. "Take a whiff," but she just moved Zukav forward.

Snook trotted alongside Ralas, his ears swiveling, taking everything in.

Vic noticed Via kept her gaze ahead, but he couldn't resist tasting and smelling the samples merchants stuffed in his face. *If they're free, then why not?* he figured.

The stink of horse manure reached their noses. The horses relaxed underneath them at the scent of their own kind. When the public stables came into view, Vic dismounted, saying, "I'm off to fulfill Kaio's instructions." He caught Afis' eye. "Afis and Alnitak: brush and wet down the horses. They deserve a good cleaning."

Afis nodded, sharing a knowing look with Vic.

"Via: take these silver pieces and get some appetizing food," he finished. "You're the best at bargaining, after all."

She chuckled. "I'd be a sorry excuse of a merchant's daughter if not."

Satisfied, Vic strode off with Snook following. Eyes restless, Vic searched the crowd. Several people walked by, but no one glanced his way. *I need to find someone to ask directions. But none of them seem…friendly.*

Or trustworthy. Snook growled at a guard dog underneath its master's table. The dog raised its head from sleeping, bared its teeth, and vibrated with a growl.

Vic shot the owner an apologetic look. *Snook, please don't.*

Someday, you may be grateful for my instincts. Someday, Vic.

A street urchin darted by. His dirt-caked chubby hands clung onto a slice of melon, and juice dripped off his chin, making Vic guess this was not the child's first fruity treat. Vic tapped his shoulder. The urchin halted and gripped his melon tighter. "Mine."

"Yes, yours," said Vic. "Just direct me to the Storyteller's home."

The urchin stuffed the melon into his mouth, distorting his face for a moment. As he chewed, he spat out, "What will you give me?"

"A coin. Hurry, please."

The child grinned, pieces of melon sticking out from the gaps in his teeth. He pointed further ahead as he said, "Just continue on until you see a brick hut leaning against the wall. He's in there."

"Purra." Vic pulled out his money pouch. The child shot him a questioning look. "It means 'thank you.' Here's your payment." Taking the copper coin into his sticky hands, the urchin folded his fat fingers over it. He bowed in an inelegant way before rushing off. *Maybe now he'll buy the melon slice.* "Come on, Snook; this way."

Snook barked and plodded alongside Vic.

As the urchin had said, they came to a hut leaning against the wall. Vic pulled on the bell, and an older bearded man answered. Vic swallowed, clearing his throat. "Kristofer?"

"Yes?" The man pushed his spectacles up with a gnarled hand.

"My name is Vic – I'm cousin to Zurze. I came to ask you about—"

Kristofer put a finger to his own mouth. "Hush, for we must go inside to talk. Everyone has ears for someone else's problems." He motioned them in. As they entered, Vic couldn't help but gasp: the entire room was lined with bookshelves, each stuffed with books and parchments, various trinkets sticking out from the gaps between books. *He must be a marvelous Storyteller, having so much knowledge at his fingertips.*

Snook stretched and lay down by the front door. His tail thumped the ground, creating a steady rhythm. Ears alert, he yawned and rested his muzzle on one leg.

The Storyteller took a smoking pipe off a decorated chest and gripped it between his teeth. "Come, sit," and he gestured to two chairs. He took two puffs from the pipe before nodding at Vic. "I've been expecting you, lad. Go ahead and ask." A vein below Kristofer's eye pumped in a hypnotic way as he spoke, beat for beat.

Expecting me?! Did Kaio warn him I was coming? "I was wondering about this bookmark," as he produced it from his pack. "I was instructed to find its owner, but I don't recognize the name provided. Perhaps you'll recall it from your many stories?"

The elderly man looked the bookmark over, handling it with gentle experienced hands. His cracked fingers, the knuckles knobby, seemed so earthy and worn compared to the exquisite craftsmanship. Vic tried to explain where he'd gotten it, but Kristofer held up a finger. "I already know, lad. Kaio was my colleague, although our relationship was much more than that."

Vic caught the past tense. "He was my mentor."

"We both lost someone important to us then. May his Yrcr avenge his death." At the sight of the name etched on the back, the Storyteller puffed on his pipe. "Aye, that's the owner's name. But, before I explain further, you must promise me that you'll not show this bookmark to anyone nor tell anyone about it or what I will say. Are we understood?"

Vic hesitated, biting his lip, but Snook interrupted his thoughts. Emotions gushed over to him, traveling in a steady rhythm to Vic through their mental bond. *My senses find nothing dangerous about him,* Snook told Vic, *and Kaio wouldn't have sent us to someone untrustworthy. Besides, I know we're both bursting with curiosity!*

Vic bowed his head, saying: "You have my word."

Kristofer smiled, pleased. "Good. Then let us continue. Only a few of us have heard of Hopacias. All who knew him on a personal level are dead – except one." The man spat into the fireplace, a short curse on his lips. Vic pondered this, remembering it for another time. "I myself have never met him," Kristofer continued, passing the bookmark back to Vic.

"But," he added, with a mysterious wink, "I know how to find him." He leaned over to the side, running his hand along the underside of the decorated chest. With a satisfied cry, he pulled out a scroll. It was tattered and secured with a red-blue ribbon. As he dusted the scroll off, the Storyteller nodded toward the chest. "Your cousin made that."

Vic got to his feet and ran his hand along the surface of the chest. Tears welled in his eyes as he felt the grooves in the wood, imagining Zurze's dusty hand curling off the wood, shaping the corners – pressing his palm against his handiwork in pride. The warmth of his cousin overwhelmed him: *I…*

What is it? Your cousin?

Snook moved to come over to Vic, but he sent a firm signal: *I'm fine. I—I don't want to talk about it.* Swallowing, Vic returned to his seat by Kristofer, who handed him the scroll. Vic looked it over, running his hand along the parchment.

"This will lead you to Hopacias." Kristofer patted the scroll in Vic's hands. "There are many who hoped for the journey you are about to take, but they were not the lucky ones," the Storyteller mused. "And then there are those, like me, who have guarded the pieces of our history that will help guide you."

Vic paused, feeling as if the scroll weighed him down all of a sudden. "But…who exactly *is* Hopacias, sir? And—and why me?"

"You have many questions, but Hopacias is the one with the answers. There isn't much more I can tell you, for fear of enemies searching your mind. But then again," Kristopher added with a smile, "you already knew that." His face grew somber. "Let me tell you something before you go: there will be trials and trouble on your way. The road to triumph is not an easy one. And the road you are about to take is a long one indeed."

Vic stood to leave. "Purra, Kristofer." At the front door, he paused, turning back. "Could I ask you a question – a personal one, if you don't mind?"

The man nodded.

"How did you learn magic? Zurze intended to ask next time he visited," Vic explained. *At least it's not a lie – just a truth without context.*

The Storyteller stroked his beard, puffed on his pipe. "Becoming a Storyteller is rare, with only those chosen learning the process. But," he added with another wink, "I didn't learn magic through the Camp, if that's what you mean."

No wonder Kaio sent me here, Vic realized. *He knew Kristofer also learned magic in an unconventional way.* "If my cousin should come by, please don't tell him the details, just tell him I'm all right."

Kristofer nodded. "I understand. May the spirits protect you, lad."

It wasn't long before Snook and Vic found themselves back among the colorful stands of the merchants – but the crowd around them moved like molasses. *Great, we're stuck,* Vic groaned when he, on accident, locked eyes with a fisherman at his stand. "Fresh fish! Just caught this morning at Bear Claw River! Want a taste, sir?"

Vic ran his thumb along his chin. "Well, I—"

"You won't regret it!" The fisherman displayed a silvery trout to Vic, who grimaced at the unseeing eyes staring hard at him.

Vic shrugged. "A sample, if you please."

The fisherman smelled of sweat and hard work and even a bit of saltwater. Pulling out a knife and chopping the fish like an expert, he began to speak, and Vic recoiled at the smell of his breath: rotting fish and beer blended together. "Some days, it seems there aren't any fish. But I am lucky. They always bite at my rod – and my pup ain't so bad either!"

Vic rubbed his temples as the fisherman rambled while still cooking. Movement above caught his eyes and looking skyward, he saw a dark eagle circling above. Its beady eyes danced along the fish being cut up. *A tamed fishing eagle – or just a hungry predator?*

At long last, the fisherman held out a cooked square of fish in his dirty palm as a wonderful aroma filled Vic's nostrils. "Go on, take a bite."

"Thank you." Vic reached to take the fish from the fisherman when he was startled by the sound of angry barking behind him. *Snook?* he projected without looking.

Shouts rang out among the crowd: "Look out! Attack dog!"

Concerned now, Vic turned. *Snook?* he asked again.

But Snook was nowhere in sight. Instead, a drooling and snarling mongrel was bounding toward Vic through a gap in the crowd. Any second, he realized, the dog would be upon him, closing its giant and strong jaws on his skin. Reacting out of instinct, Vic shielded his face with one hand, reaching for his sword with the other, as the dog lunged, mouth open and ready to snap him apart.

However, just as the dog was about to knock him to the ground, Snook rushed out from the crowd and stood between the attacking mongrel and Vic. Snarling, he was swift to latch onto the other dog's underbelly, pulling it down. With a whine of pain, the massive mongrel broke from Snook's grip and rolled away. Blood dampened its underbelly. It stumbled to its feet, and Snook growled a threat: *Stay away, mutt.*

The mongrel shook itself, snarling once again. The two dogs faced each other, pacing, circling. Their fur was bristled, teeth bared, eyes flaming with fury. Legs stiff and tails tense, both continued to circle each other, each wanting to start but afraid and unsure when to move first. After a tense few moments, the mongrel bolted at Snook who barked deep in his throat and sidestepped. He winced as the other dog tripped over his back leg. Recovering, the mongrel turned, sharp and abrupt, to then run back at Snook, who leaped back, biting down hard on the back of the mongrel's neck, while the other pawed, desperate, at Snook's chest.

The crowd parted, hurrying to get out of the way of the dogs. Others rushed over to watch, and a group of rambunctious street urchins started cheering: "Fight, fight!"

Snook toppled the other dog over and backed up. His lips curled back as he snarled, warned the dog to give up now – before it was too late. The mongrel ignored Snook's threat and went for his throat. Snook dodged the blow by jumping to the side and then latched onto the dog's side. Fur ripped off it as Snook pulled away. Blood darkened his muzzle, and the droplets hitting his tongue tasted sour. With a loud rumbling bark, Snook lunged, gripping his opponent's throat, and held on. *How does the death grip feel, mutt?* The mongrel whined, desperate to pull away. Snook closed his eyes, bit down harder, tightening his grip. Within moments, his opponent stopped struggling, and Snook felt the mongrel falling beneath him, weakened. He released his jaws and stepped back. The dog was dead.

The crowd cheered. One street urchin, upset his choice had lost, tossed a ripe tomato at Snook. It pelted him, and he jumped around, growling: *Who threw that?* But the child slipped away into the throng.

Still tense, Snook surveyed the crowd, flicking an ear back toward Vic to ensure he was safe, even though their bond assured him he was. *Someone sent that mutt to attack,* he knew, keeping it from Vic. *They waited until we were separated by the crowd before unleashing him.* Now, he projected to Vic: *The sooner we get back to the others, the safer we'll be.*

Vic was leaning back, fingers gripping the fisherman's stand in shock. He tried to control his breathing but found himself shaking. "Get away," a voice whispered in his ear, and Vic winced as the smell of rotting fish plugged his nose. The fisherman leaned closer, squinty eyes darting among the crowd. "Get away before someone brings out a knife. Lucky for you, your dog came in time – but don't test Fate twice!"

Vic shivered, still shocked. With one last glance through the crowd, he sheathed his sword and dashed through the mob of people. Snook sensed his departure and bolted after him. Both were still running when they came upon the public stables. From where he stood combing through Ralas' mane, Afis motioned them closer. "Alnitak is around the corner, talking in a rough voice with a stranger," his voice low.

Vic thanked him and ducked around Betel. A man standing next to the Alnitak caught sight of him and left in a rush. Vic watched him leave. "Are you done with the horses?"

Alnitak nodded, and Betel snorted, her breath ruffling her master's hair.

"Who was your friend?"

Alnitak froze for a brief moment. "He was admiring Betel."

He's quick to answer, Vic threw out to Snook, who snarled back.

Carrying an armful of fresh fruit and veggies, Via appeared. "Look how much I got for two silver pieces," she said, laughing, a cookie set between her teeth. "I told you, the daughter of a merchant knows how to bargain!"

"Put it all in my pack," Vic said, holding it open for her.

Once her hands were free, Via bit into her treat and produced three more. "I didn't want to spoil me alone, at that price! We all deserve a sweet treat after enduring the Plains," she added, handing them out. But when she offered Vic his, Via paused. "Vic, why is there blood on Snook's muzzle?"

Vic cursed himself. "Just a minor incident," he said in a rush, cupping his hands to scoop water out of the nearby trough. "Snook handled it." As if confirming, the dog barked, wagging his tail, while Vic cleaned his snout.

"What happened?" she demanded.

Noticing Alnitak eyeing them, Vic lowered his voice. "Snook *handled* it." Before Via could speak again, he plucked the cookie out of her hand. "Like you said: we all deserve a sweet treat."

Via frowned in frustration, but to Vic's relief, she turned away.

Vic bit the cookie in half. His eyes moved from watching Via help Afis detangle Ralas' mane to the bustling town of Armoth beyond. His eyes jumped from one person to the next as each hurried by. But then he caught sight of something that kept his interest: a black horse, with a lone rider on its back.

Absentmindedly, Vic ran his fingers over Azeri's soft hide. At that moment, he realized both stallions looked alike: Azeri and the approaching one. The stallion walked at a steady pace, no spring in his steps. His body was streaked with dirt, while the saddlebags were faded, losing their color to both suns. Exhausted, his rider leaned low over the stallion's neck; a brown hood hid his face in shadows.

The traveler rode his stallion into the stable. There, he dismounted and picked the leading rope off its back. He smacked dirt off the lead before looping it around a hitching post while calling out, "Stable boy: some water for my horse – and myself!"

Vic started: *I've heard that voice before!* Azeri's ears swung forward as if he also recognized the voice; his nostrils quivered. Then, eyes dancing, Azeri nickered at the black stallion being tied in front of him.

Everything happened all at once, quite quickly. With a neigh, Azeri sprang forward. Vic, startled by the sudden movement, fell to the ground, scrambling back to his feet. Via looked over, cried out, and sprang to Azeri's side. Grasping his long, thick mane, she tugged and tried to hold him back. At the same time, the traveler grasped his stallion's rope, pulled back, and tried to steady his dancing horse.

"Azeri! Whoa!" Via ordered, with another frustrated frown.

The traveler looked at them. "Azeri? Is that you?"

"Do you know him?" Via tilted her head.

"Yes! I didn't realize till now – but there, his one white mark." The stranger pointed to Azeri's neck.

Vic leaned closer. With a confused glance at the newcomer, Via brushed back Azeri's mane and revealed the shape of an upside down 'A'. She confronted the stranger: "How did you know about it? I had forgotten – but you? How did you know?"

When the newcomer threw back his hood, Vic gasped: *the traveler from Dugar!*

"He is half-brother to Filo, my stallion here that Azeri recognized," the man explained, patting his stallion with pride. "Azeri and Filo were close as colts, so I often brought Filo to visit Azeri whenever I passed through Levar. That white mark was how we told them apart."

"We?" Via repeated.

"The woman who owned Azeri and I."

"She was my mother," Via murmured.

"I am Qupano. I hail from Drema."

At the traveler's words, Snook perked up, wagged his tail, and barked. "As does Snook," Vic cut in, thrusting his thumb toward the dog laying down behind him.

With a smile, Qupano nodded at Snook. "Aye. So, we are of like blood, no?" Snook scratched at an itch under his chin before barking again in agreement. "And you, son. I recognize you…" Qupano rubbed his dark palm along his chin before snapping his fingers. "Aha! The lad from Dugar. I recall knowing you would be traveling…" Qupano smirked, a triumphant spark in his eyes.

Vic grinned. "You were right, sir."

Qupano's eyes jumped from Vic to Via and back again. "I met you in Dugar, but Mileda lived in Levar. So, I must ask: are you somehow related?"

Vic and Via both shook their heads.

"Incredible." Qupano raised his eyebrows. "Not exactly alike but strikingly similar."

Footsteps approached, and the stable boy came running, with a sloshing bucket full of water. "Sorry about the delay, sir," he said, stumbling over his words, bowing in an inelegant. He filled the trough with the fresh water, and Qupano tossed him a bronze coin.

Filo flicked his ears toward the trough. His nostrils quivering, he moved his eyes off Azeri and stretched down to drink. "Let Azeri join Filo, no?" Qupano asked, smiling, and untied his stallion. With a snort, Filo raised his head and neighed to Azeri, who tossed his head and glanced at Via through his thick forelock.

"Go ahead." Via patted Azeri's rump. The black stallion needed no more. He trotted over to his half-brother and drank noisily, as Filo reached over to nibble at a bug on Azeri's back.

"And you are?"

Via smiled. "My name is Via, Qupano. My mother was Mileda."

"You look just like her. But why are you so far from Levar – and without family?"

"Both my parents are dead, sir," Via said, looking away.

Qupano shook his head. "I am sorry, Via, for your loss. May their Yrors avenge their deaths. I wish I could do more."

Via shrugged, dug her fingers into Zukav's mane. "No, no. That's all anyone can do."

After an uncomfortable pause, Qupano turned to Afis. "And you?"

"Afis, sir. I come from Glasiea."

Qupano rubbed his chin. "That rock pile, hm? You must be the first I've met from there."

Afis made no reply, merely stared, and another awkward silence ensued.

When Betel neighed, Alnitak appeared from behind her. "I'm sorry, but I had to do something. Everything seemed under control, so I slipped—" He paused, took in the sight of Qupano. "Who are you?"

What was he doing? Weren't you watching him? Vic demanded.

After that mutt's attack, the one person I'm watching is you. Snook scratched at an itch behind his ear. *We should be leaving soon.*

Vic noticed Qupano still had his eyes on Alnitak He was surprised to see the traveler's face hard set and stern, with a frown. And, Vic realized, he made no answer to Alnitak's question. But in a blink, Qupano turned back to Vic, his eyes cheerful again, as he patted Filo. "And where are you headed?"

Afis shrugged, as if bored. "Nowhere."

That's what they think! Snook told Vic then projected their shared image of excitement: knocking Vic to the ground at their first meeting.

Qupano rubbed his chin again. "Well, soon you must bed down for the night. Unless you have money and want to spend it, I would advise camping by the Upper Spring. You will have water, a good vantage point if attacked, and safety from village robbers." He moved his eyes over all of them, excluding Alnitak. His eyes lingered on Vic the longest.

Out of the corner of his eyes, Vic saw Alnitak pound a fist against Betel's side – but not hard enough to hurt the mare. She snorted and shifted weight away from him.

Gazing at Filo, Qupano brushed his hand along his stallion's side. "I had better be going. I have things to trade, adventures to pursue." He mounted in one fluid motion and waved. "Good luck in yours!" Then Filo trotted into the throng – and they were lost among the sea of people. Vic watched them go, remarking, *I like him.*

I do, too, Snook agreed. *But did he say you'd met before?*

Yes, and perhaps one day, we'll meet again.

"Shall we go, too?" Via asked, untying Zukav and clicking to Azeri.

Vic mounted, and the others followed suit. "Qupano knows what he's talking about," he said while recalling: *After all, he knew – correctly, somehow – that I'd be traveling.* "The Upper Spring is our camp for the night. But first, we must make it out of this crowd!"

On his watch, Vic patted Snook's side, calling him across the mental bond. Snook awoke with a growl, but Vic put a finger to his own lips. *Hush. The others are asleep, but I want to read the scroll on my watch.*

Snook yawned, stretched, and lazily got to his feet. *Well, then, let's begin.*

Vic glanced at the embers. *I'll reignite the fire, so that we can sit here and read it. We must keep to our minds and not allow anyone else to hear.* He paused. *My eyes are weak in the dark. Is there anyone about?*

I'm quite aware how weak your eyes are, Snook said, laughing across their bond. Vic watched his ears perk and swivel, catching every sound, and his nose quiver, catching every smell. *Nothing but a hare nibbling at the clover, and a stag at the river.*

Satisfied, Vic stretched out an open palm and murmured, "Ralas."

222

The fire flared again. When Vic unrolled the scroll, he gasped: *Snook, it's full of poems! Just…poems!*

Perhaps the poems are clues that lead us to…what was the name again?

Hopacias. Vic cleared his throat, projecting the poem across to Snook:

Indeed, your quest has begun
But more dangers lurk than fun.
To begin, follow the horsehair
To the red forest of the north,
The Tree of Life hides
The underground key below.

Rubbing his temples, Vic dropped the scroll into his lap. *There's not enough to go on! What does it mean?* He groaned. *Kaio wasn't joking when he said this would unfold in pieces, like a puzzle. I just wish I could see the bigger picture!*

Snook scratched behind his ear. *No matter. Dream about what you've read, and perhaps you'll wake up knowing what to do.*

Vic sighed and shook his head. *I wish it was that easy.*

Blinking, rubbing his eyes, Vic yawned. Beside him, he felt Snook stirring, licking his chops. *Any luck with your dreams?* the dog questioned.

No, Vic groaned. *All I dreamt was that mongrel lunging at me.* Propping himself on one elbow, he saw Afis preparing breakfast, and his stomach growled. *Should I tell them what we read last night?*

Of course: Kaio said we are to trust each other. Snook scratched at an itch under his chin. *Perhaps they'll be able to read between the lines for us.*

"Breakfast already?" Vic scooted closer to the ashes, whispered, "Ralas," and watched the flames leap up again.

"Hey!" exclaimed Afis, who, while setting up the makeshift spit, almost hadn't been able to avoid the sudden flames. "Give me a little warning next time? I think you singed my arm hair."

Vic laughed. "Sorry – I was thinking with my stomach and not my head." He wiped a hand across his forehead. "And now that cuchel has made me even hungrier than I was before."

With a little yawn, Via shifted, opened her eyes. "Where's Alnitak?" she asked between more yawns.

Afis jabbed his thumb behind him, toward the Upper Spring. They could see the Alnitak's blond head almost hidden among three of the horses. "He went to water our horses." He shared a knowing look with Vic.

Straightening, Vic cleared his throat. "Good. I need to talk to the two of you – alone." Via raised an eyebrow, and Vic saw. "Yes – what I'm about to tell you we cannot share with Alnitak. We may be 'escorting' him to Polaski, but that doesn't mean we can be sharing information about our quest with him."

"Did you find out anything while in Armoth?" Afis asked.

"I visited the Storyteller, who gave me a scroll with the next step of our journey." Vic produced it out of his pack and, untying it, began to recite the verse to them.

He hadn't finished when Via let out a giggle. "Wait one minute." Going over to Zukav, the one horse Alnitak hadn't taken over to the Upper Spring for fear of being bitten, she tugged at the bay stallion's tail and returned with a strand of horsehair. "Here you go, Vic: one genuine horsehair. Follow it as it flies away!" She let go, and it sailed away on a breeze.

With a shake of his head, Vic smiled despite himself. "This is serious, Via. I don't understand what the scroll wants us to do."

She shrugged. "I wish I knew. Afis?"

He was about to reply, but then Alnitak came closer, and in haste, Vic tucked the scroll back into his pack. "Breakfast?" Afis asked, holding up the spit, as if their conversation had been nothing more than casual.

While the others' chewing turned into chatter, Vic watched a dark eagle circling overhead. *I wonder what Lilligrav looks like so high above,* he mused.

We may never know, Snook replied, tearing up his food.

Once they'd finished, they cleared the camp and walked over to the horses still at the river. Via stooped low to fill their goat horn with fresh water, and Vic gazed upstream, watching the water wind through the Plains. *What would our island look like from above?* he wondered again. "That's it!" he cried, and Via looked over her shoulder at him. He laughed, embarrassed, and pointed northward. "We have to follow the Upper Spring upstream."

"Why?" She plugged the horn, passing it to Vic.

Standing by Ralas, Afis looked over at Alnitak, who was staring at them all in confusion, and shrugged. "Okay…"

"It all makes sense now. Via, if you were a bird, what would the Upper Spring look like from high above?"

She rubbed the back of her neck as she thought it over. "A strand…of water," she answered simply. But then her face lit up. "But a poet might say a strand of horsehair! Very creative." Then she gasped – "The Forest of Ralas, or the forest of red!"

Vic grinned. "Precisely."

They'd cantered along the Upper Spring for several hours before turning their horses for a drink. Then, because Betel had begun falling behind, they slowed them down to a simple walk. They'd traveled like this for not even an hour when Snook let out a long howl. *We're being followed!* he told Vic.

Vic twisted on Azeri's back to see. "Weevils!" he shouted, and the others glanced over their shoulders. Not far downstream came a band of weevils, their steeds at a steady gallop. At the head of the group rode the same weevil commander atop his blue roan. "Do we try to outrun them or stand and fight?" Vic asked the others.

All of a sudden, Snook fell into a frenzy of frightened barking and leaped forward, starting to run. Panicked, their horses whinnied and broke into a mad gallop, Zukav screaming at the top of his lungs. As if pushed forward, Vic fell onto Azeri's neck, his head spinning when he righted himself.

Snook, what in all Lilligrav?—

But the dog blocked him out.

The human riders tried to slow their steeds, but the frightened horses would not listen. Zukav tossed his head, eyes wide in panic. Betel stretched out her neck, matching the bay stallion stride for stride; sweat appeared on her hide. Alnitak pounded his fist against her neck, begging for her to stop so he could fight the weevils. As Azeri caught up to Zukav, Via cast a surprised look at Vic. Ralas kicked as he ran, screaming in fear, and Afis held back the nausea.

Something is very wrong – but why? A loud shriek answered Vic's thoughts, and as startled as the horses, he looked up.

We're doomed.

Gryphon Killer

High above the Plains soared a gryphon, with the back end of a bloody lion but the front end of an eagle. One sun's fingers trailed along its back, igniting its feathers with golden light – a terrifying golden light. Bloodshot eyes scanned the ground below as it glided in circles. It shrieked again and stretched its legs, and both suns' rays bounced off its sharp talons, almost blinding Vic below.

Vic gulped.

Beside him on Zukav, Via looked at him in disbelief: "It's been centuries since a gryphon sighting – how is this possible?!"

How indeed.

Vic shuddered at the voice and focused on the situation at hand. *The horses refuse to listen, and the weevils are gaining on us. Is this how I die, Dark One?!*

A distant cackle entered his mind, but Snook interrupted by lowering his borders and projecting: *Listen to me. Kaio taught you many cuchels, and I know you read that book on your watch. Forget the voice and remember some magic!*

Vic let out a deep breath. *Purra, Snook,* he said before shouting, "Surg!" The weevils cried in terror as bright light surrounded them, shining deep into their eyes with blinding intensity. They reeled in their horses at the wall of light – an impenetrable force, it seemed – and the commander roared in anger.

Vic pulled another cuchel from his mind but broke off mid-recitation when he heard a shriek followed by a bark of pain. He looked toward the Upper Spring to find Snook dangling mid-air, caught in the gryphon's clutches. *Snook!*

Snook growled, teeth bared, and snapped at the gryphon's leg. The creature screamed and dropped him – right into the river. He disappeared under much deeper water.

Snook! cried Vic, wary of the powerful current. He turned Azeri's head, and somewhat reluctant, the black stallion loped toward the shore. Out of the corner of his eye, he saw his wall of light fading, but the weevils had noticed the gryphon and didn't advance. For a moment, he was relieved– until he turned his attention back to Snook. The dog hadn't resurfaced, so Vic leaped off Azeri and stumbled to the shore. "Keep your arrows pointed at the weevils, Afis; I've got to help Snook!" he yelled over his shoulder, but Afis already had an arrow nocked.

Snook! He could still feel him distantly and reached out for a sense of where the dog was, but all of a sudden, the gryphon shrieked. Blocking out both suns by closing one eye, Vic saw the creature beating its wings – but then it tucked them in to dive at him. Swallowing hard, whispering a spell to steady his hands, Vic drew an arrow, nocked, and released it. Despite the gryphon's thick fur, the arrow lodged itself in its shoulder, and the creature screamed, tumbling down through the air.

Their mental bond reignited, exploding as Snook burst from the water, gasping for breath. Relieved, Vic reached out across their bond, offering energy. *Snook!*

Snook managed to stare at him as he swam against the current, a mixture of fear and relief in his eyes. *Vic...* But then the gryphon appeared again, yanking the arrow out, and extending its claws toward Snook. The dog snapped at it, but the creature dodged, picking Snook up again.

228

"Shu!" Vic shouted, pointing at the gryphon's rump. A spark emerged from his finger and traveled above the water, zapping the gryphon. Startled, the creature shrieked, throwing Snook toward the bank.

Rushing over, Vic waded into knee-high water and pulled Snook to him. *You're going to have to help me. Please,* Vic pleaded, almost unable to lift Snook's drenched body. Snook whined, and Vic's breath caught at the sight of blood mixing in with water. He dragged Snook onto shore, where the dog collapsed, panting. There was a strong wind as the gryphon landed upstream, beating its wings before folding them in. Vic looked up, unsheathing his sword again. *How do we kill it?*

Struggling to his feet, Snook shivered and shook himself, saying boldly: *I don't give up so easily.* He projected an image of a creature trembling in fear. *Let's end this.*

With a shrill scream, the gryphon reared, uncurling its talons. Without a moment's hesitation, Snook lunged, aiming for its throat. And despite the gryphon attempting to claw at him, Snook succeeded, biting through the creature's thick fur with a snarl.

Good boy! Vic charged, thrust forward with his blade, stabbing at the gryphon's right shoulder – in the exact same spot his arrow had pierced earlier. The gryphon stumbled, as the wound reopened, gushing blood once more.

Lower, Vic! I can feel him weakening!

The gryphon dropped to all four legs, and Vic stepped back, calculating. *Release him, Snook, and keep him distracted. I'll slice his neck!*

Growling, Snook hesitated before dropping, slipping under the gryphon's stomach, and barking over and over when he reappeared. The creature clacked its beak and turned, giving Vic the perfect chance. Yelling in anger, he lunged forward, impaling the gryphon's thick fur and driving his sword hard, close to its throat. "Beu shu!" he cried, and red energy rippled across his blade. The gryphon screamed, going into shock as it staggered away from Vic. He watched it writhe in agony before it collapsed, dead. *One enemy down.*

Impressive. But a gryphon is nothing, Vic.

Vic shook his head, pushing back the trembling. In a blink, Snook responded: *Reach out to me — forget the voice.*

Walking back over to the gryphon, Vic wrenched his sword free, wiped it clean on the creature's fur, and then turned back to the weevils. The commander was pacing his roan stallion in front of his men, looking over his shoulder and grunting. Vic breathed in and walked away from the bank, Snook at his heels, blood dripping from his muzzle. *What's the plan?* the dog asked.

I didn't have time to think of one, Vic admitted. *I was too focused on you to worry about the weevils.* Pointing in anger at Vic, the weevil commander grunted to his men and with a united shout, they charged, stallions tossing their heads. Taking a deep breath, Vic closed his eyes, tapping into his mental core. *I have an idea to buy us some time.* In the physical world, he could feel the approaching hoofbeats pounding under his feet. Behind him, he sensed their nervous horses pacing, and Via shouting: "Vic, run!"

But he didn't. He waited, clearing his mind and focusing on a point in front of him. Kaio's training returned to him, and he channeled his energy into a ball, placing it at the same spot, keeping his body calm and relaxed. And then, when the hoofbeats neared his chosen point, he took a deep breath. Opening his eyes, Vic thrust his palm forward and shouted, "Beu shu!" Without fail, a wall of red energy flared up, rising from the ground and rippling toward the sky. The weevils' horses screamed and reared, tossing their heads, at the base of the wall. Their riders grunted, and the commander gave a frustrated shout.

Snook, Vic strained, finding himself pulled in different directions. *Bring Afis to me.* He could hear Snook loping away, barking in a frenzy, until he returned to him, dragging Afis along with him.

"What in bloody hell, Vic?!" Afis demanded.

Keeping his attention on the wall ahead, Vic forced himself to speak aloud: "The spell is breaking down; I don't have the strength. Keep the weevils at bay with Via."

Standing upright, Afis stretched his shoulders and readied himself for battle. "Via! Bring the horses!"

Vic dry heaved, feeling the spell breaking down and tearing at him. "Afis?"

"Yes?" he asked as he turned back to Vic, bow at the ready.

"Once again, I'm counting on you to not to let your…Bloodthirsty side…overpower you."

Afis aimed, cleared his throat. "I'm hoping for the same."

Via came up to Vic, placing a hand on his shoulder as she leaned over on Zukav's back. "Vic, stop, you're breaking out in a sweat—"

"Don't distract him," Afis hissed, two arrows aimed at the wall. "His spell is about to break, and we'll have to cover him."

Considering these words, Via took a deep breath and unsheathed her sword. "Spirits help us!"

As the last fragments of his cuchel ripped at his mind, Vic sent one final message: *Watch Alnitak.*

You have my word, Vic, Snook promised right before Vic tumbled to the ground, light-headed, as his wall of energy fizzed away. At the same time, Afis released both his arrows, striking a weevil in front right in the forehead.

Everything was a blur, fuzzy, distant. He could feel the hoofbeats under his hands pressed to the ground. He heard Afis give a battle cry and kick Ralas forward, presumably armed with his club by now. Via had left his side, also, and he found himself incredibly alone as the darkness pressed at the back of his mind. **You've used too much magic, foolish child. Did you actually think you were ready for multiple cuchels on top of each other?**

I've done it before… His vision became narrow, the ground ahead wavering.

If you keep overestimating yourself like this, Vic, you'll make my part so much easier.

And then Vic found himself almost flat on the ground, his forehead pressed into the cool dirt, as a wave of nausea overtook him. He threw up, vomit dripping from his lips, but its stench was so strong – so close to his nose – it seemed to clear his mind. He found himself regaining composure, his vision returning, and his mind focusing. The Dark One's evil laughter rang in his ears, but Vic blinked, pushed himself up despite the shakiness. *I won't give up. Manno didn't die in vain, Dark One.*

Manno?!

But the voice was fading, and Vic felt Snook's touch: *Beu.* As a swell of Snook's energy pulsed through his veins, Vic raised his head to the battle scene in front of him. He saw Afis and Via each fighting three weevils. She was weakening – but Afis seemed to be growing stronger, though Vic caught the hesitation each time Afis swung at a weevil, holding back the Bloodthirsty One inside of him. Closer to the banks of the Upper Spring waited the weevil commander and the last two weevils. Vic caught the eye of the commander, who turned his stallion's head and cantered toward him.

A horse nickered beside him, and Vic turned to find Azeri waiting, patient as always. The giant stallion stepped forward, nudging Vic's shoulder. "Good boy," Vic said with a smile, stroking Azeri's nose. He unsheathed his sword, staggered to his feet, and took a deep breath to fill his lungs.

The weevil commander raised his sword, grunted as if threatening him. *You thought you could keep me from enjoying my first battle,* Vic conveyed, as he mounted and kicked Azeri forward. *Not today, Dark One.*

From Zukav's back, Via battled three weevils. They rode their rugged horses with enough skill but struck their curved swords with twice as much. She bit her lip to concentrate. The three circled their grey stallions around Zukav. The bay, wary and watchful, snorted before kicking out his back legs. His hooves crashed against a weevil's skull, knocking him off his mount. Via ducked lower as Zukav bolted past the other two weevils. Tossing his head, he veered around, once again facing Via's opponents. The weevils pulled their horses back into rearing. They raised their swords and swiped at Zukav, and Via felt her stallion tremble when one blade cut into his hide. Her free hand flew to the wound on Zukav's chest. She felt the blood dripping through her fingers. *Thank the spirits it's not a deep cut.*

She raised her own sword and knocked it flat against one weevil's head, bruising the side of his skull. She swung again, and the weevil thudded against his stallion's neck before sliding off. He lay twisted on the ground, blood spurting from the gash in his neck, and Via had to avert her eyes to keep the lump out of her throat and back to her stomach.

A flash of silver caught her eye, and she raised her head to see her last opponent raising his weapon. Out of instinct, she thrust her sword forward, plunging it into the weevil's armpit. She managed to pull her blade back out before her opponent, his face frozen in shock, began to slide off his mount.

But another flash of silver came into her line of sight. Afis' steel club collided with her opponent's skull, the force of his blow knocking the weevil to the ground. Via pulled back on Zukav's mane, feeling her heart racing in her chest, as Afis jumped off Ralas. She saw a strange fierceness flashing in his eyes as he began pounding away at the weevil's skull, each blow from his club making a sickening sound.

"Afis, he was already dead!" she shouted, dismounting, and rushed to him, shaking his shoulders. "Stop! Stop!"

He turned to her, snarling, as he raised his club. His pupils were dark slits in his eyes.

She shrieked and fell backwards, hitting the ground.

At the sound, he blinked and shivered then his eyes returned to normal. "I—I'm sorry. I don't—I don't know what happened."

"Who—what are you?!"

He sighed, dropped his club. "Via, I—"

But she didn't hear the rest of what he said, if he'd said anything at all, for at that moment, she felt the spirits tugging at her. At first, it was a faint but insistent pull – until all of sudden, it felt as if her mind was being separated from her body. Via felt the familiar nausea return, the panicked reaction her body had to the overwhelming experience.

Bending backwards, she gasped for breath as blurred images tapped into her mind: *a black sword flaming in the center of darkness; a deafening roar, but no one around; weevils scattering in confusion, clawing at the grey stones tumbling around them.*

Then her normal vision returned, and she found herself lying on the ground, Afis above her, calling to her, but she couldn't hear. Still somewhat groggy, she turned her head, only to find herself face to face with the weevil whose neck she'd sliced, his lifeless eyes gaping back at her. She choked out a yelp, but then the spirits returned, and her eyes closed as visions played out under her eyelids.

Vic and the weevil commander circled each other, wary of each other's movements. They'd been an equal match thus far, and Vic pushed back the frustration and impatience: *Let's end this!* He lunged, driving Azeri forward, but the weevil commander blocked his blow before moving into a counterattack. Vic blocked it as well, pulling Azeri back and calculating.

A black shadow crossed overhead, and the enemy glanced up. Fear washed over his face, and he wrenched his stallion's head back. The roan snorted, foam flying off his mouth. Vic watched as the weevil commander disappeared, taking his last two riders with him. He glanced up, surprised when he didn't see anything other than a dark storm cloud. *He's afraid of…rain?*

Nudging Azeri, Vic rode him at a lope to the battle site. He dismounted and took careful steps over the bodies of dead weevils, coming up to Afis, who squatted, his back to him.

Concerned, Vic asked, "Where's Via?" but as Afis turned, he found his answer. She lay on the ground, her body wracked with spasms. *Visions!* Vic realized, recognizing her convulsions from Kaio's training. "What happened?" Vic demanded, kneeling beside her and glaring at Afis. "Why aren't you helping her?!"

"I don't know how to," he replied, Vic catching the guilt and inadequacy in Afis' tone. He paused, taking a breath. "She saw my Bloodthirsty side."

"And that caused her to undergo visions?" Vic laid a palm to her forehead but drew it back at the sweltering heat of her skin. "She's in fever!"

Afis groaned and squeezed his eyes shut. "It's all my fault."

Digging into his pack, Vic retrieved the goat horn of water and poured some on Via's face. Cupping her head, he put the horn to her lips, forcing some down her throat. She stilled, grimacing. He was about to speak when a new voice called out to them. Both he and Afis looked upstream to see a young man approaching, followed by Snook and Alnitak on Betel. Afis tensed, reached for his bow, but Vic held up his hand. *Snook?* he called out.

He's my healer, Vic. We can trust him.

"Snook says we can trust him," he echoed aloud.

Afis bristled. "A random stranger approaches a battle scene, and your dog says we can trust him?"

Vic laid a hand on Afis' arm. "It's taking you over again."

Freezing on the spot, Afis gaped, blinking. Then he sighed. "No, I'm just on edge."

"That's fair, given our latest string of battles."

As Snook lead Alnitak and the stranger closer, Vic put the goat horn back in his pack, saying: "Snook has met our new friend before. According to him, he healed Snook after your…fire."

Afis perked up, intrigued.

Vic peered at the stranger, noting an amulet around his neck. It was in the shape of a half-moon, the color of a bright blue afternoon sky. The stranger stepped around the dead weevils and knelt beside them. Vic watched the amulet swinging hypnotically as the newcomer said, "We mustn't move her. She's having visions."

Vic glanced down at Via cradled in his lap. *I know that, but how does a stranger know?* "How do *you* know that?" he asked, his tone laced with suspicion.

The young man laughed, a twinkling sound, like dozens of little bells. "I'm the one who bestowed the spirits' gift upon her."

Speechless, Vic couldn't believe it: *An elf!*

The elf pressed two fingers to Via's forehead.

Via lay unconscious, drifting in and out of visions, when she heard her name called, faint and distant. She tried to open her eyes but couldn't; her mouth formed the word "Yes?" but no sound escaped her lips. But then, in the real world, her side burned in pain – a wound from the battle reminding her of what had happened. *Awaken,* the unknown voice said while an invisible hand seemed to lift her out of unconsciousness, and she gasped for breath at the surface. Her eyes flew open, and she saw Bronté looking down at her, a tender smile on his lips. She blinked and took in Afis and Vic's faces. Afis was looking at her in worry and confusion while Vic stared at Bronté.

"What—how?" she asked.

"The spirits don't always bless us with our gifts at the most appropriate time," Bronté responded. "Help her up, Vic."

With great effort, Vic tore his eyes off Bronté and scooped Via up, lifting her into a seated position. She felt her cheeks burning at his care and tried to brush the feelings aside. *Forget it, Via,* she told herself. Wincing, her hands went to her side, pressing against the small wound that had started bleeding again. Bronté laid his hands over hers and whispered quiet words. In a blink, the pain vanished, and she thanked him.

Bronté stood and addressed them all: "Come, let's leave these weevils to the vultures and find somewhere else to camp. I have much to tell you, but here is not the place." And he turned on his heel, heading back to the riverbank.

The others all glanced at each other before following, helping Via along. "What do you think he's come to tell us, Vic?" Afis asked, and Via nodded, eager to know.

Vic shook his head in disbelief. "What's more important is how many questions can I ask him?"

Past Revealed

As they all sat around a midday fire, Vic couldn't keep his eyes off Bronté. *What—how—where did he come from, Snook?*

From where he lay at Vic's feet, Snook thumped his tail. *He seemed to appear out of nowhere, Vic. Just walked right up to Alnitak and I, where we waited upstream for your signal. I recognized him right away, but he merely led us back to you.*

I never thought I'd live to see an elf.

Bronté removed their supper – a field owl he'd somehow acquired for them – from the spit and offered it to Afis to cut up into even shares. He refused his portion with respect, saying, "I'm fasting today, but I thank you."

Vic couldn't hold it back: "Do elves often fast?" *I have so many more questions, but how do I ask them all?*

Looking across the fire at Vic, Bronté chuckled. "Only when deemed necessary on a personal level. Fasting allows us to replenish our spiritual needs." He gestured to all of them. "But please enjoy your meal. One day of fasting is a mere blink of time for me."

Afis spoke up: "I don't understand: what's an elf?"

Bronté bowed in an inelegant way from where he sat on the ground. "It is the name of my people, Afis. We are recognizable from our ear shape alone." Brushing back the strands of blond hair, he tilted his head, displaying his ears and how they rose to sharp points. "We are the keepers of magic, thus Vic's fascination."

Aware that his cheeks had flushed with embarrassment, Vic coughed and ducked his head. "I only wish to learn."

"As you shall. But today," and Bronté held up both hands, "is meant for something else." All of them held their breath, leaning closer. With a mysterious smile, Bronté gestured to Vic. "Give me the pouch of unicorn fur."

Surprised, Vic retrieved the pouch from where it hung around his neck. Kaio's words came back to him: "I'm not sure if you even need it at all, but someone will instruct you what to do if *and when* you do." *Is today the day?* he wondered, heartbeat quickening, as he handed the pouch over to Bronté.

Stroking the unicorn fur, Bronté cleared his throat: "Centuries ago, before any of my kind roamed the land, dragons ruled our world. They were powerful beings, who seemed to control the very nature of Lilligrav itself. My kind was blessed to know them, to have the strongest bond with them. But, alas, all the dragons are gone.

"Before their extinction, one of the last females was chosen to bond with the strongest male dragon – to join him as the final mating pair. She is considered a good omen by my people – for her green color symbolizes new life. After mating, she flew to our very island and laid an egg in the Wilderness Mountains. She cried out to the spirits to protect her egg, for it was, and is, the last. Then she met death and the disappearance of her race.

"But the spirits had other ideas for the last egg, as the spirits often do. Upon discovering the dragons' fate, my people sought it out and brought it back to our kingdom. There, it was guarded by the Dragon Masters for many years. But over time, it became clear that the unhatched dragonling would not bond with any of the elves. And so, my people knew the egg would have to return to the heart of Lilligrav, to humanity.

"We entrusted the egg to our most faithful Ally, who was instructed to guard it with his life. Unfortunately....man had since learned of the egg's significance and plotted an ambush. Our Ally lost it, and his elfin companion lost her life. Ashamed, our Ally retreated, and the egg was lost to greed.

"Through the years, the egg changed owners as it was stolen over and over. Some had good intentions, most had selfish ones. Not many knew the exact truth of what the egg held, but those who did attempted to awaken the dragonling inside. And yet, the last dragon refused to bond.

"Now, jerdas, here is something important: there is no such thing as a baby dragon." Bronté laughed at their lost expressions. "A dragon egg is merely a vessel for a dragon's soul. Because of this, the Dragon Masters discovered a way to protect the dragonling from harm. My people came together and uttered a powerful spell: to transfer the dragon's soul into another vessel, another lifeform.

"The night of the spell, not too many years ago, the entire island shook with the spirits' rage. Your kind calls it 'The Night of Terror,'" and Bronté paused, taking in their reactions.

Afis, of course, showed nothing but confusion; the other three looked shocked. "The Night of Terror?" Via asked. "I thought our world was ending that day." Vic and Alnitak agreed. "But we were always told to blame it on the Dark One," she continued.

Bronté sighed. "That myth isn't entirely untrue." They waited for him to elaborate, but instead he retraced back to his story: "During the spell, my people begged the spirits to choose a lifeform that would protect the dragon's soul from harm. The egg cracked, and the last dragon's soul found a new vessel. The current owner of the egg – in his rage at having the dragon stolen from him – discarded the shells...but one of his servants betrayed him and, in secret, brought them to our Ally, who had been waiting for a second chance." Bronté paused to look over at Via.

She looked up from tracing shapes in the dirt; her eyes were sad. "Kaio. So. That was his secret."

"Kai," the elf confirmed. "Kaio saved the eggshells for the day when the dragon would be restored to his proper form. He sought its new form for many, many years. Until he met all of you." Bronté stroked the pouch thoughtfully and mused, "Unicorns are known for connecting to inner souls. Hence why Kaio kept the dragon's eggshells in this pouch." Hearing the others catch their breaths, Bronté looked up and smiled. "Indeed: the eggshells lay in my palm, and the dragon – the last of his kind – sits among us."

Via perked up. "Afis?"

The elf shook his head then locked eyes with Vic. "He knows."

Feeling the heat of all their stares, Vic took a deep breath. "I do." He sighed. "Will it change anything?"

Bronté grinned. "Indeed not. The spirits have already incorporated you, Vic, into the dragon's story. Through your mental connection spell, you are bonded – and bonded you shall stay."

Mental connection? Bonded? Snook repeated.

Snook— Vic began, but across their thread, he could already tell the dog understood.

Getting up on all fours, Snook sniffed the air, looking at them all. *I always knew there was more to me. I just never had words for it.*

Now you do.

Via gasped. When Afis turned to her in confusion, she pointed at Snook. "Snook—is the last of the dragons!" she exclaimed.

Snook looked at Vic with pleading eyes. *What if I don't like being a dragon?*

Patting the dog's side, Vic shook his head. *You'll love it. I only hope you'll still consider me a friend.*

Of course, Vic.

Vic turned back to Bronté, who watched the two of them with a small understanding smile. "We're ready."

The elf got to his feet. Coming over to Snook, he bowed on one knee before the dog. "This means more than I can express, jerdas. That I have the honor of showing Lilligrav the last — and greatest — dragon is beyond my words."

In a blink, the fire flickered out, and standing again, Bronté gave them orders: "Stand back and don't look directly at whatever might occur. Even I am not aware of the power this spell may contain — and the damage therein."

Vic shivered as a familiar chill crept down his spine. When no voice tapped into his mind, he looked around, fearing what he might see: *Surely the Dark One isn't...* But all he saw was a dark eagle flying above, watching them in curiosity.

Vic turned at the sound of Bronté chanting. The elf was circling Snook, scattering pieces of the eggshell on the dog's back. He took the largest piece and after cracking it in half over his head, laid it on Snook's head, between his two pointy ears. There was a loud rumble as a flash of smoke curled and spiraled to the sky. A gold light surrounded them, and they blocked their eyes from the brightness. When the light faded, Vic found himself staring up at a mighty dragon.

Snook fanned his golden wings, stretching his neck to look at himself. It seemed that all his life he'd felt squished and now, at last, was free, able to fully stretch. He extended a zaak, curling his talons in and out, relishing their sharpness. He breathed in deep and realized how much more acute was his sense of smell — it had been exceptional as a dog, but now it was profound. Craning his neck, he took in the sight of all of them adjusting to his new appearance. He growled, and the humans stepped back, eyes wide. Then the words came — for a moment, he soaked in the incredible ability he'd never had before — and he aimed for the friendliest tenor he could muster. "Are you going to say *anything?*"

Cautious, Vic approached, hands open. *Are we still friends?*

Snook smiled, delighting in their familiar touch. *Of course, jerda.*

Grinning, Vic relaxed and laid a hand against Snook's leg. "I have no words, honestly."

"Neither have I," Via agreed as she came up beside him. "You look…incredible."

Lowering his head to nudge her as gently as he could, Snook blinked. "I wish I could see what you see."

Bronté gestured to the rushing river behind them. "Why not test out those wings of yours and see your reflection?"

"Stand back," Snook growled, extending his wings. With a roll of his shoulders, he positioned himself and then leapt into the air. The Plains shook, and Via clung to Vic to steady herself. As the wind rushed under his wings, Snook staggered a little in mid-air, unsure of how to use them properly. *I thought it would be instinctive,* he confessed.

Give it a minute, Vic reassured him. *You're still adjusting to your true form.*

Within a few minutes, Snook's wings ruffled as he flexed them, feeling the wind guide him toward the Upper Spring. There was a shining glimmer as his dragon scales caught the light bouncing off the water. Hesitant, he looked at his reflection while gliding upstream.

Purring in appreciation, Snook rolled over in midair, reveling in the sight of his muscular build, two strong wings, and numerous sharp scales. Diving closer to the water, extending his talons to feel the water ripple between them, Snook growled to display his teeth and felt a well of pride at their sharpness, their whiteness. Pulling back up, he caught sight of various colors and whipped his tail under him – it came to an arrowhead tip, with small jewels tucked between his golden scales: rubies, diamonds, emeralds, sapphires. But in the center of his tail lay an indentation, as if something would be placed there. *Interesting…*

Stretching upward, Snook hovered over the Upper Spring, craning his neck to take in all the sights around him. His new vantage point unlocked the world before him, and he discovered his eyesight allowed him to focus in on a pinpoint. He snuffled, taking in the countless scents surrounding him – thousands more than he had been able to sense as a dog. *Jerda, there's so much more now!*

Send me what you feel, what you see.

Snook projected all the various perceptions – from hungering for an antelope grazing miles away, to the chilling touch of the breeze on his scales, to narrowing his vision in and out.

He sensed Vic staggering under the weight of it all, overstimulated: *How are you able to send so much?! It's so much more than I was expecting!*

Deep within him, at the core of his mind, Snook encountered an entirely new orb – one pulsating with magic, glowing with a dim blue light. *Let's just say…you'll have to teach me more about magic.*

Vic grinned. *One question: does the Upper Spring look like a horsehair from above?*

The dragon laughed – a deep rumbling sound that filled Vic with joy. *I'll have to fly higher up to see!* Then, with a steady beating of his wings, Snook climbed upward and disappeared into the clouds, out of sight.

Squinting, Vic searched for Snook's silhouette – then spooked when the dragon's voice thundered into his mind: *Indeed, jerda!*

I knew it! Vic crowed.

From where he hung in the air, Snook bristled and then let out a tremendous roar.

All those below him covered their ears, almost falling to their knees from the sound. *Come back down here before you alert all of Lilligrav!* Vic scolded.

Somewhat reluctant, Snook tucked in his wings and returned to the ground, in a not-so-graceful landing, still learning how to balance himself properly. As he shook himself, he projected to Vic while laughing across their bond: *I suppose I'll have to work on that.*

Laughing back, Vic turned to Bronté but was surprised to find the elf had vanished. "He's gone," he said simply, but Via still turned to look.

"Not surprising," Snook and Via replied in unison.

She looked at Snook, her eyes curious. "He healed you but then just vanished?"

With a slow nod of his head, Snook raised his eyebrow spikes in surprise. "Kai. It seems to be his…trademark."

With a shrug, Vic focused his attention on Snook, grinning up at him. "I can't believe I'm standing in the presence of a dragon."

"Not for long," came a sneer, and Snook's eyes turned to slits as he growled: *Alnitak*. His sword drawn, Alnitak stood between the group and their horses. His stance was tense, on the offense, and Vic caught sight of the burning hatred in his eyes.

Stepping forward, Vic raised his open hands. "I knew I couldn't trust you."

"Yet you did anyway," Alnitak mocked, his lips curling back in a sneer.

Via joined Vic, hands also raised, trying to de-escalate the situation. "But why, Alnitak?"

When he looked at her, she saw no trace of the innocent youth she thought she knew – and his voice was harsh and cold. "You were so desperate in your desire to take another orphan under your wing, Via – it was simply too easy. When the Blood Bearers sent me—"

"The Blood Bearers?" Afis growled from behind Via.

The hairs on the back of her neck rose on end. *What—what is he? And how does he know of the Blood Bearers?*

For a moment, fear crossed Alnitak's face, Via noted. "Rudolf told me you would be involved, Bloodthirsty One," he said.

Bloodthirsty One?! Via repeated, glancing over her shoulder.

"But I have yet to see you do anything worthy of that name," Alnitak continued.

Afis grinned – a terrifying sight, so Via looked away again – as his pupils narrowed. "You'll see it today."

Alnitak took a step back, so Via took her chance: "Alnitak, what is one sword against a dragon? It doesn't have to be this way. We can help you."

In response, he spat at the ground. "Help me? The Blood Bearers are helping you by purging our world of those unworthy to be in it. I am proud to be a part of their cause, and you should be thanking them."

"How long, Alnitak?" Via asked, and Vic put a hand on her arm. "How long have you been with them?"

Puffing out his chest with pride, he said, "My father is a Blood Bearer, and I carry on the tradition of my family."

"How awful," Via whispered.

I knew he looked familiar. Afis growled. *I recognized his father in him.* He remembered the man boasting about the son he'd left behind on the main island, how he'd reunite with him once the Blood Bearers returned to exact their revenge.

"Rudolf sent you to track me, didn't he?" Afis found himself holding back the last bit of his Bloodthirsty side, his entire being rippling with the anticipation of a kill. Yet outwardly he acted nonchalant, rolling his steel club back and forth in his hand.

"Yes, but I see now that the spirits intended me to kill your dragon instead. My father will be proud to have a ntéh for a son after today."

Deep in his throat, Afis snarled. "Save it. You'll have to get through me." And then red flashed across his vision, his hairs stood on end, and the smell of blood drove him dizzy and wild. He rushed at Alnitak, though the boy fearfully blocked Afis' blow.

Via moved forward, but Vic's hand tightened on her arm, holding her back. "We have to help him!" she pleaded. "Afis is...is possessed!"

"Alnitak has my sword, and besides..." Vic paused, taking in the sight of Afis pounding away at Alnitak, who continued countering each blow – and weakening. "This may be Afis' Bloodthirsty side, but the last thing he'd want to do is hurt you." He looked at her. "If you go near him now, he just might."

"You knew about this?" Via demanded.

Vic found he couldn't return her gaze as guilt rushed through him.

Disappointed, she flung his hand off her arm.

"This is my fight," came the dragon's deep voice, and the other two looked up at him. "I've wanted to tear Alnitak apart ever since I met him, and I see now that I sensed his involvement with the people who burned down my old master's village. He came here to kill me, not Afis."

I think he intended to kill all of us, Vic inserted.

Snook blinked, snuffled. *All the same.* Hissing, he snaked toward the fighters and sliced his tail between them, thudding it against the ground.

Both Afis and Alnitak fell back, though Afis was quick to leap back to his feet, snarling. In one fluid motion, Snook curled his tail around Alnitak, scooping him up into the air. Afis yowled and lunged at Snook, hitting his steel club against Snook's zaak. The dragon roared in pain, dropped Alnitak, and faced Afis.

Vic moved to intervene – *though I'm not sure* how *I can help* – when he caught sight of Alnitak shaking off his daze, grabbing his sword again. Alnitak locked eyes with Vic and approached, blade ready.

"Listen to me, Alnitak," Via said with caution, as he drew closer, a dark gleam in his eye. "They've led you astray – the Blood Bearers. They've fed you lies when—"

"Silence!" he screamed. "I am proud to serve in my father's footsteps, and he will be proud of my achievement today!" And then he raced at them, slashing his sword through the air.

In the blink of an eye, Vic gripped his connection to Snook, feeling a new sense of magic pulsating between them, and concentrated, uttering: "Ir yoi draco!"

Alnitak flew back until he collided with Snook's side. The dragon glanced over from swiping at Afis, trying to keep the other at bay. *Vic!*

Despite the fatigue tickling the back of his mind, Vic understood the dragon's annoyance. *I won't let him harm Via,* he insisted. *As a visionary, her life is even more important than mine.*

Snook straightened at these words, noticed Via safely behind Vic. With a deep growl, he pushed Afis back, the force causing Afis to push up earth. *I don't want Afis to harm her either.*

Cursing, Alnitak approached Vic and Via once more. "Rudolf told me how magic works — keep using it, and you'll weaken. You've already used quite the number of spells today, Vic. That gryphon was my lucky accident."

Vic swallowed. *He's right. I've recuperated some since the battle, but the back of my mind is weak. I need your strength, Snook.*

Gladly, jerda. And their string tightened, becoming an iron rod. *Teach me a spell, and I shall use it to protect you.* Vic sent him an image — a page from his tome — and Snook turned, concentrating on the two of them. "Elisdh!" he roared.

Just as Alnitak jumped and swung, a transparent forcefield rose from the ground, surrounding Vic and Via. Alnitak's sword collided with it, and the impact threw him back. He howled in anger, got to his feet, and began pounding away at the forcefield. Each blow created a ripple effect, but it remained standing.

"Can he break it down?" Via asked, but Vic shook his head.

"Snook's magic is too strong — but it's also new, and I don't know how long he can withhold the spell." *How do you feel?* he inquired.

Behind Alnitak, Snook unfurled his wings. *Dizzy with a new strength I never knew. You may want to block Via's vision.*

Why— But Vic's thoughts were cut off when he saw Afis come out of nowhere, a crazed look in his eye. He knocked his club into the back of Alnitak's skull, and the boy's face froze. Alnitak fell forward, crashing onto the forcefield, blood spurting from his nostrils at the impact, his nose broken.

Via yelped, and Vic shielded her, hiding her face in his arms. *I don't want the sight of Afis to provoke another vision,* Vic thought, *not after the last one she experienced.* "Don't look until I tell you," he said, his voice firm, and she gripped his tunic.

Alnitak slid off the forcefield, and Afis' eyes flashed at the sight of Vic and Via. Vic's heart pounded in his ears as Afis lunged at the forcefield, whacking at it with his steel club. *How do we turn him back?* Vic asked Snook.

I don't know, jerda. He's never been so far gone before.

Snarling, Afis pummeled the forcefield, and Vic could see it breaking, like ice splitting on a lake – small cracks now, but the wrong kind of blow could splinter the rest. *You're losing control of the spell, Snook.*

The dragon snuffled. *I let go. Was I not supposed to?*

I've never done a personal forcefield spell, for mine would be quite inadequate. Vic flinched as a larger crack appeared from the force of Afis' swing. *But now that you've let go of the thread, the forcefield will dwindle. We must switch Afis back before that.* Tensing, Vic braced himself as Afis pulled back one last time, seeing Snook in the corner of his eye as the dragon stretched out his talons toward them, intending to scoop Afis up.

But Vic felt Via stir in his arms and before he could stop her, she had lifted her head. "Afis!" Via screamed, having opened her eyes. She broke free of Vic – despite his protests – and put two palms against the forcefield. "Please, Afis, come back to me; this isn't you, Afis," she pleaded.

The monster roared, drew back, and Via screamed his name again.

Red.

That was all Afis could see. From the moment he'd first rushed at Alnitak, Afis only saw bright red splattered across his vision.

Blood.

That was all Afis could smell. From the moment his club first collided with Alnitak's sword, Afis only had the dizzying and nauseating scent of blood clogging his nostrils.

But he hadn't heard anything – until Via's scream.

The sound pierced his ears, shattered his vision, and unclogged his nose. Losing three of his senses – and regaining them within the same breath – was deeply unsettling, and Afis wobbled under the weight. He fell to one knee, got back up, dropped his steel club as he grabbed both sides of his head. "Afis!" came Via's cry, and he looked at her through the unsettling, rocking feeling. He saw her reach for him, a hand on both shoulders, and all of a sudden, his world was righted again. He blinked, brushing back the last few traces of red from his sight. "Via?" he said, voice cracking.

She pulled him to her, enveloping him in an embrace. "It's all right, it's all right," she repeated, over and over, as Afis began trembling. He dropped his head, gulping for air, when he caught sight of an unmoving body lying among the blood-stained grasses. Pushing Via aside, Afis reached for the body, rolling it over to reveal Alnitak's frozen face – and Afis recoiled and caught his breath. "Did I kill him?" he asked.

There was a pause before Vic nodded. "Aye, Afis."

Instead of red, all that filled Afis' vision was the mocking face of Rudolf, and Afis fell to both knees as raindrops splattered against his back.

Zukavnamas

Vic stroked Azeri's sweaty neck, eyeing the Upper Spring as it churned past its shore. Knowing the stallion ached for the refreshing water as much as he did, Vic gestured to the river. "We're on the wrong side, so shall we cross and cool off?"

"The wrong side?" Via asked, shifting to face him.

Vic considered her thoughtfully before answering. She'd been awake almost all night, too unsettled to sleep after what she'd learned. Vic had confessed everything, from Afis' "birth" to their interrogation – with Afis interjecting occasionally, when not in the lowest of moods. It seemed that Via had accepted their explanation, but not long after succumbing to slumber, she'd awoken screaming from a nightmare and took the rest of the watch with a protective Zukav guarding her. Vic could see the exhaustion behind her eyes, and he prayed the spirits would provide her with deep slumber at nightfall.

"The scroll directed us to Belfg, which is on the western side of the river, and beyond that—"

"The Forest of Ralas," and Via smiled, dreamy-eyed. "I cannot wait to see it."

"I've heard it said that you'll never be cold among the trees – that it's eternally warm, like the purest flame." Vic flicked a thumb toward the river. "Shall we?"

"Race you across!" Via said, jabbing Afis in the arm. Vic noticed she'd recoiled a bit, and he sighed at the thought of Via still adjusting to the truth about Afis.

Afis groaned, rubbing his arm. "What's the point? I've got Betel to hold onto."

"True," Vic said, as he turned Azeri's head toward the rushing river. "Let's make a deal, shall we? If either Ralas or Betel cross first, you win. Twice the luck."

To Vic's surprise, Afis half-smiled. "I accept."

Azeri perked up, ears facing the river. Tossing his head, he neighed and leaped into a gallop. His hooves stuck against the stones along the shore before colliding with water.

Via rolled her eyes. "Well, Zukav," she said, leaning to her left to see his bay profile. "Shall we show them who's the real champion here?" The stallion needed no urging. With a vicious scream, he reared and chased after Azeri. Laughing, Via looked back and saw Afis nudging Ralas forward, pulling Betel along by the rope Via had taken off Zukav's neck. The mare had lost interest in many things since Alnitak's death, but even she couldn't resist the Upper Spring.

Above, among the clouds, Snook sensed a change. Never breaking the beating of his wings, he glanced downward. The three humans were now headed west – across the river – laughing as their steeds pounded through the water. Snook growled in irritation and changed direction.

He was still adjusting to flying: *an incredible way to travel but much lonelier than before.* As a dog, he'd walked alongside the horses and listened to the humans' conversations, a steady buzz of comfort. But now, as a dragon, he had to keep hidden among the clouds. He could still faintly hear their words — *yet now that I can actually speak, I can't even join in.* Of course, he still had Vic to talk to through their bond, no matter the distance — but Snook found that he missed the others throughout the day.

So, he talked to himself to keep from boredom: *While the others seek the Belfg chief, I must fly straight to the Forest of Fire. Will I feel at home there? Will it awaken my own flame?* He dug deep within himself but still nothing. *What kind of dragon can't breathe fire?!*

Vic leaned forward, until his chin brushed against Azeri's thick mane. "See you on the other side, when Azeri leads me to victory!"

"Take those words back, Vic — Zukav used to beat Azeri just circling the paddock!" Soon, the bay and black were neck to neck, with Ralas straining at the tip of Zukav's flying tail.

Water sprayed in cascading arches around the horses, soaking their riders. Vic reached over and splashed Via. She ducked out of instinct before kicking back a spray of droplets. On accident, Afis swallowed a mouthful of water. Gurgling, he spit it back out and hit Vic on the back. "No cutting in!" Vic shouted over his shoulder.

A dark eagle swooped ahead, crossing their path. Its wingtips graced the water's surface, dipping in and out with each beat of its wings. In passing, the eagle fixed its eye on Vic. Caught mid-laugh, Vic shuddered. The gaze seemed too… *Human.* But then the eagle had looked away, moving farther upstream,

Too soon, the shore was at the horses' hooves. Zukav stumbled to shore mere seconds — just a nose ahead — before Azeri. The black trotted onto the soggy ground after him. Ralas tucked his forelegs in and leaped over a wave, landing on the bank. Azeri and Zukav both nickered and padded over to face each other, snuffling in each other's breath and nipping at each other's dripping manes.

Vic reached across to Via, laughing, and they shook hands. "You won by just a nose!" Vic said, grinning. "Perhaps I should ride Zukav."

"We both know he won't allow anyone else on his back!" she teased.

Leading Betel, Afis trotted Ralas up, and the chestnut dug his front hoof into the ground. "Even with twice the chance, I lost."

"But you cooled off twice as much!" Via said, laughing.

With both suns drying their clothes, they turned their steeds to the north. Zukav settled into an easy trot alongside Betel, teasing the mare with gentle nips to her neck. Azeri plodded along on Ralas' left.

"The forest we're heading to," Afis said after a while, "it's different than the Avro Woods?"

"Kai," Vic answered. "The woods we're headed to make up what my people call the Forest of Ralas – or 'the red forest of the north,' as my scroll described it. Lilligrav's third notable forest is the Mælle Shio Surg tuk, otherwise known in our language as the Forest of Abundant Light."

"Why are they called such?"

Via answered now: "The Forest of Ralas is home to the Pllatæ Ralas tuk – the fire plant. The Forest of Abundant Light collects so much sunlight that the trees brush against the sky!" Slightly rising up while on Zukav's back, she gestured upward, grinning. "The Avro Woods has trees that do not lose their leaves in the Month of the Phoenix. The elves perceived them as dark and foreboding, hence the choice of name."

"Why did the elves name everything?"

"The elves were the first people of Lilligrav," Vic explained. "When the natives arrived, the names were translated or changed altogether."

"Natives?" Afis rubbed his temples.

"Kai. I suppose the proper term for them would be Zukavnamas. Their ancestors – our cousins – were the first to land on Lilligrav, and our ancestors – Refeonamas – followed later."

"I—I think Rudolf mentioned them, but he called them savages." Afis paused. "He mentioned skin color, but I don't understand why that matters?"

"It doesn't," Via insisted. "But men like Rudolf have used that as an excuse to do some terrible, awful things. So, we should assume that the Zukavnamas will be wary of us."

Catching sight of what lay ahead, Vic pulled Azeri in. "Speaking of," and he gestured to the north.

Afis turned to see three horsemen waiting not far off. He and Via reined in Ralas and Zukav, respectively. "Do we draw weapons?"

Vic shook his head. "We're coming into their territory, which means we must do things on their terms. Drawing weapons would give the exact opposite effect we desire."

The horsemen continued watching, while their patient stallions swished their tails. Then one took the lead and nudged his steed forward, with the other two horsemen following close by. "Lillef!" the front horsemen called, stopping his horse a few feet away. "What brings you to my village?" he asked, addressing Vic.

"We come in peace," Vic responded. "All we seek is a place to rest for the night."

"Refeonamas don't visit Zukavnamas without dark purpose," the warrior said, and his two companions drew arrows and nocked them. "Perhaps you wish to see our Fire Forest?"

Vic raised his open hands. "Your guess is correct: that is our wish, but I had intended to approach your chief about it. I assure you, we come with peaceful intentions."

As the lead warrior considered Vic's words, Via noticed how muscular and bronzed his arms were. His entire torso was covered with black tattoos, most in images she didn't quite understand. His head was shaved, except for the stiff black hair in a line down the middle. The two warriors behind him wore their raven hair in long braids down their back, and she noticed a significant lack of tattoos. The warrior in front caught sight of Via watching, and she looked away, embarrassed to be caught staring. "My father,

Chief Ralan, will hear your request, but I warn you not to get your hopes up, Refeonamas."

"Your father?"

"I am Shaman, Prince of the Zukavnamas." Then he yipped like a fire fox, and more warriors appeared to Vic's left, circling in silence around the three. Shaman turned his stallion's head and kicked him forward, rejoining his first two companions.

"I suppose this is our escort then," Vic said, prodding Azeri forward. Afis and Via did the same, with Betel following along reluctantly, wary of all the stallions around her. She turned her head, whinnying toward the open Plains.

In time, the village came into sight – a spread of simple huts. Not far away, Belfg villagers looked up from their work as the warriors rode by with the guests. One man, hunting trout with a spear, straightened as the warriors passed; picking up his basket, he ran after, shouting with excitement in another language. Women tending crops looked up when they passed. Exercising his dappled pony, a young boy looked up at the sound of hoofbeats and mounted to follow. Much closer to the fringe of the village, a woman and toddler stood from picking wildflowers.

It seems visitors are rare here. "Tell me," Vic said, turning in his seat to the closest warrior. "Does the village of Belfg receive many visitors during the year?" But the warrior was silent, looking ahead, and Vic shrugged.

At the ring of huts, Ralas shied, tossing his head and refusing to enter. Afis cursed under his breath. Snorting, Azeri nipped at Ralas and passed with ease into the village. Zukav reared once, smelling mares and other stallions. Upon crashing back to the ground, though, he entered the circle of huts.

The village bustled with life. A man slept beside several drying hides – one was a silky fox fur, red with streaks of silvery black. A pair of dogs lay tethered beside him, and both quivered in excitement at their dreams of chasing rabbits. An elderly woman hunched over her weaving, red diagonals separating the blue of the sky and green of the grass. The air hung with new scents, but Zukav only seemed interested in the one coming from a far paddock, where ponies galloped along the edge of their enclosure.

Startled to hear someone shouting in their own tongue, Vic and Via both looked over their shoulders. A crippled woman, her black hair streaked with silver, hobbled in vain after the convoy. Unable to break through the warriors, she waved her walking stick over her heads, crying out: "Greetings, children! May you bring luck!" No one else noticed her, and the group pressed on.

The procession halted at the largest hut, and Vic took in the intricate design on the hide. *The chief,* he realized, at the sight of a large painted flaming tree.

Shaman dismounted, ordering the warriors, and turned to Vic. "I will precede you before my father. Wait for my return." And then he ducked inside.

"What now?" Afis hissed between gritted teeth.

Vic shook his head. "Relax, Afis. I assume this is all for show. It's clear that the villagers are excited by our arrival. Shaman will return, and I shall present our request to Chief Ralan." Grumbling, Afis looked away, and Via reprimanded him by poking his arm.

Throwing aside the door flap, Shaman reappeared and barked an order at the warriors. They spread out, giving the visitors more space. "Come," Shaman said simply.

Dismounting, they followed him through the door flap and into the cool interior of the hut. At the other end sat the chief, cross-legged on a woven blanket. His haircut was like Shaman's, but the tips of his black hair were colored bright blue and red. Behind him stood an older woman, another blanket draped over her arm.

Shaman bowed from the waist. "The visitors, Father."

Chief Ralan gestured with one hand. "Lillef. My son tells me you bring a request to enter our sacred forest."

Stepping forward, Vic bowed. "We are grateful to appear before you,

Chief Ralan. Your son speaks true: we have come with a request to enter the Forest of Ralas."

The chief's eyes were cold as he stared back at Vic. "Why? Refeonamas are not to be trusted with the sacred powers held within."

Kristopher said not to show anyone, Vic remembered, *but I have no choice. I need to prove to them our intent.* "We are not ordinary Refeonamas," Vic began. "We are on a journey, led by a scroll. It commanded us to come to your village and enter the forest. We mean no harm to your people or the Forest of Ralas." Dropping his pack off his shoulder, Vic retrieved the scroll and handed it over to the chief.

Unrolling it, Chief Ralan broke eye contact to read the inscribed words. Once finished, he handed it back to Vic. "I had a dream last night – from the fire sprites themselves. They showed me this scroll and alerted me of visitors."

Straightening, Vic asked, "Surely they alerted you of good things?"

Tilting his head, Chief Ralan paused before answering. "Kai, but tradition still stands. Refeonamas are not allowed on its sacred grounds without a gift to my people."

Vic glanced over at Via as an idea popped into his head. "We have something to trade for permission to enter."

Patting Betel on the rump, Vic turned to Shaman. "She's a fine horse, bred in the Plains." He smiled. "In fact, I would not be surprised if some of your stock is in her ancestral blood."

Shaman rubbed his chin. "The slope of her head proves it."

Outside Chief Ralan's hut, Belfg had returned to its everyday bustle, though passing villagers still slowed to peek at the visitors. Someone had taken Azeri, Zukav, and Ralas to be watered and brushed down, but now Vic presented Shaman with Betel – their gift for entrance into the Forest of Ralas. Vic watched as Shaman inspected the mare, and catching Via's eye behind

Shaman, Vic nodded, smiling.

"Jynnx!" Shaman shouted all of a sudden, and a warrior standing by Chief Ralan's tent rushed over. "Your mare was traded to Heftka warriors, no?"

"Kai, Oono."

"Take this one – a gift from our visitors," and Shaman gestured to Betel.

Grinning, Jynnx took Betel's muzzle in his hands, breathing into her nostrils. Facing the others, he bowed from the waist. "May you find what you seek in the forest," he said, offering a hand to Via.

Surprised, she placed hers over his open palm. "Purra, Jynnx." And then the warrior turned, leading Betel away to the far paddock.

"I'm studying languages," Vic said, and Shaman raised an eyebrow, arms crossed. "What does 'oono' mean?"

"In your tongue, it translates to 'prince' of either our roots or our pride, as used here and at Heftka respectively. My cousin is the son of their chief and the prince of their pride. I am the prince of our roots."

"Roots? Pride?" Vic asked.

"They guard the lions, and we guard the forest. Sacred tasks given to us by the elves themselves," Shaman said.

"Shaman, how do you speak our tongue so well?" Via asked.

"My father and I do trade with your people often." Shaman shrugged. "It therefore seemed fitting to learn your words." He looked over their shoulders. "Where is your companion?"

Vic sighed. "He's not in the best of moods, after an unfortunate incident yesterday. I'm guessing he's wandered off to think to himself. Via and I shall find him."

"Good: Father will not like him unsupervised. When you find him, take him to the hut at the far end of the village – you'll know it by the soaring phoenix motif on the door flap. It's reserved for guests, and my grandmother Ettar will have supper prepared for you there."

261

"Purra." Vic bowed his head, and Shaman did the same before leaving the two alone. Turning to Via, Vic ran a hand through his hair. "He makes me nervous."

"I suppose the shared histories between our people has put him and the chief on edge. As you said to Afis earlier, they don't seem to get many visitors."

"But I was always told the village of Belfg is the more peaceful," Vic countered, leading the way as they went to find Afis. "Heftka's people are more aggressive."

"If you think this is aggressive, I'd hate to meet a villager of Heftka," Via said with a laugh. Then, somber, she added: "Perhaps it's just instinct — after all, if your people were slaughtered by your fairer-skinned cousins in the past, wouldn't you be a little cold, too?"

Swallowing, pondering her words, Vic nodded.

Jerda, you've forgotten about me, Snook teased, despite knowing that both of them were still adjusting to Snook's true form — for a dog could be Vic's shadow, but a dragon now overshadowed him.

Nonsense, Snook! ....where are you?

Vic could feel the dragon's rumbling laughter. *Within the forest,* Snook replied. *It seemed the best place to land.*

Chief Ralan accepted us, but we had to give him Betel for permission to enter the woods.

Do I need permission? Snook wondered.

I doubt it. Besides, who is a chief to turn away a dragon? Especially a dragon in the Forest of Ralas!

I like your logic. I could get used to this.

When we go into the forest tomorrow morning, I'll look for you.

And I'll be waiting for you, jerda.

Via interrupted his thoughts: "Do you think one of us will see a Pllatæ Ralas tuk?"

"Quite doubtful," answered a new voice, before Vic could respond.

Both Vic and Via turned in surprise, to the back of a giant hut. A chuckle came from the shadows, and a young woman emerged into the dimming sunlight. "Those flowers only bloom in the beginning of summer, and every hundred years at that." She waved her hand toward the far-off trees. "Even I haven't seen one yet."

"Who are you?" Vic asked.

Via put a hand on his arm, interjecting politely: "Please."

She laughed. "My name is Tigra of the Twirling Feather. My father is Chief Ralan."

The princess of their roots! Via thought.

Tigra was of a much more delicate build than Shaman, but like her brother, she had her own share of muscles. Instead of tattoos, her suns-kissed skin was painted in reds, blues, greens, and yellows – diagonals up her arms, dapples across her upper chest. Laughing again, she fluttered her hand around in a gesture of welcome. "I was not in the hut with my father when you appeared before him."

Via tried repeating the gesture but gave up halfway through, at Tigra's teasing giggle. "You said Vic and I won't see a Pllatæ Ralas tuk?"

Tigra grinned. "Vic most definitely won't."

"What do you mean?" Vic asked, stepping forward, confused.

"Vic won't be going in."

"What do you mean?" Vic asked again, even more confused.

Tilting her head, Tigra frowned for the first time, her eyes squinting. "Perhaps you really don't know." She tossed her hair back, gesturing to Via. "Only women are allowed inside the fringe of trees, Vic."

Disappointed, he glanced toward the far-off trees.

"As the daughter of the chief, it is expected that I shall be your guide, Via," Tigra added. "And if I've never seen a Pllatæ Ralas tuk, I'm quite doubtful that you will." She glanced over at Vic, saw his look of longing.

"Don't look so disappointed, Vic – the elves implemented the spirits' will, after all. Our men have never seen what lies inside the woods, either."

Lowering his gaze, Vic kicked at a pebble. "I understand, but still—"

Via placed a hand on his arm. "I'll be sure to tell you all about it, as detailed as I can."

Interrupting them, Tigra pointed through the village. "Ettar will not be pleased if supper grows cold; your hut is not far that way." And then she turned, slunk back into the shadows, the green of her eyes gleaming at them.

Moments later, Afis appeared, and somewhat hesitant, Via pulled him to them. "Where have you been?" she asked.

"I was wandering," Afis mumbled, eyes unfocused. "After a while, I decided to come looking for you but found myself lost among the huts. I'd almost given up when a crippled woman approached me. She…she told me…" Afis looked at them, and in that moment, Via forgot her fear. "She told me, 'Good luck, one of no race.' But how? How did she know?" He gestured to himself. "I look human!" But then his face dropped when he murmured, "Don't I?"

"You look just like us," Via reassured him. She led him into the hut, speaking gentle words.

Vic stepped to follow but turned, looking back at the forest in longing. *I won't be seeing you tomorrow, Snook.*

The weight of Vic's disappointment traveled across their bond, and Snook sent a consoling image. *I promise, jerda: we'll still find a way to see each other tomorrow.*

Visionary

Vic breathed in the smokiness of the Forest of Ralas, the crisp burnt air. *I still can't believe I won't be allowed beyond the fringe of trees.*

Don't worry, jerda – as soon as you can slip away, you can teach me all about the basics of magic. Though I must say, I seem to be revealing a natural knack for it.

In the corner of his eye, he noticed Via turning to him, from saying her farewells to Afis. She'd spent the evening consoling and encouraging Afis, and Vic was glad to see she'd accepted him, without fear. "Be careful," Vic told her, eyeing Tigra. "I don't know where the fire is, but it's called the Forest of Ralas for a reason."

She laughed. "I'll be fine." Her new crimson dress glistened in the sunlight, the golden lining sparkling. With Via's guidance, Vic had purchased new outfits for all of them, which was long overdue, as their previous clothes had gotten dirty from all the battles and traveling. Though the Belfg weaver mentioned bronze for payment, he and Via had instead agreed that her skill was worth more, so they'd spent the last four silver.

He leaned closer. Mouth to her ear, he whispered, "The Tree of Life. And an underground key. Remember those." When she nodded, he moved back, and she clapped a hand over her ear. "Did I hurt you?"

"No," she stammered, blushing. "It just…tickled."

Afis rested his arm on Via's shoulder and smiled. "Don't get lost."

"With me as her forest guide? Impossible!" Tigra scolded, appearing at Via's right shoulder.

Startled, Afis recoiled, rubbing his neck in embarrassment. "I was only joking."

With a small smile, Via winked at Afis. "I'll try not to." Then, catching sight of the many Zukavnamas gathered beyond Vic, she sighed. "I've never felt so much pressure in my life."

"Come, Via," Tigra said, pulling at her arm. "The longer we wait, the less sunlight!"

"Wish me luck," Via called over her shoulder, as Tigra led her into the woods. *Take me with you,* he yearned.

Beyond the fringe of trees, Via gasped, taking in her surroundings. "Tigra, it's—it's wonderful!"

Her forest guide laughed. "Come!"

A ray of sunlight cut through the canopy, spotlighting Via. All around her, flowers and trees basked in the morning light. Red, orange, and yellow flowers dominated the forest floor, bursting through the green foliage. Moss spread like a blanket across the ground before crawling up the trees. Tracks in the moist dirt caught Via's eye, and she knelt to examine them: fire fox. As if proving her right, a scratchy bark echoed above her. Lifting her head, she scanned the trees to see a flame-colored fox poking its head from a hole in a tree. A firebird soared into view, flying inches above her head. Closing her eyes, breathing in deep, Via took in the forest scent – like a hot summer day or a warm evening campfire. "Is something burning?"

"Not quite. Some of the rarer plants have fire dancing on their leaves, but nothing is burning unintentionally." Tigra gestured around her. "Welcome to the spell of the Forest of Fire."

"Fascinating." Via touched a flower dappled with red marks. "Everything is so...so—"

"Red?" Tigra supplied.

"Kai," and Via blushed, looking around once more. "It's quite amazing, Tigra. You're so lucky to live here."

Tigra peered through the green canopy into the blue sky. "I suppose."

"Do you not like it?" Via got to her feet, head tilted.

Tigra shrugged. "I've been here too many times, Via – you could say the forest has lost its wonder. My first visit, I bolted from Ettar. All Belfg girls enter the forest on their fifth year with an elder, but I broke free on my third year." Tigra grinned, mischief dancing in her eyes as she recalled the story. "I followed the sound of birdsong, as we hear it now. I chased foxes and fawns. But hearing the distant drums, I climbed one of these trees and looked out to see my entire village spread before me. I could see the men dancing around the fire; I could see the smoke curling into the sky. I didn't want to leave. But then Ettar found me up there."

"We're alike, you and I," Via said. "My mother often found me hiding under my father's merchant table, peeking through to watch the men trade. I also never wanted to leave, but she always found me." Via brushed stray hair from her face. "She was of your blood, Tigra – but whether she came from Belfg or Heftka, I know not."

"Your mother was Zukavnama?"

Via nodded. "Perhaps that's where I get my stubborn independence from."

"More than likely," and Tigrra grinned. "At least, I'm told I get mine from my mother."

"Where is your mother?"

Again, Tigra shrugged, looking to the sky. "She died at my birth. Shaman's mother assists Ettar with the household."

"You and Shaman do not share a mother?"

Shaking her head, Tigra scratched her back on a tree. "My father keeps many a woman. In our tribe, only those born with the firemark are considered his true children." She came over to Via, holding out her arm. On her wrist was a reddish birthmark, shaped irregularly, like a flame. "Shaman has his on his shoulder."

Via reached out and brushed her fingertip along Tigra's wrist, and it seemed to her that the firemark felt warmer than the rest of her flesh. "Does 'oono' mean 'prince' or—"

"'Chosen child,'" Tigra cut in. "Shaman is Oono, and I am Oona."

"Do you have any other…chosen siblings?"

"Just Shaman." She nodded to Via. "And you? Is Vic your only sibling?"

Ignoring the blush rising up her neck, Via ducked her head. "Vic isn't my brother."

Tigra cocked an eyebrow. "The two of you look like twins, so I assumed…" She trailed off, and Via smiled in understanding.

"Trust me, we were both shocked when we met."

"I can imagine." Tigra swept leaves off her dress. "Now then. My father told me you have been led here by a scroll. Did it direct you to something specific in the woods?"

"A tree – referred to as the Tree of Life." At Tigra's gasp, Via's eyes widened. "Do you know of it?"

"But of course! After the Pllatæ Ralas tuk, the Tree of Life is the most sacred. No one's allowed to see it without direction from the spirits." She leaned in close. "Consider yourself lucky for not having mentioned it to my father. He would have never accepted your gift had he known!" And then, before Via could respond, Tigra turned on her heel and vanished between two trees.

Via moved to follow, but a strange humming distracted her. *What was that?* A flower seeming to glow caught her attention. Colored a bright orange-red, it poked its petaled head just a few inches above ground. Kneeling beside it, Via noticed a puddle of dew glistening at the center of the bloom. Gazing into the dewdrop, she saw the humming was created by vibrating ripples flowing out of its center.

Intrigued, Via dipped her finger, hoping to create more ripples and distort her reflection. Instead, the humming ceased, and an image of a field filled with flowers and vibrant green grass appeared. *A vision?!* But it disappeared, ripples forming once again, with dark red sparkles appearing on the dew. *What*— She dipped her finger in the dew again and at her touch, the sparkles leapt out, floating past a silver birch tree. Leaning back on her heels, Via watched them zip through the breeze, stood, and moved to follow.

"Via?" came Tigra's voice.

Via froze. *I'd forgotten about her*, and a wave of guilt crashed over her.

Standing between the two trees, Tigra shook her head. "Typically, you follow your forest guide."

"Tigra, this may sound ridiculous," Via began, looking over her shoulder to the birch. "But I believe we're to head a different way." *I—I just know I'm meant to follow...*

Hands on her hips, Tigra regarded Via with raised eyebrows and narrowed eyes. "It does sound ridiculous." She glanced over her shoulder back to the two trees she'd just vanished and then reappeared between. "I'm the one who's been in the forest since my third year," she said, facing Via again. "Why do you dare to suggest I know not the way?"

Via took a deep breath. "I understand, Tigra, and I apologize. But the...flying sparkles led me to believe we must go another way."

"Flying sparkles?" Tigra laughed, and Via relaxed.

She's not too upset with me. "They're gone now, but they flew that way," and Via pointed to the birch.

"Where did they come from?"

"This flower."

Tigra knelt beside the bud, reaching out to trace the leaves with her fingers. "Incredible. It's a RalasRefeo flower, yet you saw the fire sprites' signal, when forest lore says they appear in the bloom of a Pllatæ Ralas tuk." She turned back to Via, eyes narrowed again. "What aren't you telling me?"

"N—nothing," Via stammered and moved to the birch. Just beyond the tree, the sparkles hovered in the air, like a swarm of bees. Via smiled — hearing music, she felt the fire sprites calling to her, beckoning.

Tigra appeared at her side and gaped. "Amazing."

"What?"

"You're a visionary, aren't you?"

Reaching out to the sparkles, Via nodded, distracted. "Yes…"

Before she could even touch them, the sparkles spiraled toward the clouds and zipped beyond the trees. Tigra and Via ran after them, pushing aside foliage as they passed. A red squirrel skittered up a tree, where it began scolding them. Ears flopping, a speckled fawn trotted away, joining its crimson mother in the underbrush. At long last, the sparkles stopped before a ring of evergreen trees which, with their interlocking and close branches, blocked off whatever lay beyond. Via and Tigra tried to stop in their tracks but stumbled, falling onto the ground instead.

"What in the name of Ralas—I tripped," Tigra muttered, rubbing her ankle.

Via helped her up. "Me too. But on what?" Confused, she searched for the culprit before gesturing to the forest floor at their feet. "There's nothing here."

"Something below the surface then." Brushing off her dress, Tigra glanced to the right and left, but the fringe of evergreen trees was endless. "Now what?"

"I don't know."

"You're the one who awoke the fire sprites, so my time as your forest guide is over. You're the visionary." Tigra nodded to the sparkles. "What are they telling you?"

Nothing. I don't know anything about my…gift. Humming, the sparkles shot through the ring of trees, and Via pressed her lips together. "I suppose we follow."

Pushing aside the larger branches, Tigra and Via ducked through, but the wall of pines was thick, and before long, they found themselves covered in scratches. And then both suns peeked through the dark trees, and the two women emerged on the other side.

Hidden within the Forest of Fire, Snook breathed in deep. Ever since landing here yesterday, he'd found the forest…*Intoxicating. As if something is, at long last, awakening within me.* And now, when he dug within, he stumbled upon a revelation: *Deep inside me, in the pit of my throat, lies an ember — but without a spark, I cannot breathe fire, not until that ember is ignited.*

He sighed. *Bronté mentioned I am the last of my kind, so I have no one to ask: but did the dragons often visit the Forest of Ralas? Is this where dragonlings found their inner flame?* He tried to picture his ancestors, perhaps curled up in the exact same spot, but nothing came to mind. *I'll never know the answers — and I may never discover the connection I seek.*

The snapping of a twig broke through his thoughts, and Snook raised his head. *Via?* He knew she was somewhere in the forest, but he needed to stay out of sight. *Though, again, who could turn away a dragon in the Forest of Fire?!*

Instead, a fire fox appeared from the underbrush. Catching sight of Snook, the creature paused mid-step, its nose sniffing the air. Snook stared, aware that the fox had never seen a dragon before. The creature blinked then trotted back into the underbrush.

Snook gazed into the canopy, where crimson squirrels raced along the branches. *Dragons live the longest, so none of these creatures would have ever met one of my kind.*

All of a sudden, he felt incredibly alone.

I wonder where Via is, and what she has discovered.

A field of fresh green grass stretched before them. Bursting out of the center of the meadow stood a giant willow, with trembling veils of greenery hanging off every branch. The sound of ethereal music fell upon their ears, and they saw the red sparkles dancing in and out of the drooping leaves. Whenever a sparkle lighted onto a branch, a small red faerie appeared. The faeries fanned their scarlet butterfly wings, smiling and waving at the two visitors, before vanishing into a sparkling red speck of light again.

The willow's roots dug into the ground but poked up in arches above. Glancing down at her feet, Via saw the roots extending past the evergreen trees – possibly even beyond the forest border. *So that's what we tripped on,* she thought. *Uneven footing due to tree roots but unseen from above ground.*

Various red flowers decorated the meadow, and butterflies darted through the air. Red squirrels ducked underneath the exposed roots and hid their nuts, while a red fox sniffed at the base of the willow, ears flicking. A massive red stag peered through the delicate veil, willow leaves draping over his impressive antlers.

Turning to Tigra beside her, Via saw her gaping at the sight. "You've never seen this before?"

"Never. As I said, it's forbidden." She grinned at Via. "I can't wait to tell Ettar."

"She won't believe you," Via teased.

"No one will. Not even Father. It will be our little secret." Tigra's eyes sparkled. "At last, the forest has granted me what I've wanted for years."

"A secret?"

"A gift – to be able to see something no one else has." She pointed behind them. "Back there, the forest is everyone's. It's nothing new, nothing special. But here." And she spread her arms wide, gesturing to all four corners of the meadow. "Here is something only I can claim to have seen."

Via touched Tigra's arm. "But what enjoyment is there in something only for yourself?"

Tigra shook her head. "You don't understand – of course there's enjoyment. When I step into the forest, it won't be the same clump of trees everyone else has, the same clump of trees that I've taken for granted all these years. Next time, I'll be able to remember something of my own. It's what everyone in my tribe dreams of, but only a select few are blest with." She grinned. "And besides, I'll have you to share it with!"

"Of course." Via let her eyes wander and sighed. "I just wish I knew what I was supposed to do now."

"You don't know?"

Via stepped beyond the trees, careful not to crush any of the delicate flowers, and avoided another clumsy spill from the roots. "No. Vic is the one with the scroll. That's why he wanted to come into the forest with you – he's the one who knows what we're doing, after all."

"Didn't he tell you anything at all?" She could hear Tigra following her.

The willow towered above her, and Via placed her hand against its trunk, leaning back to look through the canopy of wispy leaves into the bright blue sky. "No. Just to find the Tree of Life and that there I would find an underground key." She turned back to the grassland and gestured. "But we can't unearth the entire meadow."

Tigra put a hand on Via's arm. "Via, you have a gift. Why don't you use it?"

Via swallowed, hard. "It's a gift that terrifies me, Tigra." She shivered at the memory of her first vision, one she still wished she'd never seen. *And I can't tell anyone about it*, she remembered, chilling her.

"But why?" Tigra blinked, unbelieving. "The people of my village can only dream of a gift like yours. Our connection is to the fire spirits alone – the sprites, faeries, and nymphs. As a visionary, your connection is with all of them, fire and more." Tigra tilted her head. "You have a direct link to the spirits, their most powerful gift of all."

273

"I fear it because I never know when the visions are coming – but when they do, they're always cold and filled with terrifying images. It's not a warm and comforting gift."

Squatting beside a large root, Tigra carved a hole in the moist dirt with a fingernail. She plucked a nearby seed, plopped it into the hole, and mounded the dirt into a small hill. "Nature itself isn't warm and comforting – this seed may never grow, but at least I've tried to help it on its way." Straightening, she smiled at Via. "That's what Ettar always told me."

"Is nature supposed to help me?"

"The spirits molded nature after themselves, Via, or so the legends say. Why would their gifts be any different?" She eyed Via and then smiled. "I can tell you've lived among nature like my people. You're surely no stranger to it."

"I grew up on the Plains after my parents' deaths."

Tigra swept her arm across the meadow, taking in all of it. "Perhaps nature can help us today. Use your gift and ask the spirits." She nudged Via with her shoulder. "After all, there's a reason only you could enter the forest with me – and the spirits made that rule."

Looking once more at the giant willow, Via took a deep breath and closed her eyes. She tried to calm herself, center herself – as Vic had described in vague terms to her once – to encourage a vision to overcome her, but nothing came. Then a small touch, like a breathy whisper against her earlobe: *Embrace your gift, betel.*

Bronté? she called out.

Kai, jerda. Every visionary is linked to their spirit guide, the elf who granted their gift. I've been waiting for the day you would need my guidance.

What do I do?

The spirits can be cold and terrifying, but they can also be beautiful and empowering. Bring yourself to a peace of mind, he encouraged, *and they will answer you.*

With Bronté leading her, Via cleared her mind and dug into the silence of inner peace. But then came a gentle crackling sound, and she found herself realizing more of the world around her. She could feel an energy pulsating out of the willow tree, rippling through the ground, like a rhythmic heartbeat. Above her, she heard the faeries' singing – and it dawned upon her that the humming from the sparkles earlier had indeed been their vocal music. *It's as if there's a whole new layer to the world,* she gushed.

Indeed, Bronté agreed. *And as I help you understand your gift, the more of the spirits' realm will you uncover.*

All around her, the world seemed to be waiting on her, held in anticipation for that moment. So, she called out simply: *Show me the key, spirits, please.* She thought nothing had happened, for the heartbeat didn't even falter. But then, in the real world, Tigra gasped – and without opening her eyes, Via turned to her. "What's wrong?"

"A rabbit – it just dug up my seed and hopped away with it!"

Opening her eyes then, Via saw a brown-and-white rabbit a few hops away, brushing its whiskers with its paws. As Tigra had said, the little creature held her seed between its teeth, and as Via watched, it looked at her with its large liquid eyes before hurriedly burrowing into the ground. Via moved toward the rabbit, kneeling beside it and watching. *Don't startle, little one.* As if it heard her thoughts, it paused in its digging to look up at her, unblinking. Its nose twitched, and then it resumed its burrowing. Once satisfied, it released the seed, which fell into the hole, and the rabbit kicked dirt back over it with its back legs.

"Via—" Tigra began, coming up behind her, but she shook her head.

Via reached out her hand to touch the creature, but the rabbit moved slightly, and Via found herself pressing her palm against the cool dirt. Beneath her touch, the ground trembled as the tree's rhythmic heartbeat pulsated twice, and a swirling purple ribbon of light burst from between her fingers. Heart racing, Via kept her hand still as the purple light spiraled, leaving in its place a single iridescent bloom. "An Elva flower," Via whispered, glancing at the rabbit again. The creature stood on its hind legs, sniffing at her arm. Via released the flower from between her fingers to stroke the animal's ears, and the creature pressed into her palm. But then it pulled back, stared at her with its liquid eyes, and with a flick of its powderpuff tail, hopped away.

"What did the spirits tell you?" Tigra asked.

Facing her, Via smiled. "They don't really speak – it's more like music." Via glanced back at the willow, appreciating once more the tree's strength and beauty – and its hidden heartbeat. "Why is it called the Tree of Life?"

"Refeonamas don't know the story because my people guard it closely." Tigra leaned in closer. "This tree beats its life source throughout the entire island. The spirits planted it to keep our world alive." She tapped the iridescent flower. "But where's the key, Via?"

"My second father, Kaio, once told me that Elva flowers are the purest flower of all – and that they only bloom in places of pure magic." She cocked her head, regarding the bud. "But he also said never to pluck one." She cupped her hands around the mound of dirt again, breathing in deep. "Perhaps if I..." The flower stretched toward her, and as the petals bloomed, a miniscule brass key appeared in the center. Via plucked it from the flower and, holding it up to the light, smiled.

After a moment, Tigra cut in: "So, what does it unlock?"

"I'll have to ask Vic – but somehow, this key leads us to the next part of our journey." She saw Tigra's face droop. "What's wrong?"

"You're leaving so soon?"

"Alas, yes." Via smiled in reassurance and rubbed Tigra's arm. "Whenever you come back into the forest, remember your secret, and then you'll remember me."

"I wish I could go with you," Tigra began and then shaking her head, sighed. "But I'm not allowed to leave before Shaman has his first true child."

"Why?"

"Because until then, I shall take Ettar's place. My father may guard the forest and our people, but as a woman, Ettar guards the intentions of the fire sprites."

"Are those the fire sprites?" Via asked, pointing to the willow, but discovered the red sparkles had vanished.

"No, just flame faeries. They help guard the forest, but I didn't know they lived among the sparkles of the fire sprites." She smiled. "I've seen much more of our forest than I ever imagined I would today." Getting to her feet, she helped Via up. "Would you like to see the river? It's what most visitors ever want to see."

"I'd love to." Clutching the key to her chest, Via admired the willow tree one last time. *Purra, spirits,* she whispered.

"We should leave a gift." Tigra untied a beaded leather thong from around her neck and looped it around the root arching closest to the Elva flower. Then beckoning to Via, Tigra led the way out of the meadow, and Via smiled at the thought of the Tree of Life being underneath her wherever she went.

Once past the fringe of evergreen trees, Tigra tested the wind with her finger. "It blows this way, meaning the river is also this way. Come, before the full moon celebration begins."

Both suns had almost set by the time they came upon the river. It was wide – Via estimated twenty steps or so to cross – its water almost tinted red from the crimson-striped salmon. "Our River of Fiery Water: Gulangi," Tigra said then gestured toward the north. "It flows from the center of the forest and enters the ocean at the far northern border, beyond the forest's edge."

Peering at their reflections, Via noticed Tigra seemed to be one with the Forest of Ralas: her face blended among the brown-red of the leaves and her body was as sturdy as a young sapling, her smile reflected the sunslight that made the flowers grow, and her eyes sparkled like the fire all around them. *She needs no secret gift from the forest – she herself is its greatest secret, for she and the forest are bonded together, even if she denies it.*

Coma

His face hidden among the shadows of his cloak, Vic watched his breath forming little puffs in the air, as the wind nipped at his nose. In the distance, he could still hear the beating of the drums from the evening's festivities – with the full moon above, the Belfg villagers had spent the last several hours drinking and dancing away. Via had been exhausted from her afternoon in the forest, but Tigra had convinced her father to allow Vic and Afis to enjoy some of the prepared fire drinks.

But now, Vic thanked the spirits for the distraction the celebration created – for without it, sneaking out of the village would have been much more difficult. After Via had left that morning, Vic had felt Shaman's men's eyes on him all afternoon. He'd finally been able to sneak away with the help of a smoke cuchel, but tonight it wouldn't be necessary.

Ducking past the hut where Via was resting, Vic headed for the fringe of huts at the end of the village. Beyond that, he knew, waited a hungry Snook – patient, perhaps, but hungry, nonetheless. Guilt rushed through him at the realization that he'd forgotten his promised snack for Snook.

To his relief, the dragon didn't seem to notice: *No cuchels this time, jerda?*

I don't think any of Shaman's warriors are watching me with the celebration continuing right now. I'll be there in a moment.

Just as he was about to reach the border of the village, Shaman stepped out from the shadows, arms crossed and blocking his path. "Vic."

Vic halted in his tracks, shocked: *Where did he come from?!* "Shaman."

"My sister begs my father to allow you to attend our full moon celebration, and yet you sneak away to leave the village." Frowning, Shaman raised his chin higher. "Why?"

"I needed some fresh air," Vic answered, holding up both hands.

"I know what your companion Via came for in the forest, and even if my sister denies that she took her there, I've read your scroll."

Vic sighed, lowering his shoulders. "What do you want, Shaman? I'll never be able to convince you that I truly mean no harm to your people."

"I believe you," Shaman said simply, and Vic blinked in surprise. "But my people have long had a violent history with yours – our own cousins – and so you must understand where my suspicions come from."

"I'm learning to see it from your point of view, thanks to Via."

There was a long pause as Shaman regarded Vic, who, in the back of his mind, wished he could read the Belfg prince better. He had no desire to try a mind-searching cuchel, suspecting that the prince would defend himself, at least on a physical level. "My father doesn't know it yet," Shaman said, "but I've already begun receiving visions from the fire sprites, and they alerted me about you as well."

"About me?"

"My father saw the scroll alone, but I saw you instead. The fire sprites showed me your unique connection to our shared island, a connection that I don't understand."

Connection?! Vic repeated before stammering, "I—I don't know anything, I swear."

"Nonetheless," Shaman cut back in, silencing him with a narrowed eye. "My father says a wise chief makes allies than enemies. If what the sprites say is true, then you are one I wish to count as a friend and ally."

Relaxing, Vic bowed his head. "And I, you, Shaman."

For the first time, Shaman smiled, and Vic bit his tongue to keep from gaping. "Good." He gave a low hoot like an owl, and Vic wondered what signal it meant. "When your quest is over, I look forward to discovering what your exact connection to Lilligrav is." And then, just like his sister had the day before, Shaman disappeared back into the shadows.

For the longest of minutes, Vic stood frozen on the spot, running over their conversation in his mind. It wasn't until Snook broke in that he awoke from his trance: *Jerda?*

Sorry – I'm coming, Snook.

Beyond the village border, Vic found no warriors on patrol, and his mind went back to Shaman hooting like an owl. *Did he tell his men to leave me alone?* he wondered.

In the dark, as his eyes adjusted, he caught sight of Snook curled up far from the distant torchlight of the village. Earlier that morning, Snook had requested Vic look up a hazing spell, to conceal him from passersby. Vic had felt a twinge of jealousy at the newfound pool of magic Snook had at his disposal. "Did you bring me food, as promised?" Snook rumbled in a low voice.

"What kind of dragon can't go hunting for his own food?" Vic teased back.

"The kind of dragon who waits almost an hour for his Master to show up!" He rolled back one wing to reveal a half-eaten doe, and Vic waved for him to continue eating. "She happened to be passing by while I lay concealed in my mist, so I snatched her before she could even comprehend what was happening," Snook said with a smirk in his eyes.

Sitting cross-legged in front of Snook, Vic dug out the key from the pouch around his neck. *Via found our key,* he said across their bond to avoid Snook talking with his mouth full.

With a strip of meat dangling from his lower jaw, Snook raised his head and peered squinty-eyed at the brass key between Vic's finger and thumb. *It's so tiny,* the dragon remarked.

Quite so. Via said it came from the bud of a flower.

I thought it was underground?

I suppose that's up for interpretation. Vic untied the scroll, paused. *Anyone nearby?*

None, jerda. If I hear someone approach, I'll tell you.

Do you breathe fire yet?

Snook grumbled, as if muttering a curse. *Avro.*

Well, I need something to read by. Vic nodded to Snook's zaak. *And I trust your talons more than my fingers.*

With a chuckle, Snook raised two talons then whispered *Ralas.* A small flame flickered, hovering between the two. *Proceed.*

Purra. Vic unrolled the scroll and found the next part:

To continue, to the brother hills you must head
But, alas, misfortune and fortune both await you.
The hanging Vulture is near, with its bloody cry;
Therefore, be cautious, as is one's nature.
Dig underneath, and you will see
The door that belongs to your key.

Vic sighed. *More riddles.*

"That was all it said," Vic said, disappointed. He could feel Azeri rippling underneath him, the stallion's muscles working hard under the fierce suns. All the horses had enjoyed a few days of rest while at Belfg, but Vic could tell they enjoyed being back in the Plains even more.

Via chewed her lip, thinking. "It's clear that 'brother hills' refer to the Wilderness Mountains, for the outer ring is called the Brothers, and the inner ring is called the Sisters. But 'the hanging Vulture'…" She trailed off, shaking her head.

From where he rode Ralas between them, Afis groaned. "You know I don't understand all these things."

Vic laughed. "We're sorry, Afis. But Via's right: The Wilderness Mountains are indeed referenced in the first line of the poem. Those are the mountains guarding the far western wilderness – beyond which few have gone and come back. It's the greatest lore of Lilligrav."

"But what Vic and I don't understand is the reference to a 'hanging Vulture.'" Via shook her head. "My father and Kaio taught me much about the history of Lilligrav, but still, I don't know what that line means."

"I didn't get quite as in-depth of a history as you, Via, but my cousin was still quite the teacher." Vic sighed. "Yet I also don't know the meaning."

Afis shrugged. "Well, we should at least head in the right direction."

"You're quite right, Afis," and Vic turned Azeri's head more to the west. "We'll want to head southwest a bit, to avoid the weevil fortress."

"Those blue-skinned creatures?" Afis asked.

"Kai," Vic responded with a nod. "Their fortress is not something I want to seek out. Besides, we'll have to curve around Whirlpool River, too." *Snook, do you have any idea regarding the scroll?*

None, jerda, he replied from high above. *When I was a dog, my master and young master didn't discuss history much.*

Vic focused his gaze to the western sky, knowing that far beyond the Plains lay the more familiar side of the island – and most important: home. *We're getting closer to the other half of Lilligrav.*

And what worries you, jerda? Snook asked, sensing the underlying emotion behind Vic's words.

Deep at the back of his mind, frightening images and words threatened to creep into his core, but Vic swallowed them back – and Snook saw. *The Dark One,* he admitted.

Never fear, jerda. For as long as this dragon is awake, the Dark One won't bother us.

The next day, as both suns passed their midday meeting point, Vic pulled Azeri in at the sound of Snook's low roar. The golden dragon swooped in, and Zukav reared. "I hunger," Snook growled, fanning his wings. "Stay here while I find something to eat."

Vic nodded, but behind him, Afis grumbled. After Snook had leaped back into the sky, Vic twisted to look at Afis. "What's wrong?"

"Must we keep stopping for Snook to snack? I'm hungry, too," Afis admitted.

"He doesn't want us to wander far from him – after all, a dragon is the best protection in all of Lilligrav." Vic dismounted, patting Azeri's neck.

"While we wait, perhaps we could munch on some of the fruit from Belfg?" Via suggested. At the village, Vic and Afis had discovered Bralbas, a rare treat from the forest. "I've been so excited to taste it," Via continued, "after being too tired for the festivities."

Vic chuckled. "Tigra ensured you wouldn't miss out." He opened his pack. "I'm afraid all we have left is fruit, Afis, since we finished off the vegetables from Armoth."

"We'll get you some meat soon. The Blood Bearers didn't have 'vegetarian' in mind, did they?" Via teased, poking Afis in the arm.

Rolling his eyes, Afis cursed to himself.

Almost an hour had passed before Snook reappeared on the horizon. The ground trembled when he landed and as he shook himself, Vic approached. Lowering his snout to Vic's level, Snook uncurled his talons, revealing an antelope. "The dark eagle feasting on this buck proved little competition, and if there's anything left after I'm through with it, you're more than welcome to it."

Vic grinned. "Anything left after a dragon? We appreciate the kind thought."

Snaking his tail around himself, Snook turned away. "Find something to do while I devour my snack. I don't quite enjoy being watched."

With a lopsided grin and a shrug, Vic turned back to the others. "If it's meat you want, Afis, we'll need some new arrows, don't you think?"

Snook held the carcass down with one zaak and tore away at the meat with his teeth. He could hear Via laughing at something, and he stole a glance to see she had her head thrown back, reacting to Afis telling her about a dream last night. She'd seemed in much better spirits since her trip into the Forest of Ralas, and Snook wondered – as Vic did – exactly what she'd seen and discovered.

But the smell of bloody meat wafted into his nostrils and breathing it in, he resumed lapping up strips of meat. As he swallowed, a strange throbbing sensation began at the back of his head. He ignored it at first, but halfway through the carcass, dark circles appeared in his vision, and Snook snuffled, drawing his snout back. His head pounded, screaming in his ears. Snook groaned – a low growling sound – and Vic glanced over at him. *Snook?*

The dark spots widened, and Snook staggered back from the carcass, trying to reach out and respond to Vic. But the thread fizzled under his touch, vibrated, and threw him off. In the real world, he lost his balance and swayed. The horses reared, panicked, and Vic jumped to his feet. *Snook! Regain balance!* But Vic's words were too fuzzy for Snook to comprehend as he crashed to the ground, his head landing with a thud at Vic's feet.

Snook! Can you hear me?!

For Snook, everything faded; his surroundings blurred into one grey mess. His head made a loud popping sound, stinging his ears, and then everything snapped off – and went black.

SNOOK!

285

The fire crackled in the darkness, and Vic watched the flames rising upwards only to die, return to the mother flame, and become reborn. His thoughts lay with the dragon behind him, still unmoving.

Snook, what happened to you? As always, he prayed for an answer but again, received none. Last time they'd lost connection, a sort of blackness had invaded both their minds, the string lost in it. But now, Vic only found dead silence, as if their string had snapped.

He knew Via was watching him, but he didn't care. His mind was far too occupied with whirring thoughts to look back at her and pretend everything was fine.

"So," Afis finally said, "this is our camp for the night then."

"Yes, Afis," Via whispered, her eyes still on Vic.

"Why did you burn the rest of the meat?" He rubbed his growling stomach.

"Because no one is to eat it." Vic answered Afis' question but kept his eyes on the flames. "The meat was poisoned."

"But what's your proof, Vic?" Afis asked between stomach growls.

For the first time, Vic looked at Afis, hard. "My proof is right behind me."

"And quite visible," came a new voice, as a shadow crossed the fire.

Via put a hand on Afis' arm, lowering his hunting knife as she broke into a smile. "Bronté," she said in greeting.

"Good evening, jerdas. It has been a long time for you, but a short while for me." The elf winked in a knowing way at them, his blond hair gleaming in the firelight.

"Time passes differently for an elf, Kaio once told me," Via said.

Bronté nodded. "A month seems like a mere day in the span of centuries." He frowned, putting a hand on Vic's shoulder. "Come, Vic, lighten up. Snook is merely sleeping, and the dawn brings an antidote."

Vic raised his head. "Why must we wait till then?"

"The herb only works in sunlight. Until then, perhaps a spell to hide him from sight?" And with a wave of his arms, Bronté built up a mist around Snook.

As the elf took a seat beside the fire, Via passed him the goat horn filled with water, which he accepted with gratitude. "So, the meat was indeed poisoned?" she asked.

"Kai," the elf said simply.

Via frowned. "But by whom?"

Vic already knew the answer, but he didn't dare say it aloud. He was surprised to hear Bronté respond: "Not even I know, betel." Looking up, he found Bronté regarding him with a strange expression and flustered, Vic lowered his eyes back to the hungry flames.

"The night is young, jerdas, and with a sleeping dragon, we can't exactly move camp, can we?" the elf asked with a chuckle, and Via smiled back. "Shall I tell you a story of my people then?"

Afis perked up. "Where are your 'people,' Bronté?"

Pressing a finger to his lips, the elf grinned. "The answer is one of the greatest secrets of Lilligrav, Afis."

"Tell us the story," Via said.

Clearing his throat, Bronté waved his hands over the fire, and the flames leapt higher into the air, almost burning their cheeks. The fire flashed purple, then blue, and then returned to orange, shrinking back down. Via and Afis gasped and clapped, but Vic turned his eyes toward Snook's dark form behind him. *Wake up, Snook,* he pleaded. But then Bronté's voice drifted into his ears, and although reluctant, Vic listened.

"Many centuries ago," began the elf, "the races of Lilligrav lived together. The dwarfs mined among the minerals, and the dragons flew among the clouds. Your people explored the world, while my people guarded its magic. We lived among our great glass cities, the fragments of which can be found throughout the island. Our story begins at the start of The Separation – which my people refer to as the Bruavk – when the elves abandoned their cities to disappear forever," he ended, with a knowing wink to Afis.

"But why?" Afis asked.

Bronté frowned, sighed. "Alas, the greed of men drove us away. But tonight, I shall tell you a story of the night before the elves vanished." He leaned forward. "Would you like to hear the legend of the dark unicorn?"

"Yes!" Via and Afis said, in unison, while Vic grumbled under his breath.

"Picture this: the Avro Woods – familiar to you, jerdas. Now, forget the calm assembly of evergreens you remember, for tonight, in our story, the woods are thick with anticipation…

"Two elves rode their horses at a mad gallop through the trees. The mares strained at their bridles, forcing their way through gaps in the dense trees. Their riders lay low across the mares' backs, their faces tickled by the pine needles. On one rider's back, in a tube under her tunic, rested a letter of grave warning, and the riders urged their horses further, knowing time was short.

"In the underbrush, a shape flickered in and out of the shadows. Glimpses in the light revealed it to be a lone redbeard dwarf, riding a dwarfish donkey. He followed the elves, staying close but keeping to the shadows, a fiery flicker in his dark eyes. But the elves knew his presence, for he was their secret weapon.

"They rode for half an hour when—" Smiling in a mischievous way, Bronté halted in his story and motioned for the goat horn. Afis passed it over, and the elf drank long and hard. Afterwards, he murmured a cuchel to refill and handed it back. "Purra, Afis."

Irritated, Vic grunted under his breath. "So, what happens next?"

"Ah, so you *were* listening."

As his mood darkened again, Vic frowned at the fire. "Kai – but what of it? You can't leave a story unfinished."

"Peace, Vic," Bronté said, holding up his hands. When Vic relaxed, the elf began again: "They rode for half an hour when an unknown rider blocked their path. The intruder held up a hand, and a wave of earth flew up before the elves, spitting out stones. The elves jerked back on the reins, bringing their mares to a halt. When the whirlwind of dirt ceased, the elves paced their mares, for the elfin horses shivered with desire to begin the journey anew.

"But the intruder didn't move, and the elves were surprised to see the beast he rode: a unicorn colored as grey as the snow falling during twilight. The unicorn's eyes were dim, a sign that he'd surrendered to his rider's control. The elves knew their opponent was wise indeed, for man's horses cannot match an elfin horse's speed – but a unicorn can.

"Now, the man drew a sword and demanded of the elves: 'Which of you is Elviera?!' But they didn't answer and instead glanced at each other. So, the man demanded again: 'Elviera with the scroll; which?'" Pausing, Bronté displayed his pointed ears to them. "You know my race by our ears, and you know me by my short hair. But among my people, both male and female have hair sweeping down our backs, and therefore, our intruder couldn't tell Elviera from her male companion.

"Angered by the elves' resistant silence, the man raised his blade, the sword crackling with dark magic. 'Which?' he shouted once more. But the words had hardly left his lips when out from the shadows leaped the dwarf on his donkey. The redbeard dwarf's eyes crackled as he threw forth his spear, and his aim was true: the spearhead plunged into the man's chest, right into his heart."

All of a sudden, Bronté leaned over his knees, blond hair blocking his eyes, sides heaving as he gasped for breath. Via signaled to Afis, who, after a moment of confusion, passed the elf the goat horn again. Bronté took it, chugging water. When he finished, he looked all three in the eyes while saying: "If *and* when you should ever meet more of my kind, I urge you to never speak of this incident."

"Why not?" Afis asked, and Via mouthed a reprimand.

The elf held up a hand, breathed in deep with his eyes closed, and took another sip of water. "In my culture, an elf who cannot finish a story on a single breath of air is hardly an elf at all," he explained, ashamed, with an apologetic smile on his lips.

"We shall never speak of it, then," Via promised, throwing Afis one last warning glance.

"Now, where was I?" Bronté paused, retracing his steps, before straightening in his seat. "The dwarf's spear collided with our intruder's chest – but instead of dying, the dark Magic Master did an incredible thing. His body faded away, and his black soul blended into the unicorn he rode. The creature's hide darkened, and a new youth flared in its eyes. With a piercing neigh, the now-dark unicorn rose up, forelegs flailing. The elves whispered protection spells, and the dwarf ducked back into the underbrush. And then, right in front of them, the unicorn shivered and then vanished – a transportation spell known only to those mystic creatures. Yet the unicorn's terrifying screams haunted our riders as they spurred their steeds forward." And bowing his head, Bronté gestured to indicate the story was complete.

"Then what?" Via whispered.

"That is the story of the dark unicorn," Bronté said with a small shrug. "And that is the story I promised you. What else is there?"

"There's the scroll," came Vic's voice, and Bronté turned to him, brows raised. When the elf didn't respond, Vic repeated: "The scroll the elves carried."

"Ah, the scroll." Bronté's expression darkened, and he stared into the dying flames. "The scroll carried word that humanity was eyeing the elves' great glass cities for its own. By dawn the next day, every elf in every city had vanished: the Bruavk." He looked up, catching sight of their fallen faces, and with a small smile, he motioned to them. "But now, a new era has begun. Elves and humans *shall* be Allies again."

Via brightened. "That's what my father and Kaio always hoped for, Bronté."

He leaned over, touching a strand of her hair. "Then you must not disappoint them, betel."

Afis spoke up. "And those with no race?"

Grinning, the elf nudged him with his shoulder. "We shall never be enemies, Afis the Blood-despising One." Afis grinned back at the name.

"After all," Bronté added, "our races have never been at war."

Afis' grin widened.

Standing, Bronté clapped his hands lightly together. "Now then. The moon rises, which means you must get rest. No need for a watch – I shall plant a protection spell around us to keep us safe for the night."

Within moments, Afis and Via had tucked in for the night, eyelids flickering as the first traces of dreaming touched their minds. Vic stayed seated, poking the embers with a stick. He sensed Bronté coming up behind him, and the elf placed a hand on Vic's shoulder. "Rest, Vic. Snook shall sleep deeper than he has ever before, and with the return of both suns, we shall awaken him. Sitting here upset isn't solving anything." Then, waving his hands, the elf extinguished the fire.

Vic stared at the ashes, threw his stick into the pile, and went to bed. *Though I doubt I'll sleep much, if at all,* he admitted, his heart sinking into his stomach.

Surfacing from his slumber, Vic stretched and yawned. His dreams had just been various scenes jumbled together, like a tailor distracted while stitching. He last recalled the sound of hoofbeats while hazy images raced across the back of his eyelids. But then, as he adjusted to the dawning light, he continued hearing hoofbeats – and in a blink, he was awake, sitting up and reaching for his bow and quiver, always by his resting spot.

Inching their way into the sky, both suns cast a grey-yellow light across the Plains. Movement from the southeast caught his eye, and Vic waited. Then the faint forms of horses trotted over a hill – and then Vic made out their riders. They weren't moving too fast, but Vic knew that, very soon, they would notice the camped trio.

He nudged Afis' side with the toe of his sandal. Afis awoke with a snort. "Hush!" Vic demanded in a low whisper. "Arm yourself: we have company."

As Afis grabbed his club and bow, Vic slid over to Via and rubbed her arm. She yawned, blinking at him, still sleepy. "Good morning, already?"

Putting a finger to her lips, Vic shook his head. "Prepare for battle."

His words seemed to startle her awake. Sitting up, Via fastened her sword around her waist and passed Vic his own.

A shiver ran down Vic's spine as Afis came up behind him. "I counted almost twenty riders," he whispered close to Vic's ear. "We're outnumbered."

"When haven't we been?" Vic snapped back.

Rolling his eyes, Afis groaned. "But back then, we had a massive dog – and now our dragon is sleeping!"

Panic crept in when Vic realized his connection to Snook was still dead silent, and he spun around to find his worst nightmare realized: "Where is Snook?!"

Circling in the sky, a dark eagle glared down at the Plains below, at a hazy spot that shimmered like a mirage. For hidden somewhere in the haze lay an unconscious dragon, desperate for an antidote, but utterly without a connection to his Master.

As if Death herself had come for the last of the dragons.

-obrio-

(to be continued)

Elfin

- Ako – hate; hatred
- Avro – no; to be negative; evil (etc.)
- Azeri – to run
- Betel – beauty; beautiful
- Beu – energy [used to replenish energy aka strength]
- Bron – despair
- Bruvk – to go; to leave
- Bruavk – the Separation [when elves disappeared]
- Chinel – you; yourself
- Chinel'pe – yours; your
- Cuchel – magic [can be used with or without "dahla" to refer to magic spell]
- Dæmon – demon [ultimate creature of avro]
- Dahla – spell
- Dertic – to cure
- Deruge – (bloody) lion
- Draco – dragon [used with respect; see -nama]
- Durkva – to drain [used to fully drain when attached to "beu"]
- Dwarva – dwarf [see -nama]
- Elisdh – shield [can be used like a small force field, depending on mental strength]
- Elva – elf [see -nama]
- Espe – honor
- Etta – to give
- Fierelä – Master [as in Cuchel Master]
- Fierelä'va – [title for the High Cuchel Master, using "va" from elfin royal titles]
- Flïnaro – wound; to be wounded; to wound someone (etc.)
- Gäzarf – to fall
- Gérté – me; myself; I
- Gérté'pe – my; mine
- Grav – homeland
- Hireel – to lift up; to raise or rise (etc.)
- Hombä – to read
- Imalre – image
- Ir – to force

- Jerda – friend; companion
- Kai – yes; to be positive; good (etc.)
- Kazam – body
- Ké – and
- Kell – teeth; fangs
- Kierenata – to transfer [literally, "to give away"]
- Leyef – to grow
- Lilli – blessed [chanted & repeated word]
- Lilligrav – blessed homeland [name of main island]
- Mä – to speak; spoken
- Mælle – trees; forest; woods [includes all large plants, mainly trees]
- Nama – human [denotes one's race or species when placed at end of title or name]
- Namatéh – hero of men [gender-neutral]
- Ntéh – heroic; hero/heroine [gender-neutral]
- Nyv – this
- Obrio – bridge [or connection of some sort]; to connect
- Pe – [possession as in turn "you" to "your"]
- Pllatæ – plant [this includes all small plants, such as shrubs, fungi, etc.]
- Purra – gratitude; to be grateful; thanks (etc.)
- Qe – to communicate [as opposed to "speak" or "spoken"]
- Ralas – fire; flame
- Refeo – river; stream; spring (etc.)
- Refeonamas – humans of the sea
- Ruverb – (the color) red
- Shilek – to concentrate; to focus
- Shio – to be abundant; to have a lot; many (etc.)
- Shu – (electric) shock
- Stref – mind; mental core
- Sukrl – puddle; pool [not always water]
- Surg – light
- Té – to defeat; defeated
- Tereuk – droplet of water; teardrop
- Tigr – cat
- Tjord – to undo
- Tuk – of
- Twq'nmu – [a lower being, usually a student/apprentice]

- Viek – (the verb to be, infinitive format)
- Vieké – (the verb to be, "they" format)
- Xaniera – Master [as in owner; not to be confused with Fierelä]
- Yir – more [like the "-er" at end of words: fairer, nicer, friendlier, etc.]
- Yoi – to [a root-word sometimes, depending on use]
- Yror – spirit animal [the animal body a human spirit lives in after its death until avenged]
- Zaak – front foot (of a dragon)
- Zaam – back foot (of a dragon)
- Zhan – than [not "then"]
- Zukav – ground; dirt; mud (etc.)
- Zukavnamas – people of the land

Dwarfish

- Bläncha – the blackbeard clan
- Ecrovï – full of might
- Fũegarr – the silverbeard clan

Native/Zukavnama

- Belfg – roots [as in Tree of Life]
- Bralbas – fire fruit
- Heftka – pride [as in (bloody) lions]
- Lillef – [a form of greeting]
- Oono/Oona – chosen child [designated by birthmark]

Pronunciation Guide

- Afis // ay-**fis**
- Alnitak // ahl-ni-**tack**
- Armoth // ar-**moth**
- Azeri // a-**zee**-rie
- Belfg // belfg
- Betel // bi-**tel**
- Bronté // bron-**tay**
- Drema // drem-**ah**
- Dugar // **doo**-gar
- Glasiea // glay-**see**-ah
- Heftka // heft-**kah**
- Hopacias // hope-uh-**kai**-us
- Kaio // kai-**o**
- Levar // le-**var**
- Lilligrav // lily-**grav**
- Polaski // po-**lass**-key
- Qupano // qu-**pah**-no
- Ralas // ruh-**lahs**
- Rudolf // ru-**dolf**
- Tierm // **tee**-erm
- Tigra // **tee**-grah
- Via // **vee**-uh
- Zukav // zoo-**kav**
- Zurze // zurz

About The Author

Molly Blaeser is ecstatic to be completing a nearly 20-year writing project with the publication of her debut novel, Origins: The Snook Saga Book One, with books two and three in the works. Previously, Molly previously had short stories and poems published in various teen contests and student publications. When not escaping into her beloved fantasy world, Molly can be found caring for the zoo of animals she owns alongside her partner in North Carolina.

Where to Find Molly?

@momentswthmolly // Moments with Molly across all socials:

Facebook
Instagram
YouTube
TikTok
Twitter
Snapchat